The Praetorian File

A Novel by WA McLeod

Dedicated to my readers for whom I have written every word, and to my darling wife for whom I exist.

I wish to acknowledge the many people who provided editorial input and encouragement, especially Barbara Kramer, my dear friend, for her tireless work and optimism.

I would be remiss if I didn't mention Paddy Hatt and Gordon MacIvor, soul mates for over thirty years, who always seem to know when to wedge in an encouraging word.

Also by Allan McLeod

DEATH SPRITS
BARELY DEAD, A PAIGE HARRINGTON MYSTERY

The Praetorian File

A Paige Harrington Mystery

Allan McLeod

Duchess Publishing

This is a work of fiction. While for geographical purposes some place names are real, names, characters, dialogues, and incidents are the product of the author's imagination and are fictitious. Any resemblance to actual events or persons, living or dead, is entirely coincidental.

ISBN 978-0-6151-5066-6

To order a copy, visit http://stores.lulu.com/wammac or any online bookstore.

For Wanda and Gabe and Diane and Gideon…and in memory of Julie

When I solicited volunteers to copy edit 100 page segments of my manuscript, I had no idea that such a large and dedicated group of caring readers would leap to the fore with extensive and invaluable ideas and changes that make this a far better story. The list below contains some of these names. Because of professional affiliations or personal considerations, others chose to remain anonymous. I am deeply indebted to all, and cannot thank them enough.

Aleen Atkinson, Kingsville, TX

Brian Hay, Sidney, BC

Damian Begley, New York, NY

Gordon MacIvor, Fort Macleod, AB

Jane Abrutyn, Cincinnati, OH

Lynn Peebles, New York, NY

Tara Anderson, Staten Island, NY

Twila Tayfel, Calgary, AB

"The law does not pretend to punish everything that is dishonest. That would seriously interfere with business."
-- Clarence S. Darrow (1857-1938)

Chapter 1

She smeared charcoal on her face and pulled on a pair of black latex gloves.

On the fifth floor, the elevator stopped, and she stepped out. The door closed, and the darkness engulfed her like black water, but she dared not use her penlight lest someone see its darting beam.

She stood for a moment, clenching and unclenching her hands, waiting for her eyes to adjust, trying to get her bearings. The long winters of Fairbanks, Alaska, where she had grown up, taught her to know the dark, to listen to it, to be patient with it.

Breathe, she told herself and inhaled a few times before proceeding to the office suite at the far end, the one marked with a small brass sign that said Hebrides, Inc. There she drew the access card through the entry system slot and nudged the door open when the lock released.

The pinprick of red light near the ceiling began to blink indicating that the heat and motion sensors had started to do their job. She paused to take another deep breath, and then crept across the room. The thumping of her heart in her ears almost drowned out the whisper of the small motor that guided the awakened camera to capture all that it saw. Tonight it would see nothing but a black shadow.

Two large offices sat directly ahead. Hers was on the left. The one on the right belonged to Anne Black, her partner. She removed a key from her belt pack, unlocked Anne's door, and slipped inside. The lights of the city trickled through the oversized windows allowing her to move around quickly.

She hesitated. Anne's smells were everywhere. Was she betraying her? No. You have to do this. You can't stop. She crept across to the oversized desk and began rifling the drawers.

Click.

She froze, goose bumps racing up and down her spine. That click meant one thing—the outer door had opened. Whoever it was would be in Anne's office in ten seconds.

She pushed the outside window. Please don't let it be locked. It swung open. She dove onto the gangway that circled the building, kicked the window closed, and ran.

First, get out of sight. Then hope for another open window. Going down or up weren't options.

She raced toward the 74th Street end, staying close to the wall and keeping to the shadows, ducking in and out between the gabled windows. At the corner, she paused to catch her breath. Footsteps, running hard, headed in the opposite direction.

Recent construction blocked her path. She couldn't proceed. Her only escape was back the way she came. She dared a look. No one. She listened. A horn sounded. Tires whirred on the hot pavement five stories below. A subway rumbled. All else, silent.

Take a step. Her foot crunched on the twigs and grit. She froze. Don't stop. Take another step, and another. She began running faster than she could ever remember running.

Her pursuer must have left Anne's window hanging open. It wasn't her first choice; it was her only choice. She reached down to the tips of her toes to find one last burst of speed, one last ounce of energy to swing up and across the sill.

A coiled noose shot out of the night and circled her neck. Hot breath blew on her cheek. She smelled sweet sweat. She screamed, though only a gurgling sound escaped her throat, a gurgling sound that melted anonymously into the noises of the New York City night.

Chapter 2

My flight from Montreal landed at LaGuardia at 11:25 p.m., three hours late. The airline blamed equipment problems. It wasn't the weather because the night was perfect: not a cloud in the sky; a mere puff of wind. Even the high humidity that often visits New York City in mid-July, the kind that produces a gritty sheen of perspiration, had taken a break and let the cool air brush my arms and legs with its refreshing breath.

I gave the row of black limousines across from the main entrance a quick scan. After one more pass, I spotted my name, Paige Harrington, on a cardboard sign in the window of a Lincoln Town Car. At the same instant, the driver leapt out of the car and apologized a thousand times for not meeting me inside.

"They don' like us parking here," he said.

I assumed 'they' meant the airport police.

"Tonight, all my frens say to look out because they cracking down, towing cars. Aye coño." He shook his head and grabbed my bags. I told him not to worry. "Gracias senora," he said, and mumbled what I assumed to be a few more Spanish curse words to my bags. I spoke Spanish, fluently, so that wasn't the problem; it was just that he hadn't said them loudly enough or else had mumbled a mixture of Spanish and street argot that only a denizen of Manhattan's Hispanic boroughs would understand.

Traffic on the Grand Central Parkway was late night light, and we made it to the Waldorf Astoria in midtown Manhattan by 12:15 a.m.

The flashing message light was the first thing I saw when the bellhop opened the door to my room, and while he scurried around putting away my suitcases and turning on lights and the TV, I called the message center. The hotel's computer didn't yet realize I'd checked in, and when I got involved in a long discussion with an operator, the bellhop coughed that he was ready for his tip. All I had was a twenty, and he departed with a big smile.

After a few more moments with the operator, I was ready to give up on the message center, because I realized any calls had most likely come from my friend, Bebe Morgan, telling me where to meet her in the morning. Bebe was editor of New York-based *Madame Magazine*, an international glossy, saucy monthly that dished up fact and fancy for and about professional women at work and play. Bebe had hired me to write a story about a 'super woman' inventor friend of hers who had discovered 'some enormous breakthrough in robotics,' to use Bebe's words. I thought it an unusual story for *Madame Magazine* and I assumed more lay beneath the surface.

At last, I heard a computerized voice that said I had not one, but seventeen messages. Unbelievable, and since I was a few hours late arriving, some no doubt came from Bebe, but not seventeen, not even Bebe did seventeen.

I listened to the first. "Paige, darling, I hope your wardrobes arrived."

They had and sat neatly next to the closet. Most of my clothes were stored in my unlived-in apartment. Bebe had arranged to retrieve two wardrobes of summer outfits and have them sent to the hotel so I didn't have to run back and forth.

"And I hope your room is dandy because it's costing us a fortune. However, the real reason I called was to ask if we can we have coffee tomorrow morning. I'm simply dying for you to meet Jenny. Be a sweetheart and call me once you're settled." I assumed the 'super woman' inventor and the Jenny she wanted me to meet in the morning were the same.

About the unlived-in apartment: In January, I'd

bought an apartment in need of a ton of work in the magnificently ornate Ansonia Building on 74th Street and Broadway, on Manhattan's Upper West Side, and then promptly left for Europe, Asia, and the Middle East, with a side trip to Western Canada and Newfoundland. This was the first time I'd been back in the city since, and Bebe insisted I stay in the Waldorf until I got organized with a contractor who wouldn't cost a fortune and wouldn't take a decade to redo my new digs.

"As soon as they hear Ansonia," a friend from my Columbia University days told me, "they see big dollar signs. They know that Caruso used to live there; they know that Babe Ruth used to live there. The mere fact that these blasts from the past lived there a hundred years ago doesn't seem to register."

The next ten messages were hang-ups. The now twelfth message, also from Bebe, said, "Paige darling, I do believe I'm losing my mind. I just know I forgot to tell you when and where: 9:30 a.m., Patisserie Margot, on the north side of the grand old Ansonia Building. Take a cab to Broadway and 74th. You can't miss it."

Bebe either didn't connect with or had forgotten my more than passing acquaintance with the Ansonia. Still, it was good of her to tell me where and when she wanted to meet.

Four more hang-ups.

Finally, the last message. Peter Zane, a good friend from my Columbia University days had called call. I had called from Montreal to ask him to join me for dinner on any day of the week that didn't start with an 'S.'

Peter and I had stayed more or less in touch, mostly less. I hadn't talked to him since the previous New Year's Eve when he'd called from some wild party at a friend's apartment overlooking Times Square. Whether he'd remember was debatable.

He made his money by knowing everyone and having his finger in a lot of deals, most legitimate, a few not. As he always said, "I got three fingers in deals and two in dikes, and I don't mean lesbians." Oh, did I mention that Peter was also crass. I'd long ago given up trying to teach him political correctness—one day someone would though, likely a large lesbian, and I could only hope to be present.

That he danced the legal-illegal line wasn't a secret, and several years ago, one of his 'not legitimate' deals landed him in a country club jail for a year. His dark period, he called it. I'd never learned all the gory details.

Despite his peccadilloes, tucked away in his memory cells, he had a warehouse of business information, and if Bebe wanted me to pursue the story about Jenny Ross, he might prove to be a valuable resource. Besides, I wanted to see him again. I liked his brand of sophisticated irreverence.

His message was short. "Pager, love to have dinner. Call when you get in."

Peter never called anyone by his or her real name. I'd been Pager to him since our freshman year.

I didn't have the call-back number in my handheld. Peter was one of those people who, before the Blackberry era, you cursed because he filled several pages in your Day Planner with changed telephone numbers and addresses. I recorded this yet another new number for future reference.

I decided to call Bebe first. Her voicemail picked up.

"Hi." I said. "I just got in. I got your messages. My clothes are here; I love you for that. The room is lovely, and I love you for that too. I'm in room 1806, and I have my cellphone on. Call if you wish, otherwise, I'll see you in the morning."

That done, I started to unpack when the telephone rang. It was Bebe. I knew it would be.

"Where've you been?" she asked. "I've been worried sick."

"I went to Newfoundland with a friend, or did you

forget?"

"Yes, yes, I know all about that. Well, I mean I don't, and I can't wait to hear the juicy details, but I thought you escaped from that God-forsaken rock last Friday."

"I did, but I stopped in Montreal for the weekend to visit my brother and his new wife. Then my plane left three hours late."

"And how are the young doctors Harrington?"

My younger and only brother Brad and Lisette, his bride of three months, were residents at Montreal General.

"Montreal General has never been in better hands. Nor has Brad. Lisette is a marvel. Anyway, sorry, I should have called."

"Nonsense, Darling, as long as you're OK. I'd invite you over for a night cap, but right now, I'm with friend."

"In that case, I'll be right over."

"Good night, Darling."

I had zero interest in joining Bebe for a post-midnight drink and was glad she was 'with friend' who could occupy her mind and body so I could finish unpacking and get to bed.

Half my clothes went into the laundry and dry-cleaning pile. The rest needed ironing. I called room service. They promised the ironing by morning, the rest by 5:00 p.m. I desperately wanted to bathe, so I asked that someone come right away.

While I waited, I undressed and returned Peter Zane's call. A woman's voice I didn't recognize answered.

"I'm sorry. I think I have the wrong number."

"What number are you calling?"

I read it to her from my handheld, thinking I may have recorded it incorrectly.

"That's the number you've reached," the woman said, sounding pleasant enough. "Who are you looking for?"

"Peter. Peter Zane. I'm sorry I'm calling at this late

hour, but he said to call when I got in."

"This is Peter's number." Her voice turned cautious. "May I say who is calling?"

"Yes, I'm sorry, please forgive my bad manners; it's Paige Harrington."

"Oh Paige, yes, he said you might call." The cautious tone disappeared. "I see from my caller ID that you've arrived, and you're at the Waldorf, correct?"

"Yes," I said, "and again I apologize, but do I know you?" On New Year's Eve, I'd talked to Peter's teeny-bopper girlfriend fresh from some California beach—the voice at the other end of the telephone definitely wasn't hers.

"Now it's my turn to beg forgiveness, but Peter and I have been getting a lot of strange calls lately. I'm Dee—Dee Hunter, a friend of Peter's."

I figured the way she said friend meant 'sharing the bed' friend and wondered what had happened to Brandi or Flicker or whatever her name was.

"Peter had to go out for awhile, but he did want me to ask you to join us for dinner on Wednesday or Thursday. Peter and I leave for Europe on Friday."

I checked my watch. Even for Peter it seemed late. "I'd love to," I said, "but it's my invitation."

"Yes, of course. I'll check with Peter and one of us will call tomorrow to firm up the day and time."

Someone rapped on the door. "Bellhop," a muffled voice said. It didn't sound like the one who'd brought me to the room.

I ended the call, yelled at the door to wait a moment, and pulled on a robe, which I tied securely about my waist. Through the peephole, I saw a short man in a brown uniform and matching cap leaning against the wall and checking what appeared to be a Blackberry. I decided it was safe and opened the door.

Except for a thick moustache plastered on his happy round face, he seemed like he might be a chubby teenager. His nametag said Jorge.

"You hab ironing, Miss?" he asked with a heavy accent. The handheld device disappeared into his front pants pocket.

I checked the urge to respond in Spanish, deciding to keep that facility close to the vest, a useful secret weapon for eavesdropping on the Spanish-speaking service staff.

"Jorge, is that your name?" Now that I could see him more clearly, I noticed touches of silver in his hair and deep laugh lines around his eyes—hardly a teenager.

He grinned. "Jes, Miss. Jorge Ruiz."

"Where are you from, Jorge?"

"Cuba, Miss."

"You're working late."

"Every night, Miss."

"Well, Jorge Ruiz from Cuba who works late every night, my stuff is over there." I pointed to the two piles of clothes. "The first pile is ironing, the rest cleaning." I handed him a twenty. He grinned again, more broadly this time. The twenty went into the same pocket as the handheld.

"What time you want the ironing?"

"Is tomorrow morning at 7:00 OK?"

"Jes, Miss. Seben's OK." He wrote something on a pad that he fished from his back pocket. "Thank you, Miss. Ju call me if you need anything, OK?"

Not long after Jorge disappeared, the housekeeper assigned to late arriving guests came to turn down my bed. On my pillow, she placed two Waldorf chocolates and a yellow rose. I handed her a five. As soon as she left, I headed for the bath where I spent a long time soaking away too many hours of airports and airplanes and limousines.

Praetorian

The long Mercedes with black windows exited FDR Drive at the Brooklyn Bridge, turned onto Water Street, and headed into the bowels of Lower Manhattan.

"Driver?"

"Sir?"

"Maiden Lane entrance."

"Yes, Sir."

The car moved through the dark and deserted streets without fear of attracting unnecessary attention. Late at night, private limousines in the heart of the financial district of the financial capital of the world were more common than yellow cabs. The princes and princesses of Wall Street worked all hours and didn't ride in yellow cabs; nor did its reigning monarchs, for whom anonymity was as important as the secrecy of the billion dollar deals they cobbled together, some legal, most not.

The limo stopped briefly, and a six-inch thick steel door ascended into the fortress-like walls of the Federal Reserve Bank. An armed guard signaled them forward, and they disappeared inside. The driver and lone passenger, his head covered by a black hood, each punched in a separate code on their cellphones. No alarms rang.

Once the steel door closed, two guards came from behind a bulletproof enclosure. While they checked the inside of the vehicle and trunk with detection wands, the driver and passenger got out and stepped smartly through a metal detector and x-ray device without making any sudden moves. They were both aware that the two guards remaining behind the bulletproof enclosure gripped assault rifles with enough firepower to vaporize a human target.

"Clear," one of the checking guards said into a radio transmitter on his wrist.

The driver and passenger got back into the limo. A

second steel door opened. They moved forward and stopped. The second door closed. Again, they got out and passed through a metal detector and x-ray device. Two armed guards wearing bulletproof vests and carrying AK-47's, escorted the passenger to an elevator. One guard reached in and pushed the only button, and then said into a wrist-mounted radio transmitter, "Number Seventeen coming down." The elevator shot silently down, two-hundred feet into Manhattan bedrock.

Then the guards escorted the driver to a secure room where he could watch TV, read magazines or books from the assorted collection, or sleep. There was also a bathroom with shower. Snacks and bottled soft drinks and water were plentiful. He wasn't allowed to make phone calls or otherwise communicate with the outside world.

When all passengers had arrived, the drivers would number twenty in all. They would wait until the meeting adjourned and their passengers, still wearing their black hoods, returned: one at a time, Number One first, Number Twenty last—if in fact they all returned.

Drivers never saw one another and the only time they spoke was to respond to their sole passenger through the voice modifier in the limousines.

BELOWGROUND, Centurion Number Seventeen stepped from the elevator, adjusted his hood, and proceeded down the dimly lit hallway, his footsteps echoing eerily along the concrete floor.

When he reached the end, he stepped into an airtight chamber where his retina was scanned and his palm print read. If both didn't match, doors remained sealed and the occupant suffocated. Ten seconds passed. The seal on the exit door released and Seventeen gulped the fresh air. He advanced across a large room, past twenty chairs organized in a semicircle facing a rostrum on which was centered a throne illuminated by a single spotlight. There were twenty doors, only one of which was open. That door led to his chamber.

At 2:00 a.m. sharp, all doors opened, and twenty Centurions, unknown to each other, all with black hoods and capes and voice synthesizers stepped into the room and proceeded directly to stand in front of one of the twenty chairs in the semicircle, making sure to face the rostrum.

After a moment, a man wearing a red hood and cape—they called him Praefectus—entered and took his place on the raised platform.

The Centurions began chanting, sounding like a chorus of kazoos through their synthesizers, "Hail, Praefectus. Take your exalted place among us. Command that we do you bidding."

Praefectus raised a bejeweled mace in his right hand.

The twenty sat.

Praefectus said, also through a synthesizer, "Who brings you here this night?"

The twenty chanted, "You do, our exalted Praefectus."

"Why are we here?"

"We are here to do the work of Praetorian."

"What say you, then, my Centurion brethren?"

Centurion Eleven stood. "Oh exalted Praefectus, Centurion Eleven respectfully reports that subject has been eliminated."

"Centurion Eleven, you have the gratitude of Praetorian. Please be seated."

"Thank you exalted Praefectus."

"What further say you my Centurion Brethren?"

"Oh exalted Praefectus, Centurion Five requests permission to address Praetorian."

"Permission granted."

Centurion Five stood. "Oh exalted Praefectus, we have word the canister is missing."

A deathly stillness descended over the already noiseless room.

Praefectus said, "Tell us Centurion Five, do you present a solution, or do you choose only to burden Praetorian with a problem?"

"I respectfully beg forgiveness, oh exalted Praefectus, a solution is at hand."

"I shouldn't need to remind you what will happen if the canister falls into the wrong hands."

"No, exalted Praefectus."

"Fix it, then."

"Yes, exalted Praefectus."

"My Centurion brethren, your stipend for this night is $2 million. This sum will appear in your offshore accounts by morning. Centurion Eleven, your stipend will be $5 million in light of your exemplary service to Praetorian. Centurion Five, your stipend will be held in abeyance pending resolution of this most distasteful situation."

Praefectus raised the mace and stood. "Centurions, this meeting of Praetorian is hereby adjourned."

The Centurions stood while Praefectus left and disappeared into his private chamber, the only one that exited into a private elevator that ascended to ground level.

When his chamber door closed, nineteen Centurions glared silently—talk and touch were prohibited—at Centurion Five. Had it not been for him, all stipends for the night would have been $5 million.

The Centurions' chamber doors now opened and the Centurions retreated. Doors closed and locked. They would open one at a time beginning with Centurion One and continue until all had separately departed. They would have no further contact until the Praefectus called the next meeting.

Chapter 3

The sharp knock on my door half awakened me from a wonderful place that I had no intention of leaving. My eyes found the bedside clock. It was 7:00 a.m. I staggered part way to the door.

"Who is it?"

"Jorge, Miss. I hab your ironing."

Was Jorge the name of all their bellhops? I asked him to come back at 8:00. When he knocked again, it seemed he'd just left. I glanced through the peephole and found myself staring at the same Jorge who'd picked up my clothes the night before. I opened the door.

"Don't you ever sleep?" I asked.

"Jes I do, Miss." He grinned sheepishly. "I hab a long shift."

"You must like it," I said, watching him expertly hang my clothes. "Were you a bellhop in Cuba too?"

"No, Miss, I install alarms and safes. Here they say I no trained right." He shook his head. "They're crazy. I know more than them."

I suspected he was probably right. He came out of the closet, and I gave him ten dollars.

"Ju tip me last night, Miss. Ju don't tip me now."

"Jorge, can you find a cup of coffee in ten minutes?"

He nodded.

"Then listen to me. Last night was for last night. This is for now. Besides, my employer pays. She's got tons of money."

He grinned and took the ten. "Jes, Miss. You my friend. You tell me if you want something."

By the time I had finished showering, a white carafe and two matching cups had appeared on the small table next to the large front windows. Bless you, Jorge. I breathed in the coffee's rich aroma and gulped a few glorious mouthfuls.

I pulled the drapes aside and stared for a moment at Park Avenue, teeming below. This was it. New York City. Busy, busy, go, go, not a second to waste. A lump formed in the pit of my stomach. I ran to the closet, pulled on a freshly ironed, short-sleeved dress, glanced in the mirror, and decided that pale yellow worked well, at least for this day.

I rushed from the hotel. The front door attendant signaled a cab forward. I jumped in and told the driver to go to Broadway and 74th Street and cross the park at 66th Street. As we sped away, I glanced at the armies of people hurrying to work in the grand office buildings lining Park Avenue. This was exciting; this was fun.

Spring rains had turned Central Park into a lush wonderland. The trees bowed under the fullness of their rich green cloaks, and the grass was thick and freshly cut. I lowered the window, let the morning air blow across my face and through my hair, and breathed in the bouquets of fresh aromas. The humming of tires on blacktop made the only sound, and for a moment, it was as if the city had disappeared. Then too soon blowing horns and screeching tires and a man hollering, "Hey, watch it asshole!" broke the spell.

We crossed to Broadway and headed north.

"Let me off here," I said as we rounded the fortress-like Apple Bank Building at 73rd Street, but several police cars and an ambulance filled the roadway, and a uniformed police officer waved us on. I got out in the next block and walked back.

"What's going on?" I asked the young police officer, who was busily directing traffic and checking my legs.

"Something in one of the upstairs offices, Miss. Should be cleared soon."

I crossed Broadway and headed for the Ansonia.

Chapter 4

Patisserie Margot, Bebe's designated meeting place, is a tiny pastry shop tucked into the side of the ornate grandeur of the Ansonia Building, my future home. I decided to go upstairs later to inspect the disarray that constituted my apartment to make sure squatters hadn't taken up residence.

I pushed through the inviting French doors and stepped inside. For the second time that morning, I breathed in the aroma of rich coffee that this time danced with the seductive redolence of freshly baked croissants, muffins, and a dozen other delicacies that nestled in shiny glass counter cases.

Bebe had commandeered one of the quaint round tables and two additional chairs, her large red handbag and a black and silver shopping bag serving as territorial markers.

She wore a red sleeveless dress and matching pumps and lipstick. Her hair was blue black and she had the whitest of skin, which had always been a mystery to me since she spent every weekend at her beach house in the Hamptons.

After a loud embrace that made the other inhabitants glance in our direction, we crossed to the counter and ordered. Our cups and saucers, and tiny plates used most of the space on the tiny tabletop, although I managed to find room for my notebook and reached into my bag and turned on my recorder.

"First," Bebe said, "you simply must taste this espresso. It is, without a doubt, the best in New York."

I dutifully sipped and decided she might be right, and then we gabbed for a moment about all that had been going on in our lives in the past week. That aside, I said, "OK, what do I need to know before I meet Jenny?"

"I don't want to say too much because I want you to

see her through a fresh pair of eyes."

"What about her invention? Can you tell me anything about that?"

"I couldn't begin to do it justice, Darling, so you'll just have to wait until Jenny tells you."

"I'm becoming more intrigued by the minute. When do we meet?"

She glanced at her watch. "In a few minutes—her office is across the street."

I looked out at a green garbage truck grinding away next to the grocery market.

"Not that street—across Broadway, in the Apple Bank Building. Did you come by taxi?"

I nodded.

"Then you probably got out there."

"Actually, I got out in front of the Beacon Theater. The Apple Bank was nothing but police cars and yellow tape."

She frowned, fished her cell telephone from her bag, and punched in a couple of numbers.

"Is Jenny there?" she asked.

Her frown deepened and worked down her face.

"What about Anne? Is she there?" Her eyes began to glisten. "Anne, what's going on? I got a blob of jumble from your receptionist. What happened?"

She clutched her throat. "My God I beg of you, Anne, please tell me. Please, please tell me this isn't true."

I gripped her arm. She dropped the telephone into her bag and collapsed back on her chair.

"What on earth has happened?" I asked.

She shook her head. Her eyes brimmed with tears.

"Is she going to be OK?" a young man at the adjoining table asked.

"Yes, I'm sure she'll be fine," I said, and returned my attention to Bebe, who, for the moment didn't look at all like she was going to be fine. Her lifeless eyes met mine.

"Jenny's been murdered," she said.

Chapter 5

Had I heard correctly? The gash of shock that scarred her finely sculpted face told me I had.

"I am so sorry," I said.

Had they been close? As far as I knew, they had become business acquaintances—magazine editor meets interesting potential content subject—nothing more. I clasped her hand. She didn't pull away.

I knew a devil-may-care Bebe; this Bebe, I didn't know. I wanted to say the right words, to react in a meaningful and sincere way...for both of us because though I'd not met Jenny, I'd been looking forward to meeting her, to knowing her, to writing her story.

"Is there something you want me to do? Is there anyone you want me to call?"

She shook her head and pushed at her eyes with the bridge of her hand.

"No...I'll be OK. It's just the shock of...I don't know..."

She fished a tissue from her bag.

"When?" I asked. "I mean, how...what in the world happened?"

"Last night sometime, I guess."

Bebe balled up the tissue and dropped it into her bag.

"When Anne, —Anne Black, she's Jenny's partner—arrived this morning, she discovered one of the windows in her office open. When she went to shut it, she saw a body lying face down on the walkway."

"And no one noticed a body lying on the sidewalk until this morning?"

"Not the sidewalk—there's a walkway running around the exterior of the building's fifth floor where Anne and Jenny have their offices."

That at least made sense. Even in the worst sections of New York—and Broadway and 74th was light years from the worst—surely no one could lay dead all night on the sidewalk and not be noticed.

Her cellphone rang. She talked for a moment and hung up.

"That was Anne. The police want to see me in her office."

Chapter 6

We crossed Broadway to the Apple Bank Building. The ambulance had gone. Parked in front were three patrol cars and two black cars with extra antenna and oversized tires and red globes on top of their dashboards. A Channel 5 news truck, doors open, sat next to the plain black cars.

Men and women in casual business attire stood around the main entrance in groups of two or three, talking in low voices. Two black women, who nicely filled every inch of their jeans and blouses, smoked cigarettes held nervously in fingers that sported long fuchsia-colored nails. A thin, young white man in a white shirt and tie stood with them. Their sober young faces told me they knew what had happened.

Pedestrians walked past, some with practiced indifference and others with quizzical looks and stares. "What's going on?" a few asked. I couldn't hear what they were told, although a few departed skeptical of face; others decided to hang around; still others looked cautiously at the fifth floor windows as if seeking visual proof or a vicarious thrill.

Bebe gave her name to a young police officer and said that a Detective Kennedy had asked to see her. The young officer turned away and said something into a handheld walkie-talkie, all the while watching us from the corner of his eye as if expecting us to bolt. I tried to think how far two broads in high heels would get before he tackled us to the ground.

Static blasted from the walkie-talkie. The young officer turned it off with a showy flip and curtly told us to wait, that Detective Kennedy would be right down.

Color flashed across Bebe's cheeks. "Are you sure that's what he said, young man? I was told he wanted to see me upstairs, right now, and I rushed to get here."

The young officer gave her a long, steady look, meant to intimidate and to probably let her know he didn't like being called 'young man.' Bebe leaned forward and stared up into his big face, her way of letting him know that it would take a lot more man than him to intimidate her.

"There's been a change ma'am," the young officer said, his tone more civil and his face a touch pinker.

Bebe asked if I'd wait with her. I assured her I wasn't going anywhere. Then we fell silent and watched the uniforms and plain clothes lump into their separate cliques and have separate discussions.

"What are they saying?" Bebe asked.

I told her I couldn't hear them either.

A blonde woman elbowed her way from the building lobby, followed by a cameraman. She began firing questions. Several police shook their heads and turned away. I'd been in her predicament a thousand times, asking the unwanted question of an unwilling respondent. Thick skin was required, and she appeared to have it. She glanced in our direction.

"Shit," Bebe said. The blonde-haired woman made a beeline toward us, talking into her microphone as she approached. Her cameraman trotted along behind.

The woman shoved the microphone into Bebe's face. "Bebe Morgan, Editor-In-Chief of *Madame Magazine*. Well this is a surprise. What are you doing here? What's going on?"

"Turn everything off, and I'll tell you what I know."

The woman signaled her cameraman and lowered the mike, her eyes beginning to dart back and forth between the two of us. I figured I was next on her hit list.

"OK, spill."

Bebe shrugged. "You probably know more than I do. All I know is that someone was murdered."

The woman glared. "That's it. You made me turn off for that?"

"I didn't say I knew anything, I said I'd tell you what I know. That's what I know. The reason I wanted you to turn off your camera and mike is that I didn't want my face plastered across your news all day."

The woman wheeled around and stomped off.

"Alberta Sims," Bebe said. "Channel 5. Try and stay off her radar."

"And my guess is that's Detective Kennedy," I said.

We both watched as a big man with thick red hair, full moustache, bushy brows, and eyes that constantly shot about, barged from the building, followed by two uniformed officers.

The young officer who had confronted us walked up to Kennedy, said a few words, and pointed at Bebe.

Kennedy pulled on a pair of aviator sunglasses and marched toward us, looking too neat and tidy in his tailored suit, shirt, and fancy maroon tie, but his demeanor left no doubt he was in charge.

"I'm Detective Kennedy," he said to Bebe and asked her to meet him at the precinct at 10:30. A uniformed officer handed her a card with the precinct's address.

She glanced at her watch as if she had a choice. "Yes," she said. "That suits my time."

He asked me how I knew the deceased. I said I didn't. He said he didn't need to see me at the precinct in a way that meant he didn't want me there…or here, for that matter. Pompous ass.

A young woman in a short skirt with legs to die for raced from the building holding a tissue to her nose. All eyes locked on her as she ran to Bebe. I caught a whiff of Coco and couldn't help but notice the blue fingernails that matched her skirt, blouse, and four-inch heels. They embraced gingerly for a brief moment, as if one of them might break. Then Bebe stepped back and introduced me to Anne Black.

Anne eyed me up and down before offering a curt "Hello," then swiveled her long legs into the back of one of the unmarked cars, an activity that she knew held everyone's attention. Kennedy slid in beside her and they raced north on Broadway.

Despite Kennedy's disinclination to seeing me again, I asked Bebe if she wanted company at the police station.

"Hell yes," she said, and we hailed a cab.

Chapter 7

At the police station, while we waited for Detective Kennedy to finish his interview, I asked Bebe to talk to me about Anne Black: how well she knew her; whether she might be a suspect.

She rolled her eyes.

"I was hoping for something more verbal," I said.

"Yes, Darling, I know you were. I rolled my eyes to emphasize that Anne is a difficult person."

"So you think she is a suspect?"

"No, she's a cold-hearted bitch with a Harvard MBA an 'a don't you dare forget it' attitude. When God created Anne and Jenny, He had only one heart and one personality and Jenny got both. The first time Jenny took me into Anne's office, Jenny and I sat and talked for ten minutes while Anne stared at me and didn't say a word until we got up to leave, and then she asked if I considered myself a friend or acquaintance of Jenny's."

"What a strange thing to ask."

"You're telling me. For once in my life I didn't know what to say."

"I can't believe you left it hanging?"

"Fortunately, I didn't have to. Jenny told her I was a new friend."

"Was that the right answer?"

"Not as far as Anne was concerned. Although I think in the whole world Jenny was the only one who really understood Anne's idiosyncrasies, and she wasn't afraid to push her hot buttons."

I grabbed my notebook. "What do you mean?"

"Some time later, I discovered that Anne's greatest fear was Jenny having women friends, something that Jenny has to have known from the time they were kids growing up together."

"And yet Jenny told Anne that you were a friend."

"Exactly. She pushed Anne's hot button."

"I think that's a natural fear," I said. "No one wants to be replaced as a best friend."

"Anne Black's fear borders on pathological. Jenny told me that Anne grilled her every time she met with another woman, no matter how casually. She told me Anne wanted her to stop seeing me."

"How did Jenny react to that?"

"She laughed it off. Anne didn't intimidate Jenny."

"Were they lovers?"

"No; I hadn't meant to imply that. Anne's married to some billionaire super jock that she's reportedly head-over-heels for. Jenny is...was married to science, but she dated men—Jenny's men friends didn't seem to trouble Anne."

"Any one in particular—"

A tearful Anne Black burst from behind a closed door and started down the hallway toward us.

"Do you mind if I try to talk to her?"

Bebe snorted. "Be my guest, and use my name if you must, but I can't guarantee it will reward you with other than an icy stare."

I got up to intercept Anne. Kennedy appeared and seemed to be recording Anne Black's departure in his memory bank. I figured that after the long fleeing legs and short skirt no longer distracted him, his attention would settle on Bebe and me. It did, or at least on Bebe. He favored me with a frown. I gave him one back.

Anne hesitated as she passed by, looked about to say something to Bebe, then continued on her way.

I said to Bebe, "If I'm not here by the time the great detective has had his way with you, I'll meet you at your office," and then ran after Anne. She ignored me as I fell into step alongside.

"Anne," I said. "May I talk to you?"

She pushed her delicate nose higher and kept walking.

I took her arm.

"Get your hand off of me," she said and wrinkled her face as though encountering a distasteful odor.

"I'm Paige Harrington," I said, clinging to her arm with no intention of letting go until she talked to me. "A month ago, my best friend from the time we were in kindergarten was murdered, so I think I know as well as anyone what you are feeling, and I'm truly sorry for your loss."

"How do you know Jenny?" Her tone bordered on accusatory.

"I don't. I'm a writer. Bebe hired me to do a story about Jenny's work."

The mention of Bebe's name didn't elicit the predicted increased coolness. In fact, she relaxed ever so slightly, and I freed her arm.

"Do you feel like talking?"

Her face telegraphed 'no.' I didn't want to lose her and touched her shoulder. "Please," I said. "I'll understand if you don't, but if I decide to pursue Jenny's story, I'd value your input."

"Jenny's dead." Her eyes glistened with tears. "There is no Jenny story."

"That's not true." I fished a tissue from my bag and handed it to her. "A thousand stories will be written and told. Every network and every newspaper will want to interview you and anyone else they think can satisfy the public's desire to know every detail of Jenny's life, her work, her death, most particularly her death. Some will push you for an exclusive; some will offer money, some will just write whatever is easy, but I can assure you Jenny's story will be written...with or without you."

"They can't know about her work. Any questions about her work are off-limits."

"That won't stop them from trying, and if they can't find answers, they'll start to invent them. Conspiracy theories will abound and flood the Internet. The same with her life: what they can't find, they'll make up."

She thought for a moment, and then said, "And where do you fit in that sordid landscape of distasteful choices? Are you offering money? Will you make up what you can't substantiate? Do you demand an exclusive?"

"Why don't we sit a moment?"

"Answer my questions."

Lady, you're starting to annoy me, but if you think I'm not going to keep at you, you're wrong.

"I'm a professional journalist who doesn't pay for information. I won't report what I can't substantiate, and I don't share my data. I use only those I deem to be reliable sources, and if authorized, I name names. No magazine for which I write—I've written for most of the major names—ever changes my stories. They take what I write or they don't publish. That's my arrangement."

I expected questions. I didn't expect her to touch a hand to her hair, and say, "God, I must look a mess."

Had she heard what I said? Of course she had. This was her way of saying I'm Anne Black, Harvard MBA, and how you or the other little common people occupy your time is of little interest. Well, Queen Anne, two can play.

I stopped. "I think trying to talk to you was a mistake."

She turned to look at me.

"I'm not sure I want to write Jenny's story. Let Channel 5 and the supermarket tabloids splash her murder all over the country. No one needs to know the truth about her life, about her friends and family, about you."

She sighed. "I will talk to you for a few minutes, but not in here. I've had enough of this disgusting place."

A female police officer sitting within earshot looked up, and I got the uneasy feeling she had made a mental note of the two of us for future reference.

"Walk with me," Anne said.

We stepped out into the blinding sun and reached for

our sunglasses. Hers were six-hundred dollar *Bvlgari's*. I know because I'd looked at the same ones in Neiman's and soon found a *Kate Spade* pair on sale for five hundred less that I quickly learned to love.

"The Museum of Natural History is in the next block," she said. "Let's go there."

We both had white, paper-thin skin and didn't need a discussion about crossing to the shaded side of the street. Had I fancied the sun, I'd have walked alone.

"Rather than trying to converse as we walk," she said, "I want to be alone with my thoughts."

"Fine." That made it easy because the only thing I wanted to talk to her about was Jenny, and trying to make small talk would be painful, at best.

AT THE BACK of the museum, she found an unoccupied bench away from the madness of the hordes of tourists and locals buzzing around the crafts market and vendor carts.

"This one will do," she said, brushing the glistening slats with her hand and sitting as though she might at any second bolt.

I sat next to her, hoping I'd left the right amount of space for intimacy, though not so little that she decided to slide further away. That would have been the last straw.

We sat silently for a moment until, for me at least, the tension approached explosive. Then she dropped her face into her hands and started to cry. She wasn't the type one threw their arms around, but I had to do something. I fished a few tissues from my bag and handed them to her. She seemed not to notice. I touched her hand. She flinched, looked up, and grabbed the tissues.

"God I hate this," she said, and tried to stop sobbing. "I hate this more than anyone knows. This destroys everything."

Odd phraseology. "Is there anything I can do to

help?"

"I expect I'll be fine in a minute, but thank you."

"We can do this another time. Do you want someone to pick you up?"

"No, please, let's talk. It will help."

"May I turn on my recorder and take notes?"

She nodded as if uncertain, and then said, "Yes, I suppose so."

"Before we talk about Jenny, tell me about Anne Black. When and where were you born?"

"Fairbanks, Alaska, October 1973." Pause. "And my name was Anne Rodgers. Black is my married name."

She practically spit 'Black,' and I hoped to learn more. I didn't. Later.

"Is that where you and Jenny met?"

"We lived on the same street, we played together, we went to school together—is that germane?"

"People will want to know about the two of you. Yes, it's all germane."

She shrugged. "We left in the fall of '91, Jenny to attend MIT. I attended Harvard."

I made a few notes. She'd been watching, trying to see what I'd written. Good luck. My shorthand was a hodgepodge of several languages that only I could read. Then she stared off across the street and tapped her long, blue fingernails on the bench, making annoying clicking sounds.

"MIT was a natural for Jenny. She'd always been into science. When we were kids, she devoured every science fiction novel in the library. Her bedroom walls were plastered with Asimov robot posters and her video collection contained every robot and space movie ever made."

"Bebe said that Jenny's invention had to do with robots."

Mistake. An instant chill filled the air.

"Bebe doesn't know what she's talking about. I told

you Jenny's invention is off limits. No one knows what she was working on and if anyone says they do, they're liars."

I decided to switch back to her, a subject she seemed to prefer.

"Were you always interested in business?"

"Not passionately."

She studied me for a moment. "I've seen you before, not in person, but in some of the fashion magazines. You were a model."

"For two years."

She studied her outstretched fingers and her long elegant hand. "I wanted to be a model. That was my passion, but I couldn't leave Jenny. Even though a month older, she was the little sister I never had. I grew tall; she never made it past five-two. I got breasts, she didn't. My father is a successful business man; he loves me; Jenny's real father, a fighter pilot, died in the last days of Viet Nam without seeing her."

I studied her face. Plastic.

She continued, "Jenny's father was an aeronautical engineer, who, after his last tour of duty, planned to join NASA's robotics program. Jenny has always wanted to pursue what he never got to."

There was no question that Jenny's work involved robots, however, what that actually meant was a question for another day and another person.

Her cellphone rang. "I need to take this," she said, and stood, showing her back. I heard her voice but not her words.

She turned to face me. "I have to go."

I got up. "May I call you? I want to talk more about you and Jenny."

"I'm not sure." Painful pause. "Do you have a card?"

I gave her one and wrote Bebe's office and the Waldorf numbers together with my room number on the back.

"Thank you," I said, and extended my hand.

She pinched at it, succeeding only in gripping my fingertips, and I couldn't help but notice how cold she felt.

"Yes," she said, "Well, please don't try to reach me. I'll call you if...if I can."

I wasn't giving odds that I'd hear from her anytime soon.

A long black Mercedes appeared as if by magic and rolled to a silent stop. She spun around, strode to the curb, and disappeared into the back seat.

The driver, a large black man wearing a chauffeur's uniform, closed the door and looked at me as though recording a permanent image. A shiver snaked down my spine. I turned and hurried back toward the precinct. Bebe hadn't called. I hoped she was still there.

Chapter 8

I found Bebe pacing the sidewalk in front of the precinct. She snapped the phone shut when I got near and said, "I was about to call you."

I gave her a two-minute recap of my conversation with Anne and a three-minute discourse of the experience.

"You deserve the Pulitzer. She wouldn't have given anyone else the time of day."

"They don't give Pulitzers for asking a few questions."

"They should."

"Besides, she told me not to call, and I'm betting I don't hear from her. How did you fare with Detective Kennedy?"

"That, Darling, is why I was about to call you. With no small thanks to the irresistible and substantial feminine wiles of yours truly, he has arranged for us to talk to one of his underlings."

She slipped me a note on which someone, Kennedy I assumed since it wasn't Bebe's scrawl, had written: Constable Amato.

"How do we find Constable Amato?"

She pointed at the precinct. "He's inside now, but there is no 'we,' Darling. I have to dash."

She waved her hand in the air, and a cab, amid angry sounding horns, waving fists, and angry looks, violated at least ten traffic ordinances by dangerously whipping across traffic lanes and stopping at the curb next to where she stood. That we were in front of a police precinct hadn't seemed to matter.

"Call me when you're finished, Darling, and remind me to tell you something about Anne and Jenny that I just remembered."

"What?" I yelled after the departing cab.

She stuck her hand out of the window and waved
"Don't do this to me," I said to the air.

I watched until she disappeared around the corner, and then I turned and went inside the precinct. One of the desk constables—thankfully not the policewoman who'd overheard Anne's earlier disdainful comment—telephoned Constable Amato and directed me to the elevators. This was going to be easier than trying to dredge information from Anne Black.

The young constable waiting for me on the second floor was the same one who'd followed Detective Kennedy from the Apple Bank Building. He shook my hand and led me to a small, sterile-looking office with a rectangular table and two chairs, one on each side. Other than the fact that I could see through the one large window, the room could have passed for an interrogation space with secretly watching eyes and listening ears.

"I expected two of you," Amato said. He sat, arms on the table, hands clasped loosely, and began tapping his thumbs.

"No," I said, "Bebe Morgan, the one who met with Detective Kennedy, had to return to her office, so you'll have to be satisfied with second best."

"I'd hardly say that." He flushed, and then eyed my notebook and recorder that I placed on the table.

"Johnny...do you mind if I call you Johnny? Or would it be more proper to call you Constable Amato?"

"Johnny's OK by me."

"Johnny, I'm a journalist. I was supposed to interview Jenny Ross this morning in connection with a story I've been hired to write for *Madame Magazine*, that's Bebe Morgan's publication. Because of Miss Ross's death, I'm not altogether certain the magazine will want to continue the assignment...I don't even know if I want to continue the assignment, but I do know I won't be able to make my decision until I find out what happened. That's where you can help."

He nodded. "Yeah, a lot of people want to do stories. All the TV stations and newspapers have called. Detective Kennedy said I can answer questions with anything public."

"You're going to be busy, but then, I suppose you're used to it."

He shrugged. He was young; this might have been his first murder case, although he wasn't about to affirm or deny that supposition.

"I saw Alberta Sims from Channel 5 outside the bank. I'll bet she asks tough questions."

His big hand covered the lower part of his face, but I detected a grimace in his eyes.

"Was she in Anne Black's office?"

He looked at the recorder. "I think you'd better ask her."

I took that as a yes. Alberta Sims struck me as the type they'd have to shoot to keep out.

"My friend, Bebe Morgan, told me she thought Miss Ross had been killed last night. Is that correct?"

Nod.

"Do you know what time?"

He shrugged.

"My friend thought midnight. May I put down midnight?"

"That's what one of the CSI people said."

I had been foolish to think this was going to be an easier interview than Anne Black's. Johnny's problem was that he didn't know how much to say and he'd adopted a 'less is better' approach.

"Help me out here, Johnny, or do I need to talk to Detective Kennedy to get details?"

He shifted his large body in the creaky chair. "Ma'am, you ask your questions and I'll answer what I've been authorized to answer. I'm not volunteering information you might not want."

Despite what he'd said, I'd hit a nerve. As much as

he didn't want to give anything away, he didn't want me going over his head. "OK, was Miss Ross working late?"

"The lobby guard figured she entered the building around 11:30 p.m., just after the cleaning staff left."

"OK, that's good, Johnny. That's the type of information I like to hear, but when you say 'figured,' doesn't he know for sure? Didn't she sign in? Every office building in the city I've ever visited makes me sign in and show ID."

"This log book shows she signed in at 9:30 p.m., but the guard is positive she came in after the cleaning staff left."

"How can he be positive if the log book shows 9:30?"

"He says he knew her well."

"Did she always work late?"

"According to the guard, she came in a lot at night, though usually earlier, between eight and ten."

"And yet last night he figured she came in at 11:30. Something doesn't add up."

He shrugged.

"Doesn't the building have security cameras?"

He nodded.

"What did they show? Have you seen the tapes?"

"They use discs now."

"Ah, right, how stupid of me."

"No, it's all right. A lot of people still use tape, and everything else in the building is old-fashioned, like the log book so even I was surprised when I discovered they'd upgraded their security cameras."

"Thank you for being kind. I'll bet you know all about the latest security equipment."

"Yeah, I guess."

"What did the discs show?"

"A female, short black hair, black shirt, tights and shoes, and about the victim's size, appears on the two lobby cameras at 11:34. Judging from the video, she seemed to know the cameras' exact positions because she never showed her face."

"My friend, Miss Morgan, told me she'd been found on the fifth floor. Is that correct?"

"Yes, but on the walkway outside an executive office that perp..purp"—I fought to say the word he so desperately wanted to say—"that supposedly belonged to Anne Black."

"Did the elevator camera record anything?"

"A wad of gum had been stuck on the lens. The lab's doing a DNA test."

"What about others?"

"The security cameras in the outer office—the executive offices don't have cameras—picked up heat and motion at 11:41. They don't have infra-red lenses so all we could make out was a black shadow. A fake entry card was used to unlock the outer door at 11:40."

"Maybe it wasn't her. Maybe it was the killer."

"The shadow appeared to be her size, and when we found her, she was dressed in black, including black gloves, and her face was covered with charcoal paste. We think it was her."

"So what about the killer? What do the cameras show? Was he or she already there or did they follow Miss Ross in?"

Johnny shook his head. "The cameras and computerized entry system show nothing."

"Nothing before or nothing after?"

"Nothing before and nothing after. The guard swears no one was in the building and the victim was the last one to enter. According to the disc, the guard left his desk for a smoke every hour for fifteen minutes, but he says he never went further than the front door."

"And the heat and motion cameras in the company's offices show nothing?"

"They malfunctioned shortly before midnight."

"How convenient—didn't anyone check?"

"The alarm company noticed the problem and when they couldn't get a response, they called it in. One of our cars got to the building just as the alarm company called to say the camera system had started working again and all appeared normal. Usually our guys check anyway, but they got another call that they considered more urgent."

"What was the other call?"

"I'm not at liberty to say."

"Wasn't it on the police frequency?"

"One could try and check it there."

"But if it's there, it's public knowledge so you should be able to tell me."

The door burst open, and a red-faced sergeant, who'd not missed many meals, barged in, openly eyed that part of me visible above the table, and left the nose-wrinkling stench of stale smoke and beer in his wake.

He looked down my blouse and said, "What's going on, Amato?"

"This is Miss Harrington. Kennedy told me to talk to her."

The sergeant blew a rush of air out of his nose. "You should've asked me."

"But Kennedy's in charge and I thought—"

The sergeant smacked his hirsute, pink hand on the table. I jumped. "Next time, ask, don't think." Then he spun around and stomped out.

I said, "I'm sorry, I didn't—"

Johnny waved me off. He might have been young and inexperienced, but he wasn't about to show he'd been intimidated by the sergeant's bluster.

"Who was that?"

"Sergeant Lynch. He's OK. He and Kennedy..." He eyed the recorder and shrugged. His shrugs said a lot—too bad I didn't have a video camera.

Johnny glanced at the window behind me and nod-

ded. I looked around in time to see Lynch drawing a finger across his throat signaling Johnny to end the interview. Either that or cut my throat.

I said, "I guess that means were finished, for now."

"Yeah, I'd better go."

"May I contact you?"

"It might be better if I contact you." He glanced at
the window.

I nodded and dug a business card from my bag, wrote
Bebe's office number and the Waldorf's main number
on the back and explained what each was. He tucked the
card into his pocket.

Lynch banged on the window.

I shook Johnny's hand and headed for the door.
Lynch might not frighten Johnny, but he scared me. I
figured it wasn't beyond him to toss me into a holding
cell for no other reason than to show he's boss.

Chapter 9

To say that Bebe's office had mauve tinges was like saying a field of lilac bushes in full bloom had mauve tinges.

In her very large and very elegant tenth-floor office, we ate a late lunch seated at one end of a Deneb glass table next to large French windows that overlooked Fifth Avenue. Eight Allegro leather chairs, sat around the perimeter and a large bouquet of fresh cut orchids and lilies sat in the center. A server in a sparkling white uniform with mauve accents placed two mauve telephones to Bebe's right, laid out our tuna salad lunch, and withdrew.

"So tell me Darling," Bebe said the second we were alone, "What did Constable what's his name have to say?"

"Not until you tell me about Jenny and Anne."

She gave me a 'what do you mean' look.

"When you deserted me at the precinct, you told me to remind you to tell me something about Jenny and Anne."

She flipped her hand. "Oh that, later, it's nothing."

"I doubt that."

"I promise on mother's grave I'll tell you later."

I said, "Your mother isn't dead."

"What did you find out? That's much more important I assure you."

I told her all that Johnny Amato had told me, and then told her about Sergeant Lynch. "I'd say there's definitely friction between Kennedy and Lynch."

"I love it. Police scandal."

"Lynch isn't an attractive person," I said. "But I wasn't enamored of Kennedy either."

"You know, he's really not bad once you get to know him."

"I'll try to be kinder and gentler, but let me remind you: you were with him all of forty-five minutes, hardly enough time for an intimate relationship."

"Darling, I'm not having his children."

"Neither did you sit for forty-five minutes gazing into each other's eyes. What did you find out?"

"Detective Kennedy listens and asks. He doesn't tell."

"What did you tell?"

"Anne told you about them being friends since childhood, so I'll skip that."

"I'd like to hear you tell it."

"There's nothing to add, I assure you."

However, she did proceed to tell me what she knew, which was good, because it came from Jenny's perspective. The one thing that stood out, and that I found surprising, was Anne's generosity towards Jenny while they were growing up. I had been under the impression that Anne only took from the relationship, but that appeared not to be the case.

Some twenty minutes later, while Bebe completed her story, the server crept in and stood motionless on Bebe's far side.

"Are you finished?" Bebe asked me.

I nodded, despite having eaten little. So had she. The server took our plates and awaited further instruction.

"We have every type of coffee or tea ever manufactured. Or cold drinks. No alcohol though. I don't allow alcohol in the office unless it's the already consumed variety that doesn't show and tell."

We settled on herbal tea.

When we were again alone, Bebe said, "It's time to tell you the thing about Jenny and Anne to which I alluded before. That's what interested Kennedy most."

"I thought you said it was nothing. If it was nothing how come Kennedy is interested?"

"That's why I like you to write for me. You ask good

questions."

"Do you mind if I get my notebook and recorder?"

With a grand wave of her arm, she said, "Please, be my guest."

I placed the recorder on the table and balanced my notebook on my lap. "OK, you're on. What was it that interested Kennedy most?"

"Anne and Jenny's company is called Hebrides, Inc. He wanted to know if I'd ever seen copies of their business documents, and then wanted to know if they got along."

"Do you think he suspects Anne?"

"Everyone who has ever met Anne Black wants to suspect her of something. I do. So do you. Kennedy is no different, although I think he suspects everyone."

"What was your answer? Did they get along?"

"Like two peas in a pod, the same thing everyone else is going to tell him."

"I sense a 'but.'"

"About a month ago, Jenny asked if I knew how initial public offerings worked."

"Anne is a super smart MBA. Why didn't she ask her?"

"My point exactly. If they really did get along so famously, why did Jenny ask me?"

"Did she say why she wanted to know?"

"Anne told her Hebrides had to go public to raise more money."

I flipped to a fresh page. "What did they need the money for?"

"Jenny said it was their second phase. Their private investor initially provided $50 million on the condition that once other money was needed, it would be brought in through an initial public offering, an IPO I think she called it. I'm told that's a fairly standard practice."

"And yet, it sounds like something didn't sit right with Jenny, something she wouldn't discuss with Anne.

Did you tell Kennedy?"

"I tried to think what Jenny would have wanted, and she would have wanted me *not* to say anything that pointed the finger at Anne. When Kennedy finds out, he can point the finger at anyone he chooses: me, Dalton, their investor."

"Who is Dalton?"

"My dear sweet girl, please forgive me. Besides being one of New York City's top international corporate lawyers, he is the current love of my life." She fanned herself with her hand.

"How long did you plan on keeping him a secret?"

"Well don't feel too badly, Darling. Before last night, not even I knew he was the current love in my life."

"Was he the 'friend' you were with when I called, or are you seeing more than one 'friend' a night?"

"I've cut back to one."

"OK now that we've got that cleared up, why would Kennedy point the finger at Dalton?"

"Because when Jenny secretly gave me copies of the IPO documents that I couldn't make head or tail of, I asked if I could show Dalton, who, by the way, she'd met once before. She agreed, but only after I swore Dalton to secrecy."

I said, "And the reason for all the secrecy was that Jenny didn't want Anne to know."

"That was certainly my understanding, although she never said as much."

"What did Dalton think? Was there a problem?"

"Oh yes, there were problems, but I must insist that you ask all questions of Dalton. I know nothing, Darling; nothing."

"Did you tell Jenny?"

Her mood darkened. "I phoned her Saturday afternoon and told her we needed to meet, that there were things she needed to understand. She said she thought she knew what they were and asked if we could talk after our Monday morning meeting."

"The timing doesn't appear coincidental. Do you think she talked to anyone else?"

"I seriously doubt it—if you knew how afraid she was that Anne would find out..."

"She obviously trusted you. Did you trust her?"

"Jenny had two answers to every question: the truth or I don't know, and that precious brain of hers knew a thousand percent more than one-hundred and ten percent of the population—I trusted her one-hundred percent."

"That's why she took you into her confidence. She knew you trusted her so she trusted you."

She remained silent for a moment. I could almost see and hear her mind churning. "You would have loved her. She was so like you, I mean, not in looks and legs, my God, there's only one of you in that department, but in the way she became a best friend. You just knew she'd do anything for you and you for her."

Bebe clearly wanted Jenny's story written, but did I want to write it? Was I the one to write it? Could I find the level of passion this story needed? Had the horrible loss of my dear friend Wally Adams drained me too much? Is that what I was feeling? Why else couldn't I get my mind to wrap around this story?

Bebe had to take a few calls. I told her we'd talk more, later, closed my notebook, and turned the recorder off. Meanwhile, I'd continue to dig. Something told me I owed Jenny Ross that much.

Chapter 10

I spent the balance of the afternoon in the visiting executive's suite, a large—mammoth really, except compared to Bebe's it only rated a 'large'—fully equipped office that sat adjacent to Bebe's.

Bebe gave me a disorganized heap of stickies, mauve telephone slips, emails, and other paper scraps—droppings she aptly called them—of her many conversations with Jenny. She also plopped on my desk, a thick binder containing Hebrides, Inc.'s documents and agreements.

Dalton Croft had marked numerous passages in the agreements with a yellow highlighter and filled the margins with his notes, so while it would have helped had I been a corporate lawyer with SEC and offshore tax-shelter experience, it didn't take a genius to figure out that Dalton didn't like a lot of what he read. I told Bebe I wanted to talk to him and she arranged for the three of us to meet for dinner.

Shortly after 7:00 p.m., Bebe and I took a cab to East 12th Street in the Village, to the Gotham Bar and Grill that, though hiding behind a rather ordinary looking, green storefront, was one of New York City's finest restaurants. Dalton Croft was to meet us there, but called to say he'd been delayed. He never did show up. Bebe got even by insisting we have a $150 bottle of Pinot Gris with our wild bass and a twenty-five year old brandy with our coffee.

While meeting Dalton and having a chance to pick his brain would have been interesting, having time alone actually worked to our advantage. I started by confessing that I hadn't reached a decision about doing Jenny's story, that I wasn't convinced I was the right person, that I worried about not having the level of emotional attachment I felt the story needed, and Bebe started by trying to convince me otherwise.

She said, "Had you met her, even once, you'd be breaking down doors to find out who killed her, and why."

"I'm sure you're right."

"Listen to me Paige. I know you're spent. Your story about Wally Adams tore everyone's heart, so I know what it did to you. Let me make a proposal: you continue your research, and if by end of this week you aren't one-hundred percent certain you are the right person, I'll assign another writer."

"That's more than fair."

She stuck her hand across the table. "Deal," she said.

"Deal," I responded, "provided you do and say nothing more to convince me otherwise." This was a decision I wanted to feel in my gut, not one that responded to any sense of loyalty to Bebe; Jenny's story depended on it, deserved it.

"Deal," she said again.

I gripped her hand. "I have questions, more questions."

"I thought you might, and I'm all yours."

I had no intention of doing anything as gauche as dragging out my notebook, but I reached into my bag and turned on my recorder. "OK," I said. "We're live. Tell me about the first time you met Jenny."

"That's a good place to start: I told you that Jenny had met Dalton once before—it was a year ago at my place in the Hamptons. She came with a lawyer friend of Dalton's.

"When Dalton told me she had a PhD in computer science and advanced materials research, I wanted to kill him. My God, what were we going to talk about? Then when she spent most of the time alone reading textbooks full of complicated looking charts and graphs and working on her computer, I wanted to doubly kill him—he had his lawyer friend to talk to about all the boring things lawyers talk about and I had this mostly mute brain. Christ, she even ate lunch at her computer."

"Not an auspicious beginning."

"Inauspicious doesn't begin to cover it—it was painful, but at six o'clock when I announced dinner *in the dining room* at eight, mainly for her ears because I was damned if she was going to eat my roast duck sitting at her computer, she promptly got up and asked to help, then wanted to know what to wear. I wanted to cheer."

Even in the Hamptons Bebe demanded a certain level of formality, which included dressing for dinner. Jenny had scored big.

"After dinner, when we had coffee and cognac in the sitting room, and I wanted to listen to music, I asked if she had a favorite composer."

"Don't tell me she said Mahler."

"Yes, yes, and double yes. I couldn't believe it. And her favorite artist was Henri Matisse, but she liked all the impressionists and post-impressionists. We talked for hours, long after Dalton and his friend went to bed, and not only about music and art, everything: Alaska; MIT; New York City. The only thing off-limits was her work."

Bebe's eyes danced with excitement.

"Jenny wasn't just smart, Paige, she was brilliant, a genius, but more than all of that, she was a truly nice person and became a dear friend. She was to be our third musketeer. I couldn't wait for you to meet her."

She turned wistful for a moment, rotating the sapphire ring that occupied most of the third finger of her left hand.

"That is beautiful. Was it a gift from Jenny?"

She spread her fingers and studied the ring for a long moment. "Yes," she finally said. "I wore it this morning because of our planned meeting, but now I don't know whether to keep it on or take it off. Part of me wants to wear it; part of me wants to tuck it away in my safe deposit box, at least for a while."

"I think you should wear it."

"You know what? I think you're right."

We were quiet for a moment, and then I asked when she'd met Anne Black.

"The following week. Jenny invited me to her office—not the lab, that's off limits to everyone—in the Apple Bank Building. She had an office there, next to Anne's. Jenny rarely used hers, but apparently Anne had insisted."

"What was your initial reaction?"

Bebe leaned forward. I'd heard her hiss before—Bebe was known for her hissing—but never like this. "That cold bitch made me feel like a fool, sitting at her desk and tapping her nails, eyeing me down her tiny pointed nose like I was flotsam."

"Is that when she asked if you were a friend or acquaintance?"

"Yes, can you believe it?"

"Did you say anything to Jenny? Of course you did. What did you say?"

"I didn't want to say anything that would upset Jenny. We'd had a great time; she already seemed a good friend, and I felt she was a truly good and decent person." She shrugged. "Besides, in this business there are lots of Anne Blacks—one more or less didn't bother me all that much."

"Did Jenny say anything?"

"She said that Anne always acted that way toward her new friends, and not to give it a second thought. It didn't take a Freudian genius to know that Jenny thought the world of Anne on a whole lot of levels."

"That brings us back to the question: why did Jenny want you to look at those documents."

"Now that, my dear, is something she never got around to telling me. I respected her need for secrecy, and I respected and trusted her as a new friend."

We enjoyed an easy silence for a few moments, one we both needed.

I began to wish I'd had the chance to know Jenny, to write her story from her lips. She was beginning to grow in my mind and soul, although until and unless I saw and felt all of her; I didn't have her story within me.

I knew so little. I wanted to see and feel her life portrait. What were her hobbies, her loves and lovers? What and who was Jenny Ross, from the time she found life in her mother's womb until death left her on the walkway of the Apple Bank Building?

"Let's talk more tomorrow," Bebe finally said.

I agreed. Jenny Ross filled my mind. I suspected she, in a haunting way, would fill my dreams as well.

Dalton called as we were leaving and suggested we meet for breakfast. Bebe told him 10:30 in her office, and, because he'd stood her up, charged the $350 dinner to his house account.

Chapter 11

I got back to the Waldorf at 10:00. Forty minutes later, with Jenny Ross pushed to the back of my mind, I lay nude atop the sheets enjoying the after effects of good food and drink, a hot bath, and the cool breeze of the air conditioner on my damp skin. The flickering TV cast an eerie glow into the otherwise dark room. My eyes went deliciously shut.

The next thing I remembered was jumping like I'd been shot and grabbing the night stand telephone that attacked the silence like a fire alarm.

"Hello," I said, my brain struggling to engage.

I muted the TV. A silenced Letterman mouthed words through his gap-toothed smile, and a blue sequined Paul Shaffer dutifully laughed. I glanced at my watch. It was 11:45.

"Is this Paige Harrington?" The voice belonged to a youngish sounding woman.

"Yes, this is she," I said, curious how she knew I'd be at the Waldorf and how she'd managed to get through the hotel switchboard to my room.

"I'm sorry for telephoning at this late hour, but Brad told me you were in New York and said I should call."

"My brother Brad?" Who else? That's exactly who the caller meant. I'd kill him if this was one of his pranks. "How do you know Brad?"

"I, uh, met him a while ago. Is it too late? I'm…I don't know…I desperately need to see you."

I wanted to find out how this woman knew Brad, but that seemed secondary judging from the fear I heard in her voice.

"Where are you?" I asked, afraid my comfortable bed and I were about to part as I ventured forth to meet some unknown midnight caller.

"Please, it's important."

"Where are you?" I asked again, my legs swinging over the side of the bed as though they had a mind of their own.

After a brief moment's hesitation, she said, "I'm downstairs…in the lobby."

I don't need this, I thought, briskly massaging my fingers through my tangled hair, although going down to the lobby didn't seem a huge imposition. It could have been worse.

"Someone is trying to kill me." Her voice got little and trailed off to a whisper or a sob.

"Now wait a minute, no one is going to kill you." I pulled on a pair of jeans and white T-shirt. "What is your name?"

"Penny Munro, but it's not about me."

"Penny, where in the lobby are you?" I dashed into the bathroom and tied my hair back; brushing would take far too long.

"You can't say anything. If you say anything, they'll find out and kill you too."

I began to wonder if Penny Munro had all her gears. What did she mean, 'kill me too?' "Who else have they killed?"

"Jenny Ross."

I felt as though I'd been punched in the stomach.

"I know you're writing about her."

"Penny, for God's sake tell me exactly where you are."

I kicked my feet into a pair of sneakers. If killers, real or imaginary, didn't get her, hotel security would; a waif—why did I say waif? Because she's on the run?—in the lobby of the Waldorf had questionable tenancy, and I desperately needed to know what she knew and how she knew about Jenny Ross, including that I was writing her story. I'd have a thousand more questions by the time I got downstairs: like who was Penny Munro and what was her connection to Jenny Ross?

"I'm at the house phones next to the check-in counter."

"Don't move one step. I'm on my way."

Chapter 12

The only person standing next to the house phones wasn't Penny Munro, unless Penny Munro had suddenly morphed into a bear-like man with shiny black hair combed straight back and a big, angular face that looked like it had been chipped from granite.

His eyes were busy probing, not leering but cold and fact gathering, his brain recording every detail: red hair, long, click; five-ten, click; white blouse, click; no bra, click; stone washed jeans, designer, click; five –ten, long legs, click, click.

Leering or not, it spooked me, and I spun around and started toward the women's washroom next to the elevators. The marble floor telegraphed his footsteps coming up behind. What if he followed me inside and there was no escape? He could squash the attendant and me like bugs.

Forget the washroom. What about the elevators? An even dumber idea, if I didn't make it without him getting in the same car. Confront him, here, in the open, in full view of the registration clerks?

Defiant and scared as hell, I turned to face him and planted my hands on my hips.

"You Miss Harrington?" he asked.

"Who are you?" I didn't intend to tell him anything.

He reached into his inside jacket pocket, extracted a wallet, and flipped it open and shut, flashing something that even a high-speed camera couldn't have captured.

The wallet was on its way back into his pocket when I said as forcefully as I could, "If you expect me to do anything other than scream, you'd better show me that again so I can read it, and then tell me what I want to know to make sure it's real."

His eyes simmered with a pissed-off look, but he showed me a badge. I took it from his hand, studied it for a moment, and handed it back.

"Do you have any other ID, Detective De Groot? How am I supposed to know that just because you have an NYPD badge and ID card that you are actually an NYPD detective?"

"My driver's license with my picture good enough, or do you want to call my mother?"

"Let's see the license. Then I'll decide."

His beefy fingers burrowed into a separate section of the badge wallet and came up with his license. I alternated my eyes between his face and license and handed the license back.

"OK, Detective Herman De Groot of the NYPD, how do you know my name and what do you want?"

"A young woman by the name of Penny Munro called your room a few minutes ago. We need to find her."

"A young woman who said her name was Penny Munro called my room. I don't know anyone by that name, but she sounded desperate so I agreed to meet her here in the lobby next to the house phones. You are the only person I saw next to the house phones, and I doubt very much that you masquerade as Penny Munro. Now that I've told you one-hundred percent of what I know,"—other than the fact that Penny Munro said she wanted to tell me about Jenny Ross, which is something I'm not going to tell you or anyone else until I find out what's going on—"maybe you can tell me what you know. Who is Penny Munro and why did she call me? What has she done? Why do you need to find her?"

De Groot grinned. He had great teeth except for a wayward cusped that slanted off to the right. "I don't believe you showed me your badge, Detective Harrington."

I forced a grin that felt more like a grimace. "You started it, Herman."

He pointed to a pair of large overstuffed chairs that

faced the check-in desk. I took to the nearest one that swallowed me up; he dwarfed the second.

"Penny Munro sings and dances in clubs," he started. "Not top name places like the Algonquin or Feinstein's, although not bad ones either. She's done some Broadway stuff."

Herman didn't seem to be Algonquin or Ritz material, more of a beer and strip-club type, but what he said convinced me more than ever that I didn't know Penny Munro. I knew the Algonquin. I'd been often. I got their e-mails. I'd never heard of a performer by the name of Penny Munro.

He continued, "Sometimes Penny does drugs, gets herself into bad company."

Oh great. And my brother Brad, a resident at Montreal General, is mixed up in this? How in God's name does Penny Munro know Brad?

"We're working on a case. I can't give you particulars, but we've been at it awhile, separating the ones from the zeros, if you know what I mean."

De Groot paused, as if waiting for his wit to be applauded. I didn't.

He shrugged, and continued, "A couple of weeks ago, things started to break up, like they'd gotten wise to us."

"Are you telling me that Penny Munro is part of a drug gang or ring or whatever you call them?"

De Groot studied me for a moment. "Penny also sings at a club on the West Side, where some of the characters we had under surveillance hang out. We think Penny knows who they are, and we think she knows who their boss is."

"And she's in trouble because…because what?"

"We don't know who the boss is. No one alive knows who the boss is, except possibly Penny Munro. What I'm saying is that these are the kind of people who don't want anyone to know who the boss is."

"How do you think she came into possession of that

life-ending bit of information?" Was that what Penny wanted to tell me, that the 'boss' murdered Jenny Ross?

De Groot folded his hands, tapped his big thumbs together, and squinted.

"Jesus Herman, I hope you don't think I know anything about any of this?"

"Penny Munro is on the run, afraid for her life. Maybe you want to tell me why, out of seven million people with 212 telephone numbers, she calls you?" He gestured with his huge arm and glanced around as if the entire seven million people had gathered in the lobby.

"I know why she said she called me, but I'm not going to tell you until I know for sure."

He frowned and tapped his big thumbs again. "I get the feeling there's a lot you're not telling me."

"Are you going to arrest me?"

"If you told me everything you know, I might be able to help you figure out some things you don't know."

"And you might cause trouble, possibly for me, which I don't need, and definitely for Penny Munro."

He shrugged again. He seemed good at it. It seemed his way of saying, 'Look, I don't care, but I'll kill you if you don't tell me what I want to know.' I didn't really think he'd kill me, and he was intimidating by half compared to when I first saw him.

"She said a mutual friend told her to call."

"Did she give you the name of this mutual friend?"

"No."

"And you believed her?"

"She sounded desperate and she sounded young."

Herman gave me an odd look, as if wondering whether I was yanking his chain.

I said, "I think she was telling the truth. My friends aren't in the habit of giving my itinerary to night club performers or anyone else for that matter, including members of my immediate family."

De Groot stood then, and glared down. Why had I

foolishly thought he looked less intimidating? I quickly stood, glad of the few other people in the lobby, that and being as tall as he was.

"I guess what I told you didn't help you figure out why Penny Munro called me?"

"Let me recap, Miss Harrington." He held up his big hand and pointed to his big little finger. "One: Penny Munro calls your room, something I already know." He looked at me, and then pointed to his ring finger. "Two: You come down to the lobby to meet a girl you say you don't know, another fact that I already know." A quick glance, and then on to the next finger. "Three: You tell me you don't know who gave her your number. I already didn't know that."

He lowered his hands and looked at me hard. I refused to look away, though it was a struggle not to.

"Is that a no?" I asked.

His face tightened into a slight grin. "I'd appreciate a call when you hear from her again."

"You think I will, I mean hear from her again?"

"I'm sure of it, and I'll be real disappointed if you don't call."

"Herman, you'll be the first to know."

I watched as he walked across the glistening marbled lobby, his stride confident and strong. Though I thought he might, he didn't look back. The last thing I saw was the back of his large head disappearing down the escalator that led to Lexington Avenue.

Chapter 13

I returned to my room, doubting I'd find sleep anytime soon, and called Brad's cellphone number in Montreal. While I waited for him to answer, I crossed to the windows overlooking Park Avenue, pushed the sheers aside, and peered down, not sure what I expected to see. De Groot had exited the hotel on Lexington Avenue. I doubted he'd walk around the hotel perimeter so he could stand on Park Avenue and watch my room, though something in my gut told me he knew which room was mine.

What I saw appeared normal for a swanky avenue that ran in front of a swanky hotel in a swanky neighborhood. What I didn't see were suspicious looking characters lurking in the shadows.

A handful of taxis, some headed north and some headed south, shunted up and down on either side of the boulevard. Three waited in a queue fifty feet south of the hotel's main entrance. Two stretch limos, one white, one black sat on the other side of the entrance. Despite the late hour, but not late for New York City I reminded myself, a sprinkling of pedestrians, some in suits and fancy dresses, others in jeans and T-shirts, and others somewhere in between, strolled along the sidewalks, the hard scrabble scurry of the daytime masses suspended for a few hours.

Brad didn't answer. I left a message asking him to call concerning Penny Munro, and then rang his hospital number. The floor nurse said he'd been in the operating room for the past four hours. I didn't leave a message knowing he'd check his voicemail as soon as he was able.

Finally, I felt tired enough for sleep. Before dropping off, I turned down the telephone's ringer, fearing another blast like the one earlier from Penny might do me in; then I called Bebe's voicemail to say she shouldn't be concerned if I showed up late for our morning meeting with Dalton.

Some time later, from a comatose sleep, I thought I heard a ringing noise and decided it was part of a patchwork dream about hiding with Penny Munro under a car in a back lane near Wall Street and having my cellphone ring just as our pursuers approached. I rolled over and pushed my head under a pillow.

When I pried my eyes open at 8:00 and noticed my message light flashing, I punched the hotel's message center number. The call came in at 4:25 a.m. so I knew that while it might have been from any other person on the planet, it definitely wasn't from Bebe. Maybe Brad, I thought, though in my mind I sensed who it really was.

I played the message. Static, a loud rumbling sound, and Penny Munro's agitated voice burned into my ear. I replayed the message three times before I understood most of her words, and then again a fourth time so I could record and save it in a computer file.

"I couldn't wait for you last night," she said. "They came after me. I got away, but they're still out there looking, and they won't stop until they find me. I'll try to reach you later, but if I can't, if I don't get the chance, I'll send you a Federal Express package explaining everything." Click.

I played the message again, this time concentrating on background noises. Mixed in with the static and loud rumbling, I heard a ding-dong chime and a woman's computer-generated voice. Subway sounds, but the only words I managed to filter out were '96th Street.' I looked up a subway map on the internet. Lexington Avenue, Central Park West, and Broadway all had 96th Street subway stops. If Penny had headed north, her destination was either upper Manhattan or the Bronx; if she had headed south, her destination was either a million places in Manhattan or a million places in Brooklyn or Queens, not counting transfers and other underground connected transportation like trains and busses and airplanes that would take her anywhere in the world. Logic told me she remained in Manhattan. Logic told me she knew how best to maneuver in Manhattan, how best to hide.

I erased the message and tried Brad's three numbers in Montreal. All answered with voicemail. This time, I left the same message with all three: "Call me. It's urgent. A Penny Munro contacted me, says you told her to call. Well, good news: she has; bad news: she's either a nut job or she's got a heap of trouble."

I tried Lisette's three numbers as well, and hung up when I got her voicemail. My trying to explain Penny Munro to Brad's very new and very fiery French Canadian wife would have been difficult, but not nearly as difficult as the problem Brad would have trying to explain Penny Munro to his very new and very fiery French Canadian wife.

Then to be certain I had covered all the bases, I sent him an email. The thought of leaving a message on mother's telephone in case Brad, in a totally uncharacteristic gesture, called home, quickly dissolved. Sally Bowles Harrington, matriarch of the Harrington clan, or worse, my father, Judge P. Tillingford Harrington III, would ask far too many questions, none of which I felt physically or mentally capable of parrying.

Detective Herman De Groot's card sat on the night table next to the telephone. De Groot would love to know that Penny Munro had called again, but I decided that for now, he wouldn't. I also decided there were too many unknowns, the main one being: did Penny Munro really know who had killed Jenny Ross. Second: how did Penny know that I'd been retained to write a story about Jenny Ross? Third: if she had gotten my name from Brad, the connection didn't make sense because Brad knew nothing of Jenny Ross.

But Penny Munro existed. She might not know Brad,

but she existed, and according to De Groot, someone was definitely after her. I hadn't decided what I wanted to believe about our lives being in danger, though De Groot seemed to think that at least Penny's was. And De Groot definitely existed.

I showered, dressed, and left to meet Bebe and Dalton Croft, hoping Penny soon called again because only she had the answers I needed. In the meantime, I refused, perhaps naïvely, to accept the crippling notion that each breath might be my last. I also found it interesting that since Penny Munro's call, I hadn't wondered about whether or not to write Jenny's story. If I could believe Penny Munro, the person or persons who murdered Jenny were going to kill Penny, then me if I said anything—about what or to whom I did not know. It didn't matter. Jenny's story had become personal, very personal—and I now knew I had to write it.

Praetorian

Spaced from one to three minutes apart, twenty Mercedes limousines with black windows left the FDR Drive at Exit 3, tuned onto Water Street, and headed toward the Federal Reserve Bank.

Some minutes later, far below ground, twenty Centurions disguised in black robes and hoods gathered in a semicircle, and stood facing the throne of Praefectus.

At 2:00 a.m. sharp, Praefectus entered and took his place on the raised platform.

The Centurions chanted their eerie greeting, and Praefectus raised the bejeweled mace. The twenty sat.

Praefectus said, "Who brings you here this night?"

The twenty chanted "You do, our exalted Praefectus."

"What say you, then, my Centurion brethren?"

"Exalted Praefectus, Centurion Five requests permission to address the Praetorian Guard."

"Permission granted."

Centurion Five stood. "Oh exalted Praefectus, regrettably, the canister remains missing."

Praefectus said, "Tell us Centurion Five, how long will we be burdened with this problem?"

"I respectfully beg forgiveness, oh exalted Praefectus, but we know who has it."

"Why, then, Centurion Five, is it not here?"

"I respectfully beg forgiveness, oh exalted Praefectus, but we don't know where the actual canister is. We—"

The Praefectus waved the mace. "Enough! Centurion Five, you are hereby ordered to never again disgrace our hallowed presence without the canister."

"Yes, oh exalted Praefectus. I respectfully beg your forgiveness and that of my Centurion brethren."

Praefectus raised the mace.

"Centurions, from this night forward all stipends will henceforth be canceled pending resolution of this distasteful problem."

Praefectus stood.

Centurions, this meeting of the Praetorian Guard is adjourned."

The twenty Centurions stood while Praefectus left the room.

Nineteen Centurions formed a tight circle around Centurion Five. He had now cost them $8 million. His incompetence could not stand. When the circle opened, a gold plated sword in a black leather scabbard lay at Centurion Five's feet. He would be expected to fall on it if he didn't retrieve the canister.

He stooped, picked it up, and nodded, meaning he would comply.

The doors to their private chambers opened, and they left the sanctuary. Usually, they then departed, one at a time beginning with Centurion One. On this night, however, Centurion Five would be the last to leave. His disgrace did not allow him to take his normal turn.

Chapter 14

A man I assumed to be Dalton Croft was already at Bebe's office, sitting alone, sipping from a demitasse, his manicured pinky pointed in the air. The French cuffs of his blue and white striped shirt extended just far enough from his jacket to reveal diamond cufflinks. When he saw me enter, he deftly returned his tiny cup to its tiny saucer and glided up from his chair, his tancolored suit fresh and crisp. It looked expensive and I decided it probably was.

"I'm Dalton Croft..." he said, his delicate hand gripping mine more firmly than I would have thought possible. I wished Bebe had told me about his yellow hair. It was hard not to gape at the color and the way he had it stylishly curled at the neck. Except for shocks of white at the temples, he might have passed for a California beach denizen. His teeth flashed from his darkly tanned face, handsome in a sharp-featured way. "...and I know you are Paige Harrington except you are even more beautiful than Bebe's finest description."

Bebe breezed in looking like a cloud of powder blue with all the redolence of a whorehouse madam. "Oh, grand, I see you've met," she said, and handed me a note that read: Don't you dare say a word about this God-awful perfume. Dalton gave it to me and since he's doing this one gratis, I owe him. "Let's sit over here," she continued, and motioned to an overstuffed white sofa and chairs that surrounded a glass, kidney-shaped coffee table with a dozen pink and white roses centered on top.

After we sat Bebe said, "Darling, you look different this morning, and I like what I see, the fire in your eyes is back."

"It's amazing what a good night's sleep will do." At some point, I'd tell her about my event-filled night and my decision about Jenny.

Dalton busied himself by removing several pages of a document from his briefcase and spreading them on the table. I could see he had highlighted several parts, and copious notes filled the margins. Both the markings and the handwriting were the same as those on the documents Bebe had previously shown me.

He said, "The first thing you need to know is that Hebrides, Inc., Anne & Jenny's company, has three shareholders with Anne and Jenny each owning 25.5% and an unknown investor owning the remaining 49%."

"Why unknown?"

He looked at Bebe.

"According to Jenny," Bebe said, "Anne worked for a Boston-based investment firm while Jenny completed her PhD and finished a prototype of her brain child. When they needed money to launch Hebrides, Anne found an investor who put up $50 million on two conditions, other than owning 49% with right of first refusal to purchase the remainder: 1. the investor's identity remain secret; and 2. they move to New York where Jenny would do all her work in an equally secret underground lab.

"Jenny balked until she discovered the lab was the most advanced she'd ever seen. More I cannot tell you. Jenny swore she didn't know where it was because they picked her and her colleagues up each morning and drove them home each evening in an armored limo with windows so dark they couldn't see in or out, and they always took different routes."

"That's all we have? We don't know the 'who' and the 'why?'"

"Those, Darling, are the secrets, and as for the rest, I'll leave you in Dalton's capable hands."

Bebe excused herself to attend to some of the thousands of emergencies that commonly filled her days. I suspected her disappearance had as much to do with not sitting through a legal dissection of Hebrides, Inc. as it did dousing the 'fires of publishing hell,' as she called them.

For the next hour, Dalton reviewed the chronology and substance of the documents. He showed me an ownership family tree that had more branches than the British Royal Family.

"This isn't, of course, factual," he continued, "but representative of what an offshore ownership structure might look like, once put in place. The various holding company names I've listed are fictitious and the locations are best guesses."

"Why all the complexity? This isn't a multi-billion-dollar international conglomerate we're talking about."

"Our firm doesn't represent Hebrides, and of course if it did, I couldn't be discussing any of this with you, but to answer your question: usually it's done to hide ownership and revenue."

"Jenny seemed removed from the business side, but do you really believe Anne doesn't know their investor's identity, particularly since she was the one who found the money?"

"Sure. Our firm often represents investors who don't want their identities known. The company, individual, or government that invested in Hebrides, likely invested through a deeply veiled offshore company known only to an offshore trust agent who represents the investor and acts on his behalf. Anne likely dealt with one of the investor's long string of agents, none of whom knows the ultimate client's identity."

"Bebe told me you found problems in some of the documents."

"There were serious problems. After the planned public offering, Jenny's 25.5% interest vanished."

"What do you mean, vanished?"

He outlined various ownership scenarios, tying his comments to various points in Hebrides, Inc.'s evolution and offering documents. Precision and detail flowed from his brain in a continuous stream that ordinarily might turn gray matter to mush. Fortunately, he had a happy faculty of reducing multi-layered ownership structures muddied by tiers of offshore jurisdictions to their basics and made it easy for me to see how they'd tricked Jenny.

"I can't understand why Jenny didn't want to discuss these documents with Anne."

He shook his head. "I can't understand why anyone with Anne's educational background and experience let this arrangement pass."

"Do you think she did it on purpose?"

"Perhaps, although the one thing not evident is who ends up with Jenny's stock? If it's Anne, then yes, one might conclude she did it on purpose. For example, if I, or anyone with knowledge of how these arrangements work, passed these documents along for execution, it would be hard to argue that the sole purpose wasn't to defraud."

"Bebe said when she talked to Jenny last Saturday, Jenny already knew what the problems were. We were going to discuss them after our meeting yesterday."

"Yes, Bebe told me the same thing."

"Do you think Jenny made a mistake and confronted Anne?"

"Are you asking if Anne might have killed her?"

"Yes, I guess that would have been my next question."

He tapped his fingers together in front of his face for a moment, and then said, "Of course I don't know the answer, although I think we can safely assume that if we arrived at the question, Detective Kennedy and his forensic lawyers and accountants will soon have the same question."

I said, "The problem I have is that Anne strikes me as a person who'd never take the risk. And what's her motivation?"

"Isn't it always money?"

"That doesn't make sense. Bebe says she's married to a billionaire, and I can't imagine Hebrides being worth all that much."

"Two things contradict that statement: One, I'm not certain her husband is worth billions; and Two, rumor on the street has it that Hebrides could be worth billions."

"For what?"

He gave me a quick look.

"Sorry," I said. "I hadn't meant to be blunt, but what does Hebrides have that could possibly be worth that much money?"

"That well-kept, well-guarded secret is doubtless the root of all of the rampant speculation."

"You said her husband may not be worth billions."

"I need to get back to you on that. Something in my mind tells me his circumstances have recently changed."

"Still, it seems Anne isn't going to be short of money. If her husband isn't worth billions, it seems her interest in Hebrides is. Maybe we should be looking at the private investor."

"And I'd agree, except for one thing: the private investor has gone to great lengths to remain invisible and isn't going to be happy having light shone into every tiny crack of Hebrides."

"How soon will we know the investor's identity?"

He began re-fingering his documents. I feared he might be about to embark on more minutiae about veiled corporations and offshore tax havens, but Bebe interrupted by suggesting we adjourn for lunch.

THE MAÎTRE D' at The Four Seasons greeted Dalton by name and told him 'his table' was ready. I figured the $350 Bebe had charged to Dalton's house account at the Gotham the previous evening was small change compared to what he must spend in the Four Seasons, and I knew that Bebe had been there more than once because the maître d' said, "Nice to see you again, Miss Morgan," and Bebe said, "Thank you Enrico."

Besides a scattering of secret-service types trying to stand unobtrusively and failing miserably, dollops of the rich and famous, though ignoring us in a practiced way, seemed acutely aware of all who dared enter their hallowed midst.

When we finished our lunch and started to leave, a tall man of medium build, his impeccable long white hair in sharp contrast to his dark tan and his dark suit that screamed expensive, walked over and loudly shook Dalton's hand. I sensed Dalton cringe before bowing to the nicety of introducing this brash intruder to me. His name was Abner Dodge, and I decided I didn't like him much because he was too loud, too slick, and his eyes had done nothing but feast on Bebe's and my breasts.

"What an asshole," Bebe whispered to Dalton, and then turned to me and said, "He's the senior partner at Dodge & Drew. They represent every crooked politician in New York."

"They have other clients," Dalton said.

"Oh, excuse me. They also represent every crooked businessman. It's a large firm."

Dalton said, "I'm not about to defend Abner Dodge, but Peter Drew is a decent sort."

"Oh Dalton, stop," Bebe said. "You know you're the only honest lawyer in New York. Why do you think I love you so?"

Chapter 15

Dalton left us at Bebe's office, though not before inviting me to call with questions. I likely would, but not without Bebe's blessing. Theirs was a complex relationship with many hidden reefs, and I intended to avoid wrecking on the shoals.

I contacted the Waldorf for messages and checked my voicemail. My heart raced with anticipation when I heard Penny's voice, then as quickly, my hopes were dashed when she said she would call back and didn't leave a number.

A young woman from the reception lounge came into Bebe's office and introduced herself. She said she was sorry she hadn't realized earlier that I was Paige Harrington, that someone had called several times yesterday and today looking for me. She handed me several telephone message slips marked only with date and time.

"I apologize, Miss Harrington, but she wouldn't leave her name or number."

I told her not to worry, and gave her my cellphone number in case the unknown caller—it had to be Penny—telephoned again.

Bebe shot past with a questioning look. I grabbed her arm and pulled her into her office.

"I've decided to write Jenny's story. That's the fire you saw this morning."

"Darling, the way you grilled poor Dalton, I knew you had."

"Dalton strikes me as one who gets grilled only as much as he chooses."

"He's not that tough." She held up her little finger.

I said, "I'll bet one look from that devilishly handsome face and it is he who has you wrapped around his finger."

"Oh puleeze, Darling. This little fly has flitted far too

many miles to get trapped in a sticky web."

I LEFT Bebe's office and returned to my room. My cell-phone voicemail had a message from Brad who had called and left a 212 callback. I wondered if it was a WATS line for Montreal General and called the number. NY Presbyterian Hospital answered.

After I explained that Brad was a resident at Montreal General, a real live woman in the NY Presbyterian call center had him paged. A boyish sounding voice said, "Emergency Ward," and told me to hold while he checked his list. Classical 'telephone' music played while I waited, and my mind drifted to Jenny, to seeing Anne's tearful face as we sat on the park bench, to Detective Kennedy's glaring eyes, to Johnny Amato and Sergeant Lynch, to Penny Munro, to Dalton, to Abner Dodge—

"To what, dear sister, do I owe the unparalleled pleasure of hearing your voice on a brilliant Tuesday afternoon in New York City?"

"I love you too."

He laughed as only Brad could laugh, and hearing it made me feel good.

"Isn't this rather sudden?" I asked. "You didn't tell me you planned on being in New York."

"I didn't know until after I dropped you at the airport Monday night and swung by the hospital. The chief asked if I could take Jamie McAllister's rotation starting at 8:00 this morning at New York Presbyterian, which means something like 'if you don't you'll never work in this or any other town again' so I decided to get on the plane and head to the Big Apple. I got in at 1:30 this morning."

"And that made you too tired to return my calls?"

"Hey, big sister, I called your room twice. No one home. The next thing I knew it was morning and I'd slept in."

Had he ever not slept in?

"I guess you're forgiven. Where's Lisette? I tried her numbers also."

"Right now, sleeping is my guess. She and the hospital kept each other company all night—a lot of head trauma from a ten-car pile up on the Ville Marie in downtown Montreal—but I'm surprised she didn't return your calls. In her book, big sister, you're a ten."

"I didn't leave a message."

"That would explain it."

"What I need explained, little bro, is why one of your many, badly troubled fans of the female persuasion called me in my room last night."

"I'm crushed. How can you seriously believe I'd risk life and limb by revealing your location to any living person?"

"Does the name Penny Munro sound familiar?"

"You're serious? Someone actually called and said I'd told them you were staying at the Waldorf?"

"I'm serious. She called at 11:45 last night. I think her exact words were, 'Brad told me you were in New York and said I should give you a call.' Then she started to cry, said she thought someone was trying to kill her, and wanted to see me in the lobby." I left out the part about her saying my life might be in danger.

"Heavy duty. What'd she look like?"

"Not a clue." I told him about meeting Detective Herman De Groot.

"Do you think someone might be trying to kill her?"

"De Groot seems to think so."

"And the mysterious Penny Munro has pulled a Houdini?"

"She left a message at 4:25 this morning, saying she was safe for the moment, although she knew they were still looking for her. I think she called from a subway station, judging from the background noise. Besides a rumbling sound and bells chiming, I thought I heard a woman's voice say Ninety-Sixth Street."

"I had no idea you were an aficionado of the electric sewer."

"Don't be such a snob. During my years at Columbia, the subway and I became good friends. Besides, it's a lot better than it used to be."

"But not as quiet as the Metro."

"No, I concede that, but back to our mystery friend—Penny Munro called my room again this afternoon at 2:10. All she said was that she'd call later."

"There's supposed to be an indoctrination session for visiting slaves this evening followed by several hundred boring speeches I can do without. Let's meet for dinner, and since I'm staying in NYU's dorm—that's where one goes when the Y is full—we'll meet at your place."

"Don't give me that poor boy story. Don't forget I've been in your fancy penthouse. I know how you live, which I know is entirely due to Lisette rescuing you from that pig sty you used to call an apartment."

"Hey easy, that was a great apartment."

"Meet me at seven-thirty and wear a jacket. I'm buying."

"As long as it's round and comes in a bun, I'm happy."

"You won't be, but I'm sure Lisette will be happy to know there are two people in your life who care that you know how to eat with a fork."

"Maybe Penny Munro can join us. I'm dying to meet her."

"So am I," I said, "and not to be crass, but speaking of dying, a friend of Bebe Morgan's—Bebe's editor of the mag I'm doing a story for—was murdered last night, which may be a part of the Penny Munro story. I'll reveal all over dinner."

"Busy night in the naked city, and since when did you care about being crass?"

After I ended my call to Brad, I telephoned the

NYPD and asked to speak to Detective De Groot. Though I didn't intend to tell him about Penny Munro's last two calls, I wanted to see if he had any new information to share. I hadn't yet figured out why, but for a New York cop, he'd been overly giving in that department.

A woman answered and said her name was Sergeant Vasquez. I told her I was looking for Detective Herman De Groot and this was the number on his card. Vasquez said she didn't know Herman De Groot or any other De Groot or any other Herman and hung up.

Chapter 16

My stomach tightened into a fist-sized knot. First, I was mad I'd let De Groot dupe me, and second, I was fearful I'd been in the presence of Penny Munro's pursuer rather than her rescuer.

I picked up De Groot's card and carefully redialed the number. Sergeant Vasquez answered. I figured if I asked for De Groot again, she'd bang down the receiver, so I said, "I'm trying to reach the Midtown North Precinct."

"Well you got it, ma'am. What do you want? Who do you want to talk to?"

I told her about meeting a person who said he was Detective De Groot. "He showed me his badge and police ID and when I asked for something else, he showed me his New York State driver's license."

She told me to wait and put me on hold. After several minutes, a loud, Irish brogue rolled onto the line.

"Sergeant Daly here, Miss, how can I help?"

I repeated my story.

"I think he was impersonatin' an officer, Miss. You should come in and file a complaint and see if you can recognize him by lookin' at some pitchurs."

"I can come in now," I said, glancing at my watch. I had three hours to kill before hooking up with Brad. "How long will it take?"

"Might take a while."

"Can I start today and finish tomorrow?"

"Might be a good idea, Miss."

I got directions to the precinct, grabbed my bag and laptop, and headed for the elevators. Out front, the doorman waved a queued cab forward. I handed him a five and climbed in.

"306 West 54th," I said, "between Eighth and Ninth."

"You want the precinct?"

"Yes, Sir."

"Corner of Eighth and 54th OK. Otherwise I got to go around the block."

I glanced at the eyes staring back from the rearview mirror.

"I mean it's right near the corner, Miss, but I can take you around if you want. Costs more is all."

"The corner will be fine." I glanced at his tag. Domenico Moretti. He reminded me of Dom Caputo, a strip club owner from Calgary I'd gotten to know better than I'd intended, though as it turned out, we ended up friends.

I got out of the cab on the southwest corner of the intersection and started up the street. A handful of uniformed officers and men in suits, who I assumed were also police officers, spared neither time nor discretion in ogling. I turned and walked directly toward them, which caused much foot shuffling and changing expressions. I asked one of the uniforms, a heavyset man, who seemed like he might be the unofficial leader of the clique, where I could find Sergeant Daly.

"Second floor, Miss. Check in at the counter." He pointed to a set of double doors.

They stopped ogling, but I suspected ten or twelve pairs of eyes followed me up the steps, and I would have been disappointed to learn otherwise.

I went inside and rode the elevator to the second floor, half expecting someone to stop me for questioning. Pink-faced Sergeant Daly either knew from cameras that seemed to pop out from every corner that I was on my way up or spent most of his time watching the elevator doors because he nodded as I stepped off. "You Miss Harrington?"

He asked some questions and punched my answers into the computer that sat on his desk. When we finished, he printed a completed complaint form and asked me to sign. I looked it over and did as told. He then took me to another room with a bunch of computers and people sitting around staring at big screens. Their eyes were open, but they looked either comatose or dead. Daly talked to one of the young men who got up and walked with Daly back to where I stood.

"This here's Ajit," Daly said. "He'll show you how to search."

Ajit, a handsome East Indian who dressed American college—maroon sweatshirt that said Columbia University on the front, jeans, and bare feet in white sneakers that didn't have a Nike splash—put out his hand. He didn't have a great handshake, he didn't smile, and he didn't speak. He did lead me to a large-screened computer that sat off to one side. Daly disappeared.

It turned out that Ajit could speak. I guessed that up until he started asking questions, he'd seen no need.

His long brown fingers flashed across the keyboard as I told him what he wanted to know. When I'd finished giving him De Groot's description, he clicked search. A message box popped up that said 2,764 matches. He showed me how to advance from image to image and go back if I wanted to review something I'd already seen.

"Call me if you need help," he said, "and if you think of anything specific, like a tattoo or birthmark or scar, change the search parameters to reduce the number of hits." He showed me how.

"Before you go," I said, "What year did you graduate Columbia?"

"Ninety-five, but I didn't write my thesis until last year."

"What in?"

"AI, artificial intelligence. What about you, are you a Columbia escapee?"

"Journalism, '99. I don't have a doctorate, though it seems I write a thesis a week."

He smiled. "Maybe we can visit later. Daly said you

were in a hurry tonight." He gave me his card and wrote his cellphone number on the back.

We agreed to talk in the morning, and I left after an hour with burning eyes. So far, Herman De Groot hadn't popped up on the police computer, but I still had over two thousand images to view.

Chapter 17

In the half-hour until Brad arrived, I showered, put on a light green sleeveless dress and white heels, and was busy digging a matching bag from the bottom of one of the wardrobes Bebe had sent from my apartment, when my room telephone rang. I glanced at my watch. Perfect timing, little bro, I thought, and picked up the phone.

"Come on up and I'll show you how the other half lives."

Rather than Brad, it was an out-of-breath Penny Munro. "Is this Paige Harrington?"

"Penny? Where are you?"

"Oh, thank God it's you."

"Penny, are you OK?"

"I need your help. They have me cornered."

"I want you to listen to me. If you have a cellphone, turn it off and remove the batteries. Don't use it. They can trace your location through your cellphone."

Penny was silent for a moment.

"Are you on your cellphone now?"

"Yes..."

"Is there another telephone you can use?"

"There are pay phones, but I can't get to them without being seen."

"Where are you?"

"I'm in the main library on 42nd and Fifth."

"I can be there in a few minutes. How will I find you?" I'd been there enough to know there were several floors and a lot of rooms.

She said, "I have to keep moving. I'll have to find you. Stay on the stairways."

I started for the door, kicking out of my heels and into my sneakers. "I'm wearing a light green dress, white sneakers, and carrying a white handbag. My hair is red and long."

Penny's telephone had gone dead. All I could do as I raced out was hope she'd heard my description. I caught a cab headed south on the Lexington Avenue side of the hotel. Traffic was heavy, but moving.

I called Brad. "Penny Munro called. I'm off to meet her now."

"You're not going alone."

"Got to run. Wait for me."

"I'm going with you."

"Wish you could, little bro, but no time. Penny has bad company."

"You can't go alone. Don't be crazy."

"I've got help." I didn't, but telling him wouldn't change anything. Besides, I planned on getting help.

First, I called the 20th Precinct and asked to speak to Detective William Kennedy or Constable Johnny Amato. Amato was off duty; Kennedy was out of the building. I thought of asking for Sergeant Lynch and decided against that course of action; I didn't like what I'd seen in that guy.

I left a message for Kennedy and said it was urgent. Next, I called the Midtown North Precinct and asked for Ajit Singh. He answered immediately, and I gave him a fast run-down.

"Wait for me outside the library," he said. "I'll be there in ten minutes."

"I'm in a taxi crossing Madison and will be at the library in a minute. I can't make her wait; I have to go inside. Look for me on the stairs." I hung up.

The light at Fifth turned red. "I'll get out here," I said to the driver.

The cab pulled to the curb lane. I got out and ran, zigzagging through the Fifth Avenue traffic, ignoring honking horns and the "Hey lady, what the hell you doing, trying to get killed?" shouts. Hope not, I thought, racing up the steps and through the front door.

A mixture of excitement and fear drove me up the

staircase leading to the second floor, looking for a young woman I'd never seen, looking for people I'd never seen, people intent on killing Penny Munro because she knew who the 'Boss' was, because she knew too much about Jenny Ross and Hebrides, Inc. People intent on killing me?

A surly looking man with dirty sneakers and stained T-shirt came down the steps. I held my breath. He nodded and continued past. I noticed the book bag strapped to his back. I breathed. I was now alone on the stairs. Herman De Groot's image came to mind. Would I see him? Was he the one chasing Penny?

I stopped on the landing. The limited public space on the second floor appeared deserted. I started up the stairs to the third floor, expecting to hear Penny call out at any second, expecting to see De Groot lumbering toward me. Two dozen people of various ethnic origins were visible as I left one stairway and crossed to the other. None looked like De Groot. Any of the young women might be Penny. I had assumed she was white because her voice reminded me of a strip dancer friend from Calgary, but I knew that was naïve thinking.

I started down the stairs. Two young, Hispanic looking women followed. It was then that I realized the people chasing Penny might not be men and stopped to let the young women pass. They glanced in my direction. I clenched my fists until my nails dug into my hands. One of them smiled a beautiful white smile. They kept going. I unclenched my fists.

From above or below, I couldn't tell which, I heard a scream and a loud crashing noise. I gripped the banister. The two Hispanic women were half-way down the stairs to the first floor. They craned their necks and started to run. I raced after them.

"Ajit," I shouted.

I spotted him on the second floor with several uniformed policemen, two of whom held a struggling, young woman who screamed a string of vitriolic language at the police. He looked up and started toward me.

"I don't believe that's your friend," he said. "She was armed."

"May I talk to her?"

"I don't think that's a good idea."

"I want to talk to her."

He furrowed a brow and said, "Go for it." He gripped my elbow and walked with me toward the writhing, screaming young woman.

"My name is Paige Harrington," I shouted loudly enough for the young woman to hear.

The young woman stopped squirming, spit on me, and said, "Fuck you bitch."

The two cops tightened their grip and yanked the young woman back.

"No, that's OK," I said. I stepped out of spitting range, removed a tissue from my bag, and wiped the gob of spit from the front of my dress.

Ajit and two of the uniforms stared. "Are you OK?" Ajit asked.

"I'm fine." I hoped my stomach that had lodged itself in my throat didn't betray me.

"What're you," the young woman screamed. "Some kinda fucking hero? Well I don't need no fucking heroes."

"That isn't her," I said to Ajit. "I don't recognize her voice."

Ajit said something to one of the uniformed policemen and they took the young woman, still screaming and cursing, from the library.

"They'll check her fingerprints. We'll know who she is by morning."

"Thanks," I said. "I need to walk the stairs again."

"Are you sure you're OK?"

I realized my hands were shaking and crossed my arms on my chest. "I'm fine," I said.

Ajit and two uniformed police came with me. This time I walked through all the rooms. I figured if Penny saw me with a police escort, she wouldn't hesitate to make herself known.

We descended from the third floor. A 'library closing' announcement sounded from the PA system. I glanced at my watch. It was 7:30.

"My brother is supposed to meet me," I said. "I'd better call him."

I reached for my cellphone and noticed my bag hanging slightly open. It hadn't been before. I looked inside. A folded piece of paper sat on top. I felt Ajit's eyes watching. "I forgot my cellphone," I said, and closed my bag.

"Here, use mine," he said.

Brad answered. I told him I was OK. He wanted to know whose cellphone I had. I told him not to ask questions, said I would be at the Waldorf in ten minutes, and hung up. Ajit walked to the entrance to talk to one of the uniformed cops. I opened my bag and glanced at the note.

I got away. Call you later. P.

"Do you want us to wait until the library is cleared?" Ajit asked, walking toward me.

"No, I'm sure if she'd been here, she would have made herself known." I handed him his cellphone. "Thanks."

"I'm going up town. May I drop you?"

"My brother's at the Waldorf."

Ajit had a red Ferrari. I slid into the passenger seat and fastened the seatbelt. "The NYPD pays well," I said.

"A gift from my father," he chuckled. "I can barely afford the gas and tickets on what the NYPD pays."

"No professional courtesies?"

He laughed.

THE DOORMAN at the Waldorf extended his hand. I slid

from the Ferrari without showing all of my legs and more. Short skirts either were or weren't designed for Ferraris, depending on one's mission. Several men in suits watched with keen interest, some the car, some me, some both. Brad, wearing a navy sports jacket, gray slacks, and white polo shirt, waited on the sidewalk. His eyes were on the car, but only because he knew the legs were mine.

"Hey, not bad wheels, big sister."

"I do what I can. Glad to see Lisette has expanded your wardrobe from jeans and T-shirts."

"I even wear shoes now."

"Soon she'll have you in socks."

"One step at a time."

"What do you feel like eating?"

"Lots."

"First, I have to shower and change. I got into a bit of spitting duel at the library." I pointed to the stain on the front of my dress just below the neckline.

"Was that in the 'catfight' section?"

When I'd showered and changed, we went to Smith & Wollensky's on Third Avenue, famous for its grand portions and quality—neither disappointed. Penny Munro, though, despite heading our topic of conversation, remained a mystery.

After dinner, we hailed a cab. Brad said he would need a day to sleep off the steak.

"What time do you start?"

"Midnight. Pray for slow."

"In ER in New York City?"

"Pray hard."

I got off at the Waldorf and Brad continued on to the hospital.

Back in my room, I undressed, sat on the edge of the bed, and turned on the TV to catch the eleven o'clock news that seemed occupied with the mayor's arrival at a black-tie fund-raiser dinner in the Waldorf held earlier that evening. I watched his entourage parade in, amid flashing cameras and the general buzz that accompanies all such affairs. The announcer caught the mayor's attention and managed to articulate a handful of inane questions about the events of the evening, not seeming to realize that the mayor and his attractive companion, elegant in her long gown, *were* the event of the evening.

The camera panned back, taking in the crowd standing behind the velvet ropes and the several heavies that were never far from the mayor's side. They looked comical jammed into their ill-fitting rented tuxedos.

The next shots zoomed in to give the viewing audience a closer look at some of the happy faces applauding the mayor as he continued along to the Grand Ballroom. I was about to change channels, when one of the mayor's bodyguards clumsily blocked the view. I leaned forward to get a closer look.

"Well hello, De Groot."

Praetorian

At 2:00 a.m., Praefectus ascended the raised platform and descended slowly onto the throne. It wearied him when one of the chairs in the semicircle of Centurions sat vacant.

Nineteen Centurions began chanting, "Hail, our exalted Praefectus. Take your place among us. Command that we do you bidding."

Praefectus raised the bejeweled mace in his right hand.

The nineteen Centurions sat.

Praefectus said, "Who brings you here this night?"

The nineteen chanted "You do, exalted Praefectus."

"What say you, then, Centurions?"

Centurion One stood. "Exalted Leader, Centurion Five will not be returning. His responsibilities must be reassigned."

Praefectus nodded. "Present the urn."

Centurion One climbed the steps and approached the throne where he knelt and bowed, and held up the brass urn. "Centurion Five, Exalted Leader."

Praefectus reached into the urn and removed a numbered tag, which he handed to Centurion One, after committing the number to memory.

Centurion One handed a moist towel to Praefectus to wipe the ashes from his hands. Praefectus then gave the towel back to Centurion One, who cleaned the numbered tag, which he then gave back to Praefectus.

"Centurion One, place the urn in The Wall of Failures and rejoin your brethren."

"Yes, Exalted Leader."

Centurion One proceeded to the far end of the room. A pair of glass doors separated and withdrew noiselessly into the walls. Centurion One placed the urn containing Centurion Five's ashes next to the other eight. The glass

ALLAN M^CLEOD

doors closed and locked.

Praefectus said, "Let they be constant reminders of the cost of failure."

The nineteen chanted, "Failures, failures."

Praefectus said, "Centurions rise."

When the nineteen stood, Praefectus raised the mace and said, "Fourteen."

The others sat. Centurion Fourteen remained standing. "Exalted Leader, I am honored. I shall not fail."

Praefectus adjourned the meeting and departed the emporium. Eighteen Centurions formed a tight circle around Centurion Fourteen. When the circle opened, nothing lay at Centurion Fourteen's feet. He had been granted an extra day.

But unlike Centurion Five, his people knew how to extract information from the unwilling. He would surprise them all. He didn't need an extra day. When he returned he would have the canister.

His superior ability would be recognized and applauded. He would receive a $10 million bonus and be placed in a position to demand that he accede to Centurion Five's position.

Chapter 18

That Penny still hadn't called by the next morning had me worried. I tried to read the Times. I tried to watch CNN. I tried to work on my notes. I took off my yellow blouse and put on a green one. I looked in the mirror and decided I didn't like the color of my lipstick. I picked up the telephone and put it down, and then picked it up again. I called the hotel message operator. No calls since the previous afternoon. *Come on Penny, where are you?*

I needed something to take my mind off Penny, something to get me out of my room, and that something was De Groot. I called Ajit and asked if I could come in and continue my search. He said yes and met me on the main level. I didn't recognize him for a moment in the blue shirt with button down collar and tan slacks.

"Had I known, I would have dressed." I had on jeans and a white T-shirt since I wasn't going to *Madame Magazine's* offices.

"Yes, but I already know you dress up. I looked like a slob yesterday, and didn't want you to think that's all there was."

"Don't forget the Ferrari."

He chuckled.

I told him about seeing De Groot on television. He led me to a special computer that accessed archived news footage and brought up the previous evening's broadcasts. We reviewed the footage from the Waldorf.

"There," I said. "That's De Groot."

Ajit backed up and stopped the replay on De Groot's face, cropped it, blew it up, and copied it to a JPEG file that he attached to a police department broadcast e-message seeking De Groot's identification.

"Does this mean I don't have to look at another two thousand computer files?"

"Someone's sure to recognize him," Ajit said. "I wouldn't be surprised if he's an ex-cop, though maybe not from New York."

"Despite the badge and NYPD ID?"

"It's easy to get authentic looking fakes when you're in the business."

"But you do think he's an ex-cop?"

"From the way you described how he behaved, it sounds like he talks the talk and walks the walk."

"He had me fooled, and I've met a lot of cops. Not many from New York, though."

"Don't be too sure. I think most cops start in the NYPD or LAPD. They're the main incubators."

I didn't get into that most of the ones I knew were from Eastern Europe or the Middle East, usually private, high-paid heavies working for American corporations, the ones who didn't like me taking pictures of office buildings and chemical plants or employees. I suspected they all originally came from the FBI, CIA, or Special Forces.

I asked about the young woman from the library, the one taken into custody.

Ajit punched three numbers on his telephone, talked for a moment, and then hung up. "Her name is Juanita Sanchez. We scanned her prints and ran them through AFIS, the Automated Fingerprint Information System, part of the FBI's national system. Nothing came up."

"Is it accurate?" My image was that of a young woman who had spit on me, who would have clawed my eyes out, who would have pulled every strand of hair from my head, had she been given the opportunity. I couldn't imagine her not having a record.

"Strangely enough, the arresting officers told me that once they left the library, Ms. Sanchez calmed down and became almost ladylike."

Were Juanita Sanchez and Penny Munro the same person or had Juanita provided Penny with a diversion?

That didn't answer the question of who put the note in my handbag. It definitely wasn't Juanita Sanchez, at least not while she was in the process of creating a scene.

I mentally retraced my steps at the library, snaking through a group of young people gathered in the third floor rotunda. Had Penny been part of that group? Had she managed to slip the note into my handbag, undetected by Ajit and the two police officers?

"So what happens to Juanita now? Rikers, Sing Sing, the gallows?"

He chuckled. "A couple of her friends bailed her out. She'll likely plead guilty to disturbing the peace and get fined a hundred dollars or be given community service time or both, unless you want to press charges."

"I don't. In her spot, I might have reacted the same way."

"I'm having trouble picturing that."

"I have a younger brother who wouldn't agree."

I shook his hand, thanked him for his help, and asked how soon he expected to get a reply to his e-broadcast. He said he thought by day's end and wanted to know if I'd be in the city for the next few days.

"Until I finish the article I'm writing—probably another week. Then I'm off to the Brazilian rain forests for a month." I gave him my cellphone number. "Call me when you find the mysterious Mr. De Groot?"

"I will, but it'll cost you dinner."

"As long as I don't get arrested for bribing a police officer."

"I hadn't meant to suggest that you pay."

"Nor had I."

Chapter 19

Back in my room, I turned on my computer and gathered up my notes on Jenny. I needed to organize, chronologically, the bits and pieces from my discussions with Bebe, Dalton, and Johnny Amato, and created a spreadsheet with one column for time and date, and another for comments. I then began entering information, alternating between my notes and recorder.

Halfway through the telephone rang. I lunged, hoping it might be Penny. It was Dee Hunter, Peter Zane's friend.

Peter had gone out of the city, but expected to return tomorrow afternoon, and he and Dee wanted to know if tomorrow evening was OK for dinner. I said it was, and that I was looking forward to it.

Besides meeting Dee, I wanted to pick Peter's brain on the lengthening list of *personae dramatae* in the Jenny Ross and Hebrides, Inc. story that now included the mysterious Herman De Groot and Penny Munro, neither of whom he was likely to know, but he might know of Anne Black and her husband.

I also wanted his take on Dalton Croft and Abner Dodge, both of whom I felt confident he would know, at least by reputation.

Dee said she would call with details once Peter got back, but usually they liked to meet for cocktails in their apartment at 8:00, and then go out for dinner at 9:00 at one of the 'nicer' places. I detected a tone that said Dee didn't frequent anything other.

I WORKED for another hour on Bebe's notes, and then started on the information I had written and recorded in my session with Dalton Croft and the Hebrides, Inc. documents.

I forgot to ask Dalton the name of counsel to Hebrides, and called his office, forgetting my pledge not to do so without Bebe's approval. I was about to hang up when his secretary answered. She said he was in a closed-door meeting and asked me to hold while she went to check. The next voice I heard was Dalton's.

"I'll bet you have your secretary tell all your clients you can't be disturbed; then when you take the call they feel extra important."

"She only tells the attractive and intelligent ones," he said.

"I need to know the name of Hebrides, Inc.'s counsel. Is that something you can tell me?"

"Yes, it's a small firm. Hold on a sec."

Though he covered the mouthpiece, I heard him yell, "Mrs. Carter, get me the name of Anne Black's attorney and the firm…Right, that's the one. Thank you."

"Here it is," he said. "The firm name is Jasper, Winthrop, and Kendall. Jonathan Winthrop Jr. is also Anne Black's personal attorney, though I can't believe he put the Hebrides agreement together. His father, Jonathan Winthrop Sr., the Winthrop in Jasper, Winthrop, and Kendall, is the likely architect."

"I'll want to talk to Winthrop Jr. and possibly his father. Do you have a problem with me using your name?"

He hesitated. "No, I don't think so, though they likely won't want to talk to you about the agreements, and I'd prefer that my opinion on the documents not be stated, since our firm wasn't professionally involved."

"I won't say that we've discussed or reviewed documents, but if I need an opinion may I, or rather *Madame Magazine*, retain you, provided Bebe agrees of course?"

"Absolutely."

"You aren't keen on Winthrop Jr.?"

"Why do you say that?"

"You said you doubted he'd put the agreement together, and I thought you were hinting he wasn't capable."

"I'll have to be more careful, but no, it isn't that he isn't capable, he's not long on experience."

It was a nice try, but I wasn't buying. Dalton clearly had little use for Winthrop Jr.

"He does have an eye for attractive ladies though, so you shouldn't have any problem prying information from him."

Surely he wasn't suggesting I crawl into bed with Winthrop Jr.

"What about the father?"

"Now there you need to be ultra careful: WASPY cool on the surface, a raging pit bull with attitude on the inside, a Semper Fi type, Nam I think."

"I'll be sure to stand up straight and salute a lot."

"Don't think it won't be noticed and appreciated."

"Do you have another minute?"

"Of course."

"I should have asked Bebe, but I forgot. What is Anne's husband's name and what does he do?"

"The great Cameron Black; he does as little as possible. He came from big oil money, but whether or not there's any left, I'd need to review a file."

He'd already promised to do that—I guess he forgot.

"Shall I hold?"

"No, I'll have to call you on that one, later. What I remember is a while back we did some work that included a detailed check of the senior Black. I seem to recall that most of the money is gone, although young Cameron has a trust that pays him some money each month, albeit not enough for his life-style—he runs with the rich and famous and a year ago, the press had a good romp over his gambling problems. Two 'dark-suit' collectors trashed his hundred-thousand-dollar Humvee and told him he was next if he didn't pay up. Somehow he found the money."

"I've met Anne. I'm having trouble picturing her in that scene."

I thought I heard him snort, a very un-Dalton-like re-action. "Am I wrong?" I asked.

"If she doesn't get into the social pages of the *Sunday Times* at least twice, she hasn't had a good week. You may recall from the Hebrides documents that both she and Jenny draw two-hundred and fifty thousand a year. Anne uses every penny of hers to pay the monthly mort-gage on their fancy apartment and fund a frenetic life-style."

I thanked him and ended the call, anxious to talk to Jonathan Winthrop Jr. about his high-spending client and her even higher-spending husband. What, if any-thing, did it mean in terms of Jenny?

JASPER, Winthrop, and Kendall's web page—a stylized JWK seemed to be the firm's logo—was appropriately lawyerly looking and intelligently designed, with several pertinent information segments and a section containing each partner or associate's head shot, together with a brief bio including his or her area of expertise.

I read several, including Junior's, which lacked the long list of published books, noted articles, and corpo-rate and philanthropic directorships that the more senior members of the firm had, although not lacking the list of pedigree schools. He also lacked the gray hair or bald-ness of the others. A boyishly round face, clear blue eyes that signaled a combination of confidence, intelli-gence and mischief, and a lump of unruly brown hair all seemed at odds with the dark gray suit and maroon tie and starched white shirt that admittedly looked as though they'd been hung on his large frame for the photo.

JWK's offices were in the new Time Warner Build-ing on Columbus Circle. The firm boasted forty-five at-torneys, the majority involved with the intellectual prop-erty part of the practice. Ancient Pennington Jasper, spe-cializing in international law, had started the firm in the

the late 1940's. Winthrop Senior and Kendall joined the firm in the 1960's, both after stints in Viet Nam. All three remained active, although Pennington Jasper had to be in his 80's and Winthrop Senior and Kendall in their 60's.

I checked my file. There was no mention of Jenny having a lawyer and I wondered if she'd used Jasper Winthrop as well. I made a note to check with Bebe. If Bebe didn't know, I would have her call Dalton since I had no intention of calling him twice in one day, at least not until he had been officially retained.

I phoned JWK's offices and asked for Jonathan Winthrop Jr., saying that Dalton Croft had referred me.

A woman with an airy voice that left a rush of hot breath in my ear asked me to wait a moment.

The next voice I heard, a rich baritone, bursting with self-confidence—I thought of a broadcaster's voice—said, "This is Jonathan Winthrop Jr."

"My name is Paige Harrington. I'm—"

"Hello, Paige Harrington. To what or to whom do I owe the pleasure?"

I remained silent for a moment, waiting until Jonathan Winthrop Jr. got some of Jonathan Winthrop Jr. out of his system.

"Hello…Miss…are you there?"

"Yes, I'm here. I thought I'd wait my turn. Is it my turn to speak?"

He laughed nervously. "Sorry," he said. "I have a bad habit of doing that. Yes, it's your turn, please."

"I'm writing a story for *Madame Magazine* about women starting companies, and want to discuss agreements between founders and investors, including IPO's. I've spoken with Dalton Croft. He said I should also talk to you."

"I'm flattered. Is Jasper Winthrop involved, or does it represent any of the individuals or firms to be included in your story?"

"No," I lied.

He was quiet for a moment, and then said, "I'm going to be out of the office this afternoon. Is tomorrow morning OK?"

I didn't want to wait until morning. "It is, or, since I'm staying at the Waldorf, we could meet at the Bull & Bear for drinks if that works for you." The Bull & Bear and all its glistening mahogany and large drinks, a real business jock-of-all-ages spot, occupied the south west corner of the Waldorf on Lexington and 49th Street.

"I'm sorely tempted. What time?"

"Your call, I'm wide open." A Freudian slip that made my face grow hot, but to back-peddle would only make it worse.

"I don't know…"

"Is seven too early?"

He hesitated, and then said, "I'll have to confirm."

I gave him my cellphone number, ended the call, and marked 7:00 p.m. in my appointment calendar. I figured Jonathan would be on the telephone to Dalton, and as soon as Dalton told him I didn't have a third eye in the middle of my forehead, he'd be back in a flash. I reread his bio on the web page and closed the file.

My cellphone rang. "That was quick," I said. My caller ID told me it was Jasper, Winthrop on the line, and that meant it had to be Jonathan Junior.

"I didn't want to appear easy," he laughed. "Seven is fine. At the bar?"

"I'll be at the far end. I have long red hair, and in the event there's more than one redhead, I'll be wearing a blue dress, and in the event there's more than one redhead wearing a blue dress, you're on your own."

"I suspect you'll be my first choice, even if the bar is full of redheads in blue dresses."

"I looked at your picture on your firm's website," I said. "If you haven't changed too dramatically, you'll be easy to recognize."

"That's pretty much how I've looked since joining the firm. We have our own barber and the senior partners don't know that suits come in any color other than dark blue or dark gray. Shirts can be either white or white and we get to pick our own ties as long as they're maroon and conservative."

"I know the drill. My father is a lawyer."

"You're too modest. Ten years ago I had the great pleasure of hearing the distinguished Judge P. Tillingford Harrington's Ethics and Law address at Harvard, and just this afternoon I looked him up in the Canadian Law Directory."

"He does get around, and I think the subtitle of his Harvard talk was 'An Oxymoron.'"

We shared a chuckle and ended the call. I wondered if he'd be as easy to pry information from as I hoped. Ladies man or not, I thought, he is smart and quick. I tried to think who, among the hundreds of lawyers I'd met professionally and socially since I'd reached the age where my femininity was more of interest than my intellect, most reminded me of Jonathan Winthrop Jr.

Bobby Bryce's name shot to the top of the list: partner in his father's firm, handsome, had the world spinning in his direction, until he murdered his new wife. Well, scratch him. Maybe Conrad Ashcroft. Off and on, he's wanted me to marry me since high school, though Sara Richardson may now have him cornered. I was sure others would come to mind once I'd met Jonathan Winthrop face-to-face.

Bebe called and I asked her about Jenny's legal counsel. She knew of no one.

I told her about Jonathan Winthrop. "He's Anne Black's attorney. I'm meeting him for drinks at seven."

"Darling, do try to be a tad careful. Old man Winthrop swims with sharks and loves it."

"I'm not seeing the old man."

"From the day he was born, Junior has been groomed

to follow in his daddy's footsteps. Daddy knows who Junior sees, what he does, and with whom he does it every second of every day, and it had better not interfere with the master plan. I repeat Darling: do be careful."

Chapter 20

While trying to decide which blue dress to wear for cocktails with Jonathan Winthrop Jr., Sergeant Lynch called and totally destroyed any sense of adventure I'd started to anticipate. I assumed he'd gotten my number from Johnny Amato, and then I decided since he was a cop, he could have gotten it from any number of places.

"To what do I owe the pleasure, Sergeant?"

"There's a few things that have come up in the investigation that I thought you and me should talk about."

"I have plans for this evening, but I can come to the precinct tomorrow morning."

"We won't be able to meet at the precinct. There are certain people who know things they're not supposed to know, and seeing you talking to me would tell them more than they need to know."

Something smelled. "Sounds mysterious. What did you have in mind?"

"I'm downstairs. Can we meet for a drink? I'd sooner tell you face-to-face than over the phone."

"I'm not sure I have enough time." I didn't want to meet, but what were my options.

"It won't take long, and will help us with the investigation."

It seemed Lynch wasn't going to be easily put off. "You know, Sergeant, Bebe Morgan, the woman who met with Detective Kennedy, knows far more than I."

"Maybe she's part of the problem."

He couldn't be serious. "Come on, Sergeant, you've got to do better than that."

"I'm telling you what I know. That's why I can't talk to her or Kennedy; that's why I don't want to say any more over the phone."

He sounded agitated, and I didn't want to upset him

to the point where he came charging up to my room—that would be a lot more dangerous than meeting him in a public place.

I glanced at my watch, hating my brain for the process it had started, the process of trying to figure out how Bebe might be involved—Crazy! Crazy! Crazy!—she's not involved. Why did Lynch think she was? I had to find out.

As long as we stayed in the hotel…Peacock Alley, off the lobby in plain sight of lots of people… "Get an outside table at Peacock Alley. I'll meet you in five minutes."

I hung up and went into the bathroom to check my makeup, brush my teeth, and gargle away the metallic taste in my mouth. My face had a used car look, but from what I recalled of Lynch, his eyes seldom got that high.

LYNCH wasn't in Peacock Alley's patio area, but a smartly uniformed waiter standing near the gated entrance locked his eyes on me the instant I exited the elevator; I suspected he was Lynch's messenger.

I strode toward him with as much purpose in my step as I could muster. Lynch was surely watching, and I didn't want to appear indecisive or fearful, the juices of both currently flowing in abundance through my veins.

"Miss Harrington?"

I nodded.

"Mr. Lynch is seated at the bar inside."

My initial instinct was to go back to my room, although then I'd have to go through this…this, whatever this was, all over again in a day or an hour or whenever Lynch decided to yank my chain. Besides, I wanted to know if he had anything substantive to tell me, or if he simply used Bebe as a bargaining chip to get my attention.

"I could take you," the waiter said, "but our shift isn't

all here yet, and I'm supposed to stay out front."

I assured him I felt capable of making it on my own.

Lynch was seated on a stool at the back of the bar. He got up as I approached. He didn't offer his hand; I didn't offer mine.

"I know you said outside," he said, "but there are a lot of eyes walking through the lobby, if you know what I mean."

"This is OK, but I don't have a problem with people seeing me. Why do you not want anyone to see you?"

"I got a bourbon," he said, not answering my question. "You want something?" He snapped his fingers and said, "Yo Tommy, over here."

The bartender sauntered over. I asked him for a mineral water over ice and a lime wedge.

"I took you for a gin and tonic woman."

What did he think? A couple of stiff gins and I'd be an easy lay?

"No, I prefer single malt Scotch, but not when I'm working." Actually, I hated malt Scotch, but it was the only masculine drink, other than the bourbon he was drinking, that popped into my mind.

He shrugged and pointed to the stool next to his. I took the one next to that, leaving the one he'd pointed to vacant; that was as close as I intended sitting.

The ice crackled as the bartender poured my mineral water, an activity that took all of five seconds, but in those five seconds, Lynch undressed me several times. I picked up the glass, swiveled to face him as though his wandering eyes were not in the least upsetting or intimidating, and said, "Cheers!"

"Yeah, cheers."

His glass stayed on the bar. So much for courtesy. A group of four people in business attire, three men and a woman, came in and sat at a nearby table. Lynch glared; they paid him no mind.

"So Sergeant Lynch," I said, "tell me why you think

Bebe Morgan and Detective Kennedy had something to do with Jenny Ross's murder."

He looked around as though surrounded by prying eyes and ears, and then leaned toward me. I didn't reciprocate.

He leaned closer. "Kennedy has been under internal investigation for six months."

I almost gagged from the smell of stale smoke and other odors emanating from his clothes and body. "What has that got to do with my friend, Bebe Morgan?"

"Kennedy talked to the partner, Anne Black, and Miss Morgan."

"I know. I was there, remember."

"Don't you think it screwy that a detective under investigation jumps into the middle of a murder case?"

"Maybe he doesn't know he's being investigated."

"He knows."

"And he didn't really jump into the middle. It seems to me that he jumped in at the start."

He took a drink. His eyes said, 'Don't be retarded.' His mouth said, "What I mean is he shouldn't be involved at all."

"That still has nothing to do with Bebe Morgan."

"Let me explain." He put his glass back on the bar and seemed to be gearing up his mind for a lengthy, painful exercise. He wasn't what you'd call quick-witted.

"Don't take too long." I made a point of looking at my watch. If he noticed, he didn't let on, but in fifteen minutes, whether he was finished or not, I intended to leave.

"I, that is, we, the police, believe Ross was murdered by Anne Black and Bebe Morgan as part of a deal to get the stock of Hebrides."

I laughed.

His face darkened. I'd pissed him off. He really believed that Bebe had something to do with Jenny's murder.

"Bebe Morgan had no more to do with Jenny Ross's murder than I."

"Were you with Bebe Morgan at 11:30 Sunday night? Can you vouch for her whereabouts?"

"No but—"

"Were you with Anne Black? Were you with Dalton Croft?"

"Now he's in on it too? What about me? Don't you want to know where I was?"

"We already know?"

That brought me up short. I wasn't sure I wanted the likes of Lynch knowing my whereabouts or, for that matter, anything else about me. "What do you mean? How do you know?"

"We checked." He pulled out a notepad that, unlike Lynch, looked classy and new. "11:25, your plane from Montreal landed at LaGuardia; you took a New York Limousine car driven by one Jesus Alvarez, and he says you never left the car...and at 12:15, you checked into the Waldorf." With uncharacteristic flair, he snapped the book shut. "Oh, and we know from security tapes that Ross was murdered at 11:49, plus or minus a minute."

"You're very thorough." More than I thought him capable. I'd miscalculated. I knew better. With people like Lynch, never underestimate.

"So, as I was sayin', unless you can vouch for the whereabouts of Anne Black, Bebe Morgan, and Dalton Croft, which I know you can't, don't be so certain they aren't involved."

"And you're saying they're in this with Detective Kennedy."

I got the impression he'd already forgotten the Kennedy connection, just like I was beginning to get the impression that he'd made up everything he'd just told me about Bebe, Anne Black, and Dalton Croft. It wasn't something he'd done spur of the moment though, because he didn't seem swift enough to make up stories as he went along, or was that another underestimation?

"You think I'm wrong, Miss Harrington? You think I don't know what I'm talking about. I can tell by the way you look at me. You think I'm nothing but a dumb cop with nothing better to do that make up stories so I can get my rocks off spending time with women like you."

I stood up, rage boiling in my stomach. I wasn't naive enough to think cops like Lynch didn't exist, but in my mind they had no right to wear the badge. "Sergeant, I resent that. It's insulting and sexist."

"Yeah, and it's also true. Now sit down before I arrest you."

"You wouldn't dare."

"Yeah, I would. You see, dames like you interest me. You think the rules don't apply to you, that you can throw around your connections and social standing and good looks and poof, no rules. Well here's the scoop, Miss Harrington: when we toss you in jail with the street people, you got nothing but a body that's gonna get you a lot of attention, and dumb cops like me are gonna sit and watch the show."

One of the young business men at an adjacent table came over and asked if I was OK. Lynch tapped his arm to get his attention, let his jacket hang open enough to display his shoulder holster and gun, and flashed his police badge. The young man paled. "Get lost sonny," Lynch said.

"I'm OK," I said to the young man. "Thank you though."

I wasn't OK, I was enraged, but I had to keep my cool and get rid of Lynch. What I did to get even with him after that hadn't become clear in my mind, but it involved a great deal of groin pain.

The young man retreated to his table where the four of them started whispering and glancing at Lynch and me.

"He thinks I'm a criminal."

Lynch grinned and took a swig of bourbon. "Interesting, ain't it, how close you are to being one."

"All right, you've made your point. What's my role to be, going forward?"

He pointed to the stool. I sat. Jonathan Winthrop might have to wait.

"We need to know every move they make, everything they talk about, everyone they or you are in contact with, particularly anyone who says they know who murdered the Ross woman."

Is that his angle? Does he work for them? Is he trying to get to Penny Munro? I started to feel slighted that they'd sent this moron to lure me into their trap, but I'd miscalculated Lynch twice, I wouldn't do so again. Did he work with De Groot? De Groot likely hired guys like Lynch all the time, to do their dirty work.

"How do I get in touch with you?"

He ran his nicotine-stained fingers across his whisker-stubbled chin. "Better I contact you."

Not what I wanted, but far better than having him show up in person. "You have my room and cellphone numbers."

"Do you have anything to tell me now?"

If he worked for De Groot, he might know that Penny had contacted me, but that definitely wasn't information I intended to share voluntarily.

"I met with Bebe and Dalton today. They didn't talk about killing Jenny Ross, and they didn't talk about Anne Black." Actually Anne's name had come up several times, although I had no intention of sharing those conversations.

The longer I sat there, the more I knew they weren't involved, but I had to play Lynch's game; I didn't want to have my contact with the human race severed by getting tossed into Lynch's jail.

"You gotta make sure you play it straight with me.

These people are dangerous, and if you don't tell me everything, and I mean everything, you could get into trouble. These people are killers."

"I'm scared, Sergeant Lynch." I forced myself to touch his arm. "I don't want to be scared."

He puffed up like a blowfish. "Yeah, well you tell me the truth, and you don't need to be scared."

"But I have to see Bebe every day. I work for her. Dalton's her attorney. They're often together. What if they try to kill me?"

"As long as you don't tell anyone, and I mean anyone, about this conversation, you don't have to be afraid."

I glanced around as though they might leap out from behind a planter and attack.

"They don't know we're here. I've kept my eyes open. That's the main reason I didn't want to sit outside."

I couldn't continue pushing his buttons because he'd soon figure out I was playing him for a fool, and I didn't doubt that he enjoyed torturing and killing people. That did scare me, but I figured I'd convinced him that he had me in his trap. More importantly, he'd brag to others that he did, which might make me less of a target.

The next thing I had to do was figure out how to handle his inquiries, because by tomorrow he was sure to start calling. What I had to do was give him enough creditable-sounding information to convince him and others they had me on their side.

I got up to leave.

He studied his watch. "I'll call you at 8:00 a.m. and 8:00 p.m. each day starting tomorrow morning."

"Don't you think once a day is enough?"

"Twice a day may not be enough. This is a murder investigation. More people could get hurt."

"I don't always check my messages regularly."

"Start."

I nodded, and then left before I hit him with something heavy and hard.

I STOOD under the cool hard spray of the shower for ten minutes to wash away the Lynch grit that clung to my skin and brain. I didn't know what I'd do if he became a serious threat, because I hadn't built up a network of New York City power contacts who could keep the Lynches of the world away. The only person I totally trusted was Bebe. I had to find others.

While putting on a cocktail dress for my meeting with Jonathan Winthrop, Ajit called to ask me for drinks. Maybe he was a person I could grow to totally trust.

I told him I had to run to a meeting. He sounded disappointed. I asked if he could find out on the sly about Sergeant Lynch from the 20th Precinct. He didn't ask why, and I didn't volunteer; Ajit needed more figuring out in my own mind, before I trusted him with that kind of information.

He did ask if I were in trouble. I told him no. He told me to be careful. I told him I knew how to do that.

When I left my room to meet Jonathan Winthrop, I began to think the unsettling thought that I'd see Lynch hanging around the hotel lobby. I stepped from the elevator and glanced from side to side, then walked quickly toward the Bull & Bear.

I didn't see Lynch, but that didn't mean he wasn't there; if he intended to follow, he wouldn't do so in plain sight. Then I had another unsettling thought: any of the fifty people in the lobby might work for Lynch.

Chapter 21

Mostly men, two deep, lined the curved mahogany bar in the Bull & Bear. I checked my watch, 6:55, and walked to the far end where I'd told Jonathan we'd meet. Eyes, some respectful, others hopeful, others leering, all flattering in their way, followed me like metal balls sucked along by a powerful magnet.

Four young men in business suits had congregated around the end stool that sat vacant. I sidled past. The bartender rushed over. I ordered an extra-dry Bombay martini straight up with no fruit.

One of the young men stepped aside and asked if I'd like to sit. I gave them a quick once-over. All wore wedding bands. Harmless, I thought, but I didn't want to be surrounded.

"I'm waiting for someone," I said. "If I sit, he may never find me."

"If he's smart he'll find you," another said. His three pals nodded, as if they'd heard great wisdom.

"Thanks," I said. "What brings you to New York?" I thought I'd ask, before they asked me.

The one who had dispensed great wisdom said, "Toy show." His pals laughed.

They were having fun stringing me along.

"What about you?"

"Call-girl convention." I took a sip of my martini in an effort to keep a straight face. "This is the week we look at the latest S&M equipment."

Open mouths replaced their smiles.

"Paige?"

I recognized the baritone voice and turned to see a dark gray suit, white shirt, and maroon tie wrapped around a six-foot body with a darkly-tanned and handsome face. He'd lost at least fifty pounds since his website picture. Shark in training.

"Jonathan," I said, and put out my hand. "I wouldn't have recognized you."

"Everyone tells me I need to get my picture updated, but it's like a security blanket—it stays fat, I stay thin; it gets thin, I get fat." He laughed easily, and ordered a martini.

"Thank you for coming," I said. "You've saved me half a day."

The four young men stepped aside, eyeing Jonathan with envy because he looked rich and successful and got the expensive call girl.

We exchanged the usual pleasantries and spent a few moments on the heat of the day and New York afternoon traffic. His martini arrived.

"Cheers," he said, picking up the large, condensation dotted goblet as though it might escape.

We touched glass to glass and each took a sip. He daubed a manicured finger to his lips.

"I can't stay," he said, looking at his watch—a gold Rolex I noticed. "On the way out, my father reminded me that at 8:00 sharp, I *would be attending* a cocktail party at his and mother's apartment."

"I'm sorry to hear that," I said. "You could have phoned. This wasn't a life or death meeting."

"I want you to come with me. Had I telephoned, you would have said 'no.'"

"I might say 'no,' anyway."

"That's progress. I've got twenty minutes to convince you otherwise."

"You don't have twenty minutes, because I have to change. You, Mr. Winthrop, are out of time."

He insisted that I didn't have to change. I said I wouldn't go unless I did. A pale blue dress wasn't what I wanted to wear to an evening cocktail party with Jonathan Winthrop's parents. Blood red came to mind.

I left a twenty on the counter next to my check, and started out with Jonathan in tow.

"Maybe next time," I said to the four young men. I felt their eyes on my back until we exited the bar. A smile played at the corners of my mouth.

I asked Jonathan if he wanted to come up to my room while I changed. He said he had to make a few calls and waited in the lobby.

I put on a red Vera Wang, not because of the blood aspect but mainly because I had heels and bag to match, and I suspected the Winthrop's guests wouldn't be wearing cotton summer dresses that came from Anne Taylor. While I put on pearl earrings and a matching single-strand choker, I called the hotel answering service and left my cellphone number in case Penny called.

When I stepped from the elevator, Jonathan's eyes lit up—maybe he would tell me all that I wanted to know.

"You're going to knock their socks off."

"Too much, you think?"

"Not at all. Don't change one particle."

"I'll bet you say that to all the women who pick you up in a bar."

A standard dark blue Seville waited in front. No stretch, no tinted windows, no extra aerials, nothing ostentatious. Nor was it rented for the evening since the license plate said WINTHROP II.

"Winthrop I not available?" I asked.

He chuckled. "Actually this is Winthrop I. His had better speakers so I switched plates."

A tidy little uniformed driver complete with chauffeur's cap that hid most of his white hair waited near the back of the car. When he saw us coming, he smartly opened the rear door and extended his gloved hand.

"Good evening, Miss," he said, helping me inside.

His Scottish accent reminded me of my recent visit to the Isle of Skye where I'd gone to research the Scottish half of my father's family.

"I'm Paige Harrington," I said.

"Yes, Miss," he said.

"This is Barry," Jonathan said, climbing in.

"Hello, Barry," I said.

Barry's face reddened though his blue eyes twinkled. I suspected Barry having a dialog with Jonathan's passengers was a rarity. Smiling, he slid in under the steering wheel.

"Father's place," Jonathan said.

"Yes, Sir," Barry said.

Jonathan told me that most of the partners of the firm and several important clients would be at the cocktail party. "Socially, you'll find them disarming, but be careful—they're all considered a bunch of sharks."

"Does that include present company?"

"I'm trying to avoid the label. Some, including my father, say I've succeeded rather well on that score."

"I've grown up around lawyers, but of the small town variety."

"I've met small town lawyers. There's is a fraternity not devoid of sharks."

"No," I said, "not by a long shot."

We crossed from Park Avenue to Fifth and 66th Street and stopped at the building on the corner, fifteen stories of white limestone and brick facing Fifth Avenue and Central Park.

Barry jumped out and ran around to the curbside door, which the building's uniformed doorman had already opened. Jonathan stepped out and offered me his hand. I pulled myself to the sidewalk. The air smelled of money. The other smell was power. A half-dozen secret service types were spaced along the sidewalk and I saw several more in the lobby.

The little round doorman in his maroon and gold uniform and shiny black oxfords that seemed too large didn't seem to notice as he rushed ahead to hold the door, looking over the tops of his glasses and smiling a big smile, first at me, and then at Jonathan.

"Tough neighborhood?"

Jonathan chuckled and whispered, "Some of father's friends suffer from feelings of insecurity."

Two members of the small army got on the elevator and rode up with us, and two more met us when we stepped off, then they melted away.

As it turned out, the Winthrops' apartment occupied the entire twelfth floor. We walked through a marble gallery to the living room and dining room that extended across the Central Park side. I figured the party had started on time since we were only twenty minutes late and it seemed, based on the laughter and noisy conversation, already mature.

A tall, elegantly dressed woman with an unnaturally smooth looking face and a body that seemed too thin, stood in the doorway with a handsome sixtyish man with a patch of gray hair on each side of his tanned head. The woman stepped forward as we approached.

"I'm Mimsy Winthrop," she said, and offered her hand. "You must be Paige Harrington. We were delighted when Jonathan told us he had invited a young lady friend, but he gave us no idea you were this beautiful. We are so glad you came."

"I'm Jon Winthrop," the man said. "Now you know where Jonathan gets his powerful good looks." He kissed my hand. Head shark. "Welcome to our humble abode."

"It's magnificent," I said. "Thank you for having me."

A waiter appeared with a tray of crystal wine goblets half full of white wine.

"That's the house wine," Jon Winthrop said. "It's not bad if I do say so myself, but please, order whatever tickles your fancy."

Jonathan said, "Refusing the house wine, since father picked it, is life threatening."

Jon laughed, too loudly I thought. I took the wine. Jonathan ordered a martini.

"You live dangerously."

"I'm the only heir."

Mimsy had wandered into the midst of their guests, bumping every woman she could, nodding in the general direction of Jonathan and me. I figured I'd passed the Mimsy litmus test that doubtless had something to do with social status and child bearing ability. I'm sure everyone knew that I was the daughter of a judge, albeit a Canadian one, though a graduate of Harvard.

It took Jonathan and me a half-hour to circulate through the living room. A waiter brought a second drink, and we made our way into the adjoining library where another thirty to forty lawyers and lawyer's wives stood around in groups of six or eight, laughing at each other's witticisms.

"Scene look familiar?" Jonathan asked.

"Very," I said, "and so does the white-haired man next to the window, the one with the plaid jacket. Who is he?"

"That's Abner Dodge, the king of sharks. He's a senior partner at Dodge & Drew. My father and Abner attended Yale at the same time."

"I met him at lunchtime at the Four Seasons yesterday."

"That's where Abner has lunch, and he seems to remember you because he's on his way over."

From ten feet away, Abner said, "Paige," as though hailing a taxi. "I thought you looked familiar. Nice to see you again. I'm Abner Dodge. We met yesterday at the Four Seasons."

By now, most everyone in the room had turned to stare.

I shook his hand. "Likewise," I said. "I never forget a pretty face."

Abner laughed. "You'd better watch this one," he said to Jonathan. "She sounds like a keeper."

Most everyone had stopped staring. Dodge, Jonathan,

and I chatted about nothing for a moment, and then Dodge dashed noisily off when someone across the room waved to attract his attention.

"I've done my duty here," Jonathan said. "If you like, we can find a quiet place for drinks or dinner or both."

"You won't be disbarred, disinherited, or dismembered?"

"Being disbarred I pray for, being dismembered sounds painful, but not nearly as painful as being disinherited. However, in ten minutes my father will be in his den, smoking a cigar, sipping brandy, and watching a ball game. In a half-hour, most of the men and some of the women will have joined him. Mother will keep the rest entertained with gossip and drinks in the parlor."

When we said goodnight to Jonathan's father, he took Jonathan aside and whispered into his ear. Jonathan's face flushed, he nodded to his father, and rejoined me.

"Last minute instructions?"

"I apologize. That was rude of him."

I laughed, though I felt like kicking the old man's ass. It was rude. It was something my father would never do.

Mimsy swirled around a corner, pecked at Jonathan's cheek, and told me in a way that sounded as though Jonathan and I had become engaged, how delighted she was to meet me. It was an aggressive move, something Sally Bowles Harrington might have done—had done— to many of my dates. I glanced at Jonathan, by now pink of face as he shriveled down inside his suit. I knew how he felt...very un-shark-like.

Chapter 22

Jonathan instructed Barry to drive us to Café Boulud on 76th Street.

"When we get there," I said, "let's have a drink at the bar so we can talk about the story I'm researching. Otherwise, we'll have dinner, and we both know one mustn't discuss business over dinner, after dinner we'll have coffee and a cordial, and then, who knows, except we won't have discussed owners and investors."

"Madam, I second the motion."

"I hadn't meant to sound dictatorial," I said, and gripped his arm, holding on longer than intended. Our eyes met briefly. My face felt warm.

I don't want this, I thought. I don't need this. Please don't let him think there's anything more than a professional relationship. Say something, but not something inane. Why doesn't he say something? The weather, the Yankees, the Mets.

When we got to the café, Jonathan clambered out. I wanted to bolt also, but thought I ought to wait for Barry to come around. Instead, Jonathan's hand appeared."

I pulled myself to the sidewalk. "That was an awkward few moments."

"Totally my fault," he said. "I'm usually not at a loss for words."

"Nor am I; therefore, apology not accepted."

We shared a laugh. I wondered if his was as forced as mine.

When I crossed the sidewalk, my spine began to tingle, and I paused for a moment to glance up and down the street. What was it that I sensed? De Groot? Lynch? It had that feel.

"Anything wrong?" he asked.

"No," I lied. "Just enjoying the night."

WE WENT to the bar where we ordered martinis, and Jonathan made dinner reservations for 10:00. It was already 9:30, so that gave me a scant thirty minutes to pick his brain.

"A santé!" He touched his glass to mine.

"Cheers." I took a sip and placed my glass on the bar. "Confession time for Paige," I said. "I lied before when I told you a client of your firm isn't involved in the research for my story."

He raised an eyebrow as if to say 'do tell me more.'

"A month ago I promised Bebe Morgan, editor of *Madame Magazine*, that I'd write about a young woman PhD in engineering from MIT, who is considered one of the top aerospace engineers in the world. When Bebe and I met Monday morning, Bebe told me the young woman was Jenny Ross, that Anne Black was her partner, and that Hebrides, Inc. was their company. That is also when Bebe and I learned that Jenny had been murdered."

"Thank you for telling me." He paused and studied his drink for a moment. "Jenny's murder is a horrible tragedy. Not anyone who knew her, even casually as I did, can imagine who or why anyone would do that. She was a super nice person."

"That's what I'm discovering."

"And of course, I know Anne and Hebrides. Our firm represents both, and Cameron, Anne's husband is one of my best friends from Yale. I also need to tell you, since we're in a full-disclosure mode, I'm also acquainted with Bebe. I met her through Dalton."

"I'm sorry I didn't tell you when we first spoke, but I was afraid you'd put me off."

"And I might have, so I'm glad you didn't."

"You know what? So am I."

We looked at each other for a brief moment. It had a good feel.

"When did you first meet Jenny?" I asked.

"I met both her and Anne at Cameron's wedding. I was best man. Jenny was matron of honor. That was three years ago. The next time I saw them was when they moved to New York eighteen months ago and created Hebrides, and I've only seen Jenny once since."

I gave him a questioning look.

"At Bebe's place in the Hamptons."

Ah, so he was the lawyer friend Bebe had told me about.

"Bebe told me about Jenny's visit, but I swear she never mentioned your name."

He laughed. "I have that effect on some people."

I felt my face flush. "No, what I meant was that she was telling me about the first time she met Jenny."

I wasn't making it any better and decided to quit while I was ahead. "I know you said you couldn't imagine who might have murdered Jenny or why, but have you heard any speculation?"

"Nothing really," he said.

"Anything at all?"

"It's probably easy to think of the secret investor, since no one knows who or what that is, although for that very reason, no one can say for certain, and, even if we knew the investor's identity, there is absolutely nothing that I'm aware of that points the finger of suspicion in that direction."

"Have you talked to Anne?"

"I went to see her. She wasn't in a talking mood."

"What about Cameron?"

"He isn't in town. I've asked him to call, but that's never a certainty with him."

My look asked, 'why not?'

"We speak once or twice a year. No reason, that's just the way our friendship has always been since we left Yale."

I thought about that for a moment, and then asked, "Are you aware that Jenny had concerns about the revised Hebrides ownership and IPO documents?"

"Our firm prepared those documents."

"I saw draft copies only, although it did appear that Jenny's stock was being transferred to an offshore trust over which she had no control."

He pushed his drink aside and frowned. "Let me assure you that nothing I worked on did anything of the sort. Anne insisted that she and Jenny be protected, and that included maintaining their stock positions."

"I don't know if anyone knows what Jenny's concerns were, although assuming there was nothing amiss, who gets her stock?"

"Anne has right of first refusal at a periodically set price, currently $10 million. The company carries key-man insurance to pay the purchase price."

"So, Anne ends up with control of Hebrides."

"Yes, but if you're suggesting Anne had anything to do with Jenny's murder, that's a discussion I refuse to have."

"No, I'm not suggesting anything, merely trying to clarify a point in my mind."

"Anne had nothing to do with Jenny's death, and nor did Cameron."

I squeezed his arm. "Jonathan, listen to me. I'm not saying or thinking they did."

"Sorry. I overreacted. It's just that they're good friends."

"I'd have done the same."

He said, "To answer your question: Anne does end up with control of Hebrides if she acquires Jenny's stock."

"Why wouldn't she acquire the stock since the insurance pays?"

"If she decides she doesn't want to continue without Jenny, the investor can acquire Jenny's stock, provided he buys Anne's stock on the same terms."

"Which is currently $20 million?"

He nodded. "The same held true if either Jenny or Anne simply wanted out, except there is no life insurance to pay the arbitrated price, and the seller has to accept the buyer's terms or agree to take the investor's cash offer, which will be a deep discount over the arbitrated price."

"So the only way anyone could get their hands of Jenny's stock, if she refused to sell, is to either murder her or con her out of ownership. And that brings me back to the documents."

"And I reassert, they didn't come from our firm. I'm the only one who has contact with Anne and Hebrides, and no one would dare release revisions without my approval."

I tried to recall if anything I'd seen tied the documents to the Jasper Winthrop firm, but couldn't. The next question: if they hadn't come from Jasper Winthrop, where had they come from?

"Our firm has a reputation for being tough, but it's a Marine toughness. My father and Dave Kendall were Marines, still are I guess. Once a Marine, always a Marine. They fight to win, and they use every weapon known to man and law, but they don't fight dirty. I didn't decide to join the firm because of a great love for my father—I'm there because I respect him."

"Your father struck me as one who gets what he wants."

"Ten years ago, I probably feared him. Maybe I still do in a way, but I'm not afraid to make my own choices."

Winthrop Senior didn't seem the type to sit idly by while his only son decided to paint or write poetry or do anything other than practice law.

I asked if Jenny had sought independent counsel.

"Yes, she met with Tatiana Marchand, a fellow Eli."

"Ah, one of your people."

"Yes, but she is independent. Otherwise, I wouldn't

have referred Jenny."

"I hadn't meant to imply she wasn't. I assume she's in the city."

"She has a small office suite in Lincoln Plaza, across from Lincoln Center."

The maître d' arrived to say that our table was ready. I glanced at my watch: 10:00, already. I needed to make a quick bathroom stop, and told Jonathan I'd be right back.

IN THE ladies room I checked my cellphone messages. Bebe had called twice, Ajit once, and a name and number from area code 201 I didn't recognize. Penny! It had to be. I called the number. It rang four times, and an answering machine picked up. A few bars of a hard-rock guitar pierced my ear, followed by a young man's voice that said, "Hi, when you hear the cuckoo, leave a message or don't."

After three 'cuckoos' sounded in rapid succession, I said, "This is Paige Harrington—"

"Paige, this is Penny. I'm glad you got my message." She sounded out of breath and talked as fast as a TV traffic reporter. "I'll drive into Manhattan, if you can meet me. Take me forty-five minutes."

"Whoa. Calm down. I'm excited to hear from you too, but is that a good idea? Are you still being followed?"

"Not at the moment. Thanks to you showing up at the library, I got away. Sorry about Juanita. She feels real shitty about spitting on you."

"I figured she was your diversion."

"So can we meet?"

"I'm at a restaurant. Someone is waiting for me to join them for dinner."

"I can pick you up."

"I definitely want to see you, but I don't know how long I'll be. Give me an hour?"

"Where are you?"

"76th Street between Fifth and Madison. Café Boulud." I looked at my watch. "I'll be out front at 11:15."

She said, "I'm driving a silver-colored Ford Explorer with New Jersey Plates that read HARD ROCK V, and I look like Jessie McArdle's twin sister."

"Wait just a second; did you say Jessie McArdle, as in Jessie McArdle from Calgary? How do you know Jessie?" Jessie was my dearest friend.

"I'll tell you when I see you. Right now I've got to run, because my friend is giving me the hang up or die signal. I'll see you at 11:15."

As desperately as I wanted to call Jessie, I knew I'd already kept Jonathan waiting too long, and Jessie was usually impossible to reach around 8:00 p.m. Calgary time, because that's when her dance shift at the strip club where she worked started.

I RETURNED to the bar, and told Jonathan I needed to finish dinner by 11:00 sharp.

"This doesn't sound good," he said.

"I'm real sorry, but for the past few days, I've been trying to meet someone I haven't seen for some time." It was a lie, but the truth was far too complicated.

The maître d' led us to a cozy banquette. Jonathan explained our time constraint, and the maître said he had just what we needed, adding we'd even have time for a nice bottle of wine.

"Will I be exiled if I continue discussing our business during dinner? I'd like to see if we can figure out where Jenny got documents different from those you gave Anne."

I also wanted to find out anything more he might know about the secret investor and Jenny's thus far equally secret invention, but I'd save those zingers for later.

"Had you not, I would have insisted so we'll be

exiled together."

"And let's do this again on a night that I promise not to take calls."

"You can write me in for that rare occasion."

"It's not that bad, really."

He chuckled. "Why do I doubt that?"

I studied his face for a brief moment. Despite Dalton's misgivings, I didn't think Jonathan Winthrop a ladies man. Nor did I think him lazy. But he was smart, smart about law and in my opinion, smart about life.

The steward poured our wine. When he left, I asked Jonathan if he had any fresh thoughts about where the documents that effectively stole Jenny's stock might have come from.

"I wish I did. I'd like to see the copies you reviewed. Maybe I can tell from them."

"I'll have them sent to your office in the morning," I said, and made a note to myself.

The waiter brought the main course. I glanced at my watch. In thirty minutes, Penny Munro would be out front.

"What can you tell me about Jenny's invention?"

"About as much as I can tell you about their investor. Those are two of the world's most closely guarded secrets."

"Surely, someone has to know something."

"About the investor: no. About the invention: rumor says it's the Holy Grail of AI. I don't know if that's true or even what it means, and I'm a sci-fi nut, one of the original *Trekkies*."

I'd get back to Jenny's invention and investor later. For the moment, it seemed a dead end, though I remembered that Ajit's major was AI, and I decided to pick his brain at the first opportunity.

"Tell me about your friend Cameron. I've heard he has a gambling problem and trouble with bill collectors."

He exhaled a smile that evoked as much pain as mirth. "You mean the Humvee smashing incident?"

"I think I'd be worried if two guys in black suits and no necks took baseball bats to my car, forget about it being a car that cost $100 thousand."

"Most people would. Cameron is different. He's an only child…spoiled from the day he took his first breath, which I believe was the same day his parents divorced. His mother worships him and has always given him whatever he wants, except she doesn't have much. I mean, she's not poor, but his father is the one with the oil wells, and it's his father who doesn't trust Cameron with money."

"So where does he get his money?"

"Cameron's trust fund hovers around $100 million and earns close to $8 million a year, but the trust limits him to $10 thousand a month. Cameron figures he'll be sixty by the time his old man dies. By then, his trust fund will be in the billions, and that doesn't take his inheritance into account. So what does Cameron do? He gambles on everything, millions a year, and when his luck hits a bad a streak, he borrows."

"The last I knew, bank lending officers haven't been known to smash cars and body parts."

"He takes it from anyone who'll give it, but it's safe to say his sources aren't at the top of the lending pyramid. When he gets up to a few million and his reasons for non-payment wear thin, particularly in the gambling casinos and racetracks of the jet-set world, he smashes up a car to get his father's attention."

"Don't tell me he arranged to have his Humvee trashed."

"It's not the first; it won't be the last. We were in Yale when the first, a Thunderbird convertible, got reduced to junk. He bled on that one, but now he isn't as dramatic."

"Has he seen a psychiatrist lately?"

Jonathan laughed a good laugh. I shook my head. What was it about Cameron Black that so amused Jonathan?

Then I thought about what Dalton had said, and asked, "What if his father decides to reduce his trust fund, or disinherit him, or what if the trust goes broke?"

"Little chance of that—the trust fund is irrevocable and blue chip and the old man's string of young wives sign pre-nups. He makes sure his legal residence remains in a non-community property state. In fact, I believe he's now a legal resident of Bermuda."

That certainly didn't square with Dalton's misgivings, and I made a mental note to double check.

"You wondered before if Cameron was crazy, and I don't want you to have the wrong impression. Cameron does some crazy things, but more than anything, he wants his father's empire. He wants to prove he can run it better than his old man can, and he's probably right. He's got loads of talent. His problem is boredom and being pissed off, so he gambles, goes to the racetrack, and parties, all at places where he'll likely get bad press that his old man can read and stew about."

"Anne must be a forgiving soul."

"She parties with him when he's here in the city, but she can't afford the time to follow him to Monaco and Switzerland and Japan and Saudi Arabia or wherever he decides he wants to be."

"Until death or gambling do us part."

"The only thing I can say is, she knew his lifestyle before they were married, and I think she knew him well enough to know he wouldn't change. He's never been any different as long as I've known him, and he did love her—I mean he fell for Anne with a huge thud. She's probably the only woman he's ever loved, and I suspect that's still the case."

I doubted that meant Cameron Black remained faithful, if he even knew what faithful meant, and I found myself liking Jonathan a tad less for having a friend like Cameron Black, unfair though it surely was. Also, I knew my brother Brad, blessed with millions of dollars, had the capacity to be a Cameron Black except Lisette, Brad's new bride, would not sit idly by while Brad 'Romeoed' his way around the world; she would nail his balls to the bedpost.

Jonathan checked his watch. "As much as I'd like this to continue, it's eleven-oh-five."

My eyes shot to my watch. I'd lost track. I'd missed Penny twice and didn't intend to make it three in a row.

"Thanks," I said. "I've got to run."

Jonathan stood, held my chair, and I ran for the door with Jonathan hurrying along behind.

Outside, I told Jonathan he didn't have to wait and proceeded to the curb twenty yards behind the limousine; Jonathan walked over to talk to Barry. It appeared they were going to wait.

I didn't see Penny and her silver-colored Ford Explorer and scanned the street. My spine tingled again the way it had when we'd arrived. There were cars parked on both sides. They appeared empty, but Lynch or his henchmen wouldn't be sitting up where they could be easily spotted. I began to fear I had led Penny into a trap.

I checked my watch. It was 11:15. I stepped into the street and glanced toward Madison just as a set of headlights rounded the corner and raced toward me. I jumped back, and amid a cloud of dust, the Ford Explorer skidded to the curb.

The tinted window lowered. A blonde head popped out. There was no mistaking her; she looked exactly like my friend, Jessie.

She waved her hand in front of her face. "Sorry for all the dust," she said. "I'm Penny."

As I gripped her hand, her face paled and her eyes locked on someone or something near the front of the restaurant. What had I done? I whipped my head around fearing the worst, but saw no one other than Jonathan and Barry.

"I can't let him see me." She yanked her head back and raised the window. Tires screeched. I stepped back. She tore off up the street.

"Trouble?" Jonathan walked over, his forehead wrinkled with concern. He glanced at the Ford Explorer rocketing toward Fifth Avenue.

"I'm not sure," I said, watching Penny swerve around the corner and disappear. Who had frightened her? Who mustn't see her? Jonathan? Did Jonathan know Penny Munro?

Jonathan asked if he could drop me somewhere.

What was Penny likely to do next? She has my cell number; she knows where I'm staying.

"If you don't mind," I said, "I'm going to take a cab."

He appeared disappointed.

I brushed a kiss past his cheek. "Jonathan, I had a great time, and remember, you promised we could do this again, so you know I'm going to be calling."

That got me a smile, and he waved a taxi to the curb.

"To the Waldorf," I said, jumping into the back seat. The cab started forward. I looked out the back window. Jonathan watched from the sidewalk and waved. I waved back.

The cab headed south on Fifth. Across 59th Street, my cellphone rang. I had my notepad ready.

Chapter 23

"Did he see me?" Penny asked. "Are you still with him? Did you tell him about me?"

"Hey, slow down a sec. Are we talking about Jonathan Winthrop?"

"He knows me. If he saw me, he'll tell my father, and they'll find me again."

"Wait a minute—did you say your father? What does your father have to do with all of this?"

"I meant my stepfather. God, I'm so scared I can't think straight."

"Are you saying Jonathan knows your stepfather and your stepfather is after you?"

"Yes, that's exactly what I'm saying—oh God, oh God."

Fear dripped from every word.

"I'm certain Jonathan didn't see you."

Jonathan had been talking to Barry, and I doubted their conversation had anything to do with Penny. Besides, Penny had her head out of the window for only a few seconds and wasn't in direct light. Even I hadn't seen her clearly until I got closer.

"And to answer your other questions, I'm alone, and I didn't say a word about you, although at this juncture, I know little more than your name. Who is your stepfather?"

"I can't chance that he saw me. I'm heading back to New Jersey. Oh God, they'll trace the license plate. Now I've gotten my friend in trouble. Shit. I've got to find another place to hide."

"They can also trace you through your cellphone."

"Not any more they can't, not after what you said. Since then, I've picked up several. Every time I use one, I throw it away."

"I don't recall telling you to start stealing them."

"I think of it as borrowing."

"Where are you? Are you able to answer a few questions?"

"You must have a million."

"At least—how about starting with how you know Jessie and telling me who your stepfather is."

"Jessie and I were at Julliard together. When she went to Paris, we lost touch. A year later, after she came back to New York, I bumped into her downtown when we were both doing the drug and prostitute rounds. We were in bad shape. Maybe we kept each other alive, if you can call what we were doing living."

I heard horns and sirens over her cellphone.

"Hold on a sec," she said. "I've got to put the phone down."

My taxi pulled to a stop at the Waldorf's main entrance on Park Avenue. I ran into the foyer and deposited myself in a large wing chair in an unoccupied corner.

After a moment, Penny came back on the line.

"Sorry. The cops were stopping cars and I didn't want them to catch me talking on a cellphone. They've really been cracking down lately. Anyway, back to Jessie and me—when she left for Calgary, we were both clean of drugs and booze and had stopped turning tricks. Since then, we've stayed in touch, probably because now that we're sober, we remember promises made and telephone numbers."

My mind raced, trying to think of the name Jessie mentioned every time she talked about New York. It wasn't Penny. Something didn't add up.

"Was it Jessie who told you where I was staying?" I asked.

"Yeah, sorry about the lie. When I talked to her on Sunday and told her I'd gotten into big trouble, the biggest, she told me to call you. She said she'd talked to you earlier that day at your brother's place in Montreal, knew you were on your way to New York, and thought you were staying at the Waldorf."

Another thing she had in common with Jessie was how fast and how much she talked between breaths.

"She told me how close you are to your brother, so I used his name because I couldn't risk your not taking my call."

She could have used Jessie's name too, but that conversation was for another time. More than that, I wondered why Jessie hadn't called to tell me, but Penny had to be telling the truth. Other than Brad, who already said he didn't know Penny, Jessie was the only one who knew my plans.

She kept on, "After I called your room, one of the guys my stepfather uses for security came into the hotel. Fortunately, he didn't see me, and I made a run for it. I knew others were waiting outside, but I thought I could get into the subway without being seen. Unfortunately, one of them caught me on the platform and I screamed 'Rape!' until a cop and two guys chased him off."

"The guy in the lobby was still there when I came down. Said his name was Herman De Groot, that he was a NYPD detective. He knew you'd called my room and wanted to know why."

"His real name is Vesco, Louis David Vesco. Everyone calls him Lou or LD. He's former CIA or FBI or something like that. My stepfather keeps him and a few others on the payroll to protect certain clients."

I recalled De Groot's big face staring out of the TV, from the coverage of the Waldorf gala for the mayor. Was the mayor one of the stepfather's clients?

"It seems he uses them to not only protect clients but to follow you?"

"They're not following me. I told you they plan to kill me just like they killed Jenny Ross."

"You've got to tell me why you think they killed Jenny Ross. Ever since you mentioned it Monday night, it's been driving me crazy."

"I don't know why; I just know they did."

"But why, and who is they? Who is your stepfather?"

De Groot said that Penny Munro was running for her life because she knew the boss. Was Penny's stepfather the boss?

"Maybe Jenny found out things she wasn't supposed to know, and he killed her to keep her quiet. I know things I'm not supposed to know, and I know for sure he will kill me to keep me quiet."

"What kind of things?"

"Things that will ruin him and a lot of big people— that's why I can't trust anyone. You have to promise with your soul not to tell anyone about me."

"I'm not going to tell anyone."

"Jessie said I could trust you with my life, but I guess I had to test you for myself, to make sure."

"I haven't talked to Jessie, but she's the only reason we're having this conversation. I'd do anything for her. Right now, that seems to be to help you, though if you don't trust me, this isn't going to work."

"Please don't be upset—it's just that my stepfather knows everyone. Everywhere I turn, I see people trying to catch me, people I trusted, people I've known all my life. It's wearing me down, and I don't wear down easily."

"I'm not upset, more like frustrated at not knowing how to help, and I do want to help. I tried to find you— there are a ton of Munros in New York."

"Penny Munro is an old stage name. It helps me move around without raising eyebrows. Because of the dirt bags he represents, my stepfather is too well known for me to risk using my real name; his face is always in the papers for keeping some killer out of jail."

"You still haven't told me who your stepfather is."

"My real name is Abby Dodge—"

Abby! That's the name Jessie had said.

"—actually Abigail Sara Dodge. My stepfather is Abner Stuart Dodge who married my mother, Penelope Stuart Jamieson Dodge."

She laughed.

"This hardly seems a time for laughing."

"Sorry. Every time I say my mother's names, it strikes me as ridiculous that she's kept each of her previous husband's names, the Jamieson part being the point at which she conceived me, though Jamieson flew the coop before I was born because my mother and Abner Dodge were already rubbing thighs.

"Abner Dodge married my mother before I was born, legally adopted me, truly my lucky day, and since he couldn't call a girl Abner, though I'm sure he thought of it, I ended up being Abigail, Abby for short, which is what his mother called him."

Again she'd managed to numb my brain with her rat-a-tat delivery.

"Just so I'm clear, are you talking Abner Dodge from Dodge & Drew?"

"You know him? Oh God!"

"I've met him—twice, once at lunch yesterday and once earlier tonight at the Winthrop's apartment."

"Oh God, oh God—meeting him wasn't an accident. He's got you under surveillance. He wants to know what you're doing, where you're doing it, and who you're doing it with, or to. Look around. See anyone suspicious? He knows you had dinner with Junior, and my guess is he knows where you are at this very moment. He may even know that you're talking to me because your cellphone is bugged."

"Do you really believe he would go that far?" I scanned the lobby. There was no question he'd not go that far. I figured De Groot, or Vesco as he was now known, and probably Lynch too worked for Abner Dodge.

"He knows you're writing a story for *Madame Maga-*

zine, and he doesn't want you talking to me."

Had some insane dream locked me in its grasp? None of this made sense. Jenny Ross, someone I hadn't met, gets murdered. No one seems to know why except that it might have something to do with her stock in a company called Hebrides, Inc., stock that may be worth millions if not billions of dollars, or that it may have something to do with Jenny's invention that no one has seen or heard about.

Now, according to someone else I've barely met, Penny Munro, who is actually Abigail Dodge, her stepfather, the city's most powerful and feared lawyer, murdered Jenny. Help!

"Do you really think your stepfather murdered Jenny?"

"You don't believe anything I'm saying—I can tell."

"It's not that I don't believe you. It's just that I'm having trouble processing Jenny's murder and you and all that you've told me. You said that what you know would ruin a lot of big people. What kind of people?"

"The biggest. Abner Dodge created a highly secretive organization called Praetorian that is involved in a lot of real nasty business like political assassinations, arms smuggling, overthrowing third-world regimes, and creating civil wars, to name a few of their preferred activities. Praetorian does all the bad things everyone thinks the CIA does, except the CIA wouldn't ever get away with one-tenth of the stuff Praetorian does, because next to Praetorian, the CIA is a garden club."

Praetorian seemed more like something from a conspiracy-theory movie than a living, breathing organism.

"How do you know who Praetorian's members are?"

"I don't, for sure. No one does. But I hacked into a computer and stole memo files that contain details of a dozen or more unsolved political assassinations, arms supply deals for rebel African and South American governments, and thefts of billions of dollars in U.S. aid from other foreign governments."

"Including individuals' names?"

"No, no names. But I know the people involved are senior government and military officials. Abner Dodge calls them 'The Praetorian Guard,' and I have a sealed canister containing a list of their members—they call themselves Centurions, all of whom will go to jail for the rest of their lives if the list gets into the proper authority's hands."

"So can't you just turn it over?"

"Who to? Praetorian controls the CIA, FBI, the Pentagon, the Senate and Congress, city officials, police departments. I turn it over, Praetorian gets it back, and I'm dead. As long as I hold the canister and they don't know where it is, I won't be killed."

"Do you recognize any names on the list?"

"I haven't seen it. The metal container is sealed and has a computerized locking device that will blow if anyone tries to open it without the correct code."

"I'm not sure I want to know how you got your hands on it."

"I stole it from a hunting lodge in West Virginia that the Praetorian Guard uses for secret meetings."

Now I was certain I didn't want to know.

"Dodge doesn't know for sure that I have it—all he knows is that it's gone missing, and through the process of elimination has concluded that I may have it."

"Penny, logic tells me if Praetorian is what you say it is, any number of people could have it. Praetorian can't be without powerful enemies. Why does he suspect you?"

"I got unlucky. I snagged and broke my bracelet on the limo's trunk latch—that's how I got into the lodge—I thought I had all the pieces, but later when I tried to put it together one section was missing. He must have found it."

"And he knows it's your bracelet?"

"Not by looking at it, but it must have made him wonder what piece of a women's bracelet was doing in the trunk of the limousine that delivered him to and from the hunting lodge. He may have found a fingerprint."

"No doubt." Given her background, her fingerprints were likely in every police database in the country.

"Why in God's name did you take it?"

"Ever since I turned sixteen, I vowed to destroy Abner Dodge."

"And yourself in the process?"

"I have to admit I didn't think that far ahead."

"I don't think I want to ask the next question, but why are they after me? What have you told them?"

"I promise, absolutely nothing. The only thing they know is that I contacted you, but they don't know why."

"Other than I'm a reporter and they assume you have given me information or intend to give me information, something they'd know from our earlier telephone conversations that they were probably listening to."

She started to cry. "I'm sorry I dragged you into this, but I needed help and didn't know where else to turn. Had Jessie been here you wouldn't be involved."

"Stop it! I was merely thinking out loud. Jessie is here—as far you're concerned I'm Jessie. I love her dearly, and I'd do this for her without hesitation and I know she'd want me to do this for you without hesitation."

"It seems like you're her because I'm braver when I talk to you—Jessie made me feel brave. She was always saving me from some crazy thing, although not this crazy."

"What I'm about to say is even crazier, but I desperately needed to get my hands on those documents and the container. How soon can you get them to me?"

"Everything is in a safe deposit box. I sent a duplicate key, box number, and location to you at the Waldorf. If anything happens to me, you'll have to figure out how to get it."

"First, nothing is going to happen to you. Second, if Praetorian finds out where the container is, I can assure you a safe deposit box won't even be a minor hurdle. We have to find a better hiding place, one that Praetorian can't get at."

"It's too dangerous. I'm having trouble thinking about what to do."

"It's too dangerous if we don't. You've got to take a chance and come into the city tomorrow, or if you want, I can pick you up."

"I'm afraid we'll be seen. My stepfather has trained killers and cops working for him. That's the reason I didn't talk to you in the library. About the time my friend, Juanita, and I decided you were alone, a bunch of cops poured in through the front door. I had to ask myself if they were legit, or did some of them work for my stepfather? I couldn't afford a wrong answer, and Juanita created her spitting tantrum…so I could escape. My stepfather's people are everywhere. They don't wear signs, and if they get their hands on what I have, I'm dead."

"I didn't mean that you aren't in danger, although, surely we can take someone into our confidence. Bebe Morgan, the woman I work for, is totally trustworthy. She can help us. She knows good people. If we get enough good cops—all of New York City's forty thousand cops aren't crooks—or enough good FBI or CIA people, no one would dare touch us. But whoever it is we decide to trust, and make no mistake we need help; your stepfather is in too many places with too much power."

"You have more faith than I. I've lived in New York all my life, and there isn't one person I trust."

"Sooner or later, we're going to have to trust someone."

She laughed without mirth. "They're going to try to

make you run, just like they've made me run. They'll have you so scared, soon you won't trust anyone either. Before, when I told you not to tell anyone, that's what I meant. Everywhere you look, someone you thought you could trust will turn against you, just like they did me. You think you want to tell Bebe Morgan. Go ahead, but who might she tell: Dalton Croft, her good lawyer friend?"

"How do you know about Bebe and Dalton Croft?"

"When you live at the top of New York society, as I did for my first sixteen years, New York's really a small, boring little neighborhood with the same monied people doing the same monied things day in and day out. You said you saw my stepfather at lunch. He has lunch in the Four Seasons every day, has for years. Dalton Croft has lunch there every day, has for years. The last time I had lunch there, four years ago, Dalton Croft was there with Bebe Morgan, editor of *Madame Magazine*. You work for Bebe Morgan. I connected the dots— lunch, Four Seasons, Abner Dodge, Paige Harrington, Bebe Morgan, Dalton Croft."

"Six degrees of separation—are they really that predictable?"

"Rich or poor, most of us are except the world doesn't give a shit that Joe, the garbage man, and Pete, the subway driver, have coffee in Tony's coffee shop every morning at 4:30, have for years. When they die, their obituaries, except they won't have obituaries that anyone reads, will say: never missed a day's work in thirty-five years, had coffee in Tony's every morning."

"So I'm naïve."

"How many layers can we trust? I trust you because of Jessie, but can I trust your friends? You trust Bebe, but can you trust her friends? What if she tells someone you've never met who tells someone she's never met, and so on? You've met Dalton Croft. What if Bebe tells him? You trust him because you met him through Bebe.

I've met Dalton Croft. I don't trust him because I met him through my stepfather. The same with Jonathan Winthrop, and I've know him practically all my life."

"Still, we're going to need help. I'll figure something out without telling anyone about you or what you know."

"I'm going to lose you...I'm heading into the Holland Tunnel and someone's hot on my tail. I'll call you ...Oh God, oh God, they ta--i...co...ing...me..."

"Penny, you're breaking up. I can't understand what you're saying...Penny...Penny?"

Chapter 24

While I waited, hoping desperately Penny would call back, I sorted through my notes and listened to my recorder, trying to make sense of everything she said.

I stopped when a group of women in evening dresses and red-faced men in tuxedos laughed and reeled through the lobby singing 'Oh Danny Boy' loudly and badly. They looked my way and laughed and waved and sang some more.

No sooner had my band of wandering minstrels disappeared into the night when a heavy-set man dressed in an ill-fitting plaid sports jacket and slacks that didn't come to his shoes, walked through the foyer and sat on the far side, kitty corner from where I sat. He had a bullet-shaped head, and when he looked at me, my skin crawled.

The lobby had emptied of people...just Bullet Head and me sitting there across from one another. Where had all the people gone? Where had New York City gone? It was quiet, too quiet.

I checked my watch. It was after midnight. All the people had gone to bed, which is where I wanted to be, except for the idea of being alone in my room waiting for Penny to call.

Come on, Penny. Call damn it.

Bullet Head's eyes flicked and his eyelids clicked, or so it seemed. He folded his hands on his lap and heaved his barrel of a chest.

Enough! Whether or not that was his intention, he'd succeeded in scaring me. I hurried past the elevator banks into the main lobby where several people moved about, some customers and some hotel staff. As near as I could tell, Bullet Head didn't follow.

I introduced myself to the young man at the registration desk, and because I wanted to keep my cellphone free in case Penny called, I asked to use a house phone. He pointed to a nearby chair with a telephone on the side table and told me he'd let me know if anyone called my room. Then he accessed my room's telephone log and said there were no messages.

The first thing I had to do was call Jessie McArdle to see if Penny Munro a.k.a. Abigail Dodge was a sane person, someone I might trust. If Jessie vouched for Abby, then Abby was OK, although the more I thought about it, the more positive I was that Abby was the name of Jessie's New York friend that I'd heard her mention so often.

I called The Garter, the strip club in Calgary where Jessie worked, the strip club where I, as Tawny Lane, had danced less than a month earlier while searching for my friend's killer, the strip club where Jessie and I had become best friends.

"Tawny," she cried.

I doubted she would ever call me Paige. She'd met me as Tawny, Tawny became her friend, even the night Jessie was almost murdered and finally met me as Paige, she'd called me Tawny.

She continued, "I was so worried when you didn't call. I left you a ton of messages. Did you speak to Abby?"

Typical Jessie: rapid-fire questions that didn't sound rapid-fire because of her soft, little girl's voice, but I had long since learned her questions didn't stop until they were answered to her satisfaction.

"I'm sorry I didn't call, but I didn't get your messages."

"Oh no, you must think I'm terrible. I would never do that to you. I should have waited until I talked to you, but Abby sounded in a terrible fix, and I didn't know what else to tell her. I'm so sorry. This was such a horrible imposition. Did you speak to Abby anyway? I really and truly hope you did because I love you both so much."

"Breathe Jessie."

She laughed. "I'm doing it again aren't I?"

"Yes, but I love you just the same. And I did talk to Abby."

"Oh thank you, thank you, you and Abby are my dearest, sweetest friends in the whole world."

"I'm worried about her Jessie. She's still on the streets, and she's in trouble."

"She's been on the streets for years, ever since her stepfather raped her."

"She told me she hated her stepfather, but she didn't tell me that."

"No, I guess she wouldn't have. Maybe I shouldn't have mentioned it either, but it's important for you to understand all that she's been through."

Coming from Jessie, whose stepfather had murdered her mother, and brothers and sisters before committing suicide; that was saying something.

Jessie continued, "When Abby told her mother she'd been raped, her mother didn't believe her, and told her stepfather, who told Abby he'd kill her if she told anyone what had happened. That's when Abby left home."

"No wonder she doesn't trust anyone."

"Ooh, that's only the half of it. After Abby left, her stepfather sent some of his secret police to make sure she got hooked on drugs and booze and pushed her into prostitution. That way, with her reputation in tatters, if she ever decided to tell anyone that she'd been raped, no one would believe her.

"Her stepfather then told the world she was a delinquent, run-away daughter trying to shake down her loving stepfather; a loving stepfather who had adopted her as a baby and gave her everything a young woman of privilege might ever hope to ask for; a loving stepfather highly regarded as a citizen and generous philanthropist, all that bullshit."

Did Jonathan Winthrop or Dalton Croft suspect or know any of this? They'd both referred to Dodge as 'head shark,' but that fell woefully short of describing someone who raped his stepdaughter, got her hooked on drugs and alcohol, and shoved her into prostitution.

"Jessie, I hate to tell you this, but Abby says he's trying to kill her."

"I know. She told me. She's so scared. That's why I wanted her to call you."

"Jessie, I give you my promise: I'll do everything in my power to help her. I can't tell you what's going to happen next because I don't know, although whatever it is, I will be here for her."

"I know you will. I told her how you'd saved my life, that you weren't afraid of anything. Ooh, I'm so glad you've spoken to her."

I wanted to tell her how wrong she was, that I was probably more afraid than Abby, that I wasn't a miracle worker or caped crusader with extraordinary powers, but I couldn't. I had to let her believe. She was my dear friend and she'd suffered too much tragedy in her young life.

"Jessie, Abby needs to start trusting more people. She made me promise not to talk to anyone, but I need help. If you think of anyone you and Abby know from the past, someone she can trust, it's important."

"We didn't keep the best company."

"How well I remember, but in case you do, Jessie, you've got to call me in my room or on my cell, anytime, day or night."

"Ooh, I will, I promise. I do so hope she's OK mentally, I mean, she sounds OK physically."

"When you speak to her please tell her I haven't and won't ever betray her confidence."

"She knows that. She's just being careful is all."

After Jessie and I ended the call, I began to worry

that I still hadn't heard from Abby. I scrolled to her cell-phone number on my incoming calls and hit talk, was shunted to an anonymous voicemail, and, since I didn't know whose telephone Abby had used, I didn't leave a message.

The lobby clock chimed 12:30. For the briefest of moments, I wondered if I dared telephone Bebe, then called her number. I wanted her permission to talk to Dalton to find out what he knew about Abner Dodge and his relationship with Abby, except I couldn't mention Abby to Bebe because she'd want answers I'd promised I wouldn't reveal.

On the fourth ring, I heard a click and Bebe's voice saying, "This had better be good."

"It's Paige. Are you alone?"

"Yes, damn it."

"I've run into some complications and need to talk to Dalton."

"Tell me."

"I would sooner tell you than anyone, but you've got to trust me on this."

"But you can tell Dalton?"

"Not everything, but he might know the answer to one piece. If he doesn't, no one will."

"Ominous."

She desperately wanted to know, but I held my ground. "First, I want your approval, and second, I need to know if he is one-hundred percent, swear on his mother's grave, trustworthy."

"More ominous."

"Sorry Bebe, you're not going to drag it out of me."

"I didn't think so. Permission granted, and Darling, as imperfect as he is in a whole lot of areas, he's rich, he's not bad in bed, and I do trust him with my life."

"You might have to, you, I, and others."

Chapter 25

When Dalton answered, I said "Twice in one day is an imposition, and I want to make sure you invoice *Madame Magazine* for your time."

"And I accept only because I sense we will need attorney slash client confidentiality. For the record, though, since it is currently 12:45, you have talked to me only once today."

"That is certain to change."

"And you, dear lady, have my undivided attention."

Is he always this pompous, or just in the middle of the night?

"I'm calling to pick your brain on Abner Dodge. I need to know what type of person he is."

"That's a surprise. I was thinking more along the line of documents. What prompts your interest in Abner Dodge?"

"His daughter telephoned me."

"That's an even bigger surprise."

"You know her then?"

"Are you sure you're speaking of Abner Dodge's daughter?"

"Well, stepdaughter, actually, but yes, I'm quite sure. Why?"

"Have you actually seen her?"

Careful Paige—Abby's warnings echoed in my mind.

"No, why?"

"I wasn't sure she was still alive."

Was he baiting me?

He continued, "But you asked about Abner, not his stepdaughter."

"I should have said both. A friend of a friend told me that Abby has a lot of problems with Dodge and her mother."

"A few years ago, I read or heard that she embarrassed them by getting her face splashed across the front page of every tabloid in town."

"What do you mean?"

"Abner Dodge was livid that she'd stained his image. She was heavy into drugs, alcohol, and prostitution and hanging around with dangerous people. I guess that's why I thought she'd died or had been killed. In fact I thought I'd read something to that effect. In any event, it wasn't the type of press Abner Dodge could stomach."

"One would think he might have tried to intervene, rather than worry about his image."

"I'm sure he tried, though never at the expense of image. He probably would have liked nothing better than to have her institutionalized."

Or killed. We were silent for a moment, he probably wondering why Abby Dodge had called, and I wondering what lies to tell and what truths to reveal or bend.

"May I ask why she telephoned?"

I hated being right. "It turns out we have a mutual friend who suggested Abby call. She wants me to come to a studio to watch her dance. I used to be a dancer."

"Your list of talents is impressive."

"If it weren't for our mutual friend, I'm not certain I'd bother. This whole Dodge thing leaves me a bit cold."

"You have to admit the timing is interesting. I mean, you meet Abner Dodge yesterday for the first time, and the same day his stepdaughter calls out of the blue."

"I never thought about that. It seemed more of an odd coincidence than a related event."

"It may be, but I've learned over the years that nothing with Abner Dodge is coincidence."

"Do you think it has anything to do with Jenny Ross or Hebrides?"

"It might. Dodge or his firm may represent the secret investor in Hebrides."

"Assume for the moment that he does, would he have

me followed and tap my phones, or is that being para-noid?"

"The answer to both questions is a resounding 'yes,' if he thought it would give him a means to stop you from writing a story harmful to his client."

"Then, he could be listening to this conversation," I said, thinking I had better be careful lest at some point he begin to think me paranoid or abstruse.

"He isn't. Because of the highly confidential public offering work our firm does, our telephone system is one of the securest in the world, capable of detecting listening devices anywhere along a live communications network. It tells me if my phone is bugged, it tells me if someone is listening, and it tells me if the phone I'm talking to is bugged."

It sounded like a large dose of overkill, but I had to remind myself that this was New York City. Terrorists had struck at its heart; people behaved differently now.

"Tomorrow, I'll have yours and Bebe's phones checked and bug-proofed."

"I can't imagine we need to go that far."

"I'm going to say to you what I said to my partners: 'If you aren't one-hundred-percent secure, you aren't secure.'"

Hearing Dalton talk about bugs and bug-proofing sounded foreign to his tongue, comical almost, like a private school WASP, of which Dalton was the epitome, trying to talk *gangsta*.

"Assuming Abby's telephone call was more that a coincidence, how do you think she fits in Dodge's over-all scheme?"

"Maybe she decided to get on the payroll. Everyone used to say how sly and tough she was. Maybe she's perfecting her skills at the feet of the master."

Now that's a possibility I hadn't considered and, for Jessie's sake, didn't want to. If Abby had turned, Jessie would be heartbroken.

He continued, "A friendly word of New York City advice, if I may?"

"Please, I need the education."

"Always assume everyone with whom you do business, particularly the likes of Abner Dodge, is playing to win. It's cutthroat and usually not personal. It's the game, the fight, the contest—call it what you will. Dodge once had his mother under surveillance, hoping to find some way to discredit her because she sued him for fraud."

"Dodge Thanksgiving dinners must be pleasant affairs."

"Dodge isn't universally loved. To combat the threats on his life that occur weekly, if not daily, he is constantly surrounded by a team of secret-service types, and if he wants anyone followed, he reportedly has half the New York police force on call."

That explained at least some of the secret-service people I'd seen at the Four Seasons and in Winthrop's apartment, though I had to admit to some disappointment at not at least seeing Bill Clinton in either place.

It probably also explained my visit from Lynch. I glanced around the lobby. I didn't see the heavy-set man or Lynch or De Groot, though several others standing and sitting nearby could have been employed by Dodge. Who am I kidding? They all, men and women, could work for Dodge; they weren't going to be wearing ID badges.

I ENDED the call, more agitated than I wanted to be. Dalton had contributed greatly by making me think about Abby in a way I didn't want, although the hundreds of pieces of information that didn't fit together were equally to blame. One I could resolve right now: Jessie's missing calls.

I crossed to the registration desk and asked the night clerk to check my messages.

He scrolled through a list on his screen and soon found the missing calls, though not why they hadn't gotten into my voicemail. Since I was becoming a skilled truth bender, I explained because of not getting the calls someone had followed me, and I would feel better if one of his security people accompanied me to my room.

Well, it was partially true because I did feel better, even if the nice, wobbly old man who escorted me to my door might need more protecting than I, had we encountered anything untoward.

Praetorian

Praefectus raised the bejeweled mace.

The nineteen Centurions took their rightful places.

Praefectus said, "Who brings you here this night?"

The nineteen chanted "You do, our exalted Praefectus."

"What say you, then, my Centurions?"

Centurion Fourteen stood. "Exalted Leader, we have the girl. The canister will be ours by morning."

"Make sure that it is. You will not be granted a further reprieve."

"Yes, Exalted Leader. I shall not fail."

Praefectus raised the mace and said, "Hebrides reports please."

Centurion One stood. "Exalted Leader, the North Korean delegation has indicated a willingness to increase its offer to $50 billion dollars for a one year world-wide exclusive."

Praefectus said, "We will grant them one year ahead of Japan, nothing more."

"Yes, Exalted Leader. I will so inform."

Centurion Two stood. "Exalted Leader, Venezuela's position remains unchanged: $100 billion for five years ahead of all of South and Latin America, except Cuba, which is to be considered part of Venezuela for purposes of its bid."

"Tell them we agree."

A chorus of "oohs" sounded. It was a generous deal for the Venezuelans.

Praefectus raised the mace. The room fell silent.

"Centurions, I said only that we agree. Since Venezuela displays its greed, we shall terminate once we have their money."

The Centurions stamped their feet and applauded their agreement.

Centurion Three stood. "Exalted Leader, once Sudan receives U.S. foreign aid and the World Bank loan, they will pay and additional $5 billion."

"Give them one month or cancel their contract."

"Yes, Exalted Leader."

Centurion Four stood. "Exalted Leader, the Iranians will pay $1 trillion dollars for a Middle East exclusive. The Saudi's will match that offer. Several smaller kingdoms want in, but can't pay that kind of money and don't want to compete with Iran and Saudi Arabia."

"Tell Iran and Saudi Arabia that the cost for a Middle Eastern exclusive is $2 trillion, or we negotiate with the Israelis. Let them figure out who pays."

"Yes, Exalted Leader."

More foot stomping to show enthusiastic support. They were going to be rich beyond their dreams, and they were only getting started. United States, Europe, Russia, and China hadn't yet been approached.

Praefectus said, "Centurions rise."

When the nineteen stood, Praefectus raised the mace and said, "Centurions, $10 million will be paid to your offshore accounts."

"Thank you for your generosity, Exalted Leader."

"Fourteen, yours will be held in abeyance until the canister is delivered."

"Yes, Exalted Leader, and I shall not fail."

"See that you do not."

The others sat. Centurion Fourteen remained standing.

Praefectus adjourned the meeting and departed the emporium. Eighteen Centurions formed a tight circle around Centurion Fourteen. When the circle opened, a gold plated sword with a jeweled handle and a black leather scabbard lay at Centurion Fourteen's feet. He was the last to leave that night. At the next meeting, his car and driver would return, with either him and the canister or an urn full of his ashes and the sword.

He wasn't worried. He had the girl and she would talk. He would have the canister.

Chapter 26

I slept fitfully, dreaming about Abby being chased into the Holland Tunnel, about Herman De Groot an Sergeant Lynch and faceless secret-service agents and police and Abner Dodge and Jonathan Senior and Mimsy and Jonathan Junior. I dreamt Dalton Croft grilled me on the witness stand, constantly accusing me of perjury and demanding jail. I awoke several times sensing someone in my room. I thought of calling my new friend, Jorge, the bellhop, and asking him to bring up some 'Sleepytime' tea, but in the end, didn't. In desperation, I turned on the lights and TV and covered my head with a pillow. Morning finally arrived.

I checked for messages. Abby hadn't called. Bebe had called several times to say she'd talked to Dalton, who wouldn't tell her anything. I called her to say I'd be in the office within the hour, that I didn't want to discuss anything over the telephone. She went into orbit with worry and a thousand questions. I told her she'd have to wait.

Dee Hunter called to confirm that Peter had in fact returned to the city and they hoped I could join them for cocktails at 8:00. She gave me the apartment address on West End Avenue. I called to accept.

I ordered room service and took a long, hot shower. My breakfast had arrived by the time I'd finished dressing. I sat to eat, opened the *Times*, and switched on the TV. CNN had a long piece on foreign aid and World Bank loans that Sudan had scandalously diverted away from humanitarian projects to the military. What else is new? Channel Four had Martha showing how to use different vacuum attachments. Help.

After I'd eaten, I reviewed my notes from the previous evening and called Bebe's office with a message to have copies of the Jenny's documents sent to Jonathan

Winthrop. Then I left a message for Jonathan that they were on their way.

My cellphone rang. The caller ID read Columbia Presbyterian, which meant my brother. "You're up early," I said.

"I haven't found the bed yet."

His voice signaled trouble. "What's keeping you from your favorite pastime?"

"You'd better get up here. An ambulance delivered a critical an hour ago. I think it's that young woman you told me about."

My heart stuck in my throat. "Who, Penny Munro?" Of course it was Penny, or Abby, as she was more correctly known, except Brad only knew the Penny Munro name. Who else could it be?

"I think so. On the rare occasion when she's semiconscious, she mumbles for you and Jessie."

"Is she...OK?"

"It's touch and go, big sister. I'm sorry."

I wanted to scream.

I kicked off my heels and grabbed a pair of sneakers. "How can I find you?"

He gave me directions and added, "It looks like the people chasing her are playing for keeps, big sister."

"Yeah, I know they are." Why had I doubted her? Jessie, I'm sorry. She'll be OK. She has to be OK. "And don't worry, I know this is New York and not High River, and I'm being extra-careful."

"I have to tell you: some of what you get involved in, big sister, scares me shitless."

"That makes two of us, and little bro, you need be careful too; they won't stop until they know Penny is dead."

"As of now, she's a Jane Doe. I'll keep her a secret and nose around to see if anyone's checked our morgue admittances."

I threw my notebooks, recorder, and cellphone into

my bag, and took off running. I called Bebe from the
taxi to say only that I'd be late. A dark blue car started
following the cab, and the first two names that popped
into my mind were De Groot and Lynch. Why hadn't
Lynch called?

My cellphone rang. It was Lynch. Who else? Was he
telepathic? Was I? Not with him, I hoped. I told him
about Jonathan and the cocktail party and dinner, because I suspected he already knew about those happen-
ings. He wanted to know where I was. I looked back.
The blue car was still behind. I suspected it was Lynch. I
told him I was in a taxi on my way to the Upper West
Side to meet a friend for breakfast. He ended the call.

A half-dozen blocks later, I asked the driver if he
anyone was following. He glanced in his mirrors and
told me he'd make a circle, if I wanted. I looked back
and saw nothing except a collection of nondescript vehicles and the 104 bus.

"No," I said. "Keep going."

There was a thin line between careful and paranoia,
and I suspected I'd be dancing along its treacherous
boundaries a lot in the coming days, though for the moment, I only wanted to get to the hospital, as fast as possible.

BRAD met me at the main entrance and took me to a
changing room where I put on pale green pants, top, and
head cover. Hidden behind a surgical mask, I rejoined
him and two other similarly attired human life forms he
introduced as Tom and Zoë.

I followed them to a dark and vacant-looking corridor
in the critical care unit. Brad warned me along the way
that what I was about to see wasn't pretty. I hoped they
couldn't hear my heart pounding in my chest and see the
fear in my eyes.

We entered a dimly lit room with white curtains
pulled around each of the four beds. I sensed all but one

was empty.

"This one," Brad said, heading for the far corner. He pulled the curtains back. The person in the bed seemed tiny next to all the attached tubes and monitors, and could have been man, woman, or child hidden behind the bandages and casts, but I knew it was Abby. I reached out and touched her fingertips. They were cold.

"Is she...?"

"Jessie..."

I turned to look at the swollen mass of bandages that comprised Abby's face. "It's Paige."

"Paige..."

"Yes, I'm here. You're going to be OK."

"She doesn't know what she's saying," Brad said.

"Yes, she does," I said. "She knows I'm here, and she knows she's going to be OK."

Brad touched my hand. I wiped away my tears and let Brad hold me for a moment before I dared ask, "What happened to her?" As if he knew.

"We don't know and probably won't, unless she tells us."

He pulled the curtains closed around Abby's bed and motioned for Tom, Zoë, and me to follow. We went to a doctors' lounge behind the nurses' station and removed our surgical masks and caps.

"Has anyone been looking for her?" I asked.

Tom, tall, orange hair, a million freckles on his face and hands, said, "No, but it's early. We expect the police will show up in a couple of hours. After that, the press will start poking around, if not here, then with the police, to see what happened overnight. Usually it's the city desk guys looking for anything that will make gory copy."

"Who told the police?"

"Admitting lets them know whenever anyone who comes in appears to be a victim of a crime," Zoë, the other intern said. Olive-skinned Zoë, short and petite, had black hair done up in a tight bun atop her head and black eyes that shot fire.

I took Brad to one side. "Can you hide her?"

"No one uses that wing except for disasters. She's safe for now."

"What about the ER people? They must know she's in here somewhere."

"Maybe you'd better tell me what's going on."

"Penny's real name is Abigail Dodge. Her stepfather is Abner Dodge, an extremely powerful lawyer lacking an ethics code or anything resembling a moral compass. In fact, he probably did this."

"And we thought the judge was tough."

I glared at his reference to our revered father.

"Sorry."

"Dodge's tentacles slither down too many hallways and into too many boardrooms, and I have it on good authority that half of Washington and the New York police force are on his payroll. If you or your colleagues make the mistake of letting even one person learn Abby's whereabouts, I guarantee Dodge will find her and finish the job."

He glanced across at Tom and Zoë. "She might not make it, big sister. Her family needs to be notified."

"Dodge is her family. She has information that will destroy him and a host of powerful people, information that she promised to get into my hands, if anything happened to her. I can only hope she had the opportunity before—"

"I don't like the sound of that. What if they think you have it? Are you next?"

"I'm trying real hard not to be."

He gripped my arm. "We need to tell them," he said, motioning toward Zoë and Tom.

"You start, and I'll take over. Don't act surprised if I bend the truth. The less they know the better, believe me."

Zoë and Tom were involved in an animated discussion that they suspended mid-sentence when we neared.

"I need your help hiding Jane Doe," Brad said.

They looked first at him, and then at me.

I said, "The young woman's name is Penny Munro, which is an alias. I don't know her real name, but I do know that someone with powerful connections is trying to kill her because of what she knows, because of what they think she told me."

"Then that means…" Zoë didn't finish. Tom shifted his lanky frame. They stared hard with the realization I might be next, and then their eyes widened with the added realization that if they were caught, they might be next.

"They don't need to know," Brad said, referring to Zoë and Tom. "I can hide her."

"Not by yourself you can't," Tom said.

"I'll help," Zoë said, though not with any real sense of conviction.

I said, "I can't emphasize enough how dangerous and powerful these people are, and right now, their singular mission is to find this young woman, either to get what she has or to make sure she's dead."

Zoë stepped back a pace.

"They are convincing liars who will try anything to gain the confidence of you and your colleagues, including posing as police officers or medical professionals. Some may actually be police officers or FBI or CIA, but let me assure you, they do not have anyone's interest at heart except their own; they are being paid a lot of money to be corrupt."

Tom said, "Right now, too many people in here know about your friend's existence, but when we put our plan into place, she'll disappear physically and from the hospital's records."

Brad agreed. Zoë demurred.

"You can opt out," Brad said to Zoë. "Tom and I can

handle it."

"I'm in," she said. Her eyes flashed. I liked that.

I said to Brad, "I need to call Jessie. You asked about next of kin; she is Penny's only real family; she's the only one other than us who needs know."

I asked if I should wait in case Abby regained consciousness. They all agreed it might be days, not hours.

BRAD walked with me to the visitors lounge so I could use my cellphone. We found a private corner and I called Jessie to give her the news.

"Ooh, I've been so worried since you called last night. I just knew something bad was going to happen. She's going to die isn't she?"

"She's tough, Jessie. She isn't going to die. Think about how many times they narrowly missed murdering you when you landed in tough scrapes, how many times you got beat up and left for dead. Abby too. You always made it, just like Abby's going to make it."

"Oh how I pray you are right. My mind won't think of anything else until I know she's OK. I've got to come to New York; I've got to be there for her. Please don't say no, because as soon as I can throw a bag together, I'm heading for the airport."

Jessie had a habit of going underground and not letting people know. I didn't need that worry. "I can't say no because I'd be doing the same thing, but you have to promise to call the second you land."

A black car pulled up in front of the hospital and two street-tough, hard looking men in rumpled suits got out. I glanced at Brad. He got up to take a closer look.

Jessie said, "Don't worry. I know the streets. I can make it on the streets."

"Jessie, I don't want you to do that. This is different. These people aren't like the ones you know; they don't come and get you and take you out to kill you; they find you, kill you, and you won't even know."

Brad came back and shrugged. "MD plates," he said.

I'd bet my life they weren't MDs.

Jessie asked, "What hospital is she in? What if they find her?"

"Jessie, they won't find her. She's in Columbia Presbyterian, though I don't want you to go there either. Brad and his friends are hiding her so no one, not even I, will know her whereabouts."

"Did you say Brad? What is he doing there?"

I told her about the resident exchange program. Knowing Abby was in Brad's care made her happier. For Jessie, I prayed Abby would live.

Chapter 27

I telephoned Bebe from the West Side Highway on my way back to midtown and told her I wanted to tell her, the one person I trusted, about all that had happened, except I couldn't tell her over the phone.

"I absolutely detest you," she said. "I can't operate this way; I can't exist in a vacuum."

I scratched my nails across the mouthpiece. "We're losing our connection." I ended the call and tossed the cellphone into my bag. Until Bebe's and my telephones were swept for bugs, I couldn't risk telling her about Abby. Meanwhile, I reminded myself to use pay phones and guard my words.

The driver said there'd been a bad accident at 72nd Street. I told him to exit at Ninety-Sixth and go to the East Side, but when we got to Riverside Drive, I remembered that Tatiana Marchand, Jonathan's lawyer friend, the one Jenny had talked to, had offices in Lincoln Plaza. I decided to pay her a visit, and instructed the driver to take me to 64th Street and Broadway.

We headed south past the expensive brownstones and co-op apartments that lined one side of Riverside Drive, and Riverside Park the other, where nannies pushed strollers past kids playing soccer and basketball, where joggers, walkers, and skateboarders provided a kaleidoscope for the elderly sitting on the liberal scattering of benches. Gaggles of pre-schoolers in matching sweaters marched along, strung together on leashes to make sure they didn't dart into the street or shoot off on their own.

So many contradictions: life everywhere, as Abby lay close to death and Jenny lay dead.

I got out at the Metropolitan Opera House and walked across Broadway. A double pay phone kiosk sat on the corner. The receiver dangled in the first one and someone had scrawled 'OUT OF ORDER' on the enclosure in a black marker. I went to the next cubicle, shoved a quarter into the slot, and called Tatiana Marchand's number. A woman answered. I hung up.

THE SIDEWALK leading to Lincoln Plaza snaked through well-kept flowerbeds and lawns that hosted a generous array of trees and shrubs. A young couple sat on one of the quaint cedar benches, holding hands and enjoying the rock gardens with tiny cataracts that tumbled into pools filled with lily pads and white flowers. A gentle mist touched my skin as I passed by, and a rainbow arced down to the moist grass that glistened in the bright sun.

Inside the glass and stone lobby, the building directory listed Tatiana Marchand's office in Room 202. I took in a deep breath and started for the elevator.

"Excuse me, Miss?"

I turned and smiled at the doorman. He tried to smile back as the wheels of recognition spun in his mind.

"Do you have an appointment?"

"You don't remember me, do you?" I put out my hand.

He cocked his head and gave me the once-over. I gripped his hand.

"No, Miss, I think I would have remembered—"

"Paige, Paige Harrington." I put my other hand on top of the one I had locked in a vice grip and squeezed still harder. He responded and the corners of his mouth started to smile.

A shrill voice from behind that yelled, "Tommy," interrupted our contest.

The doorman snapped his head around. A great body in short shorts and a skimpy halter with a big kid in a stroller straddled the doorway. "My groceries will be here within the hour."

"OK, Mrs. Walker," Tommy said. I released his hand and waved at Mrs. Walker so that Tommy saw both my wave and Mrs. Walker waving back.

"I'm sure its OK, Miss…Harrington, is it?"

"Yes, but call me Paige," I said. "Thanks, Tommy."

"I'll need to call."

Tommy was a tough nut to crack.

I said, "She may not remember me. Tell her I'm a friend of Cameron Black's."

I should have said Jonathan, except she could easily call him, and I doubted he'd be pleased I hadn't told him I planned to use his name. I gambled that Cameron Black might not be as easy to track down on short notice.

Tommy hung up. "She says she don't have no appointment marked down, but you can come on up."

"Thanks, Tommy."

"Anytime," he said, and trotted off to deal with Mrs. Walker, who seemed baffled by the idea that the door had to be open before the stroller could pass through.

I got off the elevator on the second floor, which comprised rows of small offices hidden behind doors with small brass nameplates. The walls and carpet were light gray and sconces with soft lights were spaced between each door. The overall effect was one of quiet elegance.

The sign on Room 202 said Tatiana Z. Marchand, Attorney at Law. Through the closed door, I heard a muffled woman's voice. I suspected she was trying to contact Cameron Black. I pushed the brass doorbell and a chime sounded. The voice went silent.

"Who is it?" The voice neared the door.

"Paige Harrington, Cameron Black's friend."

Silence. Thinking time. Does she or doesn't she? I snuck a hand into my handbag and turned on my recorder. The door opened. A woman in a beige skirt and white blouse that touched all the right places said, "I'm Tatiana Marchand. What do you want?"

I figured Tatiana to be about five-foot-ten, which meant we were the same height, except today Tatiana had the advantage because of three-inch heels; I wore sneakers. Tatiana's hair was black and cropped short. She didn't offer her hand and she wasn't smiling.

"I need to talk to you about Jenny Ross."

"The office is closed this week. My staff isn't here."

"I won't be but a moment, I promise. I'm a writer for *Madame Magazine*. We're doing an article on Hebrides, Inc. and its two owners, Anne Black and Jenny Ross. It was something we had started before Jenny was murdered."

Her eyes iced over.

"I understand you advised Jenny regarding changes in the agreements."

"I…I didn't…look at changes."

"Has Detective Kennedy contacted you yet?" It was a bluff.

Tatiana frowned, but stepped aside and motioned me in. "We can sit there."

She pointed to a rectangular conference table surrounded by eight black-leather chairs that looked like part of the Mies van der Rohe collection. Four over-stuffed black leather chairs sat at the other end of the room around a large coffee table of the same design. Except for part of a one wall covered with small platinum and gold discs in black frames, colorful posters of theatrical events featuring pop stars like Cheryl Crowe and Avril Lavigne filled the walls. It appeared she had a lucrative entertainment law practice. So why was she mixed up in a piece of complex offshore corporate law?

Her gold bangle bracelets clinked on the glass when she folded her hands on top of the table. She didn't have a wedding ring unless the oversized ruby on her ring finger served that purpose. Her fingernails were long and bright red, the same color as her lipstick and her heels.

"I don't have much time," she said, making a production of glancing at her watch, a Cartier tank.

"I understand you wrote a favorable opinion letter?"

"No, there was no letter." She jumped up and started pacing behind her chair. "You have to understand something. I'm an entertainment lawyer." She waved her hand at the posters on the wall. "I...I saw Jenny only as a favor for a friend."

"But you told her you thought the changes were acceptable."

She stopped pacing and gripped the back of her chair, her eyes boring into mine. "What I told her was the same thing I told her every time she came to me with another change."

"And that was?"

"That I wasn't a corporate lawyer, that she should get someone else to take a good look at everything."

"And then you told her to sign?"

"I did no such thing. Anyone who says otherwise is a liar."

"Jenny thought you had."

"That's impossible."

"We have copies of all her notes, correspondence, and emails," I lied. "And Detective Kennedy is getting logs of her telephone calls. I'm certain you'll be high on his list."

The telephone rang. "I have to take that," she said, and walked to the reception desk a dozen paces away. She picked up the receiver, her back to me. I got up and studied a few posters, mostly to give the appearance of not eavesdropping when it was impossible not to. She ended the call. I returned to the table.

She said, "I really have to leave now. If you or Detective Kennedy or anyone else needs to know anything more, it will have to be heard in court."

"You told her what?"

"No more questions."

"I think you told her to sign even though you knew that by doing so, Jenny gave up her stock and all rights to her invention."

"You're entitled to your opinion, but I would strongly recommend that it not be included in your story." A red tinge crossed her face.

"Is that a warning?"

"Call it what you will?"

"So you told her not to sign."

"I told you: no more questions."

"How long have you known Cameron Black?"

"Longer than you, apparently. That was he on the phone. He says he doesn't know anyone by the name of Paige Harrington."

She walked to the door and opened it.

"Goodbye, Miss Harrington. Please don't come again." Her face darkened.

I walked to the open doorway and stopped. Our faces were no more than a foot apart. Her nostrils flared and I heard her breathing.

"Are you a friend of Anne Black's?"

"Have a nice day, Miss Harrington."

I stepped into the hallway. As she started to close the door, I said, "Oh, FYI, your doorman tried his best to stop me. I lied so don't beat up on him."

The door slammed shut. I listened for a moment, heard nothing, and ran for the elevator. Back in the lobby, Tommy had returned to his station, apparently having successfully resolved Mrs. Walker's physics problem.

"Miss Marchand seems testy today," I said, and handed him a twenty. "She may have a few unkind words."

Tommy grinned. "I get a lot of that," he said.

Outside, I ducked into a women's clothing store where, from its side windows, I could watch the entrance to Marchand's building. Five minutes later, she came out and glanced around. I stepped back. She started off at a good pace, heading north.

I decided to follow. Broadway was clogged with the usual noon-hour mass of humanity so I didn't have to lag too far, and because she was tall, she was easy to follow. She crossed 63rd Street and went to an outdoor table at Café Fiorello. I stepped behind a pillar on the far corner building and watched a man in a light blue suit stand as she approached his table. They kissed a two-cheek greeting that seemed more warmly familiar than formal. The man held her chair while she sat. I suspected I was looking at Cameron Black.

I was about to leave when the man waved and again stood. Tatiana looked around, smiled, and waved. The hair on the back of my neck bristled. Jonathan Winthrop walked up to their table. He embraced Tatiana, and then Cameron. I thought about being a bitch and joining them, but that would end my access to Jonathan, and I figured it would serve me better to know something about Jonathan that he didn't know I knew.

I walked a block south, flagged a cab, and headed for midtown, wondering if Jonathan would confront me about my visit to Marchand, or would he prefer to think I didn't know he knew?

Chapter 28

Because I wanted to check in with Ajit at the Midtown North Precinct to see what he'd been able to find out about Lynch, and to learn if De Groot, who for the moment was the only thread to Abby and possibly Jenny, had popped up on any of his searches, I left instructions for Bebe to meet me for lunch at a small 50's style French Bistro on 51st Street. Bebe hated the West Side. Had I spoken to her in person, she would have declined.

When she arrived, she hesitated at the open doorway as though she might turn and run, until I instructed my waiter, a handsome young man with shiny black hair, to take her arm and deliver her to my table.

"OK Darling, I'm here," she said, amid a swirl of attitude. "Now would you please tell me what the hell is going on?"

I had ordered a Muscadet. The waiter poured her goblet half-full and topped off mine.

She took a sip and said, "I'm waiting," though I could tell from the change in her demeanor and the way she began studying my face she'd detected something that both concerned and frightened.

"Come close," I said, lowering my voice.

She tightened the grip of the stem of her glass.

"I've just come from the hospital," I said. "Someone tried to murder a young woman who has being trying to meet with me."

"Oh dear God." She took a fast sip. "How is she…is she going to make it?"

"I'm not sure, but I'm about to tell you something I promised her I would never tell a single soul, including you, and you have to swear on your unborn child's life that you won't repeat a word to anyone, not to Dalton, not to your mother, not to your rabbi, not to anyone. If you do, my dear friend, we might end up dead."

Her lips grew tight and her eyes big.

"Swear?"

"Yes, yes, I swear, Darling, please."

"She told me Abner Dodge murdered Jenny."

"WHAT?"

Several customers stopped to stare, and she lowered her voice to a whisper. "What ever are you talking about?"

I told her about Abby, from the time or our first telephone contact up to seeing her in the hospital, about Abner Dodge, about Praetorian, about everything Abby had told me.

She leaned back in stunned silence, a combination of unwilling disbelief and skeptical belief sloshing across her face. "Incredible," she finally said. "I mean, this is…I don't know what this is. This is crazy is what it is. Have you proof?"

"The last time Abby and I spoke, she told me if anything happened to her, she would send a key to a safe-deposit box containing a list of Praetorian's investors and documents listing all of Praetorian's activities, including proof that they had murdered Jenny."

"And did you get the key?"

"Not yet."

"It might still be coming," she said. "She could have sent it last night before they tried to kill her."

"You don't know how much I hope you're right, but let's not kid ourselves: according to Abby, Praetorian is comprised of some of the richest, evilest, and most powerful and corrupt men in the United States. They will stop at nothing to ensure what they do and who they are remains secret."

She exhaled noisily and her hands fidgeted. Her ten years of non-smoking would have ended right then and there had anyone produced a cigarette.

"Dodge knows you hired me to do a story on Jenny.

Abby said meeting him at the Four Seasons and again at the Winthrops wasn't a coincidence."

"But why so clandestine? That we're doing a story on Jenny isn't a secret."

"Abby says he always studies his enemies and tries to figure out what he's up against. Dalton makes me think Praetorian and Dodge have tapped of our phones. That's why I couldn't tell you anything."

"Darling, I finally figured it had to be something like that, because I knew it wasn't me."

I gripped her arm. "Plus, he's probably having us followed."

She glanced around.

"Forget it. It'll drive you insane. He uses former secret-service types who specialize in surveillance. We'll never recognize them."

"Have you stopped to consider for even one second that if they believe this young woman, Abby, passed the information along to you, they'll be doing a lot more than listening and following."

I nodded, very aware of that truth. "I can't stop looking for Jenny's killers, and now I've added Abby to the list. To me, she's as much a part of this as Jenny."

Our lunch remained untouched. I suggested we try to eat. Bebe agreed and signaled the waiter to refill our goblets. We picked at our food.

"On my way back from the hospital," I said, "I stopped to see Tatiana Marchand, the lawyer to whom Cameron Black referred Jenny."

"Darling, you've got to stop this craziness; you've got to promise me you'll stop running around playing detective." She put her hand to her heart, and then asked, missing no more than a half a beat, "How did you find out about Tatiana Marchand?"

"I thought you wanted me to stop."

She glared.

"Jonathan Winthrop told me."

"I'll bet she was real happy to see you."

"She denied telling Jenny to sign the agreements."

"And you believe her?"

"I didn't want to, but something about her rang true. Then Cameron Black called and told her he didn't know me. That brought our meeting to an uncomfortable and abrupt end."

"No kidding."

"After she kicked me out, I waited downstairs because I was certain she had agreed to meet Cameron. A few minutes later she came out, and I followed her to a restaurant in the next block."

"Did she meet him?"

"I assumed that's who it was, particularly when Jonathan Winthrop joined them."

"Cozy."

"Not only that, last night Jonathan told me that although he and Cameron Black remained good friends, they hadn't seen each other for about a year. When I saw them today, it didn't seem that way. There were no surprised looks, no moments of catching up; it seemed more like two people who saw each other all the time."

She said, "From all that I hear, Cameron is faithful to Anne. Maybe Jonathan has something going with Marchand."

"She's a knockout and a lawyer so she might qualify as a future Mrs. Jonathan Winthrop Junior, although that would make me mad because I thought he might be taking an interest in me."

She gave me a look that said, 'Are you nuts?'

"Don't worry, I'm not being serious."

"How much of this does Dalton know?"

"He knows Abby and I talked, but not details. It's best to assume I've told him nothing."

She nodded and seemed to be thinking deep thoughts.

I said, "There are too many people and too many stories to keep it all straight. It's best to not say a word to anyone."

"Darling, you have my solemn promise: not a word to anyone."

While we sipped our coffee, I happened to glance up at the television behind the bar, immediately wishing I hadn't.

"Uh oh," I said.

"What?" Bebe asked, following my gaze.

I went to the bar and asked the bartender to turn up the volume. Bebe slid up onto the stool beside me.

"What are we looking at?" she asked.

"They've found Abby's car. I hope the envelope isn't there."

"What envelope?"

"The one Abby was going to send to me, the one with the safe-deposit box key."

Wind whipped the reporter's hundred-dollar haircut and made a growling sound in the microphone, obliterating some of his words as he stared at the camera through his designer sunglasses. "Cops," he said, "are—this very moment—the—Meadowlands, mysterious disappearance—Abigail Dodge, found wallet, keys—on Jersey Turnpike—Meadowlands Sports Complex behind."

The camera panned away from the reporter, swept across the Sports Complex, and back to the reporter.

"Miss Dodge was driving—registered Jaeger—Secaucus, She left his apartment—10:00 p.m. video surveillance cameras—Tunnel—midnight."

I took out my notepad and recorded the times.

The wind abated. The reporter continued, "Abigail Dodge is described as Caucasian, 5-foot-7 inches tall, 120 pounds, with brown hair streaked with blonde. She has blue eyes and a vertical sword tattoo on the back of her neck. Her tongue and navel are pierced and she usually wears multiple pierced earrings on each ear. She had on white sneakers, a white blouse that she usually ties above her waist, and blue jean short-shorts.

"Her stepfather, who has said her behavior may be affected by drugs and alcohol—"

"Bastard," I said. "He never stops."

"—has offered a twenty-five thousand dollar reward for information that helps find his stepdaughter. He told this network that he and Abby's mother just want her to come home where she will be safe and can receive the care she needs. Please call the toll-free number appearing on your screen."

Chapter 29

While we stood and talked on the sidewalk in front of the Bistro, waiting for Bebe's car to arrive, I noticed her eyes explode with fear and she shrieked, driving hard into me and knocking us both sprawling into a bed of shrubs and flowers that fronted the adjacent building. Before I uttered other than a grunt and figured out what had happened, I heard a loud crash and more screaming.

Strong hands held me to the ground. "Are you OK? Are you hurt?"

I didn't feel hurt. I saw Bebe getting to her feet, helped by two young men. I looked at the owner of the hands that continued to hold me down. He had a big crooked face with gentle eyes.

"I'm OK," I said, and tried to stand.

"Wait a minute," he said. "Your foot is wedged under the fence there." He tugged at my sneaker a moment and got me free. "Now," he said. "Let's try it again. Take it real slow."

His powerful arms raised me up as though I were nothing. Bebe staggered over. Other than being covered with dirt and planter detritus and being frightened to death, we decided we were OK.

"Someone, call an ambulance," a voice yelled.

"The police are here," another shouted. "They can handle it."

Sirens roared up the street and two facing police cars screeched to a stop inches away from crashing head on.

"No," I said. "We don't need an ambulance."

A black Lincoln SUV had crossed the sidewalk five feet from where Bebe and I stood. It would have hit us except for Bebe's fast action.

"It's for her," a voice beside us said.

Bebe looked at the SUV as though she were going to

be ill. I put my arm around her shoulder and squeezed. Then I saw what she saw. The SUV had squashed a woman between its smashed grill and the front of the Bistro.

The man with the big crooked face said, "She doesn't need an ambulance. She's dead."

Despite the heat of the day, Bebe and I started to shiver. Someone from the hotel next to the bistro brought us a couple of blankets.

Voices all around us shouted orders, keeping vehicle and pedestrian traffic away.

"Where's the driver?" a policeman asked. No one seemed to know. They asked Bebe and me what we'd seen. I told them nothing because my back was to the street. Bebe said all she saw was this huge black car coming straight toward us, and the next thing she knew, we were on the ground.

"Was the woman with us?" another police officer asked. We said no. One of the men who'd helped Bebe up said she appeared to be alone.

The police took our names and telephone numbers and said we could go, that they might have to talk to us later, then Bebe's cellphone rang. It was her car service saying her driver was on 10th Avenue at the corner. The police had blocked the street, so we walked the twenty yards or so to meet him, and collapsed into the back seat.

"Jesus Christ! I've never been so scared in my life," she said, after she caught her breath. "I thought we were goners."

I held her hand. It trembled. So did mine. We embraced and began crazily laughing and crying. After a moment, we recovered, at least enough for Bebe to tell her driver to let me off at the precinct, and then take her back to the office.

As we started off, my cellphone rang. Unknown caller. "Hello," I said.

A man's voice said, "Next time you won't be so lucky." Click.

"Who was that?" she asked in a way that said she didn't want to know.

I handed her the phone and let her listen. She frowned, and then said, "This is getting far too dangerous. You've got to stop."

"If I thought for one minute you seriously believed that, I'd stop in a minute. You want this story so badly you're salivating."

"Darling, that doesn't include you getting killed, so again I say, no more playing amateur detective. Let the police find Jenny's murderer. Let the police find out who tried to murder Abby. When that is done, you write the story."

"And have it appear the same time every other magazine and newspaper publishes it? No thanks. If you don't want it, I'm sure *Cosmo*—"

We stopped in front of the precinct, and I got out. When I tried to close the door, she shot out her foot and held it ajar. "You wouldn't dare."

"I've named you as the person to call in case of accident or death."

"That is not funny," she said and slammed the door.

The car pulled away. She stuck her head out the window and shouted. "Darling, do be careful!"

Chapter 30

The desk sergeant asked if I had an appointment. I lied and told him I did, and then began to wonder what the jail time was for lying to a police officer in a police station. He called an extension and wrote my name on a bar coded lapel label that said VISITOR.

"Keep this on until you leave, and then return it to me."

I nodded.

"You can go up to the third floor. Mr. Singh will meet you there."

Two constables stood in front of the elevators talking. Their conversation ceased when I approached. One of them nodded. I thought I recognized him from the library raid the previous afternoon. I nodded back.

The elevator doors opened, and a man barged out. I jumped back to avoid being knocked to the floor. He glared through wolf-like eyes that were cold and cloudy, like they shouldn't be able to see at all.

I guessed him to be in his mid-thirties. He looked dirty, he stunk of acrid BO, and his clothes hadn't seen inside a washing machine for a long time. His shoulder-length, corn-colored hair hung in strings, traces of lunch or some previous trough gorging stuck to his matted, Fu Manchu moustache. A wide scar started below his left ear and ran down across his unshaven face to the middle of his chin.

He jammed his hands into the front pockets of his jeans, hunched his shoulders, and shuffled for the front door.

I shot a look at the two constables, thinking they displayed a lack of concern bordering on dereliction. The one who had nodded previously motioned me forward.

"Are you sure one of your prisoners isn't leaving the building?"

They glanced at the disgusting mess pushing his way out onto the street. "Could be," one of them chuckled.

I'd read where cops regularly had prisoners escape, and now I knew why. All a prisoner had to do was leave via the front door. I punched the button for the third floor. One of the constables pushed the button for the fifth floor. They continued their conversation about the Yankees and Mets as though I didn't exist, as though my observations were those of an idiot. I punched the third floor button a second time, bashing my knuckle in the process.

Ajit met me at the elevator. "You're as white as a sheet," he said.

I told him that I'd almost been run down, first by a large SUV and second, by a wiry, dirty little man.

"Are you OK? Would you like some water?"

I assured him I was fine, and he led me to his office in the computer center.

He asked about the SUV. I told him the police had arrived and he'd probably soon know more than I, though it appeared to be nothing more than a car that had gone out of control. I didn't tell him about the threatening phone call because that would raise more questions than I could answer. Then, because I was still upset, I described in more detail than I'm sure he wanted to hear, the wiry, dirty little man who'd almost knocked me over.

"He was probably a subway detective. They ride around looking homeless, watching for crime."

"Do they have to stink and appear so disgusting?"

He laughed.

"I thought he might be an escaping prisoner."

He laughed again. "We have some of those too."

I didn't want him to laugh. I wanted him to be angry. I wanted to lash out, and I struggled to rein in my emotions. Nothing that had happened was his fault, and I was beginning to think I'd need his help on a lot of fronts.

HE EXTRACTED a manila folder from a stack of papers and other folders that sat balanced on one corner of his small metal desk. "I found some information on De Groot."

"You need a secretary."

"We can do it ourselves or get cops assigned to administrative duty, and I'm not about to tell a cop who's going to get his gun back in a week that I need some filing done." He flipped through the papers in the folder. "De Groot uses an alias...Louis Vesco."

What made me not tell him I already knew that piece of information? He hadn't given me cause to doubt, but neither had De Groot a.k.a. Vesco. And why would they? The art of deception is their specialty. They earn their money by getting people to trust them, and then they kill.

I wanted to ask if he'd seen the news report on Abby Dodge. I wanted to tell him Abby's story. I wanted to, but I didn't.

"What else does your folder say?"

"Here," he said, and handed over the folder. "Tuck this in your bag, and let's take a ride."

We crossed Eighth Avenue, and hopped on a Route 104 city bus headed north.

"I had Ferrari in mind."

"What we have to say shouldn't be heard by others. This is the safest way."

"Is your car bugged?"

He chuckled. "Probably not, though it is noticeable, and I don't always want my friends knowing where I am."

We got out at the first stop past Columbus Circle and walked across to Central Park.

He pointed to a bench. "We can sit if you'd rather, or continue walking."

The humidity that had already made my blouse begin to stick to my skin seemed not to affect Ajit. I glanced up. The trees blocked the sun and I felt a whisper of a breeze.

"I'd like to walk, as long as you don't mind my sweat-drenched blouse."

"It's not noticeable, and even if it were, I wouldn't mind."

He was much more complex than Jonathan though had a simpler way of being straightforward. His response implied nothing sexual; neither did it imply disinterest.

We continued toward the Fifth Avenue side of the park. I want to trust him. I need to trust him.

I said, "I already knew that De Groot was Vesco."

He looked quizzical.

"I finally met up with the girl we couldn't find in the library. She told me."

"I'm glad you had better luck finding her than I."

"She found me. Believe me, we would never have found her."

Another quizzical look.

"Penny Munro is Abigail Dodge."

"I guess I can stop searching for Penny Munro."

"I'm sorry, I should have told you, but everything's been a blur since we last spoke, or at least since I discovered that Penny was Abby Dodge."

"For some reason that name sounds familiar."

"Her stepfather is Abner Dodge." I watched his reaction. What did I expect to see? That he hadn't seen the newscast about finding Abby's car seemed a certainty.

"Not *the* Abner Dodge?"

"You know him then?"

"Of him. We travel in different circles."

"According to Abby, Vesco works for Dodge."

"She's probably told you a lot more than the file says. Vesco's personal data is confidential, which, in the lingua franca of the police department, means that only top security clearance can gain access."

"She told me Vesco, better known as Lou or LD, is former CIA or FBI. Dodge apparently employs him and a few others to protect certain clients."

"That explains the top security clearance. He's probably killed a few people that no one is supposed to know about."

"That's not comforting, considering that he and I sat face-to-face a couple of nights ago."

He started to apologize.

"Please don't," I said. "That piece of information in isolation isn't too frightening and not altogether surprising, although it is scary as hell within the context of the story I'm writing about a scientist, a woman by the name of Jenny Ross, who was murdered on Sunday night."

"Are you saying Vesco is connected to Jenny Ross's murder?"

"No, it's just that hearing that Vesco may have killed people...I tied them together in my mind. In your line of work, you see this type of thing all the time, so you process it differently."

It wasn't a lie, at least not totally. Here's how I had it figured: Vesco works for Dodge; Abby said Dodge had arranged to have Jenny murdered; Vesco is former CIA who may have killed people. My mind connected Vesco to Jenny Ross's murder and to the attempted murder of Abby, but these were suppositions I wasn't ready to verbalize.

"I've seen the Jenny Ross case in our system," he said. "Although I can't recall who's handling the investigation."

"The person I'm currently working for, Bebe Morgan, was a good friend of Jenny's. The morning after the murder, Detective Kennedy at the 20th Precinct interviewed her."

That reminded me of Lynch's allegations and the other reason, besides De Groot, I had wanted to talk to Ajit.

"Bebe Morgan of *Madame Magazine*?"

"Where did that piece of information come from?"

"Besides Penny Munro, I did a search on Paige Harrington."

"And here I worried about my damp blouse exposing too much."

"Checking on people is an occupational hazard, and you can't tell me you wouldn't have done the same."

A silence fell between us as we walked toward Fifth. To the right, like a scene on a giant stage, Central Park South buzzed with a constant stream of cars, and a dozen colorful horse-drawn carriages, some with hanging baskets of flowers, sat in a line waiting for passengers. Black and white and brown horses lazily swatted their tails at persistent flies and ate from the canvas feedbags strapped to their noses. With costumes as different from one another as their ethnicity, drivers lazed in the shade next to the stone fence that bordered the park. Pedestrians filled the sidewalks, some as if dancing a slow waltz, others stepping along as if driven by the heat of a tango.

However, the giant stage had gone eerily silent, as though muted by an invisible curtain through which the cacophony could not penetrate, and for a brief moment I didn't think about Jenny Ross and Hebrides and Praetorian and Abby Dodge.

Then Lynch again entered my thoughts and reality set in. I asked Ajit if he'd been able to find out anything.

"Not much," he said. "It's hard to get into service records without creating more questions than they answer."

I owed him an explanation and told him about Lynch coming to see me at the Waldorf. "Lynch told me Kennedy was under internal investigation and had no right getting involved in the Jenny Ross murder investigation."

I didn't tell him Lynch also suspected Bebe and Dalton.

He studied me for a moment, and I got the eerie feeling he was trying to decide whether I'd lost touch with my faculties. "What?"

"Sorry, but I know Kennedy, and I seriously doubt he's under investigation. He's one of the cleanest cops I know."

"I'm only telling you what Lynch said. Is he also clean?"

"I don't know Lynch."

The way he said it told me he knew more than I was about to find out.

"Why would a Lynch-type make a special trip to tell me to be wary of Kennedy?"

He glanced at me out of the corner of his eye.

"I know, you don't know him, but assume for the sake of argument, you did."

"Then I'd say Lynch sounds like someone who likes to throw his weight around."

"He told me he'd arrest me if I didn't do as he said."

"He can definitely make your life difficult, although unless you feel threatened, why don't you play along to see what his game is?"

"And if I feel threatened?"

"Call me, and I'll see what I can do about putting a stop to it."

"He said he'd call me twice daily for a report."

"What kind of report?"

"To tell him who I've talked to, that type of thing."

He frowned. "Is he having you followed?"

I'd screwed up. I'd probably led Lynch directly to Ajit, something he clearly hadn't anticipated.

"I'm not used to this type of existence. I don't expect people to follow me wherever I go or listen to my telephone calls."

"I'm only worried about you. Have you spoken to Lynch yet?"

"This morning was the first time, and in case you're concerned, I'm not telling him anything other than where I've been, and the only reason I'm telling him that is because he'll probably know if I'm telling the truth."

He smiled. "First, no one followed us here, and second, even if they did, I don't care if he knows you've talked to me. In fact, you might tell him you did because if he's doing his job, he'll already know you've been to see me and that we left the precinct together."

"He has people in every precinct?"

"People like Lynch get their power from a broad network of like-minded people who play by different rules."

"Now that I'm in the big bad city, I clearly need to concentrate more on what others around me are doing. Where I'm from, those aren't primary considerations."

"Unfortunately, it's become second nature here."

He motioned toward an empty bench a few steps ahead. "Remind me again of your interest in De Groot."

"Before we talk about him, I'd like to tell you about Abby Dodge."

"The girl from the library, Abner Dodge's daughter?"

"The same, but it's a long story."

He glanced at his watch. "I have time."

"Abby made me promise I'd never tell a soul, so I trust this can be strictly off the record." First Bebe and now Ajit. How many more? Forgive me Abby, but we need help.

His gaze intensified, but he didn't agree.

"Whether you agree or not, I've decided I have to trust you because I need help."

"I'll help any way I can and so long as no major laws are broken, I don't need to provide details to anyone."

"Have you heard of a group called The Praetorian

Guard?"

"Not in the modern-day context, although I studied Roman history."

"It's the modern one I have in mind, although doubtless patterned after the original."

"In that case, I plead ignorance. Why the question?"

"Abby says Abner Dodge created Praetorian as a vehicle to shield the activities of power hungry, corrupt businessmen, politicians, and military. She believes Praetorian killed Jenny to gain control of her invention."

"What's her invention?"

"You majored in AI, correct?"

He raised an eyebrow. "Correct."

"Then I should ask you because I've heard it described once and only once, and that once was a rumor, as the Holy Grail of AI. Other than that, another source told me the invention could be worth billions."

"It has to be thinking robots, although the last I knew no one was even close. Let me check with some of my *über*-geek pals who stayed with the science. They'll at least know if the rumors are out there."

"Praetorian also tried to murder Abby last night. Dodge says she's missing—it's all over the news, but the truth is they tried to kill her."

I told him everything and this time I included the threatening telephone call after the SUV had almost run over Bebe and me.

"So before, when you asked me to remind you of my interest in De Groot: other than Abner Dodge, he's my only connection to Abby Dodge and Jenny Ross."

I took De Groot's file from my bag.

Mostly, it contained news clippings showing important public meetings and galas involving the governor, the mayor, or some private sector bigwig. In each case, a steady hand had used a red marker to circle a hard to make out face in a crowd.

"Someone's got good eyes," I said.

"The originals are clearer. It's definitely him."

"What about an address. Someone outside the FBI or CIA must know where he lives. He must sleep somewhere, go to work from somewhere, buy groceries, go to bars, have a girlfriend, walk a dog, things like that. Abner Dodge surely doesn't keep him on a shelf in his office."

"There's nothing listed in Vesco's name: no Social Security Number, no passport, no driver's license, no telephones, and no apartment, all fairly typical for anyone like him."

"But we know he exists."

He reached into his shirt pocket, extracted a slip of paper, and handed it to me.

I stared at the single printed word: APTHORPE.

"It's a huge apartment complex on 79th and Broadway," he said, responding to my unasked question.

"I know the building," I said, and tucked the paper between the sheets of my notepad.

"One condition," he said. "If you see him, you must promise to do nothing without contacting me. No, let me rephrase: you must promise to do nothing without my being there."

I checked my watch. Jessie's plane was due—I had to leave.

He touched my arm. "Paige, I'm serious. You are not immune to their level of violence. De Groot is a hired killer, and guys like Dodge don't hesitate to put them to work."

"If you agree to help, you have my promise, although if I find him, I don't intend to let him get away. You also need to know I don't plan on doing anything stupid or brave or heroic. I know what happened to Jenny, and I saw Abby."

"I'll take that because it's probably as good as I'm going to get."

I gave him back his file, and we stood and walked

past 'The Pond,' exiting the park next to the Sherman statue. He hailed a cab headed south on Fifth.

"You take this one," he said, and opened the back door. My arm tingled as my fingers brushed across the soft hair on the back of his hand.

The door closed and the cab sped off. I looked back just in time to see him get into a cab headed west across Central Park South, both nervous and relieved that I had confided in him.

Chapter 31

As we progressed south on Fifth, I took out my cellphone and laptop to check and record my messages. Jessie had called saying she had arrived and asked me to phone. Brad had telephoned to say that everything had fallen into place. I breathed easier knowing that he'd hidden Abby away where no one could get to her.

Bebe reported that Dalton's security people had swept the phones, and Detective Kennedy finally decided he wanted to talk to me. She didn't say why, although my concern was less, after hearing what Ajit said about Kennedy's integrity. Telling Lynch about meeting with Kennedy would prove interesting, though.

Jonathan Winthrop had said he'd enjoyed dinner and wondered if he might have a repeat performance. Anne Black said she'd call again. I wondered if she'd found out that I'd talked to Tatiana Marchand. I couldn't wait to have that conversation.

Zoë, Brad's doctor friend, left a message asking if I knew how to get hold of Brad. She didn't leave a number. I figured whatever Brad had done with Abby he'd done on his own so Zoë and his other colleague, Tom, wouldn't get into trouble.

I downloaded the messages into my computer and called Jessie. She answered on the first ring.

"Welcome back to New York," I said.

"Ooh Tawny, I'm so glad to be here. How's Abby? When can I see her?"

I heard a click. Someone was listening.

"Jessie, love, I'll have to call you back in a two minutes." I rattled off the number on my incoming call record to confirm that's where I could reach her, told the cabbie to stop, and ran into the shopping complex in Rockefeller Center, dodging my way around the hordes of tourists and office workers until I spotted a pay phone.

"What happened?" she asked.

"I heard a click. I think my phones are bugged."

"Maybe it's this one."

"Why is yours be bugged?"

"I'm using Abby's."

This is bad. "How did you get Abby's phone?"

"I'm in her apartment in Greenwich village."

"Dear God, Jessie, you can't stay there. Grab your stuff and get out now. Get yourself down to the street as fast as you can. If you can't find a cab, run to the nearest subway. Either way, come to the Park Avenue entrance of the Waldorf. If I'm not there, wait for me, and if anyone comes near you, scream your head off."

I grabbed a cab on the fly and ten minutes later jumped out in front of the Waldorf. Jessie hadn't arrived.

A few minutes later, she hopped from a cab and raced up the sidewalk, her long golden hair flowing in the sun. We embraced for a long time before I allowed myself to take a normal breath.

"God Jessie, I was so afraid," I said, my voice an emotional mess of a whisper. "All I could think about was the last time you were in New York and almost got killed by that maniac drug dealer."

She laughed and cried. She clung to me a few moments longer. I didn't want her to let go, ever.

"I'm not scared," she said. "I'm just so happy to see you and I'm feeling so sad about what happened to Abby."

"We'd better get off the street," I said, untangling from our embrace and leading her inside. "The same people listening to our telephone calls are following us."

We dashed for the elevators.

"Where's Abby?" she asked, as we rode to the eighteenth floor. "When can I see her?"

"People are after her, Jessie. Brad has her somewhere

safe. I don't know where."

"Is she…"

I held her hand. "She's not good, Jessie. Let's not kid ourselves, but Brad and his doctor friends are taking good care of her."

We got off the elevator and walked down the hall to my room. When I shoved my keycard into the slot, the door pushed open. The hairs on my arms prickled.

I took one look at Jessie and we turned and ran, our footsteps fast and noiseless on the hallway's thick carpet. I picked up the house phone next to the elevator bank and told the operator what had happened. She told us to stay where we were, that security would be up in a matter of a few minutes.

Jessie said, "This is all Abner Dodge, isn't it? He's the worst kind of bastard."

She seemed possessed of an angry calm.

"Jessie, I'm real glad you came, but you need to understand that Abner Dodge is far more dangerous than the drug dealers and pimps that you escaped from before. Abby is afraid of him, and we need to be too. According to Abby, he has hired killers everywhere."

"Abby always over-dramatized everything."

I grabbed her arm. "Promise me as you would Deuce and Red, no heroics." Deuce and Red, who we both loved, were strippers that Jessie considered her older sisters. I doubted she would ever break a promise to me, but I knew she would never break a promise to them.

Her eyes flashed alarm. Good. Maybe I was getting through to her. "I promise," she said, "and I'm sorry, I didn't mean to upset you."

I gave her a big hug and told her about Jenny Ross and all my contacts with Abby: the phone calls, the library meeting, seeing Abby for a brief moment outside the restaurant, and Abby's last call before she ended up in the hospital.

"Abby told me not to tell or trust anyone, Jessie, and

I think it was good advice." I told myself that didn't include Bebe and Ajit.

Two men stepped from the elevator. The first was over six feet tall and wore a blue suit and white shirt and red tie.

"Are you Miss Harrington?" he asked in his officious sounding baritone.

"I am," I said.

"I'm Mr. Thomas, the assistant manager. This is Mr. Regan, one of our house detectives."

Regan was a solid five-foot-nine. His big, square head was topped by a black brush cut with a touch of silver at the temples, his bushy hedge-like eyebrows darted independently above sunken eyes, and his neck seemed not to exist. He wore a black suit, black shirt, and pink tie and reeked of cigar smoke.

"I tink it would be best if you waited here," Regan said, his voice sounding in need of a thorough throat clearing. He seemed ill at ease in our presence and glad to get started down the hallway. A gun found its way into his hand, and Jessie and I stole a glance at each other.

He crept crablike along on his tiptoes, his back glued to the wall, his big stomach occupying half the hallway. Thomas watched intently, shifting his weight from one foot to the other.

Despite the potential danger, Jessie and I fought desperately to keep from exploding with laughter.

Regan pushed the door open, his revolver extended with both arms straight in front. I felt like we'd been transported to a Law and Order episode and half expected to see Jerry Orbach's ghost floating by.

Regan disappeared inside. Thomas started down the hallway. Jessie and I followed. Near the door, Thomas plastered himself to the wall, arms spread out as if he were about to be frisked from the front. Jessie and I stepped around.

"Where you going?" he hissed.

I pointed inside the room.

"Stay here," he hissed.

I pushed the door open and gasped. Jessie covered her hand with her mouth and said, "Ohmygawd!"

"No one here," Regan said, coming out of the bathroom and shoving the gun into his shoulder holster, "but they sure raised hell with your stuff."

Nothing like stating the obvious. They had slashed pillows, mattresses, and chairs and ripped out the stuffing. Drawers and pictures lay on the floor. They had yanked the TV from its cabinet and smashed it, ripped the lining from suitcases, which had been slashed top, bottom, and sides, and emptied the two wardrobes, wildly strewing my clothes about. The walnut dining room table and chairs lay broken on their sides.

Jessie gripped my arm.

Thomas wailed something unintelligible from behind and, trying to not step on something with his big feet, came to where Regan, Jessie, and I were standing.

I'd never actually seen anyone wring their hands before, but Thomas wrung his hands. I thought he might cry, but then he sucked in a deep breath that seemed to come from his size thirteen wingtips, exhaled slowly, and regained control.

"Those responsible for this...this...this barbarism will be brought to justice." He barked orders into his walkie-talkie. "Miss Harrington, a team of my best people is on it way to help you sort through your belongings and make a list of everything that needs replacing. Mr. Regan, I want you to review the tapes, ASAP, and let me know immediately what you learn."

Regan gave Thomas a sidewise glance tantamount to the finger.

Thomas continued, "Miss Harrington, I'll arrange for another room, a suite, with the hotel's compliments."

I didn't respond. I wasn't sure what I wanted to do.

Thomas turned to Regan and said, "Mr. Regan, some-time today, if you please."

Regan said he wanted to ask Jessie and me a few questions, like who we thought might have done this. Thomas told him to do it later. Regan went off in a huff, though it was clear to me Jessie and I hadn't seen the last of him.

Jessie and I waited until the cleaning staff brushed all my clothes and packed them into two new trunks and a set of Gucci luggage courtesy of the hotel. Two bellboys arrived. One was, Jorge Ruiz. His look told me I shouldn't acknowledge I knew him.

Thomas instructed Jorge and his partner to escort my belongings and me to a suite, gave them the number, and said he would meet us there to make sure all was satis-factory.

After Thomas departed, Jorge said, "Some bad peo-ple in here Miss. Ju be careful."

Before I could respond, Regan magically reappeared with two assistants and again wanted to ask Jessie and me some questions. I told him I had no idea who might have been responsible and promised to call if I thought of something. Regan wanted to press the issue with Jessie, but I told him it would have to wait. His face darkened, and he looked about to throw down a chal-lenge, then wheeled and left, his assistants falling in be-hind.

When Jessie and I arrived at the courtesy suite, a gi-ant basket of fresh fruit sat on the dining room table and a few steps away, next to the bar, a magnum of cham-pagne protruded from a silver bucket. Thomas danced around, smoothing pillows, tugging at drapes, adjusting lamp shades, making sure all was perfection.

After offering profuse thanks, I walked him to the door. As he started away, he paused long enough to tell me that since *Madame Magazine* had made the reserva-tion, he had asked his assistant to report the 'incident' to

Miss Morgan. I slammed the door, made a mad dash for the telephone, and called Bebe's direct line. Her frantic voice penetrated my ear.

"Darling, would you please tell me what in hell is going on over there. I haven't been out of your sight for three hours and I'm hearing nothing but agony here. Some pompous ass calls to say that your room has been ransacked, that you've been moved to a suite, compliments of the hotel, and that he hopes the arrangements are satisfactory. I assured him in no uncertain terms they were not, and I'd sue the ass off him and his hotel for allowing my best writer to be exposed to life-threatening dangers."

"Bebe, I love you too, and we're fine. Jessie, my friend from Calgary, and I are sitting in a large, elegant one-bedroom suite with a basket of fruit and a bottle of champagne. The problem is I'm not certain this is where I should be."

"Well, Darling, of course you shouldn't. You must not stay there one more night. Someone knows where you are and it seems obvious the hotel's security isn't up to the task."

"Between you and me, I think it was an inside job. When their head of security opened the door to my room, I got the feeling he knew no one was inside. I mean he had his gun out and looked serious enough, but then, just waltzed in. Later, when he wanted to ask Jessie and me some questions, I got the feeling he wanted to ask about more than the trashed room."

"All the more reason for you to get out of there this instant. You'll both stay with me. End of conversation."

We ended the call, and I told Jessie what we'd discussed. She said we should leave without notifying the hotel. I agreed. The less Regan knew, the better. I'd send for my clothes later.

While Jessie and I waited for the elevator, Jorge Ruiz appeared in the hallway escorting another guest, who looked like Tipper Gore, to a suite adjacent to the one Thomas had put me in. She nodded.

"Paige Harrington," I said, and offered my hand. "We met at the Global Warning Conference in Montreal."

"I remember," she said, and smiled graciously.

Whether she did or didn't remember, I had established with almost one-hundred percent certainty that she was in fact Tipper Gore, and therefore no one would be paying my room a visit unless Tipper's thus far invisible phalanx of secret service people were horribly inept.

I introduced Jessie, then Tipper turned and continued on toward her room. Jorge gave me a knowing smile that told me he knew we were leaving, and that I could call if I needed help.

Chapter 32

We arrived at Bebe's Park Avenue apartment the same time she stepped from a stretch black limousine with a New York license plate that read CDR–6, a Coburn, Davis & Russell car from Dalton Croft's firm.

The doorman hurried out with his luggage cart. I gladly surrendered my two suitcases as did Bebe her briefcase. "Miss," he said to Jessie, reaching for her well-traveled over-the-shoulder denim duffel with wide red straps.

Jessie pulled away and said, "I'll carry it, thanks."

"Sweetheart," Bebe said, walking over and snatching the duffel from Jessie's shoulder, "Fred would never forgive me."

I introduced Bebe to Jessie while a happy Fred and his well-laden cart disappeared inside.

"You're even more beautiful than I could have imagined," Bebe said to Jessie. "Paige, we simply must do a photo shoot for your last article."

Jessie stiffened as Bebe pulled her into an embrace. They might become fast friends, but it would be at Jessie's pace, not Bebe's. Meanwhile, Bebe would go on being Bebe.

"Come, children," Bebe said, taking us by the hand. "Let us ascend to Bebe's place for a much-needed drink. Paige, Darling, what time is your dinner?"

I couldn't remember telling her I had a dinner engagement, and my face must have telegraphed that fact.

"Oh, come, come, Darling, your dinner with your friend."

"I didn't know I'd mentioned it."

"Of course you did. How else would I know?" She flipped her hand and spun away. We followed along in her *Chloe* wake.

"Eight o'clock," I said to her back.

"Where?"

"I think somewhere within walking distance of their apartment on West End Avenue."

"Oh, West Siders," she said with all the disdain she could muster.

"I hope you don't mind," I said to Jessie.

"She'll be fine," Bebe said. "Dalton insists on taking the two of us to this absolutely divine French eatery on 78th Street."

The tiny elevator grill rattled shut behind us, and Bebe told the operator to take us to the twelfth floor.

"I hate to be a bother," Jessie said. "I can just stay at your apartment."

"Not another word, dear child. Dalton and I work much better when there's more than just the two of us."

Fred had taken the freight elevator and was waiting by Bebe's door. She had him place our luggage in the front guest bedroom, a large, airy space that had two double beds and two high-backed wing chairs, ample closet space, and a bathroom *en suite*.

After our drink, I took a bath and changed into an off-the-shoulder pale yellow dress. Dee Hunter hadn't sounded like a boxy dresser, and my recollection of some of Peter Zane's past girlfriends didn't include any that were afraid to wear stylish and sexy clothes. Peter was shallow that way, one of the reasons certain women were attracted to him. I put on white pumps and took a matching handbag large enough for my cellphone, recorder, wallet, notepad, and small makeup case.

Since Jessie hadn't brought other than jeans, I loaned her a mint-green strapless dress with trailing wisps that, with her long, blonde hair, made her look like a Hollywood version of Helen of Troy.

"I hadn't planned on dining in a fancy restaurant," she said to Bebe. "I hope this is OK."

Bebe, stunning in a white sheath, glanced up. "Why did I bother? I could go nude, and no one would notice.

Forgive me, my darling Jessie, but let me assure you, you look divine."

I left them waiting for Dalton and caught a taxi in front of Bebe's apartment. While we crossed Central Park, I checked my voicemail. Brad hadn't called. Zoë had, still looking for Brad. I cursed her again for not leaving a number.

We exited Central Park on 79th Street headed west. At Broadway, we passed a fortress-like limestone building that occupied the entire block. A bell rang in my mind.

"What building is that," I asked the driver, "the one on the left?"

"I think that's the Ansonia," he said, tossing a cursory glance out the side window.

I knew it wasn't the Ansonia. The apartment I'd purchased and one day planned to live in if I ever got it remodeled was in the Ansonia; the Ansonia was where Bebe and I had coffee the morning we learned that Jenny Ross had been murdered.

"The Ansonia is on 74th Street," I said.

The driver scratched his head. "Maybe it's the Apthorpe. I always get the two of them confused."

I hurriedly dug out Ajit's note, the one he'd given me in the park: APTHORPE. Vesco lived in the Apthorpe.

Chapter 33

Dee Hunter and Peter Zane lived in a well-kept, fifteen story limestone and brick apartment building on the corner of 76th and West End Avenue. The doorman escorted me through the marbled lobby rich with period carpets and Victorian furniture. Two dozen red roses sat on a granite-topped wall table beneath a large, ornately framed mirror. Large paintings and gilded sconces tastefully filled the walls and overhead, a massive chandelier eagerly awaited darkness.

"Their apartment is to the right as you step off," he said, and reached in to push the fifteenth floor button.

While the elevator ascended, I tried to remember the last time I'd seen Peter with a woman whose name I even remembered. He'd gone though so many bimbo relationships, it was hard to keep track. Bimbos worked for him because he had no concept of other people's needs and lives.

I stepped from the elevator. There were two doors. Matching brass umbrella stands and Victorian wooden storage benches sat outside each. Paintings and wall sconces and chandeliers seemed miniature copies of those in the lobby. The door to my right opened.

A stunningly beautiful woman with long black hair pulled back in a braid said, "Hello, Paige. Welcome to our home."

Her olive skin and dark eyes leapt from the white slip dress that seemed like a gathering of clouds and fog. She stepped forward and put out her hand. The delicate aroma of orchids brushed the air.

"I'm Dee," she said, her smile brilliant and warm.

She had an armful of bangles and wore several rings that looked expensive.

"Thank you for having me," I said. "And I am so pleased to meet you." That sounded overdone. What I was trying to do was express pleasure with Peter finally having a relationship with what seemed to be a real woman.

"Please, do come in." She stepped to one side and motioned me through the doorway with a mezuzah affixed. I assumed that meant this was Dee's apartment and that Dee was Jewish because Peter wasn't. In a pinch, he claimed to be Episcopalian.

The bright room overlooked the Hudson and the apartments across the river in New Jersey. The orange of the giant sun slipping down between the buildings basted the windrows of purple clouds that filled the early evening sky.

"Peter will be right out," she said, and offered me a drink. A well-stocked bar occupied the far wall. I asked for vodka with ice.

"Peter told me you liked Grey Goose. It's my favorite also, though I'm not much of a drinker. He usually has three or four to my one."

Dee floated to the bar looking like Odette in Swan Lake, her dress a swirl. Her long, slender hands caressed the bottle and glasses. When she poured, the silver vodka seemed suspended, and then, as if granted permission, splashed into the glass and crashed over the ice.

"L'chayim!" Dee said, touching her glass to mine.

"L'chayim!" I responded.

"You say that well."

"Columbia," I said. "The guys on our drinking team were mostly Jewish. If you couldn't say l'chayim, you didn't get a drink." I thought better of mentioning that our drinking team met Friday nights.

A door closed in the rear. Dee turned and walked toward the hallway. "Hello, Darling," she said, "Paige is here."

Peter looked the same: boyishly handsome, his sandy-colored hair sliding down across his forehead on one side, his craggy face darkly tanned from hours on the exclusive golf courses of the world. He wore an open-necked blue shirt and a light gray suit tailored to advertise his broad shoulders and narrow waist. Dee stretched up to kiss his cheek. He wrapped an arm around her tiny waist, gave her a quick squeeze, and stepped toward me, his blue eyes twinkling, his teeth flashing white.

"Hello, Peter," I said. "I like your new lady, a lot, and I like your new digs."

He wrapped his arms around me, not concerned what Dee might think about the closeness and duration of the embrace.

"Darling, I have your martini ready," Dee said.

He released me and took the martini from Dee as though she were a waitress. "Yeah, isn't it great, and look at that view. Look at that boat in full sail heading up the Hudson. Wish we were on her."

Peter had been a sailor all his life. His father had a sixty-foot yacht and owned an island in the Georgian Bay in Ontario where Peter had practically grown up.

"Have you lived here long?"

"Couple of months. The woman I was with when I saw you last December finally tossed me out. Too bad she was good in the sack."

I wanted to hit him and glanced at Dee. She looked away.

"Anyway, that's when I met Dee. I guess she took pity on me."

Dee seemed hypnotized by Peter. I looked back at Peter, who seemed hypnotized by my breasts. He definitely hadn't changed. Always looking for the woman he didn't or couldn't have. I tried to recall why I liked him. We finished our drinks and Dee suggested we walk to the restaurant.

MY ENTIRE body tingled when we went up 79th Street past the Apthorpe, simultaneously hoping and fearing we'd meet Vesco.

"What a grand building," I said. "Do either of you know anyone living there?"

Peter said, "This is the Apthorpe, one of the finest apartment buildings in all of New York City. I keep telling Dee this is where we should live."

"Perhaps one day we will," she said to Peter, "but to answer your question," she said to me, "I don't believe we do."

"Earlier this week," I lied, "a friend of a friend gave me the name of a photographer who's supposed to live there. I want to use him for a shoot in connection with a story, but he doesn't appear to be listed."

"Dee, I thought you had a friend living there," Peter said.

"Darling, I know someone living there, but I'm not sure I'd call her a friend."

She didn't volunteer anything more and, for the moment, that ended the subject. As we crossed Broadway, I looked back at the fortress-like building that occupied the entire block. The wrought-iron gate led to an interior courtyard guarded by a lone security officer in a kiosk. Eventually, Vesco had to come out through that gate.

WHEN WE got to the restaurant, Peter said, "We'll have a drink at the bar first." Dee whispered something in the maître d's ear, and Peter slid onto a barstool. I made sure Dee sat between us.

"Cheers!" Peter said when we got our drinks, and gulped his martini.

"Yes," Dee said, touching her glass to mine. "Peter has told me so much about you."

Peter banged his empty glass on the counter, and Chris put a full one in its place.

I asked Peter if he knew Cameron Black.

He took another long swig and said, "Nectar of the gods."

"Peter," Dee said. "Paige asked about Cameron Black."

"Oh yeah, Cameron Black." His face wrinkled to a gin grin. "Blackie, we call him. One in a million. How do you know old Blackie?"

He had started to slur his words. I knew from the past that with Peter it wasn't the quantity of gin as much as the act of being in a place where gin got served that caused him to start acting like a jackass.

"I don't. I'm working on a story and someone mentioned his name. How do you know him?"

"Uncle Sam's navy. Old Blackie and I were on a couple of junkets together—'Kings of the Morse Code' they called us."

"I thought the Morse Code went out with smoke signals."

"We were two of the last trained to use it. Came in handy for bridge and poker." He laughed at the memory.

I said, "I've heard conflicting stories about Cameron Black."

"Lots of conflicting stories about Blackie, most of them bad...one or two good ones though." He took another swig and licked his lips.

"Darling, lower your voice. Everyone in the restaurant doesn't need to know."

I was glad she'd intervened. Had Peter and I been alone, I would have smacked him down, but Dee's presence removed that prerogative.

"Sorry," he said. "It's a bad habit of mine; one of many. Anyway, Blackie is a silver spoon guy, huge trust account. His daddy's into oil and gold. Billions. Good thing, too, because ole Blackie sure throws the bucks around."

"Honey, I'm going to the washroom. When I get back, we will go to the table."

"I'll come with you," I said.

"I might hustle up another martini while you're

gone," Peter said.

"No, you won't. Chris, I'm counting on you, no more martinis." Her voice had an edge.

When we got into the bathroom, Dee daubed at her eyes. I touched her arm.

"I'm sorry," Dee said. "He gets a little crazy."

"Don't apologize on my account. I've known Peter for a lot of years—once in a while he needs a smack, and I'm going to tell you something else: I've known most of his lady friends—you're the first one I've liked."

She smiled her stunning smile. "At this moment, you don't how much that means."

I brushed a speck of mascara from her cheek. "Good as new," I said.

"We'd better get back." Dee said. "He doesn't do well on his own, but before we go, I need a promise."

"Promise granted."

"Give him that smack if you think he needs it. I won't be offended."

We collected Peter and the maître d' led us to a large corner table. Peter ordered a bottle of white wine. After the wine steward filled our glasses, Peter continued with Cameron Black, or 'ole Blackie,' as he was now being called.

"Ole Blackie's got a gambling problem. Got his Hummer smashed up by a couple of hoods from Atlantic City or Las Vegas, I don't know for sure, maybe they were from Monaco or Tokyo. Ole Blackie screws around all over the world. Who knows? They were a couple of bad dudes."

"His father had to bail him out," Dee said.

"Yeah, yeah, ole Blackie had to hit up his trust account for a couple of mil. Drop in the bucket. Pocket money."

I said, "I heard he'd blown his trust account."

We stopped talking long enough to order. As soon as

our waiter left, Peter continued. "By the time ole Blackie gets his hands on it, there'll be so much money that not even he'll be able to spend it all. He gets an allowance, maybe fifty thousand a month. The annual income is over ten mil."

"He wastes fifty thousand dollars a month?" Dee's mouth dropped open. "You didn't tell me that."

"Hey, a guy's gotta have a few secrets."

"Peter," I said. Don't be an ass."

"You guys ganging up on me?"

Dee said, "No, my love, but we will if you don't behave."

He grinned. "Blackie's a big player—the Hollywood crowd, the A-list. You name it, ole Blackie's there, first class all the way. He flies everywhere by private jet."

I said to Dee, "I guess it doesn't take long to blow fifty thousand, if you really put your mind to it."

Dee shuddered. "That's six hundred thousand a year?"

Our salads arrived. We began to pick.

"I heard his father has fallen on hard times."

"Not a chance. I went with ole Blackie to his bank. His old man was in Bermuda with some young chick but left instructions with the Bank of Bermuda to wire the money. It was already in ole Blackie's account."

"Maybe he lied," Dee said. "Did you actually see the money?"

"He showed me his balance on the ATM. It definitely said two million and something. He also got a shiny new Hummer from his old man, or maybe his mother, I can't remember."

Our main course arrived and conversation turned to Broadway plays and museums, the latter of great interest to Dee, a self-proclaimed museum addict. After the waiters cleared our table and started serving coffee, I asked Peter if he'd ever met Cameron's father.

"Couple of times," he said, "Thanksgiving last year, I

was alone, and ole Blackie and his wife, Anne—you ever met her? Super smart lady—weren't on speaking terms, so Cameron invited me to fly to Oklahoma."

"I've heard this story," Dee said. "It's disgusting."

"Not disgusting. When I get to be seventy or eighty, I hope I can do the same."

Dee frowned.

"It was like going to see Hef at the mansion. Gorgeous young women all over the place, maids, cooks, even his chauffeur—what a looker she was: tall blonde with chauffeur's cap and tunic and hot pants and boots over her knees—hard to concentrate on an old turkey and stuffing with all those young chicks around."

"Don't forget the wife," Dee said, still not smiling.

Peter stared into his coffee and shook his head as though recollecting a great injustice. "Best looker of them all and smarter: PhD from Harvard or Stanford or Oxford, one of those '-rd' schools, and a real flirt. Likes to drive the men crazy. And the old man sits and laughs because he knows none of the guys dare make a pass at her. Rumor has it he once shot and killed some young buck."

"Charming," I said

"My sentiments exactly," Dee said.

I needed to pursue with Dalton the disparity between his description of the Black empire's wealth and that of Peter Zane and Jonathan Winthrop, but for the moment I was interested in how well Peter knew Anne Black. I told him I'd met and talked briefly with her and asked how well acquainted he was.

He frowned.

"You must know then," Dee said, "that her partner was murdered on Sunday night. Horrible! It was all over TV and in the papers."

"Yes," I said. "A real tragedy—she was so young. Do they know who killed her?"

Dee shook her head.

Peter said, "No...no, they don't have any leads that I know of."

I asked if they'd met Jenny.

Peter said, "Once, maybe twice. She was a real brain—PhD, MIT, aerospace and computer science, something like that—nice girl, not a good-looker though, and real hard to talk to."

"I didn't know you knew her," Dee said.

"I don't really. She was with Jonathan when Blackie and I went to his office."

Dee said, "The Jonathan to whom he refers is Jonathan Winthrop—"

"Yes, we've met," I said, and then kicked myself for cutting her off. I would have liked to hear unfettered what she and Peter had to say about Jonathan, but I'd blown it.

Dee called for the check that I tried to intercept, but she snatched it from the maître d's fingers and signed on the back.

"This was to be my treat," I said.

"Next time," she said. "This is my place."

"Dee's been coming here for fifteen years, ever since the place opened," Peter said.

"You're aging me now, though I first came with my father when I was still in high school, so I'm not as old as it may sound."

"That thought never entered my mind."

She smiled. "Peter, I didn't know you had such a wonderful friend. For that, I propose we have a nightcap, and then we must let Paige be on her way. We've monopolized her long enough for one night."

At the bar, I excused myself and stepped outside to check my voicemail. Zoë had left another message. That she didn't know where Brad was and considered it necessary to call continuously had started to concern me.

But the next message turned me stone cold. "Please God, this can't be happening." I tried Jessie's number.

Her voicemail answered. I phoned Bebe and got her voicemail. I left messages for both to call me as soon as possible.

I ran back inside and told Dee and Peter I had to leave. If they expected an explanation, they didn't get one. I said goodbye, raced back to the street, and hailed a cab to Bebe's apartment.

"Please hurry," I said, and again forced myself to listen to the man's voice that burned into my ear like molten lava.

"We will call in one hour. If you want to see your friend alive, you'd better tell us Abby Dodge's whereabouts."

I glanced at my watch. It was 10:35. Maybe they didn't have Jessie. Maybe she was still at the restaurant with Bebe and Dalton. I tried her cellphone again, then Bebe's. Neither answered.

Chapter 34

Bebe had just arrived home, and the doorman rang to let her know I was on my way up. When I dashed from the elevator, Bebe was waiting in the hallway.

"Where's Jessie?" I shouted.

She was close to tears.

"Honest to God, I don't know where she went. When we were leaving the restaurant, I ran to the bathroom for a moment, and when I came out, she'd disappeared."

"What about Dalton? Did he see anything?"

"We both went to the bathroom. Jessie said she'd wait out front on the sidewalk, but she wasn't there. She was gone, vanished as if into thin air. We panicked and started asking everyone outside and inside if they'd seen her. No one had. Didn't you get my messages?"

"Yes, and I tried to call your cellphone a few minutes ago."

"Who is doing this?" she asked. "Is this more Abner Dodge?"

"Of course it's Abner Dodge," I said. "Listen to this." I played the message. "He's taken her."

My mind approached meltdown. Control yourself, Paige. Think. Jessie needs you to think. Abby needs you to think. I called Ajit and told him I needed help. He said he'd be there in a half-hour.

The wait drove me to the brink. I tried to reach Brad, but got his voicemail. I didn't know what else to do other than try to find Zoë and Tom. I doubted Zoë would be of much help, since she had called four times looking for Brad. That left Tom.

I dreaded tackling the labyrinthian hospital telephone system, particularly since I didn't know Tom's last name, but I had to try. After being placed on hold six times, I gave up.

Despite Dee's not coughing up the name of her friend

in the Apthorpe, I needed to give locating Vesco another shot because now two lives depended on finding him.

I called Peter. Dee answered. She asked if everything had worked out. I told her it hadn't yet, although I expected it soon would.

"Please let us know if there is anything we can do to help."

I hesitated. I didn't know her well enough to ask a favor, but I also didn't have the luxury of time.

"Possibly; is Peter there?"

"I'm afraid he's gone to bed. I shouldn't have let him have the last brandy, but perhaps there's something I can do."

"I hate to impose, but I need to locate someone who lives in the Apthorpe, and hoped your friend might help."

"It's not an imposition at all, and I'd be happy to give her a call, though we haven't been that close in recent years. I can't guarantee a positive result."

"All I can say is that it's important."

"Yes, of course, and I'll certainly try. Is there a name or at least a description?"

I couldn't see the harm in giving her Vesco's name.

"Louis Vesco. He may also use the name Herman De Groot."

"I believe you said he's a photographer?"

My earlier lie was coming back to stick a finger in my eye. "He thinks he's an investigator, but actually, he's an investigative photojournalist, some would say paparazzi." Another lie, and there would be a lot more, because I'd keep spinning them out until I found someone to lead me to Jessie.

Dee promised to call her friend and we ended the call just as the doorman buzzed to say Ajit had arrived.

Chapter 35

I told Ajit all that had happened since our meeting in Central Park and had him listen to the voicemail message.

"Tell me again how Jessie fits into the puzzle," he said.

"She and I are best friends and she and Abby are best friends. Jessie came to New York today as soon as I told her that Praetorian had tried to kill Abby."

"And Praetorian kidnapped her?"

I nodded. "Yes, they must have taken her from in front of the restaurant."

"Did you receive the Federal Express envelope from Abby?"

"No, and I can't figure out if Praetorian tried to kill her because they thought she sent it to me, and didn't want her giving copies or talking to anyone else. Or they may think she hadn't yet sent it, and tried to make sure she never did. Although that doesn't make sense because Abby said that more than anything else, Praetorian wants the canister."

"So, where do we start?"

"I guess Columbia Presbyterian. Jessie knows Abby is somewhere there."

"She wouldn't take her kidnappers there, though, would she?"

"Not in a million years. However, if they trick her into thinking she might help save Abby's life, or that she'll get to see Abby, then she might go there. Even if she doesn't, I've got to warn my brother that their hiding place may no longer be secure."

"My car's out front."

I told him in my present state, I wouldn't make a good passenger. He tossed me the keys.

"I wouldn't let anyone drive my Ferrari," I said.

"I'm guessing it isn't the first time you've driven one."

"I owned one for a year—lost my license twice. My father made me sell it."

I pulled from the curb and took off up Park Avenue. Ajit watched the side mirror. "We're being followed," he said.

I checked and saw several sets of headlights. "Which one?"

"The brown Cadillac."

I squealed the tires in a fast right turn that threw us hard against our seatbelts. "If you're right, we'll soon know."

A set of lights whipsawed around the corner. I couldn't determine the car's make. I didn't have to. Their fast turn told me enough. My knuckles showed white; my heart pounded; the adrenaline raced through my system.

I went left on Madison and sped toward 79th. At 79th, I headed west and raced toward the park, intending to cross there. At Fifth though, I slammed on the brakes and screeched a sharp left.

"Why didn't you go…never mind, I see them." A hundred feet into Central Park, two darkened police cruisers sat on either side of the road. Ajit grabbed his cellphone and punched a few numbers.

I understood 'Hi.' After that, he rattled off a string of rapid-fire words, each one sounding like a command.

"My brother owns a fleet of taxis, and a bunch of them always hang around the Plaza Hotel looking for airport fares. Go to 59th Street and make a right turn."

The Ferrari lunged forward as I tromped on the accelerator. Behind, the Cadillac continued to follow, losing little ground. The lights turned against us at 65th. I didn't stop. Neither did the Cadillac. On 59th, I made a hard right. Several cabs lined both sides of the street.

"Keep going."

I did as instructed, then checked the mirror and watched as the cabs spread out across the street like a major wreck in progress. Drivers jumped out hollering and shaking fists at one another. The Cadillac couldn't get past. Nothing got past.

"Do you think there'll be others?"

"I doubt it. They didn't think they'd lose us."

"And the cops in the park?"

"Paid help. Likely Lynch's doing—more tactics to scare you away."

"Well they're scaring me, though not away."

"I think I told you that guys like Vesco are on Dodge's payroll because they kill people."

"I already said I was scared. That doesn't help."

"You need to know what you're up against."

I TURNED north on Central Park West rather than heading for the West Side Highway.

"Going through the streets will take a few minutes more," I said, "but we won't get trapped."

"The way you drive, I doubt they'd catch us, though I agree."

We sped up Central Park West, crossed to Amsterdam, then to Broadway, constantly checking the rear-view mirrors. No one seemed to be following.

"Are you sorry I sucked you into this?"

"I don't recall anyone holding a gun to my head."

"You're a policeman. How hard would it be for scumbags like Lynch to falsely accuse you of aiding and abetting escaping criminals?"

He tapped his fingers on the dashboard for a moment. "First, you must understand that I'm not a policeman, and second, and I hope you don't take offence, I too have a price."

Had I been betrayed? Was everyone in this city available to the highest bidder?

"OK, what's your price, and for what am I paying?"

He chuckled.

"On Monday," he said, "when Daly brought you up to look at mug shots, I thought: Is this is the most exciting woman I've ever met, or what? Since then, every time I've seen you, I've thought the same thing."

Where was this discussion headed?

"What's your price?" I asked again.

"Two dinners, one at a restaurant of your choice, one at a restaurant of my choice; mine will be Indian."

Now it was my turn to chuckle, and God did it feel good. "I already owe you one dinner. Are we talking two additional dinners?"

"No, two total."

"You're on, and I love Indian food." I hadn't told him I'd spent most of February in India doing a follow-up story on the Bhopal disaster, but for now, my mind was too full of Jessie and Abby.

We passed by Columbia University. The streets had become quiet. Cars continued coming and going, but the pace had changed. The air had grown still. The street lamps glowed softer. I reduced our speed to thirty-five.

He asked how I'd met Jessie.

"It's a long story."

"I'd like to hear it, if I'm not intruding."

I took in a deep breath. "A close friend, my best friend since childhood, was murdered a few weeks ago."

"I'm sorry, and I do feel I've intruding."

"No, I'm all right with it. Wally, that was my friend's name, Wally Adams."

I told him about Wally and High River and the chemical plant, about becoming a stripper and meeting Jessie and other strippers, how Jessie and I became best friends.

We passed a police cruiser at the intersection of Broadway and 151st Street. I shot my eyes to the rear-view mirror. Ajit did the same. The cruiser pulled out and turned south. I exhaled loudly.

Neither of us said anything for a couple of blocks.

He broke the silence. "I've been thinking more about Praetorian. Abby says she has a list of Praetorian's members and proof that Praetorian murdered Jenny. The only thing that makes sense is Abby told Praetorian she sent you the information. Praetorian knows you haven't received it yet and kidnapped Jessie to make sure you turn it over when you ultimately get it."

"Because," I said, "if they knew I already had the information, they'd simply come after me."

"I think so."

Ajit answered his cellphone. After listening for a moment, he said something rapid-fire and ended the call. "The Cadillac driver took off running."

"Can they identify him?"

"White, average height, average weight, average nothing useful. He took off too fast, and the car's been reported stolen."

"Is your brother with the police department also?"

"Why?"

"He found out pretty fast that the car was stolen."

"He knows who to call."

"What language were you speaking?"

"My family is Tamil, which means we come from Tamil Nadu in southern India, like Virginians come from Virginia. We grew up speaking Tamil; most of us don't speak anything else, other than passable English."

"You hardly have an accent."

"I spent most of my early years in London," he said with a clipped British accent, "and don't axe me bout New Yawk, where I belonged to da hood and got in baaad trouble."

"That would explain the lack of an identifiable accent."

We passed another police cruiser. "What's going on? They seem to be everywhere."

My hands tensed on the steering wheel when the two

officers gave us more than a cursory look, although the Ferrari got most of their attention. Ajit seemed unconcerned.

"Back to Praetorian," he said. "If Abby, in fact, got a chance to send the information before Dodge's people got to her last night, you should get it by tomorrow at the latest."

"Oh, shit."

"What?"

"The only place she knew to send it was the Waldorf, and the Waldorf's security staff is on Dodge's payroll."

I grabbed my cellphone, then threw it back.

"What's wrong?"

"It's bugged."

He opened the console. "This one isn't." He dialed as I said Bebe's number aloud; then handed me the phone.

"Please tell me you've heard from Jessie," I said.

"Darling, I would have called instantly. Where are you?"

"We're almost at Columbia Presbyterian. I think whoever kidnapped Jessie may have tricked her into leading them to Abby."

"Would Jessie fall for that?"

"Even if she wouldn't, I don't know where else to start, and I've got to warn Brad."

"I didn't mean to say something of no help at all."

"You're forgiven, but only because I need you to urgently contact a bellboy in the Waldorf by the name of Jorge Ruiz. He's a friend, I need his help, and I need you to go there because his phone might be bugged and you mustn't call."

"What do I do with him when I find him?"

"Abby, maybe under Penny Munro's name, sent me an envelope—she said Fed Ex although it might have been ordinary mail—and she wouldn't have known where else to send it. I'm worried that the Waldorf's security people will get their hands on it. If it's there, get it. If it hasn't arrived, have Jorge call you the instant it does."

"Darling, I'm on my way."

"Give him a fifty and tell him you are my employer. He'll know what that means."

"I know what it means. It means you've been spending my money."

"Go like the wind, Baby. Ajit and I have just arrived at the hospital. I'll call the minute I know anything, and I want you to call this number—it's Ajit's cellphone— the very moment you talk to Jorge."

Chapter 36

Ajit flashed his police credentials, and the young attendant pointed to a reserved section where we parked and headed for the elevators.

"Is that legitimate police ID?" I asked. Absent Brad, I didn't have a plan for getting inside and hoped Ajit could get us past security.

"It'll do, though I suspect you'd figure out something and move as quickly without it. I might be more useful if I knew where in this small city they call a hospital that it is we are going."

"Here's what I know: Zoë and Tom are the names of the two interns who work with my brother."

"What's your brother's name again?"

"Brad. I saw the three of them this morning on the 10th Floor of Vanderbilt Clinic."

"That's the emergency center."

"You've been there before."

"More than I want to remember."

I didn't ask; he didn't volunteer. We got off on the main floor.

Ajit looked around as if trying to get his bearings, and then said, "It's easier to go up to 168th Street and across than try to sort our way through the underground maze."

"You seem to know more than where the emergency center is."

"I worked part time on an ambulance crew my first year at Columbia. That made me switch from medicine to computers."

We went outside and ran down the street to Vanderbilt Clinic.

My cellphone rang. I glanced at the caller ID, then at my watch. My stomach knotted. It was Jessie's kidnappers.

"Yes," I answered.

"Time's up."

"Listen to me. I don't know where Abby is. I'm trying to find her. Jessie doesn't know either. Please, I need more time."

Click.

"Sons of bitches," I cried and jammed the cellphone into my bag. Tears stung my eyes.

Ajit's face asked the question.

"They said time is up. I don't know if they'll call again. I don't know what they'll do."

"Trust me; they won't do anything until they get what they want."

I know he was only trying to say something he thought I needed to hear, but what he said made sense. God, I wanted to believe.

"Come on," he said. "We'll use the emergency entrance."

We climbed to the raised platform where the ambulances backed in. Several guards, who looked like police because of their blue uniforms, stood outside or sat in a kiosk. Ajit nodded to one seated inside as we approached.

"Haven't seen you in a while," the black guard said. The guard seated next to him, an Asian, glowered and said nothing.

Ajit introduced me to the black guard, whose name was Bo.

"This here's Jackie Chan," Bo said by way of introducing us to the other guard, who continued to glower. Bo laughed.

"We need to find a couple of interns," Ajit said.

"You official tonight?"

"One of them is her brother." Ajit nodded in my direction.

Bo studied me for a moment and must have decided I wasn't a danger because he turned and said, "Jackie, hand me two of them police passes, and don't be giving me no attitude."

Jackie complied, although I figured that unlike Bo, who would say to the authorities: "I never saw no Ajit and I never saw no woman," Jackie would give us up in a nanosecond.

"This can be ugly," Ajit said as we started off, "but we'll move through quickly. Best to keep your eyes straight ahead."

We went up a tunnel that led to the second floor where we had to skirt around stretchers laden with bodies, some moaning, some screaming, some appearing very dead though still plugged into things that beeped and flashed, and some looking too healthy, like they didn't belong at all. So much for keeping my eyes straight ahead—he should have warned me about the nauseating stink of vomit, urine, excrement, and medicines.

I didn't start breathing again until we got off the elevators on the tenth floor. There, we approached a young nurse sitting behind a reception counter absorbed by a computer screen. She had a practiced indifference to the presence of human life forms.

Her name tag said 'Hanratty.' She had pumpkin-colored hair and white skin that seemed almost translucent. Ajit leaned across and poked her in the arm. She jumped and let out a yelp.

"Hi, Therese," he said.

"Jesus Christ, you scared the crap out of me. What the fuck are you doing here?" Then she eyed me with a 'who the hell are you' look.

Ajit said, "No 'hello,' no 'how are you?'"

"Hello," she said, turning her attention back to Ajit. "How are you and what the fuck are you doing here?"

"Paige, this is Therese Hanratty, a.k.a. Ratched. Therese, this is Paige Harrington. Her brother works here."

"Brad Harrington?" Hanratty's glare softened.

"Yes," I said. "I saw him here this morning. Now he's done one of his disappearing acts."

Hanratty turned to her computer, tapped the keyboard, and clicked the mouse a few times. "He's not due back until tomorrow at midnight. He switched with Zoë Collins."

"Zoë was with him this morning."

Therese picked up a microphone and paged Zoë, asking her to report to the nurses' station on the tenth floor. "If she can't," Hanratty said to me, "she'll call or have someone call for her."

"The other person was Tom."

"Tom Baird." Therese checked the computer again. "He's away until tomorrow at midnight."

Same as Brad. In my mind, that meant they were both with Abby. I heard a muted chime and a light flashed on Therese's desk.

"Yes," she answered. "His sister wants to talk to him...No, she's here." Therese looked up at me in a way that said Zoë wished I weren't there. "Right, I'll tell her." Therese hung up, inhaled deeply, and said, "She can't see you now, and doesn't know where Brad is."

The hair on the back of my neck bristled. How could Zoë call a bunch of times to ask Brad's whereabouts, and now refuse to see me? It made no sense. I shot a 'help me' look at Ajit.

"That's it?" Ajit asked. "Come on, Therese, you can do better than that."

"Sorry," Therese said. "She's in the OR."

I didn't think Therese had lied, she said exactly what Zoë told her to say, but Zoë had lied. Therese knew it, Ajit knew it, and I knew it.

"She's not in the OR," Ajit said. "Come on, for old-times sake, where is she?"

Therese shrugged. "I'd like to help, but you know what'll happen."

Ajit smacked his hand on the counter top.

Therese's body flinched, her eyes grew big, her white eyelashes fluttered like she might begin to cry.

"Sorry," Ajit said, "but since when did you care about rules?"

Therese stopped fluttering. Her face darkened. "Since they've been downsizing by the hundreds and I had a kid. I need my job or two people starve. Me, I could stand it." She looked down at her hefty body. "But my kid can't."

"Christ, Therese, I didn't know you got married."

"I didn't, schmuck. I got pregnant. I had a kid. And you were studying to be a doctor. Didn't they tell you how babies are made?"

"Congratulations. Boy or girl?"

"Boy."

I turned to Ajit and said, "Come on. I've got an idea."

When we were out of Hanratty's earshot, I asked, "Where would Zoë be if not the OR?"

"In the lounge."

"How do we get to the lounge?"

He nodded at the door beyond the nurses' station. "It's locked and entry is controlled by Therese."

"What time does she finish her shift?"

He looked at his watch. "Midnight."

I checked my watch. Ten minutes to twelve. "Do they all change then?"

"They have staggered shifts, but out here they change at midnight."

I whispered my idea into his ear. He told me what I had to do, and we got in the elevator and went to the main floor. At midnight, we got back into the elevator and went back to the tenth floor. Ajit went to the nurses' station. The nurse, Therese's replacement, got up and went with him down the hall. After they disappeared, I ducked around the corner, hit the door release button Ajit had told me about, and pushed my way inside.

There, I paused for a moment to get my bearings. Ajit said the lounge door was at the far end on the right. I took off at a purposeful pace. The several people I encountered, all hospital personnel, I assumed, based on their attire, paid me little or no attention.

I shoved through the door that said 'Doctors' Lounge.' Zoë was there along with several others. She jumped up and started toward me. She wasn't smiling.

Before she had the chance to go on the offensive, I said loudly enough for all to hear, "We can talk here, or go somewhere private, your call."

She hesitated.

"Where's Brad?" My stomach geared up for a fight.

"No need to raise your voice," she said, glancing at her colleagues.

"This isn't my raised voice. You want to hear my raised voice? WHERE'S BRAD?"

Now, everyone looked.

Her glare intensified. "Come with me." She started for the door. I followed. She led me to an empty room. As soon as we stepped inside, she slammed the door.

"You didn't return my calls," she hissed.

"You didn't leave a number."

She seemed perplexed. "I thought I did."

"Well you didn't. I've been trying to find out about your Jane Doe all day. I've been trying to find Brad all day. Every time I got a message from you, I prayed you'd leave a number. Believe me; I desperately wanted to talk to someone who knows what the hell's going on."

"Sorry, I…"

"It doesn't matter now. Is your Jane Doe patient OK? Where is the patient?"

"I think she's still alive. I don't know where Brad and Tom have her hidden, but as far as I know, they're with her. They've arranged their times so they're not due back here until midnight tomorrow."

"A friend of mine is missing. She's also the patient's best friend. I think she came here to find her."

She nodded her head in the direction of the nurses' station. "The nurse said a young woman had inquired."

"When? Do you remember what time?"

She glanced at her watch. Her eyes were red and baggy. I recognized the look: an interne about to drop from exhaustion. "Within the last half-hour."

That meant after 11:30, between 11:30 and midnight—it had to be Jessie. "Do you know where she went?"

She shook her head.

"Which nurse. Was it Therese Hanratty?"

"I think so."

I wondered if Ajit and I could catch Hanratty. I started for the door.

"Others have been asking about the patient."

I spun around. "Who, do you know?"

"The police." She folded her arms across her chest, and her tone had turned accusatory. I didn't know what her problem was, and I didn't have time to find out. If she wanted a fight, I'd give her one.

I asked, none too patiently, "Did you see them? Did you talk to them?"

"What's she done? One of them said they wanted to talk to her about a murder. Is Brad hiding a murderer?"

I stormed forward, not stopping until our faces were inches apart. She blanched and pulled back.

"Listen to me," I said. "Those weren't police. They're the ones who tried to kill your Jane Doe. They're after her because she knows who murdered Jenny Ross. Did you read about that? It was in all the papers, on TV. They're after your Jane Doe because she knows powerful people who will continue killing to keep their identities secret."

She bit at her lower lip and let her arms fall. "I didn't think Brad would...goddamn him. Why didn't he tell me?"

"Because he didn't want to get you into trouble. I gather you talked to them, the ones asking about your patient."

"That's why I tried to reach you. I wanted to know what was going on."

"What did you tell them?"

"I told them exactly what Brad said to tell them: that I didn't know. That I didn't have a young woman patient. One of them called me a liar and told me they were going to report me to Dr. Sklar, one of the hospital's directors."

"How many were there?"

"Two groups of two. One came in the morning, around 11:00, the other later this afternoon, probably around 5:30."

"Can you remember what they looked like?" I wished I'd kept pictures of Vesco and Lynch. Damn, Lynch was overdue to call. Well, screw him. What could I tell him that he didn't already know?

"I'll never forget the one who called me a liar. Besides being obese, he had the coldest blue eyes and a horrible wheeze. His front tooth was broken, and he needed a bath. The only thing I remember about his partner was that he was tall and thin. The other two were ordinary: not fat, not thin, not tall, not short...just ordinary. No, wait a minute, there was also a third man who came in alone."

"Did they give their names? What did they look like?"

"The last one was small and angry. The others were big and pushy." She shook her head. "It's been crazy here, hardly time to think. They flashed ID, although I had already assumed they were cops and wasn't terribly interested in their names. I told them I didn't know anyone who matched their description. As I already told you, one called me a liar, and I suspected the others thought as much."

"I doubt they'll report you; they were trying to scare you."

"Well, they succeeded."

"When is your shift over?"

"Not until morning, eight o'clock."

"Do you live alone?"

"Now you're scaring me."

"I'll pick you up in here at eight. Meanwhile, do not talk to anyone, no matter what. If I'm late, don't leave. If I can't make it, I'll send someone else. You'll be safe with us."

She stared as if I'd slapped her across the face.

"They think we have something they want. As long as they think that, they won't kill us."

"That isn't the least bit comforting. I saw our Jane Doe when she came in. She'd been tortured. The people who did that to her are sick."

"We're staying in a high-security building on Park Avenue, and while I can't give you any guarantees, I think you'll be safe there, as long as you don't do anything stupid or heroic."

"You mean like you and Brad are doing."

"My dearest friend in the world has been kidnapped. Her dearest friend is your patient. Brad is my brother. With us, this is personal. Not so for you. Your being involved was accidental, and Brad is trying to put a lot of distance between you and the patient."

I could see her mind churning.

"Sorry, I've got to run. We need to catch Therese." I gave her Bebe's home and cell numbers. "Call either of these anytime. Bebe is a trusted friend and my boss. She will know where I am, and if you hear from Brad, tell him to call me because I'm going nuts."

She started to follow me to the nurses' station.

"It will be best," I said, "if everyone thinks we had a confrontation. Tell your colleagues I'm nothing but trouble and should be avoided. Make them believe we're not on the same team. The people after your patient have eyes and ears everywhere—they pay people on your staff to spy on each other."

She stopped dead in her tracks.

I ran back to the nurses' station where I found Ajit charming the midnight-to-eight nurse, who looked about ready to start ripping off her clothes. Her glare told me she wasn't happy that I'd appeared.

I asked Ajit if he knew where Hanratty lived. He asked the nurse, whose nametag said Daphne Nubbins, if she had Hanratty's address on file. Daphne looked something up on her computer and printed out a sheet that she handed to Ajit as though I didn't exist.

"She usually takes the M4." Daphne said.

I knew the M4 well—it was the bus I'd taken when I was a student at Columbia.

"Come on," I said. "We've got to try and catch her."

We ran for the elevators. "What's going on?" Ajit asked.

"I think Jessie was here, and I think Therese talked to her. Maybe she remembers something that Jessie said, or knows where she went. Also, Zoë said some men were demanding information about badly injured patients. They may have talked to Therese."

The elevator came and we jumped on.

"According to Zoë, five people were looking for Abby, and I wouldn't be surprised if Vesco was one of them. Another one sounded like Sergeant Lynch. I want Zoë to look at both pictures."

"They think Abby is alive?"

"If Praetorian believed for a second that she's given everything to me, nothing else makes sense other than they want to make sure she's dead."

We raced to Ajit's car.

Ajit said, "No matter how we slice this, you are Praetorian's next target."

"I know," I said. "It's hard to escape that reality."

Chapter 37

Therese Hanratty lived on 123rd Street between Broadway and Amsterdam. Ajit drove. We passed three M4 buses headed south on Broadway. I thought I saw Hanratty on the last one. Ajit tried Hanratty's home telephone but got no answer.

"I wonder what she does with her kid," he said. "You'd think if she had a sitter, the sitter would answer."

We pulled up in front of a red brick apartment building that had seen better days. A group of young men, mostly white, congregated on the corner, smoking, drinking beer from cans, laughing.

"Don't inhale," Ajit said.

My nose twitched. Marijuana. We were still in Columbia University territory—student housing, students on summer programs, glassy-eyed students partaking of the cannabis sativa plant, doubtless for medicinal purposes.

"It seems eons ago," I said, "and at the same time, like it was a week ago."

"I drive through here once a month just for the high."

"To say nothing of getting college girls agog over a handsome man driving a red Ferrari."

He chuckled and turned off the ignition. A few minutes later, Therese Hanratty rounded the corner, carrying a shopping bag in one hand and her handbag slung over her right shoulder. One of the young men on the corner walked toward her and said something. She said something back and kept walking. The young man returned to his pals and they laughed. I wanted to go over and kick their collective asses.

Ajit stepped from the car and leaned against the front fender, sheltered from the streetlight by one of the robust honey locusts that lined the block. Halfway to the building, Therese looked in our direction and hesitated. Ajit walked out into the light.

Therese continued forward, her steps becoming uncertain. When she drew closer, I got out and stood on the curb.

"What do you want?" she asked.

Ajit reached for the shopping bag. She let him take it. "We need your help. We need to find Paige's friend. Zoë thought you may have talked to her within the last hour."

"She's twenty, blonde, probably wearing jeans, T-shirt, and sneakers. No, wait, she probably still had on the dress she wore to dinner, a green strapless…I'm almost certain she didn't have a change of clothes."

"Yeah, I saw her, a real looker, except that she was messed up."

"What do you mean 'messed up?'"

Therese stepped back a pace.

"Sorry," I said. "I didn't mean to snap. It's just that I fear she's gotten into trouble."

"Her dress and hair were mussed, like she'd been in a good tussle. At first I thought she'd been on a long binge, but I didn't smell alcohol and she seemed to know what was going on. She said she was looking for her sister. She said her sister had been badly hurt in an accident and brought to the hospital. I called Zoë, but she got upset and told me to stop bothering her; that she didn't know anything about a young woman who'd been in an accident."

"Did my friend say anything else? Please, it's important. I need to find her."

"There was a man with her."

This wasn't getting any better. "Are you sure he was with her?"

"Yeah, he was with her all right, but stayed back, like he didn't want to be seen. I didn't get a real good look."

"Big or small."

"At first he looked small, and then when she left and they got onto the elevator, I remember thinking he looked big." She shook her head. "I'm sorry. I'm not being much help."

"Think, Therese," Ajit said. "Did she say anything at all, anything that seemed unusual?"

She thought for a moment. "I don't think so." Then she took her shopping bag and started toward the building. When she reached the door, she stopped and put down her shopping bag. "Do you have a number, in case something comes to mind. Sometimes things pop into my head when I least expect it."

I wrote Bebe's home and cell numbers on a notebook page to which Ajit also added his cell number and handed her the piece of paper.

"Where's your sitter?" he asked. "No one answered your telephone."

Therese picked up her shopping bag and looked up. "My mother lives in the apartment right above mine. She keeps her until I get home."

The seventh floor sat in darkness. "No lights on," I said.

"She turns the lights off when she watches TV."

I was about to say, 'no TV glow,' then thought better of it. We said goodnight and went back into the Ferrari. I asked Ajit if he thought she was lying.

"I don't know, but she's definitely stealing."

"What do you mean?"

"When I took the shopping bag from her, it weighed a ton, so I glanced inside. She had a scale and a couple of endoscopes."

I raised an eyebrow.

"They steal it and sell it. It's a big problem for hospitals, millions of dollars a year."

"But why?"

He shrugged. "Low pay, high costs, financial problems, the usual."

I shook my head. I'd felt sorry for her. Now I wasn't sure what I felt.

"At the hospital, didn't she say she had a boy? Is she lying about having a child?"

Ajit called Daphne Nubbins.

Nubile Nubbins, I thought, the one who so openly desires his body.

He spoke to her for a minute, and then turned to me. "She definitely has a baby boy, or else she goes to a lot of trouble to bring someone else's kid around to show off."

I glanced back at Therese's building. "Let's wait a few minutes."

A darkened Mobil service station sat on the next corner. Ajit parked behind a row of cars against a chain link fence. We got out and started back toward Therese's street, staying out of sight by keeping close to the buildings.

Across from Therese's apartment, we ducked in behind a row of overgrown shrubs in front of a brownstone that had no lights inside and only a small outdoor light with limited incandescence.

Ajit looked at the paper Nubbins had given him. "Her apartment is 6C."

The lights in the sixth-floor, right-front apartment were on.

He said, "My guess: that's her apartment."

A large man came to the window and looked down at the street, first one way, and then the other.

"Why is there a man in her apartment and why was he sitting in the dark?" I thought of Vesco, and then told myself that every large man in the city wasn't Vesco.

We ducked down further. The man in the window turned, appeared to be speaking, and then walked away. Therese's lights went out.

Two minutes later Therese came out, and the man had her by the arm. When they passed under the front light, I caught a glimpse of the man's face and saw a red brush-cut on a big head.

"It's not Vesco," I whispered. "But it sounds like one of the guys Zoë described."

They got into a car parked midway up the street and pulled away.

"Stay down," Ajit said.

I didn't need prompting.

A dark blue Chevrolet with New York plates passed by and turned south on Broadway. As soon as they were out of sight, we jumped up and ran to the Ferrari. Ajit grabbed his cellphone and talked rapid-fire Tamil. I understood 'blue,' 'Oldsmobile,' and 'New York.'

"Did you get the license plate?" he asked.

"Only that it's a New York plate with six letters or numbers, the first three are B's or 8's; I'm pretty sure the last three are 675."

He said something else in Tamil and ended the call.

We drove around for an hour, searching, but the blue car had disappeared. Ajit's taxi brigade had no better luck.

With my Blackberry, I accessed the Internet white pages and located a telephone number for Mrs. Timothy Hanratty at Therese's address. Using various pay phones so I wouldn't leave a trail to Ajit or me, I tried the number several times, but got no response. Finally, we went back to Therese's building and buzzed Mrs. Timothy Hanratty's apartment, #7C. No one answered.

We also buzzed Therese's apartment just in case but likewise, got no response. We walked to the corner and used the pay phone to call Therese's number one more time. Ajit didn't leave a message when her voicemail answered.

"I don't know where else to look," I said.

We headed south toward 86th Street and started across Central Park to the East Side. I called Bebe, who had left several messages. She'd been to the Waldorf to see Jorge, who told her nothing had arrived.

We exited the park and turned south on Fifth. I looked for cars tailing us or police cruisers hiding in the park. It had been three hours since our mad race to ditch the Cadillac, though it seemed like no more than a few minutes ago.

A man and woman about my age strolled hand in hand along the sidewalk next to the park, laughing, enjoying the warm night air and each other's company. I longed to do the same, even if only for a moment, to stop worrying about the delicate thread of life from which fate had suspended Abby, and the cocoon of fear and uncertainty that surely entombed Jessie.

No I didn't. I wanted only to find Jessie, unharmed, and learn that Abby was going to recover, fully. I asked Ajit if the hospital had security cameras that could have recorded Jessie's visit. He cursed himself for not thinking of it sooner.

Chapter 38

Bebe said Dee Hunter had phoned and wanted me to call when I arrived. I glanced at my watch. It was 2:15 a.m. My stomach had the vacant feeling it got when it expected bad news.

As it turned out, the urgency had to do with her friend, Amanda Diamond, leaving for Albany in the morning and being away from the city for a week. Amanda Diamond was the person Dee knew who lived in the Apthorpe.

I felt bone weary. "By the time she gets back it will be too late."

"Amanda feared as much, so she asked if you could come to see her first thing. She suggested 7:00 a.m. That way, the two of you can have a couple of hours before she leaves."

Finally, something appeared to be working. With renewed energy, I telephoned Ajit and asked him to pick up Zoë and bring her to Bebe's apartment. He said he would.

Bebe overheard and began waving her arms.

I told her about the people harassing and threatening Zoë because they thought she knew where Brad had hidden Abby.

"She's frightened and she lives alone. I told her she could stay with us until…" I collapsed onto a stool, suddenly wanting to go to sleep and not wake up until everything was OK.

"Darling, stop this instant. We'll find Jessie, and Abby will be fine, just you wait and see. And of course Zoë is welcome."

"Yes, I know she is, and if I haven't said thank you lately—thank you. I don't know what I'd do without you."

"You would perish, Darling, like everyone else that

doesn't have me on their side." She frowned and added, "I guess I didn't help Jenny much, though."

"Now you stop. This is all about trying to find Jenny's killer. If it weren't for you, no one would be giving her one tiny thought."

"Then why do I feel so useless? I put you in the Waldorf where some barbarians ransack your room. I invite you to stay here so you'll be safe, and Jessie is kidnapped."

We both needed sleep before we pounded ourselves into the ground.

"Believe me when I say that no one in the world can keep tabs on Jessie. I've seen her disappear with round-the-clock guards watching every move. And another thing: she knows the streets of New York better than anyone, and will escape at the first opportunity. Will she come back here? Probably not—she'll stay out there and do what she has to do until Abby is safe."

I couldn't be certain if what I said gave Bebe any comfort. It didn't help me much. All I could do is pray Jessie got an opportunity to escape safely, one where she wouldn't have to risk her life, because I knew she would try, regardless.

"It's all getting so complicated, and I'm in way over my head. I'm not giving up, but I need you to think of the most omnipotent people you know, people you would trust with your life, with all our lives, because I fear if Praetorian unleashes its dogs, we don't stand a chance."

Praetorian

Praefectus raised the bejeweled mace.

The nineteen Centurions took their rightful places.

Praefectus said, "Who brings you here this night?"

The nineteen chanted "You do, our exalted Praefectus."

"What say you then, my Centurions?"

Centurion Fourteen stood. "Exalted Leader, I have the canister. It has been returned to its rightful place."

The Centurions stamped their feet and applauded.

Praefectus raised the mace and said, "Centurions rise."

When the nineteen stood, Praefectus raised the mace and said, "Centurions, $10 million will be paid to your offshore accounts."

"Thank you for your generosity, Exalted Leader."

Praefectus said, "Centurion Fourteen, please rise."

Centurion Fourteen stood and threw out his chest. "Yes, Exalted Leader?"

Praefectus said, "Because you have fulfilled your promise, your account will be $20 million richer."

"Thank you, Exalted Leader." Was he also going to be promoted to Centurion Five's position?

Praefectus said, "Please step forward to the Circle of Heroes."

Centurion Fourteen walked to the hallowed space at the foot of the Dais of Praefectus and stood on the engraved stone that measured ten feet in diameter, its quadrants separated with inlaid gold marking the points of the compass: North pointed at Praefectus. Centurion Fourteen knelt on the red and gold rug placed in the center. This was it. The promotion was his. He'd earned it. The fact he didn't have the canister was of no consequence. He would have it soon enough and no one need know.

He had kidnapped the Hanratty woman. He had taken her baby. It was only a matter of time until she disclosed where the two young doctors had hidden Abby Dodge. He had contacted the writer, Harrington. She would do as told to save her friend.

When he was finished, they'd beg for mercy. And then he'd have the canister and they'd all be dead. No one would know.

Praefectus said, "Centurions, please gather around the Circle of Heroes."

Centurion One approached first and laid the gold-plated sword with a jeweled handle and a black leather scabbard at Centurion Fourteen's feet. Centurion Five wondered who would be given the honor of touching the blade to his shoulders, thus officially recognizing his elevated position. Would it be Praefectus, or would he pass the honor to one of the others?

Praefectus called Centurion One up the steps to kneel at his feet, and handed a rolled parchment to him. Praefectus ordered him to stand. Centurion One did so, and then opened the parchment, nodded, and returned to the circle of Centurions. He took the sword from the scabbard.

The eighteen began chanting and tightened the circle until Centurion Five could no longer be seen. Centurion One raised the sword over his head and brought it down with a vicious swipe. The eighteen continued chanting faster and faster, then spread their circle until it was completely open.

Centurion Fourteen lay on the carpet next to his head. touched a button on the arm of his throne, the Circle of Heroes opened in the center and the headless body, head, and bloody carpet dropped one hundred feet into the raging fire of the furnace below.

A Praefectus aide appeared and took the bloody sword and scabbard from Centurion One's outstretched hands. The aide would clean and sharpen the sword before the next meeting, and make it ready to perform its assigned task.

Praefectus raised the mace. All grew silent. Who would volunteer to embark on the journey that had already claimed two of their brethren? Who would vie for the honor? They all would, for they were Centurions of the Praetorian Guard. And they would not fail. They would return with the canister or gladly accept death in the only honorable way: by their own hand. Never would they stoop to the cowardice of Centurion Fourteen.

Centurion Nine was chosen. "You honor me, Exalted Leader, and I shall not fail you and my brethren; I will bring the canister."

Praefectus raised the mace one last time that night to adjourn the meeting. His heart was heavy. Centurion Fourteen was his blood brother.

Chapter 39

The wrought-iron gates leading to the Apthorpe's courtyard were open, and I strode in as if I belonged. A guard kiosk sat ten feet inside at the edge of a vast expanse of flowers and shrubs spilling from professionally cared-for planters, the one in the center hosting a large fountain of the sort you might expect to see in Rome, absent exposed genitalia.

I told the guard I had an appointment to see Amanda Diamond just as Dee Hunter walked up. I hadn't expected her.

The guard asked if we needed directions. Dee said, "No," and then said to me, "I hope you don't mind."

"No, of course not," I said, because I couldn't think of any reason I didn't want her there.

Amanda's huge apartment was a collection of soft yellow and quiet white elegance that bespoke peace and serenity. Not so Amanda. She flitted like a hummingbird. Everywhere, five-foot-one-inch Amanda in her red pantsuit and platinum blonde hair and bare feet, poked, pointed, and picked, all the while chirping, and smiling. Smiling is what she did best with her bright white teeth and full, red-lipped mouth and sparkling brown eyes.

She and Dee shared an awkward embrace and said how much they'd missed seeing each other, and then Amanda was off again, grabbing a piece of graph paper that sat next to her computer.

"Dee gave me a general description of the person you're looking for," she said. "Here's a list of the Apthorpe's residents as of the end of June. I've deleted the names that couldn't possibly be Vesco because of sex or age."

"Were you up all night?"

"I wasn't, but I gladly would have been. This is the most interesting thing I've done in years."

I wondered if she'd think that way if she knew the truth about Vesco.

She motioned me closer and ran her finger down the pages.

"Every one of those not deleted is a possibility, though I know some of them well and can't imagine them being the person you're looking for."

I opened my laptop and brought up a computer file that contained several Vesco pictures. Amanda studied each.

"I believe I've seen him. The question is, where? Not here, but in the neighborhood."

"I'm sure he lives here," I said.

She laughed. "He probably does. I see my neighbors on the street more often than in the building or courtyard."

She thought for a moment, then her eyes lit up.

"Starbucks." She shouted. "On 81st Street. Stephen—he's my ex—and I used to have coffee there every morning." She looked at her watch. "It's only a couple of blocks. He might be there. Let's go."

"He'll recognize me," I said.

"Not if we hide that delicious red hair," she said.

She shot off down a hallway and returned with a blonde wig that looked a lot like the one I'd worn as Tawny Lane in my stripper days.

WE HURRIED the two blocks to 81st Street. Inside, Dee went to the order counter, and I checked the dozen or so patrons seated around the tables. Vesco wasn't there. Amanda cornered an open table at the front windows. From there, we could watch everyone entering and leaving.

A few minutes later Amanda whispered, "Don't let's all look at once, but I think that's him, the man with the dog."

I glanced up. Smoke billowing from his Sherlock

Holmes pipe, a man in a tan suit with a bulldog on a heavy-duty leather leash walked up the street. He looked straight at me, and I feared I'd been recognized even with the wig, though I managed to not jerk my head away to hide my face.

"It's definitely him," I said.

He tapped his pipe on the curb, tied his dog to a parking meter, and came inside, newspaper tucked under his arm. After he got coffee, and what appeared to be a raisin bran muffin, he sat several tables away facing the side windows and opened his paper. Neither Amanda nor I dared look—Dee told us he didn't so much as glance in our direction.

"A little warm for a suit jacket," Amanda said.

"Hides his gun," Dee said.

"Are you serious?" Amanda asked.

As far as they knew, Vesco was a photographer, and I pretended not to hear their exchange.

A cellphone rang. It took a moment before I realized it was the debugged one I had taken from Bebe. When I saw it was Ajit's number, I told Dee and Amanda I had to take the call, and went outside.

I told him I'd found Vesco and assured him I intended to do nothing other than talk to him, to find out where Jessie was.

"Paige, I've just dropped Zoë off at Bebe's and I'll be there in ten minutes. Don't do anything until I get there."

I was about to agree when Amanda dashed out of Starbucks and raced across Broadway. I told Ajit I'd have to call him back, and ran over to join Dee, who had followed Amanda outside. She told me Vesco had bolted from his table so quickly they almost missed him. Then he tore outside and jumped into a car that sped off up 81st Street.

"Amanda thinks she can get their license plate number when they stop at the light."

"His dog's still here," I said, glancing at the dejected-looking animal staring across Broadway in the direction Vesco had gone.

While we waited for Amanda to return Dee said, "I get the feeling Vesco is more than a photographer."

"Yes, he is, and I'm sorry for not telling you the truth. For now, I can only say I've got more than a peck of trouble."

We saw Amanda at the next block jogging toward us. "I hadn't meant to pry," Dee said.

She was entitled to know. The problem was I hadn't figured out how much to say.

"I got it," Amanda said, and rattled off a number that I hurriedly wrote in my notebook.

She continued, "It might have been a government car. I think the license plate is federal government."

I looked at the number.

"It's not that I think the number is unique," she said, "but the plate looked generic, and the car with its extra antennae and big tires and driver with his button-down look gave the whole picture a secret agent feel. Your guy and a look-alike sat in the back wearing dark glasses and talking on their cellphones. On 79th, they turned and sped across to the West Side Highway, swerving around cars like they were standing still."

I glanced at the time. Soon she would be leaving for Albany, and I'd be back in this mess alone. "I wish you weren't leaving. I could use some help."

She said, "I'm not. I called my brother and told him not to expect me."

I gave her a quizzical look.

She shrugged. "First of all, Dee and I decided we like you. Then we figured there is a lot more to Vesco than you can tell us, so we decided to help. And just so you know, we're not just a couple of stay-at-home busy bodies; we do know a lot of rich and powerful people."

"When I said before I could use some help, I should

have said: I wish I could accept your help. This whole mess I'm in…it's too dangerous."

I couldn't let them think that this was some ladies' neighborhood detective club that followed coffee-drinking fat men with bulldogs. They needed to know that Vesco and others might murder them.

"Why don't you tell us what you can and let us decide," Amanda said.

"The only thing I can tell you for now is that these people are killers, they've kidnapped my best friend, and I think Vesco knows where she is."

They looked at each other and back at me. Who am I kidding? They won't help. I had no right to expect them to.

Amanda said, "We should start by waiting inside and keeping our eyes on the dog."

I raised my eyebrows. "I expected to see you taking off up the street."

Amanda said, "Dee used to be in the Israeli army, so I know you haven't frightened her, and you'll have to come up with bigger guns to scare me away—I used to handle big celebrity wives' divorces, where some irate husband was always threatening my clients and me."

"How about Abner Dodge? Is he a big enough gun? Vesco works for him."

They shared a look. It was Dee who spoke, her voice steely cold, "Besides his many other failings as a human being, Abner Dodge is a closet anti-Semitie. Amanda and I are Jews."

"He's a closet Nazi," Amanda said. "Oh, he's charming. Make no mistake about it. Publicly, he embraces rich Jews because they give a lot of money to the charities that Dodge attaches himself to, like the opera, art galleries and museums, schools and universities, hospitals, you name it, but at the end of the day, he is as anti-Semitic as they come. No, my dear, you'll have to do better than Abner Dodge to send us running."

Clearly, I'd run into two of the best allies I could possibly have in my war against Abner Dodge. With Dee and Amanda, it wasn't moral, and it wasn't ethical. It was personal.

"I think its time to tell you a story that on Tuesday night I promised a young woman, who feared for her life, I'd not tell a single soul. She said if I did, I would be putting my life in danger. She said the people I told would betray me, just as the people she told had betrayed her. The reason she said that is that so far in her young life—she's twenty-two—she's found only one person to trust.

"The reason I'm breaking my promise to her is that two nights ago, someone tried to kill her, and almost succeeded. That young woman is Abby Dodge, Abner Dodge's stepdaughter. She told me that Abner Dodge is the one trying to kill her."

Amanda gasped.

"Why are you shocked?" Dee asked.

"His own stepdaughter..."

"Remember who we're talking about," Dee said, her look and voice so full of hatred, it gave me pause.

"Dodge's people have kidnapped my friend, Jessie, because Abby and Jessie are best friends, and they think Jessie will take them to Abby."

I told them about Abby and Jessie. I told them about Jessie and me. I didn't tell them about my brother, Brad, and I didn't tell them about Columbia Presbyterian Hospital.

Dee asked, "Where is Abby? Is she OK?"

"Yes," Amanda said. "My goodness, that poor girl."

"The people looking after her have her in a safe place. I don't know where that is, and I can only pray that she's OK: her doctors weren't sure she'd make it."

Dee asked, "And what about your friend, have they contacted you?"

I swallowed hard. "Not since last night. They said I

had run out of time. I have to find Vesco and find out what he knows. He's the only lead."

"Why not Dodge?" Amanda asked. "We must know people who know him."

Dee said, "I'd like nothing more, but we'd never get near him. No one gets near him. You know how bullet-proof he is."

"Then that leaves us with Vesco," Amanda said. "Sooner or later someone has to come for the dog."

Chapter 40

Twenty minutes later, a young man who looked to be in his mid-teens, clearly oblivious to the fact he was being watched, unhooked the dog.

"I know him," Amanda said, and went out. After a moment, she motioned to Dee and me to join her.

"This is David Amaroff," she said by way of introduction. "He lives with his parents in the Apthorpe, and he has the keys to Vesco's place, except to him, Vesco is Taylor."

"The dog's name is Ed," David said. "I walk him when Mr. Taylor is away.

"Does he go away often?" I asked.

"Yeah, lots, though I don't walk him all the time. He has other walkers."

"Did he say when he's coming back?"

He looked at me quizzically.

"When he called to have you get Ed."

"Oh, I never talk to him. Some woman always calls, and she never says when Mr. Taylor will return."

"What's normal, David?" Amanda asked.

"A few days, a week, a month—it's never the same."

We went with David back to Taylor's apartment. David opened the door and Ed disappeared down the hallway.

Amanda said. "Come on. This layout is the same as mine, only in reverse."

"I don't know," David said. "Mr. Taylor told me to never go inside. I'm just supposed to unleash Ed and leave the leash on the door."

"Will you tell?"

"No, I guess not." David's cheeks flushed pink.

"He might have it wired," I said.

"Stay low to the floor," Dee said, "No higher than the dog. If anyone comes, we'll pretend something happened to the dog."

Amanda and I dropped to our hands and knees and followed the same route Ed had taken, wishing he'd been a Great Dane. I looked back after we'd gone a few feet, and directed Amanda's attention to the alarm panel with blinking lights mounted on the wall behind the door.

"I'd say it's active," I whispered, hoping Ed didn't decide to jump up on something or stand on his hind legs, both of which seemed feats beyond the physical ability of his little stubby legs and big blob that served as his body.

"What are we looking for?" Amanda asked, crawling down a long hallway. I followed, glad that Vesco, or whatever his name is, liked lots of carpeting.

"I guess anything that tells us where to find him, when he's not here."

We bellied our way into each room, including the master bedroom and attached bathroom.

"This guy isn't all bad," Amanda said, keeping her voice low. "I mean, look at this place."

Someone had made the beds. Nothing was out of place. The air was redolent of furniture polish and not a speck of dust had settled on the endless gleaming wood. It looked unlived-in, even the kitchen where Ed squatted on a tidy braided rug next to his food and water bowls, and watched us with toad-like eyes.

"He must be gay," Amanda whispered.

"Hmmmm," I said. That thought hadn't occurred to me—a gay murderer. Almost unfathomable, if not oxymoronic.

We crawled back toward the door where Dee and David waited, then detoured into what looked like the den. Papers in neat piles sat on top of his desk, and his telephone message light blinked.

"We need to find some way to deactivate the alarm," I said.

The telephone rang. Ed barked. Amanda and I froze. Clearly, the alarm wasn't set for sound. Dee stared through the open door and held her breath. We listened to what we assumed was Vesco's voice say, "Please leave a message," then another male voice said, "We haven't found the girl, but she isn't dead, or at least she isn't in a morgue." Pause. "And you might want to check on the kid who walks your dog. According to the guard, three women went with him up to your apartment." Click.

We made it back to Dee and David in record time. David's hands shook as he closed the door and turned two keys, one of which I was certain deactivated the infrared sensors or else Ed, despite being height challenged, would eventually set them off.

When we were finally able to draw a normal breath, Dee wanted to know if I recognized the caller's voice. I had not.

"Remember, David, not a word to anyone," Amanda said.

"Are you kidding?" He studied the three of us for a moment, possibly thinking we were deranged and wondering if we'd cost him his dog-walking job. Had he known who Vesco was, he'd be worried about a lot more. I handed him a twenty. He wouldn't take it.

Amanda said, "David, I don't want you to worry about Mr. Taylor. I'll speak to him and tell him you had nothing to do with it."

Motion at the guard's kiosk caught my attention. Ajit! I forgot to tell him we'd left Starbucks. He strode across the courtyard, and I hurried to meet him. I wanted to tell him privately what had happened and explain about Dee, Amanda and David, but first I wanted to beg his forgiveness, on hands and knees if necessary.

"I'm sorry," I said. "That was really stupid of me."

He squeezed my shoulders. "You had me worried."

"I won't do it again, I promise."

He grinned, and I thought I'd melt. After my heart slowed, I gave him a quick recap. He said he'd talk to the guard, and then wanted to know if we'd spotted any cameras in Vesco's apartment.

"Shit! How could we have been so stupid?"

"Maybe he didn't have any," he said.

"Now you're being kind. Of course he had cameras. We just weren't smart enough to think about them."

"See if you can find out the name of the security company. I might be able to retrieve the images."

I wasn't sure I wanted to make a return visit, although I knew I had to because when Vesco checked the tapes, he'd know we'd not only accompanied David but that we'd been inside.

When I told Dee and Amanda what had to be done, Dee volunteered. She didn't get an argument. David volunteered to go with her. I think he was more afraid of letting the keys out of his custody than he was brave.

While Dee and David were gone, Ajit returned from what I'd noticed had been an animated discussion with the guard.

Amanda said she had to make a few phone calls and went back to her apartment, though I suspected she did so more to give Ajit and me privacy.

"He talks to Vesco's people," Ajit said. "But he swears he never speaks to Vesco."

"Can he find out where Vesco is?"

"He'll do what he can. It turns out he's from our province in India and knows my brother, so I think I can trust him. Plus, I think some of his family is illegal, and I can help him with their papers."

Dee and David returned and gave the alarm company information to Ajit. He made a phone call and went to tell the guard that AAA alarm would be making a service call within the hour.

I asked David if he knew the other walkers.

"The guard guys know who they are," he said.

"Mostly it's a scary-looking old woman who looks like a prison warden. I've see her a few times."

"When does Ed get his next walk?"

"Probably around noon—when the woman called this morning, she said she already had someone for later. I think it will be the old woman."

Ajit had returned and asked if the old woman had to check in with the guard.

"She's supposed to, but I don't know that she always does. She rolls in like a tank, and no one, not even the guards, want to get in her way."

"David," Amanda said. "When she shows up, or if Mr. Taylor returns, I want you to call me. I'll pay you for your time."

David looked at me. "Sure," he said," but you don't need to pay me."

"David, the lady I work for pays. Take the money."

Ajit nodded and winked at him. David said, "Well OK." I could tell he thought a lot of Ajit.

Before Ajit left to return to the precinct, he wanted to know my plan.

"I'm going to ask her how to find Vesco."

"I want your word that you'll call me as soon as she arrives. If she is part of Praetorian or works for Dodge, she'll likely be armed and know how to kill."

I nodded.

"Do I have your word?"

"You have my word."

Chapter 41

Ajit had no sooner left than my cellphone rang. I glanced at the unknown number, a shiver wanting to make its presence felt. Was it Jessie's captors? I answered, fearful of what I might hear.

"The blonde wig doesn't do you justice."

"Who is this?"

"Mr. Vesco says to tell you he's sorry he had to run. It would have been fun to see what you and your two girlfriends had planned."

I looked around. He knew about the wig and Amanda and Dee, he had to be watching.

"What do you want?" I asked.

"What do you want?" he shot back.

"You know full well what I want. I want you to release my friend. She has nothing to do with any of this."

Amanda had rejoined us, and she and Dee were going crazy with curiosity. I covered the mouthpiece and whispered, "One of Vesco's men."

"Bastard," Amanda mouthed. Dee remained stoic.

"And we had nothing to do with your friend's disappearance," he said.

"That's not the way I have it figured."

"That you don't believe us is your problem, but we may be able to help."

"The way you helped Abby?"

Silence.

I pressed on. "The only way you can help is by letting Jessie go free."

"Mr. Vesco will agree to meet provided you agree to come alone. He's not interested in having the police show up, intent on his arrest, nor is he interested in saying what he has to say to your girlfriends or others—this has to be between you and him."

"Vesco wants to meet," I whispered to Dee and

Amanda. They frowned and shook their heads, Amanda vigorously mouthing "No No NO!"

"How do I know I can trust you?"

"You don't, just as I don't know I can trust you."

"Where," Amanda said.

"Where do you want to meet?" I asked.

"In one hour in the Staten Island ferry terminal."

"Are you serious? In one hour? I don't even know how to get there."

"It's not difficult; your friends there can tell you."

"Hold on a sec." I said.

"No, I won't hold. I thought you might be more anxious to save your friend. Goodbye."

"No, wait don't hang up. I'll be there. How will I find him?"

"He'll find you, and don't wear the wig." Click.

Dee said, "You're as white as a sheet. What did he say?"

I told them.

Amanda punched her fists to her hips. "Well, it doesn't matter what he said. You're not going all the way over there alone. I'm coming with you."

Dee said, "We can't. He'll be watching. That's why he's picked Staten Island. To make sure she comes alone."

Amanda wasn't convinced.

Dee added, "He can follow her on the train, and watch her in the New York ferry terminal, on the ferry, and in the Staten Island ferry terminal. It gives him four check points. He knows what he's doing. She has to go alone or he won't show."

I glanced at my watch, my stomach already getting the knot it always did when time became critical. "How long is the ferry ride?" I asked.

"Which train does she take?" Amanda asked.

A man, early thirty's I guessed, sat across the courtyard working on his laptop. "Give me a moment," Dee said. She walked over to him, bent down to give him the full benefit of her delicious cleavage, and whispered in his ear. He nodded, and his fingers flew across the keyboard. Amanda and I assumed he was bringing up a subway map and Staten Island Ferry page. Dee studied his screen for a moment, thanked him by touching his shoulder in a sensual way, and rejoined Amanda and me.

"Simple as can be," she said. "Take the local to South Ferry and follow the signs. The ferry leaves every fifteen minutes and takes twenty-five minutes to cross the harbor—if you leave now, you'll make it in plenty of time."

WE PARTED company at the top of the stairs leading down to the 79th Street station. The local arrived a few moments later and when it pulled into 72nd Street, I switched to the express. By the time I got to Chambers and switched back to the local, I had forty-five minutes to reach Staten Island. The 'running out of time' knot in my stomach grew larger.

Prior to the next stop, which was Rector Street, the subway conductor announced that anyone wishing to exit at South Ferry had to be in the first five cars and to remember that moving between cars was not only prohibited, the doors were locked.

Panic set in. I knew I wasn't in one of the prescribed cars. Then he said that passengers could move forward at the Rector Street station. My panic abated.

At Rector, I dashed from the car I was on and sprinted to the third or fourth car from the front, I wasn't sure except I knew it was one of the first five. Still, I had a nagging feeling I'd miscalculated until the very moment we arrived at South Ferry station and the doors opened.

As it turned out, the ferry terminal, a new airy, glass and shiny steel beam structure, sat at the top of the subway stairs. Once there, I followed the masses up the escalator to the second level, trying to shake the uneasy feeling that each pair of eyes watched my every move. Somewhere in the five hundred or so people: tourists, Staten Island residents, and whoever else chose to be on the ferry that morning, at least one pair was most certainly watching.

I peered through the windows at the huge three-decker ferry—The John F. Kennedy, it said in large letters painted across the top deck—waiting to take us across New York Harbor, past the Statue of Liberty to Staten Island.

I made my way to a spot near the head of the crowd congregating around Gate 1, and when the glass doors slid open, I moved along in the crush of people, out across the wide footbridges into the closed-in main deck. There I walked past rows and rows of brown wood benches, past the snack bar and more rows of benches, and out onto the open, front apron.

After a moment, when the ferry moved out into the water, I grasped the railing. I glanced at my watch. Thirty minutes to go. I'd just make it.

I looked around at the fifty or so people standing with me in the open air. I figured I could forget the couples and those who looked like they couldn't wait to get home to bed after a night shift at some thankless job in the city. That left twenty who might have been my tail, not counting the thousand or more inside. Forget it. He had to find me, not the other way around. Still, I took another look.

I decided to check the upper deck with another two hundred passengers, half inside, the other half opting to sit or stand around the exterior walkway. It was going to be a hot day, and I decided to stand for a few moments to let the refreshing ocean air blow though my hair.

"Lots of water traffic this morning."

I jumped. His voice startled me.

"Sorry," he laughed. "I didn't mean to sneak up on

you that way."

Handsome in a grungy way, weathered face, easy smile—I guessed him to be in his late-thirties or early forties. He wore well-traveled jeans, white t-shirt and sneakers and had a back pack. Under normal circumstances, I decided he could sneak up on me any time he wanted.

"No, it's just that my mind was elsewhere. I'm looking for someone."

"Too bad for me, but hey, that's the story of my life: right place, wrong time." There it was: that devilishly handsome smile again. He turned and walked aft. I went back inside, and while I was in the exploring mood, went to check the lower deck.

I climbed down the dungeon-like stairway. The colors seemed darker and the walkways narrower, with sinister little alcoves. Two passionate lovers had taken over one, oblivious to the fact or not caring that they were in plain view. Elsewhere, groups of boisterous young men, black and white, predominated and gave me an uneasy feeling of being an easy target.

I continued on to the other end and hurried up to the main deck and back to the front apron. There I gulped in the fresh air and waited for my heart rate to resume its normal rhythm.

The ferry neared Staten Island. I wanted desperately to phone Amanda and Dee to assure them I was OK, to hear their encouraging voices, but feared Vesco's tail or tails would think I was tipping someone as to my location.

So far, I didn't know where to go once I got inside the terminal. Someone would have to make himself known to me soon. The young man from the upper deck walked out. I wanted to ignore him, but I couldn't. He nodded. He probably thought I'd lied to him about meeting someone. Right place, wrong time. I nodded back. Please don't come over and talk to me.

I watched the huge pulley wheels turn and lower the footbridges. The water swirled below, dark green and angry. After a moment, the attendant released the rope, and we surged into the terminal. I had no idea where to go and simply shunted along in the crowd, following what seemed to be the majority.

Someone gripped my arm, hard, and pulled me aside. I stifled a holler and turned to look. It was a policeman in uniform. For a brief moment I thought it was Lynch, but it wasn't.

"Are you Miss Harrington?"

Another uniformed cop appeared, holding a straining German Shepherd on a leash that looked far too flimsy.

"I am," I said. "Are you going to let go of my arm?"

He released his grip and smiled. Not Lynch for sure, because Lynch didn't smile. "Sorry, but I didn't want to lose you." Nor did Lynch ever apologize, but that didn't mean they weren't on the Praetorian payroll. "Mr. Vesco will meet you outside. Go through that door and wait by the square benches to your right."

There were other doors I could have gone out, but not with the two policemen and the German Shepherd watching.

Once outside, the benches weren't hard to spot. There were about ten of them in a row and all sat empty. It didn't matter which one I chose to sit on—anyone within a hundred yards would easily see me. I picked the third one from the terminal entrance and sat facing the water, feeling like a tiny spec of nothing as I looked across at the mammoth loading cranes of the ports of New Jersey.

Several giant container ships glided past in the distance, some headed in, others back toward the Verrazzano-Narrows and the Atlantic.

I checked my watch. It had been an hour and ten minutes since I'd talked to Vesco, and I began to look around at the scattering of pedestrians making their way to God knows where. None paid me one iota of attention. If Vesco or one of his hired killers were present, they weren't making themselves obvious.

After another fifteen minutes passed by, and I'd inhaled all the seawater smells an harbor views I could tolerate, my neck stiff from glancing this way and that, I called Amanda and Dee. Anyone watching would already know I came alone so seeing me use my cellphone shouldn't cause great alarm.

In a panic, Amanda told me the woman who worked for Vesco had telephoned David. As David has suspected, someone else would walk Ed at noon.

It was a few minutes to ten. I could easily make it back to Amanda's apartment by noon, and told her I'd meet her there.

I dashed back into the terminal half expecting the two cops to intercept me. What I'd do if that happened, I hadn't yet figured out. I called Ajit and told him what was going on.

"This is how you keep you word?"

"Sorry, I didn't have a choice. He said to come alone, but he didn't show."

Ajit agreed to stay on the line in case the two cops gave me a hard time. I joined the line waiting to board the ferry for the return trip, and didn't see the two cops. I told Ajit I'd call him later.

Unless you count me about going crazy with worry, the return trip was uneventful until we were ten minutes from Manhattan. That's when my cellphone rang. It was Vesco's man.

"He didn't show," I said. "Where's my friend, Jessie?"

"Mr. Vesco can't see you today. You will be contacted."

"Please, I need to talk to him."

Click.

Chapter 42

I needed to talk to someone before I lost my mind, and that someone was Bebe. She was aghast that I'd gone to Staten Island alone. That didn't surprise me. What did was she telling me that Lynch and two of his minions had stomped their oversized feet and undersized brains through her apartment.

Was I to blame? I owed Lynch a report, but he hadn't called, so now what was his game? To let me know he still had the power...that he knew where I lived...that he could close in whenever he wanted.

"You should have called Dalton."

"Oh, believe me, I called him first thing, but of course he was out of the office, and Lynch said if I made him come back with a search warrant, he'd fill the hallways with a very loud and angry SWAT team that knocks things, like doors, down. I do want to live here a while longer."

"He's not still there, is he?"

"I should say not. Dalton finally called and put him on the run."

"Did Lynch want to know where I was?"

"Why would he want to know that? What, pray tell, have you got going with that clod?"

"He's got a bee in his bonnet that I'm somehow trying to interfere with Jenny's murder investigation, so he phones twice a day to get a report of my comings and goings." It was all a lie, but I didn't know how to explain the ludicrous notion that, in Lynch's warped mind, she and Dalton were suspects.

"I'm calling Dalton," she said. "He's harassing you."

"Please don't. I can handle Lynch. I need to keep playing him to find out what he knows."

Another lie, but if she called Dalton and Dalton called Lynch, Lynch would snatch me from the streets and stick me in a cell full of hookers before nightfall just to get his rocks off.

"Darling, this is insane. I told you to stop playing detective. I can't let you do this."

"Listen to me. I've got to keep on doing what I can to find Jessie, but I promise to call you every chance I get. If at any time you haven't heard from me for more than let's say five hours, call Dalton and tell him Lynch may have arrested me."

"If you think I'm waiting five hours, you have another think coming. Two hours, Darling, or I'm calling reinforcements."

"Make it three."

She caved, on the condition I explain to Dalton why he had to stay away from Lynch, at least on my account. I told her I would and had no sooner ended the call than Lynch phoned wanting to know where I was and what I was doing.

I wondered if he knew about my wild goose chase to Staten Island. Well, he wasn't about to hear it from me, so I told him I was visiting a friend on the Upper West Side. He didn't press. Maybe Dalton had shaken him, though I knew not for long. Guys like Lynch didn't shake and didn't quit.

I phoned Dalton and told him I thought Lynch's visit to Bebe's apartment had more to do with me than with Bebe, but that I wanted him to steer clear because I didn't want to lose access to Lynch.

He seemed bemused by my detective activities, and that got my dander up, but he did agree to stay away.

I was about to end the call before I said something untoward when he said, "You are not going to believe this—Cameron Black has been arrested for Jenny's murder."

"What are you talking about?"

"It's on our police wire."

"You're right; I can't believe it. What else does it

say?"

"Bear with me, the message has just this minute arrived...it doesn't say where or why, only that he was arrested an hour ago. Nothing has been put out to the press yet...wait, this is interesting, Lynch was the arresting officer."

"No way."

"I'm serious. Sergeant Lynch headed up the unit that made the arrest."

This was crazy. Cameron Black was being set up. Praetorian remained the only logical candidate. "How good is your source?" I asked.

"It's factual, if that's what you mean. We make it our business to know when anyone gets arrested."

"May I have a copy?"

"It needs editing. After that, I'd be happy to send a copy to Bebe's office."

"It'll get lost there." I gave him my e-mail.

"I'll have to clear it with Bebe just to remain politically correct. I'm sure you understand."

I knew he was right, yet I wanted to kick his pompous, politically correct ass. I wanted to, although like Lynch, I needed ongoing access to Dalton.

To change the subject, I asked, "Do you know of an organization called Praetorian?"

"Not since what...Rome in the fourth century?"

"I think Praetorian is the private investor in Hebrides and had something to do with Jenny's death. I also think it kidnapped Jessie and arranged to have Cameron Black arrested."

"No, I most certainly do not know of this modern-day Praetorian. My God, Paige, that's quite a list of accusations. Do you have proof?"

"No, unfortunately. I'm hoping you might do a little poking around?" I was still annoyed about him not sending the wire copy and added, more sharply than intended, "I'll tell Bebe, so you can clear it with her."

He mumbled something about being sure it was OK, and this time I ended the call promptly.

I called Ajit to ask if he'd seen a police wire about Cameron Black's arrest. He said he had and was about to call.

"Does it say anything about Lynch being the arresting officer?" I asked.

"No, I've told you everything it says. Why do you think Lynch is involved?"

"Bebe's lawyer read a report to me a moment or two ago in which he said Lynch was named as the arresting officer."

"You could be right about Lynch, although the report I have is the official version, and it says nothing about Lynch so I don't know where Bebe's lawyer gets his info. Maybe he has someone on the inside that adds not-for-publication data."

For some reason, that left an odd feeling in the pit of my stomach right next to where the Praetorian stuff sat. I told him I'd call later, then before heading into the incommunicado subway, I squeezed in a call to Amanda to let her know I was on my way.

Chapter 43

As soon as I got to Amanda's, I told Dee about Cameron's arrest. She phoned Peter and asked me to talk to him. He was clearly upset and wanted to see Cameron as quickly as possible. I promised to help him figure out how to do that.

Also, I felt I owed Dee and Amanda further explanation. Dee, because Peter through Cameron was now at least tangentially involved, and Amanda, because her image was likely on Vesco's security cameras, and I'd placed her and David at risk.

I told them all I knew about Praetorian, omitting only Abby's location, and any mention of the canister and documents. I told Dee that Praetorian had likely arranged for Cameron to be arrested—I didn't know why—and I told Amanda that Vesco was likely one of Praetorian's hired killers, and I feared I'd placed her and David in considerable danger.

Dee said, "I thought Vesco worked for Abner Dodge."

"Praetorian is Abner Dodge," I said.

They each took a moment to chew on that piece of information.

"Other than Dodge, who no one can get to, Vesco is the only thread to Praetorian and Jessie. If I can't find Vesco, I can't find Jessie."

Dee said, "Amanda and I have both done a lot of work with complex offshore tax shelters, me in real estate and she with husbands and wives trying to hide assets. We know the players in those arrangements. Maybe we can help you find another doorway into Praetorian."

I was afraid to believe, but neither was I going to cast their offer aside.

"There is one caveat," I said. "You can't let anyone know what you're doing, because if Praetorian finds out it will do all in its power to stop you."

"What about Stephen?" Dee asked Amanda. "Do you think he might help?"

"Yes," Amanda said, "he might."

What part of 'not saying anything to anyone' had they failed to comprehend?

"Stephen is my ex," Amanda said.

This was getting worse. Telling Dee and Amanda was dangerous; telling their friends was forbidden; telling their ex-spouses was insane.

As though reading m mind, she continued, "I understand fully that you don't want anyone to know about Praetorian, but Stephen is the most powerful person I know, and I'd trust him with my life—just not my girlfriends."

I had to say 'no.' This had spun out of control.

"I don't know...can he be trusted? I'm worried that too many people are getting into the loop. Someone is going to make a mistake."

Dee said to me, "He's a senior attorney with the State Department in Washington. Stephen Rattner, maybe you've heard of him."

Amanda said, "He doesn't speak to his own reflection in the mirror. If he had as many ethics about marriage as he did about his damn job..."

Ajit hacking into computers—they might bump into one another. And what about Dalton? Since I'd mentioned Praetorian to him, he'd surely start to poke around. So what, as long as they kept their mouths shut? Ajit would, for sure, and I could only hope the same for Dalton and Stephen.

"Paige," Amanda said, doubtless sensing my ongoing indecision, "Stephen has a powerful position. He knows who, how, and what makes Washington work. If Praetorian has top-level government and military connections, he will know, or can find out. Now, having said that, you must understand he might not be able to help for all kinds of conflict of interest reasons, but I can assure you if anyone can help, he can."

"Call him," I said, "but you'd better let me do the talking. I want to be sure he understands what I think is going on."

Amanda called. Stephen wasn't in his office. She'd no sooner told us he'd call back when he did. He couldn't talk other than to say he'd be happy to meet me at 4:30 p.m. at the U.S. ambassador's office at the U.N. He said an aide would pick me up and get me past the security maze. I gave him Bebe's address and telephone numbers.

Chapter 44

David called from the security kiosk to say the old woman had arrived to walk the dog. I told him to stay put and yanked on the wig.

Amanda said, "I'm coming with you."

I hated having to tell her I didn't think she'd add much, other than make us appear obvious and scare the old woman off. Fortunately, she sensed my reluctance, and decided instead to get her car and wait on the street in front, 'just in case.'

She said she had a dark blue Mercedes convertible. I told her to keep the top up. Amanda in a convertible did not project the level of inconspicuousness I had in mind.

When I approached the kiosk, the guard eyed me with respect bordering on awe now that he knew I was a friend of Ajit, and pointed us to a nearby bench that he busily wiped clean of a layer of New York City atmosphere.

We sat but a few minutes when David whispered, "That's her," and started to get up.

"In a minute," I said, and waited until the woman and Ed passed through the gate and turned south on Broadway. Then we followed.

She turned west on 78th Street, and was halfway down the block by the time we rounded the corner.

"She's circling the building," David said. "That's usually what Mr. Taylor wants me to do, so Ed doesn't have to cross the streets."

That made sense. Ed wasn't built for jumping out of the way of fast-moving traffic. We continued to follow to West End, across 79th, and up the incline back to Broadway.

When we came onto Broadway, I spotted Amanda and her blue Mercedes near 78th Street, not a good undercover vehicle, but at least it didn't have plates that said AMANDA. She was unrecognizable behind dark glasses and the baseball cap pulled down to her ears.

When the woman and Ed entered the courtyard, I told David to wait by the kiosk and ran to catch up.

"Ma'am?" I said as she neared the doorway to Vesco's wing.

She didn't stop. I touched her arm and said, "Ma'am, please excuse me, but I'd like to ask how I can find Mr. Taylor."

"You no touch," she said swinging her big arm away and turning to glare. Ajit's warning filled my mind. She looked like a killer.

"Sorry, but it's very important that I contact Mr. Taylor." I was talking louder and slower as though that might enable her to understand.

"Don't know. No talk."

To me she appeared Eastern European, and I didn't know any of the Slavic languages well enough to put together an intelligible sentence.

She turned her back and barged inside, dragging Ed along like a sack of potatoes. I went back to the kiosk and called Ajit to tell him what had transpired.

"When she comes out," I said, "I'm going to follow her."

He repeated what by now was becoming his usual litany of precautions. I told him I wasn't planning anything heroic and promised to check in regularly, though I'm sure he was beginning to question the reliability of my promises.

Since the only one I had to hide from now was the old woman who'd seen me as a blonde, I removed the wig and gave it to David. He asked to come with me and, to appease his obvious disappointment when I told him no, I asked if he had a cellphone I could borrow for the day.

He produced one from his front pants pocket. "Do you know how to work it?"

I flipped it open. "It's the same as one of mine." I snapped it shut and put it in my bag. "And I promise I won't answer any calls that aren't from you, Amanda or Dee. I'll bet you get a lot of calls from girls. I don't want to get you into trouble."

His cheeks flushed pink. "Nah, just some guys and my mom. The guys will hit on you; tell 'em to get lost. I'll tell my mom so she knows."

At the same moment I saw the woman exit the building, the guard alerted us to stay back and began a running commentary on her movements across the courtyard. When he said she'd gone out the gate, I squeezed David's arm, said "Wish me luck," and started after her.

"Zol zion mit Mazel, but are you sure I can't come with you?"

"No, I'm not," I said, "but I need you here more."

Though there wasn't time, what I really needed was Ajit. Following this woman, who looked more capable of murder than anyone I'd ever met, through the streets of New York to God knows where didn't rank high on my to-do list, but where she went might give me the clue I needed to find Vesco and Jessie.

I ran to catch up in case she headed down the stairs into the subway, where she could easily disappear in the masses of people. Instead, she went to the bus stop and peered north as if searching for an approaching bus.

I slipped into Chase's ATM area located immediately behind the bus stop, and stood next to the customer service counter where I could see her but she couldn't see me. In the ensuing few minutes, she checked her watch several times, again looked up Broadway, and then headed for the subway. I dashed from the bank and ran down the stairs.

A Number 1 train had pulled in a few seconds earlier, and I heard the door-closing chime. I elbowed my way along the platform and dove through a closing door. The train lurched forward. I staggered and managed to grab the pole just as I was about to be pitched to the floor "Sorry," I said to the back of a woman I'd banged into.

The woman turned and gave me an ugly look. I froze; it was she. I tried not to gasp and moved to the far doors where I stared out into the passing darkness at the dirt walls and wooden beams of the tunnel, keenly watching the woman's reflection. She seemed preoccupied and paid me no attention.

At 42nd Street she got off, crossed to the other side of the platform, and stared off into the black hole of the express tunnel. I watched to make sure she didn't dash back onto the local. A headlight approached. A few seconds later, the express train rumbled in and squealed to a stop. Passengers rushed off and on. The doors closed. Everyone jockeyed for position. There were three people between the woman and me.

She got off at 14th Street, walked to the 12th Street end of the platform, and climbed the stairs. She crossed to the south side of 12th and headed east. I followed fifty paces behind.

At Sixth Avenue, she hesitated and checked her watch, then crossed with the light. Two brownstones past The New School, she stopped and looked back toward Sixth. I don't think she suspected anyone was following her, still I ducked into the foyer of an apartment building directly across the street.

"Help you, Miss?"

I turned and faced the doorman. "Yes, I'm looking for my friend, Jessie McArdle, but I must have written down the wrong address. I thought this might be her building."

I glanced across the street. The woman opened the gate in a black wrought-iron fence of a vacant brownstone with large tarpaulins hanging from scaffolding, holes where windows and doors had been, and a large dumpster in front that overflowed with building scraps. She picked her way around debris and down a few steps to a doorway tucked under the front stairs. For the longest time, she seemed to be fiddling with a key, but finally got the door open and stepped inside.

"Sorry, Miss, no one lives here by that name."

I gave thanked him for his help and crossed the street, keeping my eyes peeled on the sub basement windows for signs of activity. The downstairs apartment that the woman had entered appeared as lifeless as the rest of the building, except for intact windows, dirt-caked and covered with blinds though they were.

Through one of the open spaces on the parlor floor, a worker wearing a blue hardhat and smoking a cigarette looked down at me.

"Hello," I called.

He pushed his hardhat back on his forehead far enough to reveal a head full of black shiny curls, and stepped to the opening where the main doors would one day go. Grinning broadly through a sweat and dirt-stained face with teeth so white I had to squint, he gave me a thorough going over.

"Is anyone living downstairs?" I asked.

He shook his head and motioned with his arm toward the shell of a building behind him as if to say 'Are you crazy?'

Two more workers in hardhats looked out of window spaces on the upper floors. One of them said something down to the first one that I didn't understand, though I thought it was Polish.

The first one replied in the same language.

They laughed. The first one, in heavily accented English, said, "Come back at Christmas," and they laughed again.

Chapter 45

I walked back fifty yards to The New School where students were milling about with phone calls. or smoking and drinking coffee, or talking. I called Amanda. She'd seen me go down into the subway and tried to catch up, but the train had already left. I told her where I was.

She wanted to know what to do, but I hadn't yet figured out what I was going to do, other than call Ajit and hope he arrived before the woman decided to leave. I ended the call, telling her I'd phone later. She warned me to stay out of the brownstone.

I called Ajit. He had tired of waiting and was already in the Ferrari, sitting at the light on Ninth Avenue and 54th Street. He said to wait, that he'd be no more than ten minutes.

"Uh-oh."

"What's going on?"

"Someone's coming out of the brownstone." I pressed myself hard against the front of The New School. "I think it's the man we saw leaving Therese's apartment last night."

"Paige, don't you dare move."

The man started up the sidewalk.

"He's coming this way, and he's looking right at me and patting his chest."

"He has a gun. I'm calling for backup. Get inside the school and lose yourself. There are lots of hallways, lots of places packed with people. Don't let him corner you, and keep your phone on."

If he indeed had a gun, I didn't like the idea of hiding among young people and glanced around for an alternative. There wasn't much time; the guy was in front of the adjoining building and coming fast.

"If I stay on the streets, I can outrun him."

"He might not be alone."

I looked at dozens of students using cellphones and figured reception inside was nil. "I might lose the connection." I said, and dashed into the school. "He's still coming. How soon can you get here?"

"Five minutes, no more. If I lose…trying until…stay off…right number…"

"Ajit, I can't hear you. Ajit?" My voice bounced back, the connection had been lost.

I raced up the stairs, pushed through a set of doors, and started down a long hallway, staying close to the wall. I dared a look back. The man burst through the front doors, his head jerking from side to side. The desk guard said something and started to get up, but the man kept coming.

He looked up the stairs. He'd seen me. I took off running. Ahead on the left, a door opened and three or four young women came out, their arms laden with books. I went in.

Mistake, bad mistake. It was the woman's washroom. I was trapped. My only hope was that he hadn't seen me.

Two young women stood at one end of the row of sinks hurriedly dousing cigarettes—joints, I breathed marijuana. Glazed eyes in dark sockets stared back, not as concerned as I thought they ought to be over the possibility they might be busted. Maybe they were too high.

"Get into the stalls," I said. "And stand on the toilet so no one can see your feet. A guy is chasing me. He's got a gun."

Still they stared.

Loud commotion and shouting from the hallway got their attention.

"Hurry," I said, and they dashed into the stalls. "Lock the doors." It wouldn't do much good, but if it bought them a critical few seconds…

The front door banged open and the man barged in.

I screamed, "Hey! You can't come in here."

He stopped, momentarily confused.

"Get out," I screamed,

His eyes turned cold.

"Why you follow woman?" He spoke the same broken Eastern European English as the old woman.

"Are you crazy man? I wasn't following no woman." I took a couple of steps. He blocked my way.

"What's your problem, man?"

The shorter of the two girls came out of a stall and tried to run past. He punched her full in the face with a loud crack and she sunk to the floor with a groan. Blood spewed from her nose and mouth and started to form a pool on the white tiles.

"Don't," I cried, and stepped forward to help. He swung around and caught me alongside of the head with a vicious swipe that sent me sprawling into the open stall nearest the door. More surprised than hurt, I struggled to get up.

He raised his hand again, this time as a fist that looked like a huge wooden club. "Why you following woman?" His face got redder and droplets of spit flew from his mouth.

"I told you…"

He pulled a gun.

"OK, OK," I said. "I'll tell you."

Behind him, the taller of the two girls crept up. She had something big and heavy looking in her hands. I had to make sure he didn't see her, but he also needed to step back a pace so she could get a clear swing.

"I need to come out first," I said, and took a step forward.

He waved the gun. "You not come out."

I didn't have a choice. I took another step. He edged back and raised the gun. At the same moment, the tall girl lunged and swung with both arms. He must have caught a glimpse because he turned his head. Mistake; the toilet tank top caught him square on the forehead with a loud thunk.

He staggered back against the stall, his arm slicing the air. There was a deafening bang. A bullet smashed into the ceiling, and the gun flew from his hand, ricocheting from the wall and clattering across the floor under the row of sinks. He slumped to the floor like an amorphous blob.

"Don't ever fuck with my friend," the tall girl said, and threw the tank top to the floor next to his head. Then she turned to aide her friend who had managed a sitting position. "Here baby, let me help you." She ran some paper towels under the water, pressed them gently to the injured girl's nose. The two of us helped her stand.

The shorter girl stared at the crumpled body of the man. "Holy shit," she said to her friend. "You got him good."

"Are you going to be OK?" the taller girl asked me. "You're white as a sheet."

Adrenaline had started racing through my system like an avalanche and my insides were shaking like a leaf, but I'd recover.

"Don't worry about me," I said. "What about your friend?"

"She's tough. She has nine brothers."

"Well, you better get out of here unless you feel like talking to a lot of cops. Take your friend to St. Vincent's emergency room. Do you know where that is?"

She nodded and they took a couple of steps toward the door. The taller girl eyed the gun. I told her I'd look after it, picked it up with a paper towel, stuffed it into my bag, and followed them out.

The hallway hadn't yet exploded with curiosity, though we attracted a number of concerned glances because of the bloody paper towels the shorter girl held to her nose.

"Is she all right?" a student-type asked. The taller girl said she'd banged her nose on the sink, and the two of them kept walking toward the main entrance. A young man wearing a tie asked if he could be of assistance.

"Are you on staff?" I asked.

"I'm professor of sociology," he said, as though he'd created mankind.

"Some guy's out cold in the woman's bathroom. You should call the police."

His mouth dropped open.

"Now!" I said.

A security guard ran down the hall shouting, "What's going on? What's going on?"

I said, "A guy chased two girls into the washroom. That gentleman"—I pointed to the young professor who had run into an office to make the call—"is calling the police."

Another guard came running up the stairs. He was the one who should have stopped the guy in the first place, but he was old and looked physically incapable of stopping anyone.

"I've already called the police," the young professor announced, returning to the hallway. "They're on their way."

"Are you a student here?" another voice, a man's, asked.

"I heard a loud crash, like porcelain smashing," I said, avoiding his question. "Then the two girls came out and left the building. The man never came out."

"But are you a student here?" the man asked again.

"You might have a killer in that bathroom, and you want to know if I'm a student?"

He backed away a couple of steps and looked at me as though I'd slapped him. He didn't know how close I'd come. The hallway filled with students.

I turned my attention to a third security guard plowing up the hallway. At least he appeared capable of inflicting damage if the bathroom guy regained consciousness and wanted more trouble. "There's a man in the bathroom," I said. "He was after two girls."

"Is anyone else in there?"

"No, I'm sure he's the only one. The two girls ran out."

"One of them was bleeding," a student volunteered.

"She was with them," another said.

With the same ferocity, the guard eyed both the door, and me, and then removed his two-way radio from its belt attachment.

An older man in a suit walked up. "Mr. Crabtree," he said, "I think you ought to wait for the police."

Mr. Crabtree eyed the washroom door again. "That's probably a good idea," he said, "although I'm going to stay here in case he decides to come out."

The older man nodded.

"Might be a good idea to get all these people outta the hallway just in case," Mr. Crabtree added.

In the confusion that followed, I made a beeline for the front door, not wanting to get trapped into answering a bunch of questions with a gun in my handbag. As I went out, two police officers came in. I looked up the street toward St. Vincent's and saw the two girls headed in that direction.

Ajit screeched to a stop behind a police car and leapt out.

"Paige, are you OK? I heard the 911 call a minute ago. What happened in there?"

I inhaled deeply a couple of times; then gave him a blow-by-blow.

"What did he want? Did he say?"

"He wanted to know why I was following the old woman."

"Is that the brownstone?" he asked.

I nodded. "He came out that door." I pointed to the one under the steps leading to the parlor floor, "The same one the old woman went in."

"The woman still in there?" he asked.

"I don't know." The workmen were busy hammering and sawing. "They'd know."

A police officer came out of the school. His nametag said Moran. He seemed to know Ajit and stopped to give him a report.

"Some guy got decked with the top of a toilet tank. I think he'll live, but if he ever wakes up, it'll be a while before he sees straight."

"Who's the guy?"

"ID says he's a P.I. Name's Dirk Palmer. I better call it in." Then he turned to me and asked, "Were you the one in the washroom?"

Before I could answer, Ajit said, "No, she wasn't."

The cop gave Ajit a 'you shitting me?' look and went to his cruiser.

As soon as Moran was out of earshot I said, "I got the guy's gun."

"What?"

"When the girl hit him with the toilet top, his gun flew across the floor. I picked it up on the way out."

"You'd better give it to me."

I removed the gun, still wrapped in a paper towel, from my bag. "It went off. They'll find a bullet in the ceiling."

Ajit took it to Moran, told him about the bullet, and said a girl running from the school had dropped it. "It belongs to the guy, Palmer. He came from that building," Ajit pointed to the brownstone fifty yards distant.

Moran said to Ajit. "What do you want to do? We've got to follow the ambulance and keep Palmer under wraps until someone takes him off our hands."

Ajit told him to radio for backup.

Chapter 46

While we were standing there, a black Lincoln Town Car, a limousine for hire, came up the street and stopped in front of the brownstone. Before anyone had a chance to react, the old woman, with a large bundle under her arms, tore out and jumped into the back seat, and the limousine sped away.

Ajit ripped the microphone from Moran's hand and barked several commands, then told Moran and his partner that they should go ahead with Palmer. Three cruisers with six officers were on the way.

We started up the street toward the brownstone. Ajit said, "One of the cruisers will intercept the limo, and when the others get here, we'll find out what's in that basement."

One worker saw us coming and made a dash for a pickup truck. Ajit hand-signaled a police cruiser coming the wrong way up the one-way street to cut him off. Two officers jumped out, handcuffed the worker, and stuffed him into the back seat of the police car. Then the two officers, pistols drawn, yelled at the other workers to come down. After a few moments, they had taken three more into custody.

Two other police cruisers arrived and four officers with pistols drawn started for the sub-basement suite, Ajit among them. I was surprised to see a pistol had found its way to his hand. One of the officers told me to stay on the sidewalk.

"If you think I'm waiting out here," I said, "you're crazy."

An officer about twice my size blocked my way. "I can't let you go in there, Miss."

"Start shooting then, because I'm going."

"No, you're not, and I'll cuff you to the cruiser if I have to."

I wanted to fight. This was my story. I was the reason they were here.

"You can listen," he said, and turned up the volume on his two-way radio.

I strained to hear through the static of the two-way. Then I heard "Body! Dead!"

I lunged forward, every cell in my body screaming, 'PLEASE, GOD, NOT JESSIE.'

The policeman grabbed my arms.

"Clear!" another voice shouted.

I broke free and ran. Inside, I looked wildly around trying to find Ajit. He stood near the back, in the kitchen area, next to a kneeling officer. I moved forward. Ajit tried to stop me. I forced myself to stare at the body on the floor. Tears filled my eyes. I brushed them away, took another look, and then spun around. My throat filled with vomit. I dashed to the kitchen sink and threw up.

Ajit came up behind and gripped my shoulders.

"It's not Jessie," I mumbled. "It's that girl from the hospital, Therese."

"Yes," Ajit said.

"That old woman has her baby."

"They'll catch her."

"Ajit, I'm sorry. I led them to her. I let her get murdered."

He cupped my chin and forced me to look at him. "You had nothing to do with it. By the time we talked to Therese, they were already waiting in her apartment. They thought she knew where Abby was."

"Do you think she did know? Do you think she told them?"

"The woman can tell us."

"Why did the woman have her baby? When did they get the baby? Therese didn't have her baby with her last night."

"Those are things the woman and Palmer will have to

tell us. Meanwhile, I'll have someone check Therese's mother's apartment."

"You don't think…"

Ajit told one of the police officers about Mrs. Hanratty. I dug my notebook from my handbag and read off the address. The officer spoke into his two-way radio and said someone was on the way.

The officer in front of the brownstone reported to Ajit that they caught the old woman, who was now in custody.

I asked, "Does she have the baby? Is the baby OK?"

"The baby's fine, Miss. He's with the limo driver."

I needed no other excuse to get away from Therese's dead body and went out to the limo. I glanced at the woman in the back of the cruiser. She seemed smaller and older as she sat staring at the floor. A lot of people had congregated, some gawking into the police cruiser, some trying to look into the brownstone where Therese's body lay, some just standing and not appearing to look at anything. More police cruisers arrived.

A TV news truck tried to get closer, then stopped and several people with cameras and related paraphernalia streamed out. I recognized the woman cursing up a storm and giving directions: Alberta Sims from Channel Five, the same one who'd pushed her way into the Apple Bank Building the morning of Jenny's murder.

"Keep everyone back," a man in a suit and dark sunglasses said to the constable. "Where's the body?"

The constable pointed with his thumb over his shoulder and said, "Basement."

The suit looked up at the building's shell. "Jeez, thanks, Martinelli, I thought maybe it was up there."

Martinelli's face reddened and he muttered, "Asshole."

The suit asked, "What's with the kid?"

"Someone's coming to get her," Martinelli said, and

left to attend to his crowd control assignment.

I opened the limo's front door on the passenger side. "Whew." The smell almost knocked me over.

"I know, Miss. It's bad." The limo driver seemed to be trying his best to keep the baby amused with pens and keys and a plastic Jesus on a chain.

"What's your name?" I asked.

"Jose Hernandez."

"I'm Paige Harrington."

Jose nodded. "This your baby?"

"I knew her mother."

"That policeman, he thinks he's a girl," Jose said. "He's no girl, but he need food and clean diapers. That old woman, she no understand English."

"Everything OK?" Ajit had walked up to the limo. He stepped back and put a finger under his nose.

"Not totally," I said. "The young constable over there said someone is coming to get him. This is Jose. He's been looking after him."

Jose nodded. "Sorry, Sir, I try to keep heem from crying, but he need food and clean diaper."

"Someone will be here soon," Ajit said.

A moment later, a tall, attractive black woman with a doctor's bag ran up. "I'm Doctor Houston from Children's Services. Is this the baby?" Bouncing along behind her was a shorter woman carrying a larger bag.

I slid out of the front seat, Dr. Houston slid in, the aroma of her expensive perfume quickly gobbled up by dirty-diaper stink that she seemed not to notice. She snapped on a pair of latex gloves, and a stethoscope appeared as if by magic. "Mercedes," she said to the woman carrying the larger bag, "as soon as I'm through here, we need to get her cleaned and fed."

"He no girl," Jose said.

Dr. Houston shot him a look that would have killed a lesser man.

"Yes, Doctor," Mercedes said.

I watched as Dr. Houston listened to what seemed like a hundred different spots and gently poked at the tiny, dirty, writhing body. "There, there," she kept saying.

Jose had retracted as far against the driver's door as one could, perhaps fearing Dr. Houston might again turn on him, though I suspected he was trying to put a greater distance between his nose and the baby.

After a moment, Dr. Houston jumped out and announced that the baby was fine. Mercedes reached in, wrapped the baby in a white blanket, and hurried up the street to a waiting car, Dr. Houston right behind her.

"He no girl," Jose said to the departing duo, lowering all the windows and stepping out for much needed fresh air.

"Jose," Ajit asked. "Where did the old woman want you to take her?"

Jose reached in and pulled out a clipboard from under his seat. He handed it to Ajit.

Ajit studied the form. "Columbia Presbyterian Hospital—is that right?"

"That what she say."

"She was going to drop the baby and run," I said. "I think she'd had enough."

"But why way up town? St. Vincent's is two blocks away."

"She must have known Therese worked at Columbia Presbyterian. Maybe that stuck in her brain."

Ajit took a call. I knew from the look on his face that they had found Therese's mother, murdered.

I had suspected as much. It didn't sadden me. Seeing Therese saddened me. Both frightened me because of what they meant for Abby and Jessie. Praetorian employed murderers and would keep killing until they got what they wanted. I had to be close to next on the list. How many more would I pull along with me?

Ajit said, "She was probably dead when we were up

there last night since she didn't answer her telephone or the intercom."

"I guess so," I said. "That's why Therese went with that guy. They had her baby."

I looked at the woman in the police car. "What's the connection to Vesco? Do they all work for Praetorian?"

Ajit walked over and spoke to her for a moment. When he returned, he said, "She's not in a talking mood, yet. Maybe she'll change her mind after she's sat in a cell for a few hours." Then he turned to Jose and asked, "Did the woman pay by credit card?"

"No, Sir. She give me cash. Fifty dollars."

"Did your dispatcher give you a name?"

"They tell me a man, Mr. Palmer. I ask the old woman where is Mr. Palmer? She get angry, say never mind, baby sick, to shut up and drive."

Alberta Sims strode up. Our eyes met in a brief moment of recognition, and then she shoved her microphone in Ajit's face. Her two-man camera crew went back and forth between Ajit and me, more on me, drawing a glare from Alberta Sims.

"What's going on here, Detective?"

I glanced at Ajit. Why had she called him detective?

"Sorry, Alberta, but the guy you want is inside."

"Not Henderson?"

"He's the one."

"That son-of-a-bitch."

"That'd be him."

Alberta cursed some more and stormed the brownstone.

"Why did she address you as detective?"

"It's an old title."

"What's the new one?"

"I don't have one. My job is to bridge intelligence and research. I suppose you could call me a liaison officer."

"But you were an honest-to-goodness street detective,

right? That's why all the police know you. That's why you have a gun."

"I was. Someone pushed me in front of a bullet intended for a hugely popular cop, so they called me a hero, and when I got out of the hospital six weeks later, I retired from street duty."

"This better not be a line."

"The cop I saved is now Chief of Police—that gives me far more clout that any position I ever had or will have, or would or could ever warrant."

"So who pushed you?"

"Never did find out."

"The cops in the park last night didn't seem all that enamored of your power or greatness."

"I doubt they were real, but even if they were, as popular as he is, the Chief isn't universally loved."

"So once in awhile your magic doesn't work."

"Once in a while."

"And what about the cruisers we saw on the way to the hospital? They seemed to be paying us a lot of attention."

"They knew it was my car. They saw me in the passenger seat. Their interest was you."

"Did they call you this morning to find out who your chauffeur was?"

"They asked. I told them to cool it."

"And here I thought you were nothing but a magna cum laude PhD in computer science with a major in AI."

"You've been prying."

"I checked the Internet, Columbia, classes of 1995 and 2005. For research purposes, it would have been helpful had you written your thesis the year you graduated."

The police car with the old woman pulled away and headed toward Fifth. "How soon will we know what she has to say?"

Ajit shook his head.

We got in the Ferrari. I stared up the narrow tree-lined street with cars parked on both sides, at the people, including hundreds of New School students milling about on the sidewalk, at the blinking lights of the police cars, at the yellow tape strung around the brownstone. I heard the bursts of sound from the police radios. With its siren eerily silent, the ambulance with Therese's body left, and my fear for Jessie's life intensified.

Chapter 47

There was one thread to Jessie, however fragile, that I had to pursue, and asked Ajit to take me to Bebe's apartment. Zoë had to help me find Abby. If Abby had recovered enough to speak, she might be able to tell me something, one tiny thing about Praetorian that would lead to Jessie. It was a real long shot, but I had run out of options.

Ajit's phone rang. It was Bo saying we could view the surveillance videos.

I looked at the time. If Stephen Rattner didn't cancel, that gave me three short hours. For what—another long shot, another fragile thread? Would the people on the surveillance videos tell us where else to look?

My question concerning Stephen Rattner didn't last long. Bebe met us at the door of her apartment. Stephen Rattner had called to confirm that he would have someone pick me up at 4:00. I told her that Ajit and I had to go to Columbia Presbyterian, but first I had to talk to Zoë.

Zoë sat on the sofa, black shadows puffed under her bloodshot eyes. I told her about Therese. She nodded and looked away.

"I'm sorry," I said.

She started to stand, then sat back down. She clasped her hands around her knee and reached for a cushion to hold on her lap. Her lower lip began to quiver. She set the cushion aside. Her eyes filled with tears.

"I feel it's my fault," she cried. "Why did they pick her? She didn't know anything."

Ajit said, "Therese always wanted everyone to think she knew more than she really did. Perhaps she said too much to the wrong people."

"Zoë," I said, "You can't blame yourself for what happened to Therese. What you can do is help me find

Abby, that's the name of your Jane Doe. My friend's life depends on what Abby might be able to remember or tell us."

She blinked away a few tears.

"I'm also worried that because Therese was tortured, she may have been forced to tell the people who killed her where Brad and Tom have Abby hidden. They've got to move or their lives too could be in danger."

Zoë said, "Therese couldn't possibly have told anyone where to look—I'm the only one who knows what Brad and Tom were planning, and even I don't know where they took Abby."

"Think, Zoë, think real hard. These people are murderers. Four lives are in danger, two of them your friends and colleagues. You must know something."

She leapt up, her hands clenched at her sides. "Why do you think I know anything? I agreed to help your brother, but that's all. I didn't think anyone would get killed. I can't…I'm afraid."

"We're all afraid. Abby's afraid. She was on the run. She told me they were trying to kill her, and they finally caught her. Therese had been tortured. I saw her body. It made me vomit. Her mother was shot once in the forehead. Jenny Ross was strangled. The killing won't stop unless we find a way to stop them."

She slumped back down and started sobbing uncontrollably. "I don't want them to find me. I don't know anything."

"Have you used your cellphone since you've been here, or told anyone, anyone at all, where you are?"

She shook her head.

"Make sure you don't. Use one of Bebe's phones if you absolutely must call someone, but whatever you do, be careful what you say."

"I have to be at work Monday morning."

"News flash, Darling," Bebe said, "you aren't going back to that hospital until this mess gets straightened up;

you shall stay here, and that's final."

"I can't do that. They expect me there."

"We have a whole day-and-a-half to figure something out," Bebe said, "but if we haven't, you, dear child, are not going anywhere, particularly not back there."

Ajit asked, "Are you seeing anyone, boyfriend, girl-friend, anyone who's going to know you're not at home for a day or two? What about family and friends?"

"Will they go after my family?"

"No, right now they're concentrating on Paige, but we don't want your family or anyone pushing a panic button and alerting the authorities that you've gone missing."

She said she lived in a walkup, could be gone for a year, and no one would notice. No boyfriend, no social life, the only red flag would be if she missed her rotation at the hospital. Ajit said she likely wouldn't have to, but if she did, he would fix it.

Zoë was spent and Ajit and I had to get to the hospital to review the surveillance tapes. Jonathan called as we were leaving and said he needed to see me today, as soon as possible. His voice sounded drum tight, and I agreed, although didn't set an exact time because I had no idea how long I'd be with Stephen Rattner. Later was the best we came up with.

Chapter 48

Ajit and I made it to the hospital in record time. Bo had the surveillance information ready.

"Does anyone know you took these?" Ajit asked Bo. "We don't want you getting into trouble, and we don't want anyone to know we're looking at them."

"These here are copies, and only Jackie Chan over there, he know."

"Is he OK?" Ajit asked so only Bo could hear.

"Oh, he bitch and moan, but he owe me 'cause I ain't never tole immigration 'bout his sorry ass." Bo looked at Jackie and laughed, then handed Ajit a disc.

"This here's the one you be lookin' for." The label said '10th floor, right, yesterday, 1600 to 2400?' He shoved it into the DVD player.

"How long you expectin' to take?" Jackie Chan asked.

"As long as it takes," Bo said. "Keep your shirt on." He said to me, "He's jes mad 'cause he can't see his favorite show, 'cept he don't got no favorite show. He just bitchin' to hear hisself bitchin'."

The screen flickered and the DVD started. "This here's the fast forward," Bo said, "and this here one's to stop. If you need to go back hit this here one."

"Jesus Christ," Jackie Chan said and jumped up. "You think they never seen a DVD before?"

"Now, Jackie Chan, don't you go gettin' pushy and mean, or this might take all night."

Video quality, though black and white, was excellent and gave both distance and close-up shots. The first two men, who approached Therese's desk, never looked at the camera. We zoomed in for a better look, but couldn't make a positive ID. They turned and walked toward the elevators. Bo switched discs. The elevator camera got a perfect front shot. Now we knew what they looked like, but we didn't know who they were. We knew who they weren't: they weren't Vesco and Therese's killer, Dirk Palmer.

"I might be able to match them with our system," Ajit said to me. "Bo, can I take this?"

Bo said, "I don't see no disc. Jackie Chan, you see a disc?"

Jackie Chan grunted.

After a few more minutes of fast-forwarding, we found Vesco.

"I thought he was going to be the loner," I said. "I'd sure like to know who's with him."

"I'll see if I can find a match."

"They look the same; they walk the same way; they dress the same—I think they went to the same finishing school." It was probably the man in the car with Vesco when he raced away from Starbucks.

"Quantico," Ajit said. Quantico is the Marine base where FBI recruits are trained. "They look FBI."

The next face that caught my attention was Dirk Palmer's. My mind flashed back to him hitting the shorter girl and me in the washroom. He would have killed the three of us. I shivered.

"That's Palmer."

He took a closer look.

"I'll never forget that head," I said.

I pulled out my notebook and flipped through several pages.

"What are you looking for?" Ajit asked.

"I'm trying to figure out why I thought someone matching Taylor's description was the loner." I scanned my notes. "Yes, here it is. Zoë gave us the wrong information. She said a bear-like guy came in alone, and I though she meant Vesco, but it was this guy, Dirk Palmer, he's the guy who came in alone."

We went back to the point where the camera picked up Palmer and studied everything he did up until he left.

"Look, he and Therese had an argument," Ajit said. "Why didn't she tell us? She was afraid, that's why. Goddamn it, Therese, we could have saved your life."

"She didn't trust us either," I said, "unless saying her baby was a girl when she'd already told us it was a boy was supposed to tip us off."

Ajit said, "Look at the way he's waving his arms. Look at his mouth, and then look at Therese. She's shying away, looks about to cry, then she leans forward, tells him something, and points. What's she pointing at?"

"The window. Another building, possibly the Women's Hospital."

"Any sound with these?" Ajit asked Bo.

"Supposed to be," Bo said, "but what's supposed to be and what is, is different."

I said, "That might be where Therese started making things up, sending Palmer off on a wild-goose chase."

"If she pointed at the Women's Hospital, it wasn't an illogical guess."

One thing we didn't need was for them to get lucky before we got lucky. I looked at the close-up one more time.

"If that guy's real name is Dirk Palmer, I'll eat my Papakha."

"You think he's Russian? Is Praetorian Russian?"

"No, I still think Praetorian is Abner Dodge and the power he represents, but some of their hired killers could easily be Eastern European, like ex-KGB in need of a paycheck."

We fast-forwarded to 11:30. Zoë said Jessie had shown up between 11:30 and midnight. We found her; she'd arrived at 11:35. We'd missed her by ten minutes.

I dropped to Bo's tattered chair, my arms limp. I wiped at the tears that should have been in my eyes, but they were too tired to cry. How could we have been so close then and now so far away?

"At least last night I knew she was coming here. Now, I don't know where to look."

"I'm sorry, Miss," Bo said.

I got up and looked at the disc again, trying to see the man with Jessie. He seemed to know precisely where the cameras were, and made sure to stay out of range. There wasn't even a good body shot, but with the bits and pieces we were able to see, it didn't appear to be Taylor or any of the other heavyweights.

"Wait a sec," I said. "What's that?"

Ajit zeroed in for a closer look.

"Do you see it?" I asked. "Another man's shadow, there, on the wall?"

He peered over my shoulder and touched his finger to the screen, to the shadow. I wasn't crazy. That's why Jessie hadn't made a run for it; there were two of them.

I went back to my notes. Therese had described only one man, and the man on the video next to Jessie fit her description. The shadow on the wall, though probably distorted, was of a much larger man. Had Therese not seen the second man?

"It doesn't help," I said. "There's no way of knowing who they are." Now the tears that wouldn't come before easily filled my eyes. "We'll never find her."

Ajit gripped my shoulders with his powerful hands and assured me we would. I didn't want him to let go. I wanted to believe, but Jessie's trail grew colder, and I still had no idea where Brad and Abby were.

Chapter 49

Ablack Cadillac, with State Department seals on both back doors, arrived promptly at 4:00 p.m., a scant few moments after Ajit dropped me at Bebe's apartment.

Though I strode from Bebe's building with all the false confidence I could muster, I misjudged the single step down to the main sidewalk and practically fell into the arms of the young man standing smartly at attention on the curb.

"I'm Norman Barton," he said, catching me in his powerful arms. "I work for Under Secretary Rattner."

I mumbled something of an apology he either didn't hear or chose to ignore. We shook hands.

Barton was textbook CIA: close-cropped, clean-shaven, and wore a light gray suit with button down blue shirt—all that and the gun on his belt that I'd seen when he saved me from an ignominious sprawl.

I heard no communication between front and back, and the partition remained closed and visually impenetrable. That there was a driver at all was evidenced only by the fact that we pulled away from the curb and expertly negotiated our way through heavy afternoon traffic.

We arrived at the U.N. at 4:20, and had Stephen Rattner not sent Norman Barton or one of his brethren, I seriously doubt I could have navigated the security gauntlet.

Once inside, he led me to an executive office with large windows overlooking the East River. A young woman in a crisp gray pant suit, who also looked CIA, told me Under Secretary Rattner would be but a few moments, and to make myself comfortable. She disappeared leaving me alone...and not at all comfortable.

Was I being naïve? What made me think Stephen Rattner could or would help untangle the Praetorian maze, particularly if the composition of Praetorian was, as Abby suspected, corrupt senators, congressmen, and senior Pentagon officials—who's to say Rattner wasn't one of them?

I walked across to the large windows and shielded my eyes from the bright afternoon sun glaring off the East River. Several small boats buzzed around; two scows, one going up river and one going down, were being shoved along by tugboats; a sailboat, I guessed 150 feet long, knifed through the swirling green water beneath the 69th Street Bridge; a helicopter darted off from the 34th Street heliport and headed toward the Manhattan Bridge. Rather than standing here waiting for Stephen Rattner, I'd rather be on any of them, even the scows—

"Paige…"

I spun around. "Mr. Under Secretary." It had to be Rattner. Who else would know my name? Chin up, chest forward, I stepped forward and thrust out my hand. His grasp was firm and friendly. "Thank you for seeing me."

"Not at all, and please call me Stephen."

Next to tiny Amanda he seemed a giant. I guessed he was six four or five and well built, a football player came to mind. His white shirt was open at the neck and his tie slightly askew. His black oxfords glistened and his navy-colored slacks, I suspected part of a suit, were sharply creased with no tell-tale late afternoon horizontal wrinkles at the crotch or backs of the knees.

He had a great smile and his large eyes danced. A lock of stylishly long blonde hair fell lazily across his forehead and brushed an eyebrow. Amanda had erred in leaving him unattended…ever.

"I've got a bit of a problem," he said. "Although it's not an insurmountable one if you're up for another car ride. I've got to catch a helicopter downtown and don't have many minutes to spare."

NORMAN Barton, the young woman in the gray suit, and two other young men led us through a maze of internal hallways to a side exit where three black Humvees sat, each with two people in the front: a driver and passenger.

Rattner and I got into the middle Humvee. The person on the passenger side turned and asked Rattner if his plans were firm. He said they were, and the young man advised that fact to others I assumed to be in the vehicles in front of and back of ours by barking, "good to go," into his wrist radio.

"Sorry for the charade," Stephen said. "It goes this way whenever Madame Secretary is out of the country."

"I'm sufficiently intimidated and impressed," I said.

"Feel free to talk here. No one can listen, and nothing is recorded."

I had no choice except to take at face value what he said, although I did cast a glance at the two in the front seat. Stephen reached for a console, clicked a switch, and the privacy panel closed. Certainly more of the charade, but I'd come here to talk, not to worry about people listening.

I started by telling him of Bebe hiring me to write about Jenny Ross. He remained expressionless and I therefore inferred Jenny's was a name he didn't know.

Mistake number one.

"Jenny was murdered the night before I was to interview her."

He remained silent though an eyebrow inched up.

"I didn't connect my interview to Jenny's murder until I received a telephone call the next night from a young woman, who said both her life and my life were in danger from people she identified as Praetorian, the people who'd killed Jenny.

"That young woman is now fighting for her life in the intensive care ward of a local hospital. And just in case that wasn't enough to convince me, last night Praetorian kidnapped my friend and threatened her life if I don't stay away. Then today at lunch time, Praetorian tried to kill Bebe and me by running us down on the street."

He studied my face, perhaps with the same feeling of skepticism I'd first had when Penny called my room with tales of men in hot pursuit who wanted her dead.

"I know. Initially, I didn't believe it either."

"No, it's not that. I guess I'm wondering why you've approached me rather than the police."

I asked if he knew of Praetorian.

"No, why don't you tell me?"

The veins in his neck twitched, or was it my imagination? Then he leaned back like someone who knew what I was about to say, rather than someone who wanted to hear something new. Now I became certain the neck vein twitch had been a 'tell.' He'd lied. He knew of Praetorian. The next question: how much did he know?

He was too clever by far for 'cat and mouse' and I seriously doubted undoing my blouse and batting my eyelashes would give someone of his power in the 'single woman capital of the world' much more than a lukewarm tingle. I decided to tell him what I knew and fire my questions—answer or not, his option.

"Going to the police wasn't and isn't an option. Praetorian, in addition to its corrupt constituency of powerful business and legal interests, senior Pentagon people, congressmen, and senators, also has countless senior police and members of the city government on its payroll."

He leaned forward. Was he now interested, or surprised I knew as much as I'd just stated?

"What did you say Praetorian's interest is in all of this?"

"I believe Praetorian orchestrated the murder of Jenny Ross to gain control of her invention, which has been described as the 'Holy Grail' of artificial intelligence.

"I further believe Jenny threatened to prevent Praetorian from selling her invention to foreign governments hostile to the United States, or if not to prevent the sale, to at least make a lot of people aware of what Praetorian planned."

He chuckled. It was a trap. He wanted me to get angry and he'd succeeded. He wanted me to blurt out inane and stereotypical defenses that he could easily pick apart and start my brain running on 'crash and burn,' and he hadn't succeeded, though I struggled mightily to remain silent. I looked straight ahead, hoping the anger in my gut didn't communicate with my face. The next voice I warned to hear was his, except it wasn't.

"Do you know Abner Dodge?" I asked.

My question was as good as silence because I don't think he expected it, and I already knew his answer, except he would answer with a question, something else I already knew.

"What's his connection to Praetorian?"

"The young woman who told me our lives were in danger is his stepdaughter. She told me Abner Dodge is Praetorian."

Neck vein twitch, big time. A nagging fear that talking to Stephen Rattner hadn't been a totally wise decision filled my stomach. I didn't know him; I didn't know his contacts. I wasn't even certain how well Amanda knew him, at least not any more. After all, they were divorced and living apart, he high up in the rarefied air of Washington, she in New York. For all I or anyone else knew, he might be an Abner Dodge confidant, except for Dodge's reputed anti-Semitism; and I wondered how deeply those feelings ran, or was that another deception? One thing for certain, Abby would never have talked to Stephen Rattner, and on that score, I had betrayed her.

Our vehicle slowed. I feared we'd reached his destination without my discovering one way or the other if he might be of assistance. I glanced out the side window, as did he. "Brooklyn Bridge traffic," he said, as though reading my mind. "We have a few moments."

A few moments for what—more circling, more thrusting and parrying, more lying?

"What exactly is it you want me to do?" he asked.

"If I can't figure out how to stop Praetorian, I'm afraid my friend will be murdered. I need to know if there are persons of reason anywhere within in Praetorian upon whom I might prevail, with whom I might plead my friend's case. The only name I have is Abner Dodge, and if his stepdaughter and others are to be believed, he is the antithesis of the voice of reason."

"Why doesn't Praetorian come after you? I mean kidnapping your friend is all rather dramatic, but it's you they want."

"Before I answer, I want you to tell me one thing."

"I will if I can."

"Are you part of Praetorian?"

"I can't answer that?"

"Can't or won't."

"Can't and won't."

"Why doesn't that surprise me?"

"Had I said 'no' would you have believed me?"

"Probably not."

We slowed again. We had arrived at the heliport.

Barton jumped out of the lead Humvee and opened the door. Rattner signaled him to wait a moment and the door promptly closed.

"When you talked about Abner Dodge's stepdaughter, you mentioned a list of Praetorian's investors. Is it safe to assume you never received that information?"

"I can't answer that." I said.

"Can't or won't?"

"Had I said 'yes' would you have believed me?"

He grinned.

Whether he believed me or not, Praetorian had to think I had the list, otherwise my life expectancy numbered hours if not minutes.

"I will contact you," he said. "Meanwhile the more Praetorian thinks you know, the safer you and your friend will be."

"How much does Praetorian think I know?" I asked.

"You continue to believe I'm part of Praetorian?"

"You didn't deny it."

"Nor did I affirm." He paused. "My guess, and it's purely a guess, is quite a lot."

"One more question, if I may? How do I get home from here?"

He tapped on the window and Barton opened the door. "Mr. Barton will see to that, or if you are concerned, there's always a taxi or the subway. Either way, you have my word you will arrive safely."

That should have been comforting. It wasn't.

Chapter 50

Although Stephen Rattner was a dangerous person because of his power, I decided he could be trusted, or perhaps I decided I wanted to trust him, and I opted for Norman Barton and the Cadillac as my mode of transportation. This time, though, Barton got in front with the driver and left me alone in the back surrounded by my thoughts and a lot of dark glass.

I started to think now that Stephen Rattner had left me dangling and nothing else was getting me close to Praetorian and Jessie, the powerful connections of Jonathan's firm were fast becoming my last, best chance. But, and it was a big but, though I was sure Jonathan would do all in his power to make his father available to me, would his father want to help?

Talking to Cameron Black began to seem like another possibility. By all accounts, he wasn't stupid. He had to know who had set him up and why.

Though I continued to suspect that whatever I said in the back seat of a State Department vehicle would be listened to and recorded, establishing a time and place to meet Jonathan hardly seemed information that would mobilize a vast force of men and women in flak jackets carrying assault weapons.

Besides, I had the distinct feeling that Barton was under orders to do more than accompany me safely back to Bebe's apartment, and wherever and whenever Jonathan and I decided to meet would soon be known by many people.

Truth be known, I didn't want anyone following me around reporting everything I did to groups of faceless jackals that wanted only to feed off my carcass, although in present circumstances and given a choice between Lynch, Praetorian or the CIA, I would have opted for the latter.

Still, when Jonathan answered, I told him that beyond setting a time and place to meet we shouldn't say anything because I feared my telephones had been tapped.

He suggested I come to his office.

I asked if I could talk to his father and when he said his father wasn't there, I asked him to meet me at the steakhouse bar on Third and 49ᵗʰ. Besides knowing it well, it offered two advantages: lots of people, and it was not a venue of Jonathan's choosing. Not that Jonathan frightened me, but after Stephen Rattner and the CIA, I needed the comfort of a familiar place with real people.

THE BAR was over half full, not so many as to rob us of the ability to have a discreet conversation yet enough for protection should I need it, though from whom or what I didn't know—Jonathan? I seriously believed I could physically best him if he tried anything.

I claimed two stools, ordered vodka on ice, and dug my notebook from my bag. Jonathan arrived a few minutes later. In between 'hello' and 'how are you,' he ordered a martini that he practically gulped down, and then gripped the edge of the bar until his knuckles whitened. He seemed to be trying to think through the best way to say whatever it was he was about to say.

After what seemed a long moment, he blurted out, "Cameron's been arrested for Jenny's murder."

I told him I'd heard.

"Whatever you think, he didn't do it."

"Whoa, big boy, slow down, I'm on your side."

He tried to grin.

"Have you seen him?"

"Twice this morning, with Anne the first time—what a disaster, with Anne seesawing between rage and fits of sobbing."

"What did he say?"

"I asked him a few questions. He wouldn't answer."

"You said you saw him twice?"

"About two hours later I went alone and bumped into Tatiana Marchand—the lawyer to whom I referred Jenny?"

"Yes, I remember her name." I'd never asked him about the luncheon meeting he'd had with Tatiana and Cameron—another time.

"She told me if I was smart, rather than ask a bunch of stupid questions, I'd listen because Cameron had plenty to say."

A group of three men and three women got up from their seats at the far end of the bar, and bumped and sidled past. Several said, "Excuse me, our table's ready." One guy brushed his arm against my breasts. Not an accident. "You're welcome," I said. His date or wife turned and glared. Screw you lady, and good luck.

I turned back to Jonathan.

"Cameron wasn't as talkative as Tatiana had led me to believe he might be. In fact, he remained surly, but he did tell me if I seriously wanted to know why he'd been stuck in jail, to talk to my father, to find out for myself what was going on."

Was Jonathan's father part of Praetorian as Abby had said? Is that what Cameron wanted Jonathan to find out?

"Immediately after I left, I went to see my father."

He took another few sips of his martini as if needing time to organize his thoughts again.

I felt like giving him a poke. "What happened?"

"At some level, I think my father might be involved, or know who is."

"Involved in what?" I began to wonder if Jonathan even knew of Praetorian.

"I'm not entirely sure. He fired two files across his desk: one was labeled Hebrides and contained the documents I'd prepared; the other was labeled The Praetorian File."

My heart skipped several beats.

"What was in Praetorian's file?"

Would it tell me who'd murdered Jenny Ross? I saw poor Abby's battered and broken body. Would it tell me who tried to kill her? I felt the nausea of seeing Therese lying in a pool of blood, her blouse ripped open, the burns on her breasts, her eyes bulging out, and the bullet hole in the center of her forehead. Would it tell me who murdered and tortured her?

I thought of the man in the bathroom at The New School. I felt his disgusting hands touch my body. I thought of the old woman with Therese's baby tucked under her arm trying to escape. Would it tell me who they were? Would it tell me how to find Vesco? I thought of Bebe and me outside the bistro. Would it tell me who tried to run us down?

Most of all, I heard Jessie's screams. Would it tell me how to save Jessie?

"There were only old news clippings dating back to the Regan Administration."

My energy slipped away.

"What in God's name have a bunch of old clippings to do with anything? What were they?"

"They were about Iran Contra and Oliver North, and I don't know what they have to do with anything. I can only think there's more information, that the file was a history lesson of sorts."

"Didn't your father have an explanation?"

"Unfortunately—"

I so didn't want to hear that word. I'd heard enough 'unfortunatelys' and 'I don't knows' to last me several lifetimes.

"—I was only part way through when Pennington Jasper called him to a meeting, and a Pennington Jasper call is several notches above a call from God."

"And you honestly don't know what Praetorian is?"

"As near as I can figure, it was the group that secretly funded the Iran Contras, and was dismantled when

Oliver North and others went to prison."

I said, "It might have been dismantled, but it wasn't killed. Praetorian continues to exist, and continues to be involved in a lot of nasty business like political assassinations, arms smuggling, overthrowing third-world regimes, and creating civil wars."

He gave me a look I'm sure was mostly reserved for the mentally damaged.

"Praetorian is the secret investor in Hebrides, and I believe it intends to sell Jenny's invention to the highest bidder, likely a government that is an enemy of the U.S.. I think Jenny tried to stop them, and that's what got her killed."

His mouth asked, "Is this true?" His face still said, 'you're crazy.'

"I have no proof, no one has; but I think Cameron has it figured out, and that's what he wants you to discover: that he had nothing to do with Jenny's murder; that Praetorian murdered Jenny and set him up."

I could tell his mind had gone into overdrive.

I asked, "Can you get me in to see Cameron? I need to find out what he knows."

"I doubt he'll tell you."

The back of my neck got warm. "I'm sure I can get into see him on my own if you don't want to help."

"It's not that."

"What then?"

"I don't want him talking to anyone until the charges against him are dropped."

Now the back of my neck got hot. "Listen, don't get prissy on me. This is your non-conformist friend, Cameron Black, we're talking about. Neither you nor anyone else can control what he says. Besides, it sounds as though you haven't had much success."

"If I get you in to see him will you tell me what he says?"

"What if I say no?"

The expression on his face tried to be a grin, but became a frown.

"Fine, I'll do this on my own." I pushed off the stool and started for the door.

"No...I..."

I stopped and said back to him, "In fact, it would be more useful to me if you had your discussion with your father. Find out everything he knows about Praetorian because there's a whole lot you don't know. Jenny and Hebrides and Cameron only scratch the surface."

I turned and strode toward the door. Outside I raised my arm to hail a cab.

"Paige, please let's not do this."

I spun around. He had followed me outside.

"At least let Barry drive you."

A cab whipped to the curb and stopped. I reached for the door.

"Please, I'm sorry for being a shit. I'll get you in to see him."

I turned to face him. "No strings."

The cabbie rolled his window down. "Miss, you coming?"

"No strings," Jonathan said.

I threw the cabbie a five. "Sorry. I just got a better offer."

"I'll ride with you as far as my office," Jonathan said, "I want to hear everything you know about Praetorian—unless you'd sooner be alone, in which case I can easily grab a cab."

"I'm not that mad."

Besides, the more he knew before he talked to his father, the better.

Chapter 51

Along the way to Jonathan's office, I decided as soon as Jonathan and I parted company, I would call Ajit and have him meet me at the precinct. Jonathan may or may not get me in to see Cameron. Ajit would.

Meanwhile, I didn't have much time to arm him with Praetorian information, and started by saying, "Before I tell what else I've learned about Praetorian, I want you to understand that a lot of it is hearsay, albeit informed hearsay, and some of that hearsay says your father might be involved."

He studied me for a long moment, and then said, "If, as you imply, Praetorian was responsible for Jenny's murder and is involved in illegal activities, I can deny without fear of contradiction, from any quarter, that my father is not involved. He is ethical to a fault."

"Then I apologize, but please don't let that color your opinion of what else I am about to say."

"No need to apologize, and I won't."

"The young woman I met on the street the night we had dinner was Abby Dodge, and Abner Dodge sits at the pinnacle of Praetorian."

"You're not serious."

"Yes, very."

He said, "I have to tell you that I thought Abby had disappeared from the face of the earth—there were reports that she'd committed suicide. Then yesterday, it's all over the TV and papers that her SUV was found abandoned in the New Jersey Meadowlands, and Abner Dodge was offering a big reward for her safe return. Say what you will about Abner Dodge, he's been extremely tolerant and generous when it comes to Abby."

I seriously wanted to hit him. "Why do you say that?"

"It's no secret that Abby was a wild and troubled teenager: alcohol, drugs, I even heard prostitution. At

some point, maybe five years ago, the papers were full
of a big blackmail scheme whereby she tried to get Abner Dodge to pay her a million dollars."

"Would you like to know the truth?"

He looked askance in a way that told me his version
was the truth.

"Five years ago Dodge raped Abby—that's why she
left home."

"I don't believe it."

"Believe it. And let me tell you the truth about Abby
and drugs, alcohol and prostitution: to totally discredit
her in case she ever decided to point fingers, Abner
Dodge got her hooked on drugs and alcohol, then
pushed her into prostitution as a means to support her
newly acquired habits."

"I—"

"Let me finish. Then in a final act of kindness he
manufactured the blackmail scheme and sent a battery of
paparazzi to splash the story across the front pages."

"I really can't believe this. I mean, I believe you believe what you're telling me, and it well may be true, but
you have to admit it is rather unbelievable."

"This is Abner Dodge I'm talking about. The one you
and others call the 'head shark.'"

"Yes, I know, but this, this is way beyond head shark.
Praetorian I can almost believe, but rape and the other
things…I mean, Abby and I practically grew up together
—I would never have suspected."

"Too bad for Abby that no one had the balls to check,
no one believed in her, no one dared take Dodge on."

"I know that's aimed at my father and me. I have no
excuse for not finding out the truth except youth and ignorance. I can't speak for my father except to say he ab-
hors all that Abner Dodge stands for, and I can only assume he saw no reason to investigate. You can call that
ignorance too, if you wish."

"Though abhorrent, he seems to get invited to cocktail parties," I said. It was a low blow, but I was having difficulty figuring out how so many continued to embrace an individual so hated.

"That, I can assure you, was orchestrated entirely by Pennington Jasper. My father has not voluntarily socialized with Abner Dodge for ten years."

"I don't recall seeing Pennington Jasper."

"He came after we left. Mr. Jasper usually times his arrivals to coincide with every one else's departures—some say he records the names of those who left before he arrived."

"Eccentric?"

"That may be kind. The stories about Pennington Jasper are legion."

We were silent for a moment until I said, "I'd like to get back to Abby."

"Yes, sorry, do you know where she is? The news says only that she's missing."

"She's not missing, and Abner Dodge knows she isn't because he sent someone to kill her early Friday morning."

A look of disbelief again lodged on his face.

"Believe me, it's true. I saw her."

"Where is she?"

"At the moment, I don't know, but, if she is still alive, she's safe."

"You mean she might be dead?"

"I hope and pray not, although when I saw her, it was touch and go."

He shook his head. His shock appeared genuine.

I continued, "Two days ago someone tried to run Bebe and me down while we stood on the sidewalk. They missed us, but killed a woman who just happened to be in the wrong place at the wrong time."

"I saw that on the news—the one in front of the bistro. Are you sure it was meant for you?"

"A man phoned immediately after to tell me next

time I wouldn't be so lucky. Is that sure enough?"

"This is all so insane."

"There's more. Last night, Praetorian kidnapped a young woman named Jessie McArdle, Abby's and my best friend, because they believe Jessie knows where Abby is. They told me they would let Jessie go when they had Abby."

"And you honestly believe Abner Dodge and Praetorian are responsible?"

"Are you certain you and your father aren't involved in Praetorian? You seem doggedly unwilling to accept that Dodge is capable of treason and murder on the scale of Praetorian."

"As to my father, I don't know what he knows about Praetorian, but I do know he isn't part of it. He's not involved in murder and arms dealing and selling secrets to hostile governments."

We arrived at the Time Warner complex. Jonathan got out and stood with the door open.

He said, "As to Dodge, while I'm still having trouble believing what he did to Abby, I don't doubt for a moment that he is fully capable of masterminding Praetorian. And as to my dogged unwillingness, I intend to immediately discuss Praetorian and Dodge with my father, and you can be assured I'll have both barrels loaded not with birdshot but with cannon shot."

Bravo, but will he do it? He closed the door. I rolled the window down.

"Call me if you want to talk to my father," he said. "Though you may remain apprehensive about his relationship with Dodge, my father isn't the one you need worry about."

The limo pulled away with the two of us looking at each other, perhaps he, like me, wondering what more we could have or should have said.

Chapter 52

After leaving Jonathan, I contacted Ajit, and he was waiting in his car in front of the precinct when I arrived.

"Fancy taxi," he said, hopping from the Ferrari. He glanced at the limo's plate, WINTHROP-1, as Barry pulled away. "Why do I know that name?"

"A law firm Bebe uses," I lied. I didn't want to get into the whole Jonathan thing. "Thanks for coming."

"Glad for the break—looking at pictures of Russians with big heads and brush cuts only goes so far."

"Nothing?"

"If they haven't quit their jobs, I've still got a few people still searching."

"What about the old woman and the guy in the bathroom?"

"The guy in the bathroom's still in St. Vincent's. The old woman is at the 6th Precinct. Neither has volunteered any information."

We started inside. I felt uneasy and told Ajit I hoped I didn't meet up with Lynch and friends. He assured me Lynch was off duty and his friends wouldn't do anything other than tell Lynch I'd been there.

After Ajit cleared me to see Cameron, and a police officer led me to a room with gray walls, ceiling, and floor. Nothing like making depressed people feel more depressed.

A ceiling-to-floor Plexiglas panel that I assumed was bulletproof ran down the center, with a metal shelf and chair on each side. The room was humid and smelled of stale cigarette smoke and human agony. I sat uneasily on the metal chair, and couldn't help but wonder how many thousands of downtrodden behinds had sat there before.

A door opened on the other side and Cameron, dressed in orange prison garb shuffled in, trying to see who wanted so desperately to see him. He smiled because he saw an attractive woman, not because he recognized me. To my knowledge, he'd never seen me before.

He sat opposite and picked up the headset. The guard told us we had ten minutes, and left.

"To what do I owe the pleasure?" he said.

I understood why the great Cameron Black mesmerized Jonathan and Peter. He had a swagger, a wayward mass of dark brown curls, his blue eyes grabbed and held on to everything they touched, and his white teeth sparkled from a full, confident mouth. His skin was golden brown as only the skin of the rich can be; his arms were muscular and his body trim. I took a deep breath and swallowed.

"I'm Paige Harrington."

His eyes flickered, signaling brain reaction.

"Yes, that Paige Harrington, the one who talked to Tatiana, the one doing a story on Jenny Ross and Hebrides. I need to ask you a few questions."

"What makes you think I have anything to say, particularly to you?"

"Jonathan Winthrop, whom I've gotten to know, thinks you should," I lied. "And Peter Zane is one of my oldest and dearest friends. Neither they nor I think you had anything to do with Jenny's murder; we think Praetorian set you up."

"Gee, you think?"

"Yeah we do, and before you start feeling too sorry for yourself, Praetorian tried to kill Abby Dodge, and kidnapped a friend of Abby's, who also happens to be my best friend—they've threatened to kill her also."

He studied me for a moment. "And you want me to tell you all about Praetorian so you can march out and rescue your friend."

"That's exactly what I want, although I might be able to help you in the process."

He forced a hateful, mean laugh. "I don't know what magic you think you possess or what power you think you have, although in the unlikely event we do have anything to say to each other, I would suggest we whisper so the big ears in this human garbage dump don't hear."

I nodded.

"What do you know about Praetorian?" he asked.

I quickly told him Abby's story, including her relationship to Abner Dodge.

He asked, "What do you know about Abner Dodge?"

"Only the little I've been told, by Abby and others."

"Let me put him in perspective," he said. "Abner Dodge is the most sinister and powerful person in New York City. He is the least sinister and powerful person in Praetorian."

"I thought he headed it up."

He laughed. "Praetorian can't be stopped. Praetorian destroys whomever or whatever it chooses, and that includes individuals as powerful as Dodge. Do you understand?"

I nodded.

"When they decide the time is right, you and your friend will be destroyed just like Jenny and Abby, only it sounds as though Abby wasn't so lucky if she's still alive, because now she has to die again."

I heard a hollow sound in my ears when I swallowed, and my throat hurt.

"I can't stop trying," I said.

"Then you are more naïve than you appear. I'm in here for murdering Jenny. It doesn't matter that I didn't, and it won't matter if I hire the best lawyers in the world. I'm going to jail for a long time where one of my soon to be new best friends will stick something sharp into my innards, and I'll die not because people like me represent everything the people in here detest, but because Praetorian will make it happen."

"I don't think you're as brave as you sound."

He forced the same hateful, mean laugh that this time made me mad.

"In fact, I think you're full of it. I think that despite your bravado, you are scared to death. I think you've given up. Praetorian isn't that powerful. It might like to think it is, but it isn't. You're not thinking clearly so you've bought into the bullshit. If you want to get out of this mess, start thinking like you're going to get out, or else you're right, you'll soon be dead."

"Who the hell are you?"

We were no longer whispering.

"I'm someone who's going to find her friend. I'm someone who isn't going to let Praetorian win. Who the hell are you? You can't be the Cameron Black Peter and Jonathan can't stop talking about. That Cameron Black might be a lot of things, but I didn't hear quitter, and I didn't hear coward."

A door opened and the guard walked in. Cameron leapt up and screamed into the receiver, "Listen, bitch, I'll tell you who I am: I'm a guy who never wants to see your ass in here again." Then he smashed the receiver against the divider.

I jumped back. I felt my eyes grow big and my stomach lodge in my throat. I dropped the handset back into its holder. The guard grabbed Cameron and shoved him from the visitor's room. At the door, Cameron wrenched free and shouted an obscenity that looked like, 'Fuck You.' The guard gave him a final vicious shove that sent him sprawling into the hallway behind the visitor's room.

I stood for a moment, fighting to stop shaking, to collect my thoughts, and to figure out what had triggered his sudden rage. Then I spun around and left. I don't remember if I ran or walked, but it didn't take me long.

WHEN I rejoined Ajit, he could see I was upset and

asked if I wanted to talk. I told him 'yes' but not here.

He took my arm and led me outside. I called Jonathan to tell him he was right, that Cameron didn't have much to say to me, that I'd take him up on his offer to talk to his father. He didn't answer. I left a message on his voicemail.

Ajit wanted to know what Jonathan had to do with Praetorian.

I told him about Jonathan and that, although I had no proof, I believed neither he nor his father nor the Jasper Winthrop firm had anything to do with Praetorian.

I added, "It's probably insane, but I need to talk to Praetorian to find out what they want from me that will save Jessie's life. All my other attempts have failed— Dodge is the only one left, and I'm going to ask Winthrop Senior to help me. If Dodge has a peer in this city, someone he might listen to, it's him."

"Isn't that placing a lot of trust in a person you don't really know?"

"If Abner Dodge and Praetorian are as powerful as I and Cameron Black and everyone else thinks they are, then I'm in no more danger sitting across the desk from Abner Dodge and Jonathan Winthrop Senior than I am sitting here. There is no place I can hide."

He turned off Central Park West and headed into the park. In a few moments we'd be at Bebe's.

He asked, "Do you want to talk about what happened back there with Cameron Black?"

I didn't, though I knew it would help get it off my chest.

"You mean how he called me a bitch and tried to smack me in the face with the telephone."

"I'm sorry you had to go through that—I should have warned you that it happens more often than not. A lot of anger and feelings of betrayal and helplessness are present in that room, feelings often manifested through outbursts of violence and rage."

"Don't apologize—I should have been smart enough to know the guards and Plexiglas panel weren't there for aesthetic reasons."

"They have a purpose."

"Yes, and you're probably going to wonder if it's crazy, though now that I think about it more, I believe it was all staged. I believe Cameron has more he wants to tell me, but not directly. I believe he was trying to tell me to stay away, to send a messenger."

"Paige, you have to understand something: from the moment I met you, I stopped wondering if anything in which you're involved is crazy."

I squeezed his arm and said, "Thank you."

"I'll talk to him if you want."

"I appreciate that, but there are only two people he trusts. One is Jonathan, who wears an attorney-client confidentiality crown of thorns. The other is my good friend, Peter Zane. Peter and I were at Columbia together—maybe you know him—and somewhere along the way, he and Cameron became fast friends, although Peter has done time for financial fraud and will likely need clearance."

Ajit didn't know Peter, although on my say-so he did promise to get him in to see Cameron.

Chapter 53

I phoned Peter to let him know I'd arranged for him to see Cameron, although I first needed to tell him about my intriguing jailhouse visit. He was with Dee and Amanda at the Apthorpe, and Ajit and I made a fast detour. I phoned Bebe to tell her of our change in plans, mostly hoping, wishing, and praying she might have news of Jessie. She didn't.

We were four blocks from the Apthorpe when Amanda, in a state of high anxiety even for her, called, telling us Vesco had returned and had taken Ed for a walk, and that Dee and Peter were following. She had Dee on her other phone. Vesco had gone to Starbucks on 81st Street, where we'd lost him before.

I didn't want Vesco to spot me and disappear again, so I told Amanda we were heading for Riverside Drive. Amanda said Peter would meet us at Dee's apartment.

PETER was already in the lobby when we arrived. I introduced Ajit, and Peter shepherded us to the elevators. Ajit said he'd wait in the lobby, but Peter wouldn't hear of it.

We declined his drink offer. Peter grabbed a beer. Then Ajit changed his mind and had a beer also. Male bonding. That made Peter happy.

Never one to rush into the task at hand, Peter ushered us toward the west facing windows of the living room. For a moment, we stood and looked at the millions of twinkling lights across the black and mighty Hudson.

"New Jersey looks pretty good...at night," Peter chuckled.

I wondered how many times he'd used that line.

He motioned us toward the huge overstuffed sofa and sat kitty-corner in a matching chair.

"So tell me, you saw old Blackie, how is he holding

up?"

"You don't seem all that concerned." Why did that surprise me? Nothing concerned Peter.

"Jeez Pager, it's just hard to imagine him in jail for murder—I mean drunk and disorderly is one thing, but murder, and Jenny of all people—never happened, never!"

"Well, you're right; he didn't murder anyone. He's in jail because a secret society known as Praetorian set him up."

His forehead wrinkled into a question mark.

"Praetorian is the secret investor in Anne's company, Hebrides, Inc."

"What has that got to do with Blackie? He's never had anything to do with Anne and her business."

"I don't know. Praetorian controls a lot of evil power and doesn't explain its actions to anyone."

He remained silent, studying and turning the beer bottle in his hands.

I asked, "What about money? You said before that Cameron gambled big time. Could it be that Praetorian loaned him money he didn't or couldn't repay?"

"No way—one phone call to his daddy, and his money problems are solved."

Ajit's cellphone rang. He looked at the number and said, "Excuse me. I need to take this."

"Sure," Peter said, as though Ajit planned to take the call in our presence.

"I think he'd like some privacy," I said.

"Oh, right, sorry. Yeah, use the den down the hall on the right, or you can use the terrace. Nice night. See more of New Jersey."

Ajit opted for the terrace and stepped outside.

I asked Peter how well he knew Anne.

"She doesn't like me much. Told Blackie she doesn't want me hanging around him and their friends. She figures I lead Blackie astray, bad influence and all that."

"Well, I can't blame her for thinking that, but she strikes me as a first class snob, so I wouldn't worry too much."

He chuckled.

"Have you ever heard of Tatiana Marchand?"

"You get around. How'd you meet Tits Marchand?"

"How nice?"

"Hey don't kill the messenger—that's what everyone calls her."

"She's a lawyer friend of a lawyer friend who thought she and Cameron might have a bit of a thing going."

He laughed.

"Why? Is that so crazy? She's a smart, attractive woman, and more than a little sexy, the kind I should think Cameron would find attractive."

"That may be true, except I have it on good authority that Tatiana found Anne more alluring and the feeling wasn't exclusive."

"You mean they're lovers?"

"That's what I hear."

"I thought Anne was the greatest in Cameron's eyes."

"She probably is, although he's no longer the wind in her sails. That ship sailed a long time ago."

If Anne and Tatiana were lovers, that cast everything in a very different light. Had they schemed to steal Jenny's stock? Maybe they saw it as a way to finance a life of luxury together, absent Cameron and his enigmatic billions. Then why didn't Jonathan know or at least suspect what was going on?

"Do you think Anne is capable of murder?"

"Ho! That bitch is capable of anything. If there was money to be made, Anne would murder her own mother, and the story on the street is that tons of money is involved. All she ever wanted from Blackie was his money—that's what I tried to tell Blackie and anyone else who would listen."

I wasn't totally convinced. Even if Anne and Tatiana had murdered Jenny to get her stock, I was certain they hadn't tried to kill Abby, and had nothing to do with murdering Therese and her mother, kidnapping Jessie and coming after Bebe and me—that was all Praetorian.

It made more sense to think that Anne agreed to sell Hebrides to Praetorian and Jenny said no, so Praetorian murdered her knowing that Anne inherited the stock.

"Do you think you can get Cameron to name names? Is there a person or persons he thinks murdered Jenny and set him up?"

"If I ask, he'll tell what he knows."

"You'll have to be careful. He's convinced that Praetorian has spies everywhere, and he's probably right."

"Just tell me how to ask the question so I don't end up in an adjoining cell. I'm starting to like it here." He sipped his beer and his eyes took in the elegant surroundings. "And I already know I'm not good inmate material."

"I'll think of something."

Ajit returned and asked me if we might speak privately. Peter stood and reeled down the hall, saying he had to use the little boy's room. Peter wasn't drunk; he just had a faulty gyroscope.

When we heard the bathroom door close, Ajit said, "That was a detective from the Sixth Precinct. As you suspected, the woman is Russian, an illegal."

"What is an illegal Russian immigrant doing walking Vesco's dog? Do you think he's illegal also?"

"When you talked to Vesco, did you detect an accent?"

"Yeah, Brooklyn or the Bronx maybe, but not Russian."

"The old woman says she doesn't know anything about the man who chased you into the school."

"That makes no sense," I said. "I saw him come out of the basement."

"Well, he remains comatose."

"Do you think it time for a few of your friends to talk to Vesco?"

"Where is he?"

I called Amanda. Vesco was still in Starbucks. Ajit made another call, and then said he had to leave to meet the two detectives who were already on their way.

Peter wandered back from the hallway and wanted to know what was going on. I told him Ajit was a cop and had to leave to meet a couple of colleagues.

Peter eyed Ajit partly with suspicion and partly with awe.

Ajit headed for the door. "Thanks for your help," he said to Peter. "Do you need to walk me down?"

"No," Peter said. "They let anyone out." He walked Ajit to the door. "Getting in's the problem. Took a month before they'd let me in without clearing with Dee."

I called after Ajit. He said he'd let me know when it was safe for me to put in an appearance, and disappeared into the hallway.

"Good man," Peter said. "Good man."

"I've known him only a few days, but I trust him, almost as much as I trust you."

"You've known me longer."

"You mean I should know better by now."

He chuckled.

"I like Dee. I hope it works out between you."

He shrugged. "Yeah, she's a good person, smart, rich—all the things I'm not."

"Don't forget sexy and beautiful."

"Yeah, that too."

"Listen, are we squared away on Cameron? You know what I want?"

"Yeah, just need your laundry list." He tapped his fingers on the table. "Don't forget to come and visit if I get arrested."

I looked at him. "Do that again."

"What?"

"That, the finger tapping."

"Sorry," he said. "It's an old navy habit."

"That's it."

"What?"

"I just figured out how you're going to communicate with Cameron."

He looked curious.

"Morse code—didn't you tell me that you and Cameron communicated bridge and poker hands in the navy?"

"We'd be rusty, but it could work. I think I remember enough. Blackie's probably about the same as me. Yeah, it could work."

He looked excited about the idea.

"How soon tomorrow can you see him? Timing is way past becoming critical."

"You want to come with me?"

"I'd love to, but I don't think that would be wise. I think Cameron was trying to warn me to stay away. Besides, given what the two of you have to do, it will work better if you're alone."

He looked at his watch. "What's the earliest they'll let me in, without getting arrested, that is.?" He chuckled.

"You won't think it funny when you see Cameron."

"Just nerves—police stations and jails scare me more than most things; don't forget, I've been more than an overnight guest."

"I should say I'm sorry, though I heard you deserved it."

"Yeah, I had it coming."

He'd never told me a lot of the detail concerning his eighteen-month incarceration. It's the only thing from his past that seemed an embarrassment. I'd heard it had something to do with money laundering and mail fraud.

"I'll check visiting times with Ajit."

"Earlier the better for me," he said. "I think Dee has me slotted in for brunch with some of her friends."

He'd changed. The Peter of old wouldn't have gone to a brunch to save his soul. No, that's not true; the Peter of old didn't get invited to many brunches because he usually misbehaved after a few drinks or showed up already three sheets to the wind. To him, brunch existed as a socially acceptable excuse to have booze with breakfast.

Ajit called moments later to say that the two detectives arrested Vesco and had taken him to the mid-town precinct. Ajit wanted to meet at the Apthorpe.

Peter put his drink down. "I'm coming with you. Dee's there. I should walk her home."

"I'm impressed. Someone has managed to domesticate Peter Zane."

"Nah, just want to see the Apthorpe's courtyard again. One of a kind."

"B.S."

He grinned.

WE MET at Amanda's apartment. Ajit arranged to get Peter in to see Cameron at ten, and then Ajit and I left.

When I de-Ferraried in front of Bebe's building, Ajit took my hand, his warm brown skin against my cold white skin. I felt a stirring inside. I wanted him to take me into his arms. I needed him to make love to me. I looked into his sad, dark eyes that reached deep within my soul. Was he thinking the same?

Then his police radio buzzed, ending the possibility and the idea. I stepped to the curb and watched him roar away up the avenue.

Chapter 54

I stood on the sidewalk for a few moments, trying to fight off the web of frustration that wanted to wrap me in its steel-like threads. I wouldn't admit defeat. I would find Jessie. When Ajit's taillights vanished from view, I went inside. The doorman touched the tips of his fingers to his cap. "I've let Miss Morgan know you're on your way up, Miss Harrington."

I crossed to the elevator, my feet feeling encased in lead. I needed several hours of uninterrupted sleep to recharge my resolve and hoped Bebe and Zoë were already in bed.

Zoë was; Bebe wasn't, and Dalton Croft was there. For a brief moment, my heart soared thinking he had news of Jessie, but Bebe's look said he didn't, and my interest in whatever he had to say ceased.

Worse, Bebe announced she was going to bed.

When Dalton reached for his briefcase I emitted a long, silent groan.

Despite it being almost midnight, he was dressed as though he might be fresh from the pages of GQ, particularly his suede loafers.

After we shook hands, he smiled with all his teeth. Bebe said goodnight and disappeared down the hall. Her bedroom door banged shut, and I started to wonder if they'd had a spat.

"She's tired," Dalton said.

"She's not alone," I said, hoping he'd get the message. "I hope you haven't been waiting long."

"Not at all, and I'm sorry for not calling, although in my defense, I didn't know until awhile ago that I wanted to see you."

"Why is that?"

"I didn't get the information on Praetorian I want to share with you until after 8:00, and I'll be away until

Monday so I didn't want to wait."

Hearing Praetorian made my ears perk up and the weariness drain from my body.

"Praetorian is an offshore company registered in Vanuatu, some God-forsaken island about three-quarters of the way between Hawaii and Australia, the point of the exercise being, apart from avoiding taxes, to hide its ownership from the peering, prying eyes of world."

Dear God, please have him spare me the minutiae. "Yes but who owns Praetorian?"

"Now that is the question, isn't it?"

"Yes, it is—I already know it's an offshore company."

"Alas, Praetorian was created by people who don't want their identities known."

Now I became weary again and angry. "I can't believe you rushed over here late Friday night to tell me two things you knew I already know?"

His face flushed. "I came here to make certain you understand the extent to which people like Praetorian's owners might go to remain invisible."

"How is that different from other off-shore companies?"

"Quite different, if, as you speculated earlier this afternoon, Praetorian murdered Jenny, kidnapped Jessie and had Cameron jailed. Other offshore companies, at least those I've worked with, haven't resorted to such draconian measures."

"No, I suppose not."

"No supposition involved Paige. Clearly, these aren't people who will take kindly to having daylight shine on their activities, let alone being identified in your story."

"Well everyone can stop worrying because I can't prove a thing. Whoever set up Praetorian did his job well."

"Because of the questions it would raise, they won't want Praetorian mentioned either."

"Then we have a problem—Praetorian is part of my story."

"For your safety, I strongly suggest you leave it out, or refer to it as an offshore company rather than by name."

"I'll think about it." Though he and I both knew that Praetorian was going into my story unless Bebe over-ruled, and he and I both knew she wouldn't.

"I hope you do. I'm worried that anything you write will extend to Bebe, and I wouldn't be able to survive if something happened to her."

"That's not fair, and you know it. If I choose not to write a word, Bebe will hire another writer and insist that Praetorian be a part of the story, so if you insist on playing the guilt card, you'd better play it on Bebe."

He fluffed up like a little bird and made 'getting ready to leave' motions.

"I'm sorry," I said. "I didn't mean to lash out it's just that I'm frightened for Jessie and keep hoping to learn that she's safe. When I saw you here with Bebe I thought you'd come to tell me you'd found Jessie. To find out otherwise is depressing."

"Fair enough, and just so we understand each other, I worry about both you and Bebe. I don't want anything to happen to either of you."

Then he let out a deep breath and glanced at his watch. "My goodness, will you look at the time?"

He closed his case, and I walked him to the door.

"Thank you for not making me wait until next week," I said.

"I do hope you will reflect carefully on all I said and help Bebe make the right decision."

I forced a smile, and closed the door as he turned and strode down the hallway.

Chapter 55

Bebe lay propped on her bed amid a mountain of silk cushions and scattered work papers. She peered at me over the tops of her reading glasses.

"He's gone," I said, "though for the time being I've lost any hope of finding sleep. You up for a run?"

"Darling, are you mad? The only running this good little Jewish girl has ever done involves chasing after a good man, although lately you can draw a line through good."

"Dalton's not so bad, once you get past the lawyer part."

"There's always a catch."

I chuckled and turned for the door.

"Oh," she said, twirling her glasses, "please stay out of the park. I don't want to leave this wonderful repose to traipse off to some morgue to identify your battered body. We've had quite enough of that to last us a good long while."

"Thanks. That's just what I need, but don't worry, I know the pathways."

I crept down the hallway to my room, past Zoë's door that sat ajar. Her heavy breathing emanated from the darkness.

I changed into a pair of jogging shorts and a heavier pair of sneakers designed for running. On my way out, I hesitated when I heard a noise, and then decided it had to be Bebe going to the bathroom.

I entered Central Park at 79th just below the Metropolitan Museum and followed the well-lighted footpath west toward the Great Lawn. The presence of other late-night joggers kept me from feeling isolated or afraid.

After a few moments, my legs felt more limber and I increased my pace, my long legs shooting out in front, my white sneakers flashing semaphore-like against the blacktop. I passed several men, who innately increased their speed. One pulled alongside.

"Want company?"

I looked at him trying to decide if I wanted to run alone or if I wanted a buddy, which might be wise given the time of night. He ran easily and hadn't squeezed out his words between gasps. His muscles rippled and his skin glistened with perspiration. He wasn't a gaunt distance runner, rather a finely sculpted athlete.

"Think you can keep up?"

White teeth flashed from his handsome black face. "You run well, better than most, but I'm in shape. If I fall back, keep going."

"This is my pace."

"Suits me—it feels right."

We ran silently for a half-mile, our sneakers touching the asphalt with a muted sound like brushes on a drum.

"You run here regularly?" I asked.

"When I'm in the city. You?"

"I've been traveling more lately," I said.

"I'm from Jamaica. My name is Bob."

I had already guessed from the musical lilt in his voice that he was either Jamaican or Trinidadian. "Paige."

"Your accent tells me you're not from here."

"No, Canada originally."

We reached the Great Lawn. "This is as far as I go," I said.

"I'll go back with you. I've had enough, also."

"I'm glad you decided to keep me company. I thought more would be out."

"Saturday night is often quiet," he said. "Too many parties."

"It's eerily quiet."

"It is," he said, "but I've never seen any trouble in this section."

Women knew better. Trouble happened everywhere

in the park, rarely, but everywhere. We headed back toward Fifth, both of us still running easily. I increased the pace.

"You didn't ask me what I do," he said as we started back.

"If you want me to know, you'll tell."

"I don't want you to know, but my boss does."

A prickle of fear crept across my skin.

"I work for Abner Dodge."

Boom, boom, boom, my heart thumped in my ears. Maintain the pace, I told myself. Concentrate on keeping your eyes forward.

"What's your function: murder, kidnapping, or intimidation?"

Watching from the corner of my eye to make sure he didn't move closer, I counted ten paces before he answered.

"Mr. Dodge wants you to stay away from Praetorian."

I counted ten paces and said, "Did I hear an 'or else?'" I decided he looked military and figured he was either CIA or FBI, which meant he was probably trained to kill people with his bare hands. Fifth Avenue was five hundred yards ahead. I couldn't outrun Bob, or whatever his name was.

Ten paces. He said, "Mr. Dodge will hand the person who killed Jenny Ross over to the police and will make sure those who harmed Abby receive what they deserve. If Abby agrees to remain silent, he will leave her alone."

Ten paces. "What about my friend?"

Ten paces. Silence.

"What about my friend?"

"I don't know about your friend."

It was two hundred and fifty yards to Fifth Avenue. There were a handful of walkers and joggers within earshot.

"She's been missing since last night. I think Dodge

knows where she is."

"I'll find out. What's your answer?"

"No answer until I know about my friend."

"Mr. Dodge doesn't like not knowing."

"Tell Mr. Dodge that neither does Paige Harrington."

A lone runner approached. I moved to the left edge of the pathway forcing the lone runner between us. If Bob planned to rough me up, he'd have to do it in front of a lot of people walking and driving down Fifth Avenue. By the time the lone runner passed, the park exit was twenty-five yards ahead.

I increased my speed again and glimpsed to my right. Then I turned my head for a better look. Bob had disappeared. I stopped and studied the terrain. There was no sign of him anywhere. I crossed Fifth Avenue and headed for Park. My heart hadn't stopped pounding, and it wasn't from the running.

It was twenty-five past midnight when I walked into Bebe's apartment. Bebe's light was off. Zoë's room remained dark. All was silent.

I took a thirty-second shower and collapsed nude on the bed where I lay staring into the darkness. My eyes began to close. I heard a scream and leapt up, grabbing my robe from the chair. Another scream, it was Zoë. I raced into her still dark room, realizing I had nothing to use as a weapon.

Zoë cried out again. In the semi-darkness, I could see the inert lump under the white sheet. Otherwise, the room appeared empty. I hurried to her bedside.

"Zoë," I whispered.

She moaned.

"Zoë," I whispered again.

She stirred and turned her head.

"Can you hear me?"

"What…what's wrong?"

"You're having a bad dream."

I brushed the hair back from her forehead with the

back of my hand. She felt hot. I felt her nightshirt. It was damp. The bedding felt damp also.

"Are you OK? Do you feel sick?" I turned on her bedside lamp.

She said she felt fine. I asked her if she wanted the air on. She said she did. I crossed to the control switch on the far wall and selected the highest fan speed and lowest temperature setting. Instantly, the room felt more comfortable.

I returned to her bed and sat with her, watching her troubled face as she tried to engage her mind. Tears came to her eyes.

"Everything will be all right," I said, and squeezed her hand.

She nodded and tried to find a trace of a smile.

I helped her into a dry nightgown and after a few moments went back to my bedroom, desperately wanting someone to hold my hand. I ached of loneliness, and a sense of hopelessness washed over me. I thought of Jessie and prayed she was safe. I thought of poor, battered Abby. And Brad, and prayed they were safe.

That Brad hadn't called began to gnaw at my insides and I began to imagine all types of horrors that he'd encountered at the hands of Abner Dodge's muscle men. Then I finally got it: he hadn't called me, but he had definitely called his wife, Lisette. Otherwise, Lisette would have mobilized all the police forces from both countries in a massive manhunt—to say nothing of TV, radio, and newspapers. Why hadn't she called me? Because Brad told her not to...he's worried Dodge has my phones tapped; he's making sure Dodge doesn't find him and Abby.

Yes, of course that's it. That's why he hasn't called. I wriggled into the sheets and pillows trying to find a comfortable place, and my eyes grew heavy. Then I thought of Bob from Jamaica and my eyes popped open, sleep again a fickle companion.

Praetorian

Praefectus raised the bejeweled mace.
  The eighteen Centurions took their rightful places.
  Praefectus said, "Who brings you here this night?"
  The nineteen chanted "You do, our exalted Praefectus."
  "What say you then, my Centurions?"
  Centurion Nine stood. "Exalted Leader, by day's end, I shall have the canister. If I fail in this task, please grant me the honor of taking my own life before this exalted altar."
  Praefectus raised the mace. "I too feel you shall succeed Centurion Nine, and your request is granted."
  Praefectus adjourned the meeting.

Chapter 56

Iawoke with a start. The clock on the night table blinked 7:30 in big red numbers. I jumped into the shower. Pinpricks of water poked at every square inch of my protesting body and slowly brought it back to life. Gobs of shampoo that smelled of lilac ran down my face and plopped onto the tiles. I massaged with soaps that smelled of roses and orchids. For a brief moment, I thought of standing there for the rest of time.

Bebe ended that notion by announcing breakfast. She said she'd been up for hours, though I suspected it had been more like ten minutes, but I did smell coffee.

I brushed out my hair, tied it into a ponytail, and pulled on a pair of white slacks and white shirt. The unkind mirror told me I needed some color, and I tied a green scarf loosely around my neck.

Zoë and Bebe sat at the kitchen counter. Zoë wore another borrowed Bebe outfit, this one a red sleeveless dress. It looked good on her and I said so. Bebe wore a flowing robe, fluffy and pink like her bedroom and bathroom. I told her she looked dreamy.

She said she knew, and then added, "I asked Zoë if she thought I looked like a madam in this outfit. She said no."

"She doesn't know you well enough to tell you the truth."

"Oh thank God, I thought I had lost my touch."

"What's this?" I extracted a folded piece of paper from beneath my saucer.

"Those are your messages. Neither sounded urgent, so I didn't waken you."

"Why did you write URGENT then?"

"Well they said they were urgent, but they didn't sound urgent. Go ahead, you won't bother us."

The first was from Ajit. I called him, and he told me

Vesco had been released.

"Why?" I wanted to know.

"I'm not sure. What they told me doesn't make sense."

"What did they tell you?"

"That nothing connected him to the old woman and the man in the hospital."

"Why was the old woman in his apartment?"

"Vesco said he doesn't know who she is. He said his regular walker must have asked her."

"And they believed him?"

"Apparently."

"Did they find the regular walker, or do they just say 'oh, OK, sorry we made a mistake. You can go now?'"

He remained silent for a moment before he said, "I don't know."

"I don't mean to be sarcastic, but he's the only thread that connects me to Jessie, and you've let him go free." As if they could hold him because I thought they should.

"I know, and I'm sorry. I asked the detective in charge if he thought Vesco would be amenable to letting us talk to him."

My heart beat faster. Maybe we hadn't lost yet. "And can we?"

"He's to let me know, but it probably won't be until later today."

"I don't know whether to scream or sit with my head between my knees and bawl. Maybe I'll do both."

"I wish I had better news." Pause. "Do you want me to pick you up, I'd be glad to play chauffeur."

"I've decided I have to see Abner Dodge. He's the only one who can tell me what I need to know."

Silence from Ajit. Bebe looked at me like I'd grown another head. Zoë tucked her neck in like a turtle trying to retreat into its shell.

"But I don't expect anyone to take me; I can take a cab."

"You'll do no such thing," Ajit and Bebe said simultaneously. "I'll get Dalton's car," Bebe said. "I'll take you," Ajit said.

Bebe already had her cellphone open. I waved her off. I told Ajit to come to Bebe's and we'd figure out a plan.

I called the second number on Bebe's list, though I doubted he would answer.

"This is Stephen Rattner."

I hesitated, thinking it was his voicemail, and then realized it wasn't. "This is Paige Harrington. Thank you for calling."

"Are you on a secure line?"

That sounded ominous. "As a matter of fact, I am, or at least one that isn't bugged."

"I apologize, but I really didn't get a chance to look into Praetorian until earlier this morning. Also, FYI, I told Amanda of our meeting yesterday, although I haven't told her or anyone else what I'm about to tell you, and I think it wise if what I say be for your ears only."

"All right," I said, "though I hope she doesn't ask. I don't lie well." Often, but not well.

"You need a couple weeks of basic Washington, DC training. Here, we call it 'telling a different truth,' not 'lying.'"

There are too many people, including me, telling different truths, I thought.

He continued, "I just don't want her caught up in this. What you're involved with is very deadly and ticking bomb. Everyone thought the Washington lawmakers had diffused Praetorian when Ollie North's covert operations ended. Praetorian was the private bank used in the Iran Contra Affair."

"I gather it wasn't diffused."

"No, it's still out there, bigger and more dangerous than ever, and I fear fatal to anyone who tries to discover its secrets."

"Its secrets are well guarded. I haven't turned up anything beyond the name."

"With good reason. Praetorian is probably the most protected of all offshore companies, and will do whatever it takes to make sure no one penetrates its veil of secrecy."

"Like murder Jenny Ross, and anyone else who tries to interfere."

Bebe and Zoë's heads shot up.

"Anyone it deems a threat," he said.

I knew he meant me.

"I strongly recommend you stop trying to find out who these people are. Your life is in danger, and you are endangering the lives of others."

And now he meant Amanda.

He continued, "Amanda told me you are one of the most put together and courageous people she's ever met, and coming from her that's high praise; and the only reason we're having this conversation.

"Paige, I urge you: don't discount what I'm saying. Praetorian despises daylight. Praetorian is the type of group that assassinates all threats. I suspect you are alive because you are a minor annoyance, or they think you have something they desperately want. If you become more than a minor annoyance, or they find out you can't harm them, they will kill you before breakfast and not think twice."

For a moment, my mind felt like it was about to blow its circuits. Still no answers, only Praetorian killing everyone.

"Paige?"

"Yes, I hear what you say, and I don't know how or what I'm going to find out, but I can't stop. My brother and my best friend are missing; three women have been murdered, another young woman has been beaten, almost to death. I can't stop."

"Think of the others."

"If you mean Amanda, maybe it's you who should think of her. She knows the risks, and I couldn't stop her if I tried. In my book, she is one fantastic lady."

He remained silent for a moment, and then said, "You're right, and as I said, I don't want her involved, but I know she won't become uninvolved—she thinks the world of you. For my part, I'll keep digging."

Amanda, Bebe, Ajit, and me vs. Praetorian; what a joke. And it was only going to get harder. The closer we got, the harder Praetorian would push. I had to try to keep Praetorian away from Brad and Abby and find Jessie, but Rattner was right, I had no business endangering Amanda and Bebe and Ajit.

Part of me wanted to crawl into a hole. A larger part wanted to claw at someone, to rip his eyes out. No one should have that much power to make others feel afraid.

Bebe said the minute the telephone left my hand, "You have our attention. Would you mind telling us who is killing whom; would you mind telling us how our insignificant little lives might come to an abrupt end."

"That was Steve Rattner with the State Department in DC."

"You mean Under Secretary Rattner?" Bebe asked, her eyebrows shooting up as only hers could.

"The same. I met with him yesterday and asked him to look into Praetorian. He fears Praetorian will kill us if we get too close."

"Isn't there a euphemism for kill that sounds less fatal?"

"I'm the one giving them a problem, and I believe that if Praetorian comes to get anyone, it will be me, but we, all of us, have to be concerned. Steven Rattner said that Praetorian assassinates world leaders so I don't need to tell you how long they'd hesitate to eliminate us."

Bebe threw out her chest. "Well Darling, if they try to take this little Long Island Jewish girl out, she won't go without the loudest scream they've ever heard."

Zoë looked about to melt.

"I can't let them make me quit. I've got to find Jessie and Brad, except I can't be worrying about dragging you and Zoë and Ajit and others into my mess."

"Well Darling, if you think I'm letting you do this on your own, you are badly mistaken."

She gave me a long hug. We were crazy. We were poking our righteous little stick right square in Praetorian's giant evil eye.

The doorman rang. Ajit had arrived.

Zoë continued to sit like a frightened mouse, her big round eyes nervously darting to and fro as though killers might step from behind a drape or leap from a closet. I watched her swivel from her stool and cross to the windows in the living room where she stood with her arms folded across her chest, her hands clutching her elbows. She began shaking like she was cold, and then turned to face Bebe and me. She was crying.

"I can help you find Brad and the girl," she said, tears streaming down her cheeks.

I strode toward her, not sure if I wanted to embrace or strangle her, hoping I'd heard correctly, afraid I hadn't.

"I'm so sorry," she said, "but I've been so afraid of what they might do to me that I didn't want to get involved."

She covered her face with her hands and began sobbing loud, shaking sobs.

I grabbed her arms and pulled her hands from her eyes. "Zoë, talk to me. Are you saying you know where Brad and Abby are?"

She shook her head 'no.' "But I can find him. They have to be hiding somewhere that Tom knows because Brad doesn't know the hospital." She rubbed her eyes with the backs of her hands. "And I know every hiding place Tom knows."

I shook her arms. "Please tell me how we do this, and tell me now. We've got to get to them before…before the others."

Bebe answered Ajit's knock and ushered him into the kitchen.

Zoë said, "I'll have to do it alone. If the girl's condition has improved, they could be in a hundred different places and are likely moving around. If she's still critical, their options are more limited."

Could she be trusted? Up until this moment, she hadn't acquitted herself well, but she could have continued to sit quietly by and done nothing, said nothing.

"I don't know…"

She grasped my arm in a firm grip. "You doubt that I can do this, but I can, I'm no longer afraid, and you don't have a better option."

Her eyes, though red-rimmed, were now determined, demanding that I let her do this.

"Ajit can take you."

"If anyone's watching, it'll be better if I take the bus. Not many nurses get delivered to work in Ferrari's."

"I'm as much afraid that anyone watching might try to intercept you."

"I know more ways of getting into that hospital than any other person. Trust me…no one will know I'm there, and no one will know when I leave."

"What about security cameras? If Praetorian believes Abby is still in the hospital, it will have people watching all the cameras."

"Several times a year interns coming off long shifts decide to put a few drinks away. On occasion, a few drinks become many and challenges are made that can't go unanswered. Without raising so much as a security guard eyebrow, I've wheeled interns and patients up and down hallways in wheelchairs and on gurneys. I've staggered down hallways on crutches and walkers with my bare ass hanging out of a hospital gown. I've carried bedpans full of chocolate bars defiantly held up to the cameras for the guards to see. So even if they're on high alert, they're so conditioned to such sophomoric activity, I don't expect trouble."

"I need to know that they're safe, but I don't want us leading anyone to them."

"Believe me, no one will know. I'll find them, make sure they're OK, and tell them to stay put for another day or two. Then, as soon as I'm out, I'll call you and come back here."

"If my friend Jessie isn't there, I need to know if Brad knows where she went."

"I'll call as soon as I know something, anything."

I wanted to squash her in the biggest bear hug imaginable, but instead I gripped her hand. "Thank you," I said. "Thank you for doing this."

"I'll need to change into my own clothes. Showing up in this wouldn't be the smartest thing I've done." She looked down at the bright red dress.

When Zoë went to change, I told Ajit about Steven Rattner's call. Ajit said he was also in until the end, so I could forget about trying to convince him otherwise. He said he'd drop Zoë at a bus stop within a few blocks of the hospital. That would get her there a lot quicker than having to take the bus or subway the full distance.

"They're likely following your car," I said.

He called his brother's taxi dispatcher who sent a cab and arranged for one of his drivers to pick up Ajit's car.

After they left, I called Jonathan Winthrop to see how soon I could talk to his father. He said he'd call me back within the hour. More delays.

I looked up Abner Dodge's law firm on the Internet and wrote the address and telephone number in my notebook. The telephone rang. Bebe had gone to take a shower. I picked up.

Jessie's screams burned into my ear.

Chapter 57

O h dear God, my worst fears, why is this happening? "Please don't hurt her," I cried to the man's voice that came on the line.

Jessie, my dear sweet Jessie, please be OK. "She hasn't done anything. Please, I beg you, please leave her alone."

Fear paralyzed my mind. I said things out of a need to fight, to keep him talking in his eerily disguised voice, hoping against hope he might give up some clue to their whereabouts, but mostly because I didn't know what else to do.

"Let me talk to her. Let me come to see her."

"When we get what we want you will see your friend."

"Why did you take her? Why didn't you take me?"

"You can get what we want. She will make sure you give it to us."

"I told you I don't know where Abby is. As soon as I find out, I'll take you to her."

"We'll find Abby soon enough. Right now we want the metal container. You can see your friend when you bring the container to us."

I didn't know enough curse words to do justice to how I felt.

"Please let me talk to her."

"Say goodbye. Do what we say and it need not be your final goodbye."

"Please don't hurt her. You can have what I have. I'll tell you everything, and I'll stop the story."

"You've unleashed too many dogs."

"No one knows who you are. I promise."

"Where's the canister?"

"It's in a safe place."

"Listen, I'm going to let you hear your friend scream

one more time and then I'm going to ask again."

"No, please—"

I clenched the receiver and gritted my teeth. Tears ran down my cheeks as I again listened to Jessie's tortured cries.

"I've got the canister. You want it, come and get it, and bring Jessie. When I get Jessie, you get what you want."

"Describe it to me."

"I don't have it right here in my hands. It's in a safe place. I have to get it."

"Say goodbye to your friend."

"No, please don't. I have it."

My mind flew back to things Abby had said about the list. Or was it Jonathan, or Steve Rattner? It didn't matter. I had to come up with something and pray.

"It's a metal tube with a computer activated seal."

The telephone went silent. Please God, make me right. I strained my ears to hear sound, any sound, breathing, background noise...

"Paige..."

Every nerve ending writhed as I heard Jessie's pain. "Oh sweetheart, please forgive me, I'm so sorry."

"Don't let them get Abby—"

"Enough," the man said.

"Please, I beg you, don't hurt her."

"That will depend on you, Miss Harrington, though I promise if you do not deliver that canister with its seals intact, you and your friend will be dead by day's end."

I thought of Jessie's and my friend, Dom Caputo. He knew how to deal with these people. He knew how to wield dark power. I wished he were here. I wished he could grab the telephone and say something like 'You lissen to me you dick with no brains, right now your life is worth a nickel but you hurt Jessie, you won't have a life because I'm gonna squash you like a cockroach, one stomp and your guts will be all over the city. Capice?'

"I promise you this: If you hurt Jessie, our friends will hunt you down. They know how to play your game better than you do. Praetorian will be nothing but a bad memory."

"You think some Paki cop is going to stop us?"

"Come for your list, and bring Jessie."

"We give the orders. Starting now, use your smart mouth less and your ears more."

I heard traffic noise: a horn, tires whirring fast on pavement and a siren.

"Do you understand?"

"Yes, yes I understand."

I heard a bell, a church bell chiming a hymn.

"Be in the parking lot at the 79th Street Boat Basin at 3:00 p.m., and bring your cellphone." Click.

I threw the receiver down. I didn't want to cry, but I couldn't hold it in.

Bebe came out from the bathroom. She held me close while I told her what had transpired.

"Where is the canister?" she asked. "Is that what I was supposed to get from your friend Jorge?"

"Abby said she'd send a safe deposit box key. What good does that do us on a Sunday?"

"Let's start by getting hold of Jorge," she said.

The woman who answered Jorge's cell phone asked me to hold. I handed the call off to Bebe and telephoned Ajit. Zoë was already at the hospital, and he was on his way back.

Bebe remained on hold. Jonathan called. He wanted me to come to their offices, and said he'd send a car. I told him I'd come only if his father was available to talk about Abner Dodge and Praetorian. He said his father was available and had a critical piece of information.

I still had time until I had to be at the Boat Basin unless Jorge had received the key from Abby and we had to start racing all over the city.

"What's the critical information?"

"He has the list of Praetorian investors."

My heart stopped. "What did you say?"

"He said to tell you he has the list."

"Jonathan, I need to know what he means by having the list. Does he have the list of Praetorian's investors? Is that what he's saying?"

"I...I'm not sure."

"Have you seen it?"

"No. Only he and Mr. Pennington know of its existence, but he assures me it is the list, and he then told me he has other information you need to hear."

I couldn't afford not to go. "How soon can the car be here?"

"I expect less than five minutes."

That meant he'd dispatched the car before he'd called. I hated being taken for granted, but now wasn't the time for that discussion.

Bebe signaled that Jorge was on the phone. I told Jonathan I'd be ready when the car arrived and ended the call.

I spoke to Jorge in Spanish and asked what he had received.

His voice crackled with excitement, and he rattled on a mile a minute in Cuban-American Spanish that my ear struggled to translate.

"The key from your friend, it arrived just after I talked to Miss Bebe. Your friend say it from a bank, but it no come from a bank; it come from a hotel."

"What do you mean it came from a hotel?"

"I hope you no mind, Miss Paige, but when I get the key, I think it look like a Waldorf key but the numbers no match, so I call my friends at the other hotels and they call their friends."

"No, no of course I don't mind, but didn't you have an address? My friend said she would send the key, box number, and address."

"No address, just a piece of paper with a number on it

and a key inside held with a rubber band. But we find it. Last night we find it, but my friends say Mr. Regan from the Waldorf, he coming to get it this morning so I go there after my shift at midnight and take it. I hope you no mind, Miss Paige, but I was afraid that Mr. Regan, he get it."

"Jorge, I could kiss you. Is there a metal tube?"

"Si, si, and an envelope, a large envelope full of papers."

"Where are you? Can you bring them to me?"

"I'm in Queens, at my home. I just get up. I was going to call you when Miss Bebe, she call me."

"Jorge, please, can you take a taxi and come here right now?"

"My son, Roger, he drive me."

"Please hurry. My friend's life depends on it."

"My son, he drive fast."

I gave him Bebe's address and told him he wasn't to give the box or tube to anyone except me. The doorman buzzed then, to announce the arrival of the limousine.

I debated. Go or wait for Jorge. What did Jonathan Senior have that I needed? Jorge had the metal tube containing the list of Praetorian's investors. That's what Praetorian wanted. What list did Jonathan Senior have? What other information? I asked Bebe what she thought. She told me that if Jonathan Senior said he had something I should know, I should listen.

I called Jorge back and told him to give the envelope and tube to Bebe if I wasn't at her apartment. Then I explained everything to Bebe and asked her to call my cellphone the second she had the envelope and tube in her possession.

"Yes, yes, yes, Darling, now go."

Chapter 58

Jonathan met me when I stepped from the elevator. I followed him through the reception area, as intimidating and regal as I expected, with its walnut-paneled hallway and large framed pictures of serious looking men in black robes. We walked past elegant offices whose large windows offered up a grand portrait of Central Park, Lincoln Center, and the entire Upper West Side up the Hudson to the George Washington Bridge and beyond. Each office door had a name etched on an oval-shaped brass plate. One said Jonathan Wainwright Jr.

It was pin-drop quiet. His footsteps showed on the carpet as clearly as though we were walking on new-fallen snow. I glanced back. So did mine. Why weren't there more?

"Didn't you say your father was here?"

"Yes…and others."

We walked a few more paces. Still no sound.

"I'm sorry I didn't pick you up," he said over his shoulder, "but there's been a lot going on and I couldn't get away."

I detected uncertainty in his voice and asked if I'd put him in a difficult spot with his father.

He looked back and either grimaced or smiled, it was hard to tell—I decided upon the former.

At the end of the hallway, we entered another reception area more richly appointed and more intimidating than the first, with Louis XIV period furniture and what appeared to be original oils. Amongst the collection, I recognized a Picasso and New York street scenes from the Ashcan group. Beyond, three sets of double doors led to offices that I decided faced Central Park. The unmistakable murmur of voices emanated from the open center set and caused me to hesitate. Jonathan motioned me in.

I shot him a questioning look. He nodded assurance. I stepped through the open doorway and froze. Looking directly at me sat Vesco in one of the dozen or more chairs circling the boardroom table.

I wanted to turn and run, but my feet seemed entangled in the carpet. With a smile that I calculated to be one part fiendish and one part phony, Jonathan Winthrop Senior got up and strode toward me. Jonathan Junior's hand pressed on my back propelling me forward.

"Paige, thank you for coming," Jonathan Senior said, taking my hand and pulling me along. "It seems you've uncovered a bit of a viper's nest."

The others seated around the table stood. He introduced George Kendall. George Kendall was black. That surprised me because I was certain I hadn't seen a black face on the Jasper Winthrop web page. Nor had I seen a Jewish name. To the contrary, I remembered thinking JWK epitomized a white-shoe WASP firm like one finds in Canada or England.

"And this is our mentor, Pennington Jasper," Jonathan Senior said with overdone reverence. George Kendall stepped aside, revealing a stooped little man with wispy white hair and ice-blue eyes, who extended a bony little hand bearing a disproportionately large diamond pinkie ring.

Other than a dark gray crocheted shawl draped across his shoulders, Pennington Jasper, like Jonathan Senior, Jonathan Junior, and George Kendall, wore the Jasper, Winthrop, and Kendall uniform: a dark gray suit, white shirt, and maroon tie.

"Young lady, you honor us with you presence," he said in a surprisingly strong voice. "Won't you please have a seat?"

I dropped like a stone into the indicated chair. He then held out his hands and motioned the others to sit, which they promptly did. He took the chair next to me.

Jonathan Senior sat to my right, George Kendall and Jonathan Junior to Pennington Jasper's left.

"I've favorably known your father for fifty years," Pennington Jasper said.

"Yes, after seeing from your website that you were at Harvard at the same time, I spoke to him. He regrets that the two of you haven't stayed in contact."

"Please wish him well when you next speak to him."

"Thank you," I said, for the moment far more concerned with what was about to happen and who the other men were, all of whom were looking at Pennington Jasper and me.

Seeking some measure of support, some clue as to what was about to happen, I glanced at Jonathan. He studiously avoided not only my gaze but also my presence.

That angered me, and though a breath shy of petrified, I didn't see why I needed to sit on my hands like some frightened school girl. Besides, didn't I have a right to know why they'd asked me to come?

I said to Pennington Jasper, "Sir, I'm not at all sure why you've asked me here."

He studied me for a moment as if trying to decide whether to answer while I squirmed like a fly in a web watching the spider inch closer.

"You may not know exactly why you are here, young lady, but I feel certain you have surmised that it has something to do with Praetorian."

I knew exactly why I was there: to seek help in rescuing Jessie, though it wasn't my turn to state my case so I nodded, fast becoming less certain of the breadth and depth of my understanding of Praetorian's power.

"Let me explain," he continued. "After 9/11, secret citizens' advisory councils to combat terrorism were established in major cities. There are nine in all, each composed of senior military, police and government agents, and an elder statesman from the community handpicked

handpicked by the President. These councils report only to the President and guide him with their recommendations. This is the New York Council, and I am the President's appointee. Of late, all of our attention has been focused on Praetorian."

My muscles tensed. Since Monday night I had received a dozen or more warnings about Praetorian, and as seriously as I thought I'd taken them, I obviously hadn't taken them seriously enough. It also made my puny efforts laughable.

I dared a glance around the table. Except for one man seated half way down on my right, wild-looking with shoulder-length, stringy blonde hair that didn't go with his forties something age, the others either wore military or police uniforms, or suits and ties.

Pennington Jasper added, "You of course know Jonathan Winthrop Senior and Junior and George Kennedy. The others will be introduced as we go along."

While I wondered where it was we were going along to, my eyes came to rest on Vesco, and Pennington Jasper must have noticed because he said, "Ah yes, I believe you are also acquainted with Special Agent Rockwell."

I began to suspect Pennington Jasper's eagle eyes missed nothing, not a twitch, not an eyelash flicker.

"Only briefly." I figured, Rockwell (a.k.a. De Groot, Vesco, Taylor, and the hundreds of other aliases he no doubt had) could provide an addendum if he chose to do so.

The vein-lined paper-white and paper-thin skin on Pennington Jasper's face ever so briefly wrinkled into a chuckle, and I suspected he and the others knew every detail of my meeting with Rockwell and my subsequent feeble attempts at tracking him and Praetorian down.

My attention moved back to the misfit. His cloudy gray eyes that made my blood run cold locked on mine. The growth of stubble didn't hide a gash that ran from above his left ear to his chin. I quickly shifted my focus to a blank spot on the wall near the ceiling.

Pennington Jasper cleared his throat and continued, "Praetorian has been on our radar for many months, and we had prepared a plan of action that, over time, would have neutralized its distasteful activities. Fortunately, or unfortunately, your activities of the past week forced Praetorian to make one or two uncharacteristically rash moves, and we believe it is now propitious for us to strike right at the heart of this beast."

An almost indistinguishable murmur and nodding of head signified collective agreement.

"And we think you can help us."

My stomach tightened and I heard my mouth start to say words that my brain hadn't sanctioned. "Sir, my friend Jessie McArdle has been kidnapped. My interest starts and stops with getting her safely back. If what you are suggesting accomplishes that, I'm interested; if it doesn't, I haven't the luxury of time." Then, to stop my legs from shaking, I clutched the backs of my thighs with both hands.

"We may be able to help you do that if you agree to help us."

I nodded.

The man sitting across from Rockwell spoke up. "I'm Oswald Ziff, Deputy Director of a special unit within the agency with responsibility for terrorist activities. Next to me are Special Agents Baxter and Gold."

Ziff, Baxter, and Gold, unlike Rockwell, looked trim and muscular and sculpted. None smiled—that they had in common with Rockwell.

"As Mr. Jasper said, we can help you if you help us."

"I'll do what I can, but I won't endanger Jessie's life."

"Has Praetorian contacted you?"

"Yes, by telephone. They—"

"Did anyone record or try to trace the call?"

I hated that he cut me off mid-sentence. If you don't value my input, don't ask questions.

"Not to my knowledge."

"Are you saying you did not have anyone listening to your telephone calls?"

"No, did you?"

"Miss Harrington, straight answers will do a lot more to secure quick resolution."

And I hated even more that he thought he had the right to lecture me.

"Agent Ziff, you can bend my answers any way you wish, however I can assure you, all my answers are straight. I want your help finding Jessie, but you're not going to knock me back and forth like a tennis ball. If anyone listened to my telephone calls, they did so surreptitiously. On Tuesday, we had our telephones swept for listening devices, although I suspect others could have been installed since then, possibly some of your own."

Davis, Baxter, and Gold huddled. A few of the others had whispered conversations.

Davis said, "Please understand Miss Harrington, we want to help save your friend, and although we do have a lot of knowledge on what has transpired between you and Praetorian, your confirmation is vital to ensure we have the right facts."

"Yes, and I'm sorry. It's just that I fear time is running out."

Davis asked, "When were you contacted last?"

"This morning, not more than an hour ago—a man telephoned Bebe's apartment." Though certain they knew, I explained Bebe and my relationship to her.

"Are you certain the man who called is the one holding your friend?"

"I heard her screams, and Jessie and I exchanged two or three words. He definitely has her."

"What does he want you to do?"

"He wants me to deliver a sealed metal canister."

Again Ziff, Baxter, and Gold huddled. I had to assume they knew of the canister and were comparing notes.

Ziff looked up and asked, "Do you have the canister?"

Why did I least trust Ziff and his two sidekicks? Because they gave me the creeps and reminded me of the type of people who always hid behind their leaders: they were finger pointers and blamers, and I felt disinclined to be truthful. What was the worst that could happen? Well, they could torture and kill me, render me off like a terrorist to a secret prison in a torture tolerant jurisdiction, although that seemed a bit of a dramatic stretch.

Then, I thought, since Bebe had talked to Jorge on her cellphone, and Jorge was at his son's place, chances seemed good that Ziff and his pals didn't have those two phones tapped, and therefore didn't know the metal canister was currently on its way to Bebe's apartment.

"That is the one thing I hoped to get here."

When several around the table checked their watches, I got the feeling they were wondering if I wasn't running out of time, something they shouldn't have known, but probably did.

"When and where is it to be delivered?"

"To the 79th Street Boat Basin, today at 3:00, but I guess the way a lot of you checked your watches, you already know that."

A man across from Ziff, next to Rockwell spoke up. "You are very observant, and yes we do know about the meeting. That's how we believe you can help us. I'm Admiral Upton, head of the U.S. Coast Guard. Next to me is Grady O'Shea, head of operations for New York Harbor. Next to him is Inspector Battaglia of the NYPD Harbor Unit. Together, we have a dozen unmarked boats in the harbor and rivers and our people are on another six, moored at the outer landings of the Boat Basin. The man who contacted you is currently on one of the two rivers or in the harbor."

"When he makes his move we'll be ready," Inspector Battaglia said.

"I hope you won't take this the wrong way, gentlemen," I said, "as ready as you may be, my concern lies solely with my friend's safety."

"And so it should," Pennington Jasper said, "just as these men's concerns lie in dismantling Praetorian and The Praetorian Guard."

"Sir, I don't much care what they do after she's free."

"If you can accept the word of an old man, I promise that action taken against Praetorian will not further endanger your young friend's life. I cannot say the same of you however, because you have a dangerous part to play."

"With or without help, I expected my life to be in danger. May I know your plan?"

The misfit in the jeans and tee shirt leaned forward and rested a confident, bronzed hand on the table. "That's where I come in," he said, his voice whispery and cold like it blew up from the depths of a dank cave.

My eyes locked on his, unable to waver. His presence bespoke power and authority, just as his attitude bespoke a disregard for power and authority. The muscles in his arms flexed when he moved and his pecs rippled.

"I'm Xavier Lance, retired, U.S. Army. The boys brought me in to coordinate this whale hunt."

Of course you are, I thought. He looked as much ex-army as Hulk Hogan.

"Here's how it's going to play out: You will go to the Boat Basin as instructed. The person who contacted you won't get off the boat, but will instead ask you to come to him. He'll use Jessie as bait. What I mean by that is she'll be where you can see her. She'll also have a gun pointed at her head that you may or may not see."

I swallowed. "What if he's not alone?"

"We don't expect he will be. That's why what you do and how you do it are extremely important. One false move, and you and your friend will get hurt."

I guessed all eyes in the room, like mine, were riveted on Xavier Lance. I guessed that, unlike mine, their stomachs weren't about to toss breakfast. Hurt was another euphemism for killed.

"That makes me feel better."

"Those are the facts. Everyone, especially you, needs to know the risks. This is a scary business. If you're scared, that's good."

I didn't know how to respond. I swallowed and possibly nodded.

"The Boat Basin is a collection of old wooden walkways that don't inspire a lot of confidence. They're crooked and wet and slippery. I noticed when you came in you're wearing sneakers. That's good, because trying to maneuver with heels or even hard-soled flats would be far too treacherous."

Everyone except Xavier Lance and me glanced down as though he might see my sneakers through the table.

"He wants you on the walkway, as far from shore as he can lure you, and he knows you will come to him because you want to save your friend." His brows furrowed, intensifying his gaze to laser-like beams. "It's important you understand that he plans to kill both of you."

"I have that picture," I said.

"To make sure we can get our people placed, what you have to do is take a long time getting out to the boat–it will likely take you a long time anyway because of the perilous walkways; though you need to pause periodically and keep talking to him. Make him show you that Jessie is OK, ask to see her walk, wave to her and get her to wave back. You must make absolutely sure that her hands and feet aren't anchored. Is that clear?"

"She's going to jump?"

"You both are. The instant you hand off the metal canister containing the list."

"I told you I don't have the canister, so I'm assuming you do."

Oswald Ziff nodded at Pennington Jasper who slid an aluminum-looking tube about two inches in diameter and a foot long across the table. It was locked with an impressive-looking digital combination device with blinking numbers.

The tube was air light. I rotated it in my hands, wondering if it resembled the one Jorge had. Did Jessie's captors know what the original looks like? Or was this the original. Maybe Abby never had the original.

"We suspect he'll want you to remove the list and hand it to him."

"What if he doesn't?"

"He will remove the list. Whether he looks at the list or tries to open the canister, he's eliminated."

"How do I open it?"

"Only he knows the correct number sequence. If he wants you to open it, he'll have to give you the combination."

Now I had a problem: if this wasn't the original canister, the numbers he gave me wouldn't work, or were they trying to trap me into revealing the existence of another canister? "Are you certain the numbers will work?"

"Any sequence will work."

That confirmed in my mind that this canister was a fake. Did it even resemble the original? Would the guy on the boat know the difference? Given a minute, I could have thought of a thousand other reasons why their ruse wouldn't work and Jessie and I'd end up dead, but I couldn't figure out an alternate workable plan.

"Once you get the lock open, flip the metal cap and remove the paper roll inside and hand it to him."

I gripped the canister in my left hand until my knuckles whitened.

"Go ahead and give it a try. See and feel what it's like to work the lock and removed the contents. Do not unroll the paper, however, because it should appear untouched, and that's the way you must hand it over: tightly rolled."

The fact that twelve pairs of eyes became focused on my hands that began to feel like flippers, was probably nothing compared to how they'd feel when I stood out on the water slicked pier.

"What numbers should I use? I mean, give them to me the same way the guy on the boat might."

"Center six, far left ten, far right two, near right eight, near left eleven, then center five."

He may as well have spoken Ork because my mind had frozen.

"I'm sorry. Can you repeat that?"

"No, that's good. He won't expect you to know what to do. Remember, the numbers aren't important—just make sure to follow the sequence."

He repeated the numbers and sequence, and the lock popped open. The list inside felt like art paper, and it easily slid out. I left it rolled and dropped it back inside, closed the cap and snapped the lock.

"What happens when he looks at the list?"

"In that brief instant when he takes his eyes off you, you must hit the water and scream at Jessie to do the same."

Getting the canister open and removing its contents suddenly moved way down on my list of concerns.

Ziff said, "We believe you're up to the task, otherwise we wouldn't consider this course of action."

Of course they'd done a detailed check on my background and knew I was a professional swimmer. Had they done the same for Jessie? "Is Jessie?"

Ziff said, "Neither of you will have a problem with the water."

Xavier said, "Not losing your nerve is the hard part."

MY MIND turned to mush. I asked him to repeat the steps. He did so, slowly and clearly. I had to make it work. I had to do whatever I had in my power to save Jessie.

But still the lingering question: which is the original canister—this one or Abby's? It was easy enough to imagine the members of this special President's Council had the clandestine power and means to get the original from whatever repository Praetorian had chosen for its safekeeping, except that thinking left two questions un-answered: why had Vesco been pursuing Abby, and why had Abby almost been killed: not for something of no value?

Why hadn't Bebe called to say she got the canister from Jorge? Had something happened?

Even though apart from me, he was the most insig-nificant being in the room, he was still my original host, so I turned to him and said, "Jonathan, I need to make a call."

He looked at Pennington Jasper who nodded.

Jonathan said, "There's a phone in the ante-room," and led the way.

Through the small window in the ante-room door, I sensed every eye watching and every ear straining to hear. I turned my back and called Bebe.

"Darling where in the world are you?" she said, her voice shrill with anxiety. "I'm going mad here with worry. I've called you a hundred times."

"First, did Jorge deliver the canister?"

"Yes, yes I got it. It's ticking away here in my hot lit-tle hands, like a bomb."

"Describe it to me."

"What do you mean, describe it to you?"

"Color, shape size, everything."

"It's a metal tube. About a foot long and two inches

in diameter. One end is sealed with a lock with five blinking numbers that look like they can be set with dial-like wheels."

I held my breath. "What color?"

"Black with orange numbers."

I tried to swallow the lump in my throat as I turned and stared at the brushed aluminum tube with red numbers lying on the table next to Pennington Jasper.

"Now answer my question," she said. "Where are you? Why didn't you answer my calls?"

"I'm with Jonathan at his offices. They must have the conference room sealed so no calls get in or out. Don't worry, I'm OK."

"I hope you're keeping an eye on the clock."

"Every second, believe me."

Two obviously different canisters—which was real? I kept thinking that surely these powerful men with their network of powerful contacts had a greater ability to provide the Praetorian list than Abby.

I RETURNED to my seat next to Pennington Jasper and said to no one in particular, although I was looking in Xavier Lance's direction.

"Gentlemen, I need to know if this is the real canister containing the real list."

I picked up the brushed aluminum canister, while everyone stared as though I'd asked about a generations-old dark family secret involving incest.

Pennington Jasper asked, "Are you aware of other canisters, Miss Harrington?" The look on his face had turned icily neutral and his skin seemed the blue-white of skim milk. I glanced around the table at the other faces that before had been receptive and now were in-scrutable as granite.

"I have just been made aware of another."

The scraping sound on leather seats betrayed the shifting of visually inert bodies.

Xavier Lance glared across the table at Ziff, who pointed to the canister in my hand, and said, "That is the original. That is the one Praetorian wants."

Heads nodded. I didn't believe them. They would shove their mothers in front of speeding trains to get what they wanted, and right now I decided what they wanted was to have me deliver the canister in my hand. I glanced at Jonathan. He looked away. Did he know the canister in my hand was a fake? Did he know they were sacrificing Jessie and me to get their target?

Pennington Jasper asked, "And where, young lady, is this other canister?"

I wanted to tell him where he could go; I wanted to yell and scream and tell all of them where they could go, but I reined in my anger and held my tongue. The location of Abby's canister, the original, would remain my secret.

"Somewhere between the Bronx and Manhattan."

Though he tried to smile, his eyes flashed impatient anger. I tried not to feel intimidated. Who was I kidding? I was scared to death. These people could squash me like a bug. Praetorian could squash me like a bug. But I wasn't going to give in, not to Pennington Jasper and not to Praetorian. Jessie was all that mattered.

"That's not very useful, is it," he said.

"Mr. Jasper, what's useful is giving me a chance to save my friend's life by giving her kidnappers what they want. Is this the original; is this what they want?"

Jonathan Junior flinched. He'd heard me raise my voice before, and he knew it could get a lot louder.

"It is critical that we examine your canister," Xavier Lance said. "It's the only way we can determine with one-hundred-percent accuracy which is the correct one."

He'd just again confirmed what I needed to know: theirs wasn't real.

I slid the canister back to Pennington Jasper. "Gentlemen, if you want the original, you'll have to get it from Jessie's captors."

Pennington Jasper said, "Miss Harrington, I'm afraid we can't let you turn it over to them. There are too many lives at stake; the security of the country is at stake. You have to think of that; you have to put that ahead of your friend's life, ahead of your life."

"With all due respect, Mr. Jasper, you and your high-powered assemblage here can do that. I can't and won't. I'm delivering the original canister in an attempt to save my friend. After that, I don't know what happens, but you're not stopping me from trying."

"Are you really that brave?" Pennington Jasper asked.

"They'll kill both of you," Xavier Lance said.

A chorus of agreements sounded and heads nodded.

"No, I'm not brave, but if I don't try, if Jessie dies because I didn't try to save her, I'm worse than dead. You have to understand that I'm not afraid to die if I do so while trying to save her life."

"We can simply take it from you," Xavier Lance said.

"Then that's what you'll have to do." I hoped he didn't sense my legs again shaking uncontrollably.

"Young lady, will you excuse us for a moment?" Pennington Jasper asked.

My response neither was expected nor of any concern since he and several others were already getting up to leave. Jonathan Junior remained, as did several of the uniformed men and one of the gray suits, all of them watching me as if I might make a run for it.

I got up and walked around to where Jonathan Junior sat. He started to get up. "Don't," I said so only he could hear. "I just came to tell you that I think you set me up, and if you've got any guts, you'll help me get out of here. I'm out of time."

He stood and turned away from the others. "I didn't set you up. They told me they had what you needed. I can see now they didn't, but what good would it do for me to start hollering and banging my fists on the table. You're the one who has to do the convincing, and I think you're doing a superb job."

"I can't get out of here if they don't want me to."

"That's an understatement, but I will tell you this: if they try to incarcerate you, they'll have to take both of us. I'm not walking out of this room until I know that you're free to take your canister to the Boat Basin."

"Are you being truthful?"

THE DOOR behind us opened and Pennington Jasper led his entourage back to the table. Everyone remained standing. I returned to where I'd been seated but like them, remained standing. If they planned on taking me into custody, now would be the time. I glanced at Xavier Lance. Nothing. I glanced at the others. Nothing. I turned to face Pennington Jasper. It was his show.

"You are a brave, if stubborn young lady, Miss Harrington, and we have decided we will help you save your friend."

My heart sped up, if that was possible. I wanted to hug him, almost.

"On one condition: that Special Agents Baxter and Gold go with you to check your canister before you hand it over to your friend's captors."

He may as well have punched my stomach.

"Mr. Pennington, I can't do that, and gentlemen, please don't take this the wrong way, but there are only two people I trust with my canister. Here's how it's got to be: if you want my canister, you'll have to get it after I use it to save Jessie."

The ones who had left the room glanced at each other.

"I know you can take it from me by force before I get to Jessie, but that's the only way you're going to get it. Now, I'm running out of time so please let me do what I need to do."

Pennington Jasper's bony hand cupped his chin. After a few seconds that seemed like several minutes he said, his voice barely audible, "We will comply."

Did I dare trust them? It didn't matter. I had no choice. Jonathan Senior and George Kennedy had their battle faces on. I got the feeling they were on my side and hoped I wasn't seeing only what I wanted to see.

Xavier Lance spoke. "You will stay at Miss Morgan's apartment until 2:30. A cab will pick you up and take you to Riverside and 79th. From there, you will walk under the highway to the Boat Basin. The cab driver will point you in the right direction. We suspect Praetorian will have people onshore watching everything you do, every move you make."

I started to feel a different set of nerves, the ones wrapped in steel. This had to work.

"Don't worry, we know who they are, but we can't risk them seeing us and contacting the boat, or Jessie's problems intensify."

I nodded.

"Don't take a handbag or cellphone."

Problem number one. "I have to take my cellphone. That's how he's going to contact me. He told me to bring it."

Lance thought about that for a moment, and then said, "Wear what you're wearing now and keep your shirt tucked in so they won't think you're carrying a gun or anything else around your waist. Carry the cellphone in your shirt pocket where it's highly visible. You don't want to be digging in your jeans for something they can't see."

What he said made sense. Everything he said made sense, except the doing of what I had to do.

"What happens after we hit the water?"

"The Coast Guard and NYPD boats will move in to take out anyone else on the Praetorian boat and pick the two of you up."

"What happens if Jessie's hands and feet are bound?"

Lance said without hesitation, "We'll have to move quicker."

I looked into the eyes of each man standing there. If Jessie and I died, I wanted them to know they'd let us down. Like that mattered to them.

I turned to Jonathan and said, "I'd better go."

HE ACCOMPANIED me out and downstairs to the waiting limo. I told him I was afraid for Jessie's life. I told him I was afraid of screwing up this one slim chance to save her.

He gripped my shoulder. "I watched you up there. Even my father and George Kennedy, despite once being Marines, are now just lawyers. You, you had the same fire as Xavier Lance and the others. Without you, none of this takes place, and they all know that. They know you're going to kick ass."

"I wish I felt the same way."

"You will, trust me. Besides, I expect to see a lot more of you when this is done."

I half-stumbled when he pulled me into an unexpected embrace. As awkward as it felt, for the briefest of moments I wanted to hold on, to never let go, but I could not.

"I'll call the instant they pull us from the water," I said. It was a promise that, unkept, wouldn't generate life-long guilt because I'd be dead.

"I'll be waiting," he said.

Chapter 59

When I told Bebe and Ajit of Xavier Lance's plan and what I had to do, Ajit demanded he be allowed to come until I explained that Praetorian's people would have the area blanketed and seeing anyone other than me would imperil the plan.

"Darling," Bebe said, "no matter what you say, you can't go alone. Need I remind you that you are a journalist, not a Navy frogman?"

"I didn't bargain for this, but that's the way it's got to be. If Jessie's going to have any chance at all, I've got to do exactly as Xavier Lance says."

Ajit disappeared into the den. He said he wanted to track down Zoë, but what he really wanted to do was get out of Bebe's and my line of fire—we had managed to wind ourselves as tight as piano wire.

Bebe had been pacing ever since I got back. I told her to stop, because seeing her like a tiger on a hunt made me feel more like prey than I already did.

"I need to do something," she said.

"Try to keep my mind occupied."

"How do you propose I do that?"

"Sing, dance, or tell me something funny about Jenny. Right now, my mind thinks it might not see tomorrow."

We stared at each other for a moment. I brushed my eyes with the back of my hand. "I'm sorry," I said. "I don't handle pending death well."

She pulled me into an embrace. "No one but you would do this, you know."

"Yeah," I said. "You would."

OTHER than being dead, I didn't need to think what would happen to Jessie and me if Xavier Lance's plan failed. What about Brad and Abby? Would they be dead? What about all the other people who knew about Praetorian: Bebe, Dalton, Peter, Dee, Amanda, all the people at Jasper, Winthrop, and Kendall; the list went on. Would they be dead? Praetorian can't kill everyone. That was beyond my comprehension.

Is this what I'd be thinking as I stepped along on the water-slicked, uneven wooden pier toward Jessie's captors? No, I couldn't. I had to believe, more than at anytime in my life, I had to believe. One wrong thought, one split-second delay, and Jessie didn't stand a chance.

The telephone rang shaking me from my mental black hole. Bebe talked for a brief moment and hung up.

"That was Dalton. He's in Washington, but says to tell you he will have the information you requested by tomorrow or Tuesday."

"It's not urgent—just information on Cameron Black's inheritance."

THE DOORMAN buzzed to announce Peter Zane and Dee Hunter's arrival.

"What are they doing here?" Bebe asked.

"He's been to see Cameron and wants to tell me what Cameron said. I tried to reach him and tell him not to come, but couldn't get hold of him."

"I'll send them away," she said.

I glanced at my watch. "No, let them come up. It'll help fill the time."

Bebe and I went to the hallway to await their arrival.

"Now who's pacing?" she asked.

I blew out a lungful of air.

"They don't know of Xavier Lance's plan," I said to Bebe by way of telling her I didn't want them to.

I TOOK Dee and Peter into the front room and Bebe joined Ajit in the den.

I flinched when Dee touched my arm with the tips of her fingers. "Sorry," I said, forcing a smile. "This whole

Praetorian mess has jangled my nerves."

She nodded a knowing look. I asked Peter to tell me about his visit with Cameron.

Dee gave him a concerned look and brushed at his forehead. "It was a stressful meeting."

Peter said, "He hopes you understand why he yelled at you like he did."

"I have no problem with that." I glanced at my watch, something I figured I'd be doing at least every minute until I left to keep my appointment with death.

"We're keeping you," Dee said.

"No, it's just that I'm in a bit of a serious time box. Peter, do you have something more to tell me."

He took a notepad from his shirt pocket. "As soon as I got out of there, I wrote everything down. I even told Dee not to talk until I finished so I didn't forget anything." He began flipping pages.

I fought off the urge to look at my watch again, and then looked anyway.

"Here," he said, tearing off a page and handing it to me. "This is the name of Blackie's private banker. Call him. He'll tell you what you want to know about Blackie's money."

I looked at Peter's scrawl. Jason Walsh III, Senior Vice President, Private Banking Division. I couldn't imagine a JP Morgan private banking officer giving me the time of day let alone particulars of Cameron Black's trust account, but at the moment I didn't care.

Peter continued flipping back and forth through his notes. Dee must have sensed my frustration and told him I didn't have time. His face reddened, but he kept flipping.

"Voila!" he said, ripping off another page and handing it to me. "These are the people who set him up."

I snatched it from his hand just as Ajit ran from the den. "She's found them," he said, and raced for the door.

Dee and Peter looked to see what was going on while

I ran after Ajit, my heart pounding in my chest. I caught him at the elevator.

"They're not at the hospital," he said. "Brad and Tom got Abby out of there last night when someone discovered their hiding place."

"Is Jessie with them?" I knew she wasn't, he hadn't said she was, she was being held by Praetorian, but I had to hope.

Ajit shook his head. "Sorry, only Abby."

"Are they in a safe place? Praetorian wants them dead."

"Yes, totally safe. I've dispatched one of my uncles to stay with them, and I've got two cars of detectives meeting me."

I wanted desperately to see Brad, but it seemed he was safe. Jessie wasn't. "Be careful they don't find you," I said.

He told me he'd mobilized his brother's taxi fleet, doubting anyone in Praetorian spoke Tamil so his cousins could holler and shout all they want and no one would have a clue what they're doing or where they're going.

I ran with him out to the sidewalk just as a yellow cab swerved to a stop. The driver looked like Ajit, only unshaven and a few years older. White teeth shone from a broad grin.

Ajit said, "This is another uncle with a really long name that no one can pronounce so we call him Sam."

Sam shot out a big, hairy hand. "I've been hearing a lot of very fine things about you so I am very pleasing to meet you."

Ajit jumped in the back. Sam hit the fare button and grinned. "He won't be paying but we are wanting everything to be looking not fishy."

With that, they sped away and melted into the busy Sunday afternoon traffic.

Another taxi stopped and my heart began palpitating.

I checked my watch and brushed the beads of perspiration from my forehead.

The doorman came out and talked to the driver."

"He's early," I said, and felt a full-blown panic attack coming on.

Xavier Lance had every move, every breath timed to the second. This was no good. The cab couldn't be early.

The doorman pointed to the next building and the cabby moved ahead.

"I'm sorry, Miss Harrington, he wanted 860. They always do that because the building numbers are on the ends of the awnings and they're hard to see from the street."

I went back to Bebe's apartment amply reminded how unprepared I was for my assignment. Bebe asked if I needed a drink or something to calm my nerves. I did, but I didn't want to risk it.

"Where is the canister that Jorge brought?"

She disappeared down the hallway. I figured she had it locked away in the wall safe in her bedroom.

Dee and Peter joined me in the foyer. I apologized, and asked if I could catch up with them later.

Peter asked "Did you look at the names?"

I removed it from my shirt pocket. The ink had run, it was hard to read. "I'm sorry. I've got to leave."

Bebe returned with the canister. I gave her Peter's list and asked her to put it with my notes.

Dee grabbed the paper from Bebe's hand, and said "I think you should at least take the time to look at it since Peter and Cameron took a big risk."

Bebe was irate. No one grabbed anything from her hands. I shot her a look that said 'cool it.'

Dee shook the paper in front of my face. "Look at it, damn it."

Now I was irate and turned on Peter. "What the hell is going on?"

"Look at it," Dee screamed.

I took it from her hand and scrutinized the smudged letters, wondering what had set her off, and then deciding I didn't have time to wonder.

When the first name began to register, I felt as though my brain were caught in a vise. "This can't be right," I said. "Not Pennington Jasper. I've got to telephone Jonathan."

"You haven't time," Bebe said. "Let me do this. Let me straighten this out. You've got to go."

"But you don't understand. If Pennington Jasper is involved, I'm walking into a trap. Xavier Lance's plan is Pennington Jasper's plan."

"You said it yourself: this can't be right, and you've got to get downstairs because you're out of time. Let me talk to Jonathan. If it's a trap, I'll call your cellphone."

My cellphone. I touched my shirt pocket to make sure I had it.

Bebe reached for the kitchen wall phone.

"I can't let you do that," Dee said, taking a pistol from her bag and aiming it at Bebe. "Get away from the telephone. Peter, look after your friend."

I stared at Peter. "What is this?"

The doorman rang.

"Don't answer," Dee said.

"Listen Darling, if I don't answer, he'll be up here with a carload of cops—house rules. Is that what you want, and would one of you mind answering Paige's question so we'll both know what the hell is going on?"

"That call is for me," I said. "My taxi is out in front, and I don't plan on being late."

"We can't let you do that." Peter grabbed my arm.

I tried to pull away, but his grip was firm. I looked at Dee, who seemed to know how to handle the gun she waved in her hand. Of course she did. Hadn't she been five years with Mossad?

"Get over here, both of you," Dee said, motioning with the gun toward the front room. "Go ahead Peter, tell her."

Peter shifted nervously. This was Dee's deal—he was her pawn just as I was Xavier Lance's pawn.

"Tell her." Dee spit the words.

"We can't let you deliver the canister." He tried to take it. I pulled away.

"Give it to him." Dee pointed the gun directly at my head.

I figured even if she was a lousy shot, which I doubted, she couldn't miss from five feet. My only hope was Peter.

"Peter, if I don't deliver this, my friend Jessie is going to be killed. I can't let that happen, so if you and your girlfriend plan to stop me, you better have her start shooting, because I'm leaving."

BANG!

I jumped. The bullet whizzed past my ear. I heard it smash into the wall behind and snapped my head around. A bullet hole sat dead center in a nine inch picture of Bebe's mother. I glared at Dee, a Dee I didn't know, not the Dee who'd introduced me to Amanda and helped me track Taylor and his ugly dog. That Dee was warm and caring and elegant and sophisticated; this Dee was cold and distant and calculating.

"I didn't miss," Dee said. "I aimed at the old bag, and the next one is for you if you so much as look at that door."

"Peter, would you please tell your overwrought girl-friend that I don't scare easily. Shooting a picture is easier than shooting a person. I'll bet she's never shot a real person."

Dee laughed a bitter laugh.

I took a step toward the door.

"Don't," Peter yelled and lunged at me. Dee fired another shot. I reeled and heard a clanging sound. Peter lay on the white carpet, bleeding from a shoulder wound. Dee, out cold and bleeding from a large gash in the side of her head, lay sprawled across the foyer. Bebe glared down at her, holding an olive oil decanter like a tennis racket, poised to swing again if necessary.

"I'll teach you to shoot my mother," Bebe said to Dee's inert body. "Only I'm allowed to do that." Then she turned to me and said, "Now get out of here so I can clean up this mess."

Peter groaned.

"Why, Peter? Please, just tell me why?"

Bebe grabbed my arm. "Later for that Darling; go save Jessie."

"No," I said, pulling free. "I've got to know if there's a Jessie and a boat."

I knelt beside Peter.

"I didn't think she'd go that far. I thought we were supposed to scare you away."

"Why, for Christ's sake?"

"Abner Dodge is her uncle. He controls all the family money; his ruin will destroy them."

"But she...she said he he hated him."

"All part of the deception...only a few people know the connection."

"Peter, I need to know one thing: did Cameron give you Pennington Jasper's name?"

Peter grimaced from pain, said, "No," then passed out."

Bebe shoved me out the door.

Chapter 60

This time the taxi at the curb was for me. I got into the back and looked up at the hooded eyes smoldering in the rearview mirror.

"What happened to your shirt and slacks?"

I glanced down. My right side looked as though it had been splattered by red paint. Peter's blood.

"My friend thinks she's Jackson Pollock."

"Looks like blood," he said, and pulled away, remaining silent until we entered Central Park. Then he said, "I'm to let you off on the near corner of 79th and Riverside. You're to walk from there."

"Yes, I understand."

"General Lance asked me to go over the steps with you one more time. I'd like to do that now so when we get to our destination, you'll be prepared and can exit the taxi without appearing overly suspicious and uncertain."

"That sounds like a good idea," I said, swallowing the taste of bile that had worked its way to my throat.

"You look nervous. You're biting your nails."

I stopped.

"Take a few deep breaths, and then we'll start."

I breathed as deeply as I could and noisily so he'd know.

"Try to picture yourself actually doing what you have to do. That way, when you actually do it, your mind will think it's already done it before and you won't panic."

I doubted doing it a hundred times would help. "Yes, Sir."

"When you get out of the taxi, walk west on 79th Street. That's straight ahead from where you'll be getting out."

"Yes, I know west."

"Picture it in your mind. You'd be surprised how

many wests there are when you panic."

"Yes, I see it."

"You'll enter a pedestrian tunnel that leads under the West Side Highway. Continue on that walkway, down the stone stairs to the parking area where the boat owners keep their vehicles. Remember, people live there, on houseboats, so there will be activity: kids, dogs, bikes, baby carriages. There will be Sunday walkers, tourists, families looking for a place to have a picnic. Can you picture it?"

"Yes," I said, my eyes closed.

"The parking lot will be half full. Some people will be getting into cars, some people will be getting out of cars, some cars will be coming, some will be going. Picture it."

"Yes, Sir." I kept my eyes closed, forcing myself to concentrate on every detail.

"Some of those people will be ours, some will be theirs. Don't look at anyone. And don't think you'll be able to tell who's who, because you'd be wrong. Don't try to act as though you're not nervous—they'll expect you to be nervous."

I opened my eyes and glanced at the rearview mirror. "I won't have any problem with that," I said.

"General Lance said your instructions are to wait in the parking lot for a telephone call?"

"That is correct, next to the guard booth."

"After they call you, they will call the guard, who will let you in. The piers are low and boat wakes constantly splash them with water. The wood is old and slippery. Walking is tricky, so keep your head down and concentrate and you'll do fine. People not nearly as agile as you do it every day."

Not with a hundred guns pointed at them. I closed my eyes and pictured the guard booth and the wet, old boards. I pictured myself walking toward a boat at the far end of one of the wet, old piers. I pictured Jessie standing on the deck of that boat with a gun at her head. I pictured myself asking the person holding the gun to let Jessie walk around so I could make sure her feet weren't anchored, I pictured myself waving at Jessie and making sure she waved back, hoping she wasn't bound hand and foot. I pictured handing the canister to the person holding the gun—no wait, I'm supposed to open the canister and remove the list and hand the list to him—I pictured seeing him looking at the names. I pictured him staggering back with a little round hole in his forehead. I pictured myself screaming at Jessie to hit the water. I pictured myself diving sideways into the water.

"Do you see it? Do you see it all?"

"I don't see my friend hitting the water."

"She'll make it. You scream, and she goes in. You'll both hit the water at the same time. If there's more than one of them, and we think there are, they'll be neutralized before either you or your friend come up for air."

There it was again, their preferred euphemism for killed. Neutralized wasn't a euphemism for what would happen to Jessie and me if this plan didn't work. We'd be shot dead, plain and simple.

"What if she's bound hand and foot?"

I'd asked before. I needed to ask again. I needed to see Jessie hitting the water.

"She'll make it even if she's in chains. Tell her to roll. The important thing is for the two of you to get out of the line of fire because there's going to be a lot of bullets flying around."

We passed the Apthorpe. I thought of Amanda and wondered if she knew about Dee, if she knew what had happened, if she knew why Dee had to do what she had done. Dee must have known all along that I would unmask Abner Dodge. That's why she wanted to help. She needed to stay close; she needed to know how close I got. Abner Dodge hadn't needed to have one of his people like Lynch watch my every move; I'd managed to find a pair of his eyes and ears all on my own.

We crossed West End Avenue. My heart began to race faster than ever before in my life. The cab slowed and pulled to the curb. The driver flipped the meter off. I handed him a twenty; he handed me a receipt and gave the twenty back.

"Your change," he said. "Good luck, and don't worry, you'll make it. A lot of good people are watching your back."

I stepped from the cab and walked to the intersection. Riverside Park teemed with humanity of all stripes. The walk light came on. I crossed Riverside Drive and continued west toward the underpass. Children's happy sounds filled the air, a wisp of barbecue smoke titillated my nostrils, and a soft breeze brushed at my face. The taste of vomit soured my throat.

Maybe it was the idea of entering the pedestrian underpass with its mounds of bird droppings that smelled like metallic mold and the stench of human urine. I held my breath and started in—the dank, shaded air seeming to penetrate my skin. I increased my pace as I saw two homeless men dirtier than dirt lying on flattened cardboard. Neither one stirred as I passed by. I couldn't tell if they were dead or passed out. They looked dead. I didn't want to see dead. I shivered and hurried the remaining few steps into the sunlight. There I shivered once more, but for a different reason: I had now entered the parking area.

Eerily, it was exactly as I had it pictured in my mind, even the colors of the cars, though I knew that impossible.

I continued toward the chain-link fence that protected the Boat Basin from the general public. The guard's station was located at the north end, behind a locked gate. I glanced at my watch. It read 3:01, but I always ran two minutes fast.

I threaded my fingers through the links and looked at

the river. Boats of all sizes moved about, some buzzing like angry water insects, others sailing silently like graceful swans. I took my cellphone from my shirt pocket and held it in my hand. In the other hand, I clutched the canister.

I swallowed hard several times. Second by second, I steeled my nerves for the cellphone's ring. Still, it jolted me to the bones when it rang. I fumbled to answer and dropped it at my feet. In a flash, I scooped it up and flipped it open.

"Yes," I said.

"Do you have the canister?"

It was the same eerie voice that had called Bebe's.

"I have the canister. I've kept my part of the bargain, now please let her go."

"That will depend on you, and in case you have any heroic ideas in mind, we know where your father and mother, Superior Court Judge P. Tillingford Harrington III and Sally Bowles Harrington, live; we know where your brother, Dr. Bradford Harrington and his wife live...shall I go on?"

"They've got nothing to do with this."

"At the moment your brother has something we want. Until we get it, they have everything to do with it."

An icy hand closed around my stomach. He'd changed the rules. "That wasn't the deal. You said—"

"We make the deals. You're in no position to deal."

"I don't know where he is." I scanned the water, looking for the boat.

"Your smoked-meat Indian friend does."

I hoped for the chance to rip his eyes from their sockets before a bullet parted his brain.

"Call the sahib and find out where they are. You've got one minute." Click.

I stared at the dead telephone. Tears of rage bleared my eyes as I punched in Ajit's number. Please God, answer, and please God, have Xavier Lance and his people listening.

Ajit answered and wanted to know what was wrong. I told him they wouldn't let Jessie go until they know where Brad and Abby were.

"I've got to tell them," I said.

"Are you sure you want to do that?"

"No, I'm not sure. I'm not sure of anything right now, but I have no choice. I've got to do this one step at a time, and telling them is the now step."

"They're in the Psychiatric Institute building, sixth floor, but Abby can't be taken from the hospital."

"I'll call you," I said, and hit the 'end' button.

Ajit would know Pennington Jasper's coterie of heavyweights was monitoring my calls, and Ajit's contingent of detectives and cousins would do what they had to do to protect Brad and Abby. For the moment, Jessie had no one but me.

My cellphone rang. Please let this be it. No more changes.

"Yes, I'm here."

"Where are they?"

I repeated what Ajit had told me.

"Hold on."

"You were smart to tell the truth," the voice said after a few long moments. "You see, you can't win. We have people everywhere."

"What now?"

"Keep your phone to your ear."

The guard came out of his little box and opened the gate. He pointed to the pier on the far left. "Down there," he said.

I looked where he pointed. A large sailboat, I guessed over a hundred feet long, moved silently toward the last mooring space. I hadn't seen it before. It had seemingly materialized out of the glimmering reflection of the sun on the river.

The voice said, "I see you've spotted us. Start walking, and throw the phone into the water."

"Where's Jessie?"

"You'll see her in a minute. Start walking and dump the phone in the water or what you'll see is a dead body."

I tossed the phone.

"If you hurt her, I toss the canister," I said, and stepped onto the pier. It wasn't as wide as I'd pictured, but the treacherous footing was exactly as I'd seen in my mind.

I concentrated on each step, fighting the urge to look at the boat. Xavier Lance's words ricocheted in my mind: *Take a long time getting out to the boat, pause periodically, keep talking to him, make him show you that Jessie is OK, ask to see her walk, wave to her and get her to wave back—make sure her feet aren't anchored. Is that clear?*

Yes, I thought, crystal clear, except I no longer have my cellphone so I can't keep talking to him. How many more flaws would the plan have?

I paused and looked up. I didn't see Jessie and was over half way to the boat. This didn't seem right. My mind said Jessie was supposed to be on deck. I took a few more cautious steps, Then two figures emerged from the boats cabin and walked aft, stopping half way. Was it Jessie? At that instant, the sun reflected from a mane of golden hair. Yes!

Thank you, God. I shuddered in a deep breath and hoped my heart didn't explode. So he'd know I had it, I held the canister aloft. He waved me forward. I stopped ten paces from the boat.

"You're not here yet."

"I want Jessie to tell me she's OK."

The man jabbed Jessie. I tried to see his face.

"Paige, you don't need to do this. I—"

The man slapped Jessie across the face with the back of his hand.

"Paige…" She staggered and fell.

The man grabbed her arm and pulled her up.

I took a step, wanting only to physically attack him, to tear at his face, to punch him until he stopped moving, until he couldn't hurt Jessie.

"Let me see her walk. I want her to wave to me."

I still hadn't determined if her feet were anchored.

"Get your rich girl ass out here or your friend has taken her last steps."

I know that voice? Why won't he look in my direction?

"The boards are slippery. I'm afraid of falling and losing the canister."

He shoved Jessie against the cabin wall. She cried out. "Paige it's—"

He punched her, she staggered a step, and her knees buckled. Blood trickled down the side of her face, but her feet weren't anchored.

"Stop it you bastard. You've got to stop. Don't hit her again."

He put the gun to her head.

"I'll put a bullet in her brain if you don't hand me that canister and I mean right now."

"Here. Here it is. Take it and let her go."

He turned as I took the last few steps. A black hood covered his face.

"Why are you doing this?"

He jabbed the gun harder against Jessie's head.

Jessie's eyes were clear and flashed anger. Good, no fear, no defeat. Why didn't that surprise me? I leaned forward with the canister in my outstretched hand.

"Here, now let her go."

Using Jessie as a shield, he lock-stepped forward. I kept my hands in plain sight. Jessie hesitated. He jammed his gun hard into her back of her neck. Her head snapped back.

"Ow," she cried. "You asshole!"

Good Jessie. Stay mad.

I stepped back. "You get this when you let her go."

"He's going to kill us both," Jessie screamed.

He raised the gun to strike Jessie in the head.

"You touch her I toss this."

He stopped.

"You can kill us both, but you won't know where this will end up."

"Give it to me."

He stayed behind Jessie. I stretched out, making sure the canister remained out of reach.

"Wait. I'm supposed to open it and remove the contents. This isn't right."

He yanked Jessie's arms up behind her back until she cried out.

"OK, here. Now keep your end of the bargain." Jessie's eyes told me she knew I had a plan.

His arm snaked around. "Step closer. Do you think this is a game?"

Jessie bucked as he jammed the gun into her back. Her hands were tied but not her feet.

I did as he demanded. Please God, let Jessie know when to get out of the way.

His fingers closed on the canister and his hand snaked back behind Jessie. He glanced at the computerized locking device.

"NOW, JESSIE, INTO THE WATER!"

I saw him look up and heard gunfire as I threw myself hard to my right and down. Just before hitting the water, I saw Jessie reeling toward the side of the boat and prayed she hadn't been shot. Had I been shot?, I didn't feel anything except the cold water assaulting my body.

I swam underwater to the protection of the pier and, using the wooden struts running between the posts, pulled myself away from the boat. Jessie had gone in on the other side. I crossed under the pier and tried to see through the murky water. My lungs ached. When they reached the bursting point, I surfaced under the pier where there was only about an inch of air space, sucked in a deep breath, and went back under.

Something long and black sliced through the water less than a foot away. Logic told me it couldn't be a shark, but my mind screamed with fear and I kicked and squirmed to move away.

Through the green murk, I saw Jessie scissor stroking toward the pier. She hadn't seen whatever it was in the water that now moved between us. I pushed with all the spring I could muster and drove into the intruder's side. The intruder buckled and turned. I saw a pair of surprised eyes staring at me through a mask and a wicked looking spear gun pointed at my head. In a split second, the spear gun jerked to one side and the dart shot past, missing my head by inches. That's when I spotted the NYPD insignia on the black rubber suit and gave a thumbs-up.

Jessie surfaced. A second later, I bobbed up and gulped air. A second after that, the frogman in the black rubber suit surfaced.

"You guys OK?" she asked, pulling her mask free.

I looked at Jessie. She looked at me. We made our way through the water toward each other, unnoticeable tears streaming down our water-soaked faces.

"Thank you God, thank you God, thank you God," I said, and threw my arms around her neck and kissed her forehead and cheeks and nose and mouth. We clung to each other, shivering from the avalanche of adrenaline roaring through our systems and the cold river water wrapped around our bodies and the mountains of fear that hadn't yet been expunged from out brains.

Running footsteps sounded on the pier.

"They're OK," the lady frogman said. "Pull them out."

Muscular arms reached down and plucked us from

the water as though we were twigs. They wrapped heavy gray blankets across our shoulders and around our shivering bodies, and we couldn't stop laughing and crying.

We were hustled along the pier to the parking lot that had suddenly burst at the seams with flashing lights and a dozen people in handcuffs being led away to waiting cars. Xavier Lance walked up like he'd been on a Sunday stroll.

"Good work, both of you," he said. "Take them to that ambulance." He pointed to a dark blue limousine that looked more like a hearse than an ambulance except it had the Homeland Security logo plastered on the doors.

A yellow cab screeched into the parking lot. Hands tensed, weapons became ready. Ajit jumped out and flashed his police badge. Everyone stood down. Behind him ran Brad, who didn't stop until he had both Jessie and me engulfed in his long arms.

You've got to stop doing this," Brad said. "One of these days I'm not going to be here to bail you out."

Same old Brad. God it was good to see him. Ajit stood several feet away. His brother, Sam, walked up and draped an arm across Ajit's shoulder. Then what I assume were cousins, about twenty of them, crowded around looking first at him, then at me, and then back at him, and laughing like kids in a schoolyard.

Ajit started forward. I freed myself from Brad and Jessie and ran to him. We embraced for a long while, neither uttering a word. I breathed in his man scent and felt his wonderful body press to mine.

Jonathan ran through the parking lot shouting, "Paige, Paige."

I pushed away from Ajit. "Over here." I waved, and he came running up. I said, "I'm sorry I didn't call, but they made me toss my phone."

"We were in constant contact with Lance so I knew you were safe. I couldn't get here fast enough."

His big arms swallowed me up. Over his shoulder I saw Ajit take a step away, uncertain. I pulled free and said, "Do you remember my friend, Ajit?"

Jonathan's smile melted. He stiffly shook Ajit's hand. Ajit responded, like opposing diplomats of the cold war era. Jessie and Brad joined us. Some of the icy atmosphere melted.

Three gurneys with covered bodies wheeled past. I walked over to where Xavier Lance stood amid a group of his squad or hit force or whatever he called them, to ask who the man on the boat with the black mask was.

"They were all masked," he said.

"The one that held Jessie. The one giving all the orders. I thought I recognized the voice, even through his attempts to disguise it."

A black sedan roared into the parking lot, sirens blaring, tires screeching, dust and bits of gravel flying through the air. Again, several of Lance's people tightened their grips on their weapons.

Bebe jumped from the back seat and ran toward me faster than anyone in three-inch heels had ever run, all the while flapping her hands trying to keep the cloud of dust from landing on her geisha-white face and ruby lips.

"It's my friend," I shouted at Lance before they decided to shoot.

She had already started crying by the time she threw her arms around my neck. So had I. Then she grabbed Jessie and held her so tightly I thought she'd break.

"Praise the Lord," she said finally freeing Jessie. Rivulets of black ran from Bebe's eyes down across her cheeks. "You're both OK. I was afraid I'd be too late."

"Too late for what?"

"As soon as I found out, I knew I had to take your place. I knew he wouldn't dare kill me."

"What are you talking about? Who wouldn't dare kill you?"

"It was Dalton. Dalton kidnapped Jessie. He murdered Jenny. Detective Kennedy told me not more than ten minutes after you left. He heard my 911 call on Dee and Peter and came to get me."

"Bebe, I love you dearly, but you're making absolutely no sense."

It wasn't Dalton's voice that had talked to me on the phone and it definitely wasn't Dalton on the boat. I glanced across at the black police car. Detective Kennedy and his partner had gotten out and headed toward Lance.

"Dalton is behind the whole thing," she said. "Had I been paying attention none of this would have happened."

"He wasn't the one on the boat with Jessie."

Bebe's forehead wrinkled.

"Was Dalton on the boat?" I asked Jessie.

"I don't know. They wore masks and never talked out loud, except the one you saw with me, and he definitely wasn't Dalton."

I walked over to Xavier Lance and told him I had a couple of questions. He took me aside so we were out of earshot of the others.

"Ask away," he said. His face had turned to granite and his eyes expressed no emotion. This was a different Xavier Lance.

"Was Dalton Croft on the boat?"

"I don't know."

"Who was?"

"I don't know."

"Did you recover the canister?"

"No."

I peered into his eyes. I may as well have tried peering into the eyes of a statue. I spun away and returned to where Bebe and Jessie stood talking to Brad, Ajit, and Jonathan.

"Don't go far," Lance called after me. "I want you

and your friend at Mount Sinai hospital to be checked over ASAP."

I wanted to tell him to go to hell, but I suspected that's were he and the rest lived. I told Bebe the guy in charge said he didn't know who was on the boat, that maybe it wasn't Dalton.

"Thank you Darling, but that ship has sailed. He might not have been there physically, but based on everything Detective Kennedy told me, I'm convinced he's the one calling the shots. He is Praetorian."

She was a lot more convinced than I was. Until I knew the identity of the three on the gurneys, I'd reserve judgment about whether or not Dalton had been on the boat, and even if he had been, Praetorian was a lot bigger than him. But Bebe had no reason to think or know that; she hadn't been in Jasper, Winthrop's offices; she hadn't seen the firepower amassed, wanting desperately to get their hands on the Praetorian canister.

Chapter 61

The next morning, Jessie and I went with Brad to Columbia Presbyterian to see Abby. According to Brad she remained critical, but she looked a thousand percent better than when I'd seen her on Friday morning. She still had bandages covering her face, but the number of tubes had been reduced to four or five.

Detective Kennedy placed a round-the-clock guard on Abby's room since Dalton Croft hadn't been found. I told him Abner Dodge was the bigger threat as far as Abby was concerned. He said a warrant had been issued for Dodge.

He arranged for Jessie to stay with Abby. Jessie still had cuts and bruises that needed medical attention and he figured, wisely, that she would only agree to stay in a hospital if Abby occupied the neighboring bed. Brad said he would release Abby in ten days to two weeks. Jessie planned to take her to Calgary.

"They can drive, take the train, or take the bus," he told her, "but they can't fly, at least not for a couple of months. Her Eustachian tube is damaged and we had to repair a few blood vessels. Both are prone to damage from unnecessary physical stress such as that caused by rapid changes in air pressure. She could also experience serious respiratory problems."

Jessie said they'd go by car. I decided to go with them. My story on Jenny would be finished by then, and I could assist Jessie with Abby and the driving. Meanwhile, I'd stay with Bebe. She needed help processing Dalton's betrayal.

Bebe asked Zoë to move in on a more or less permanent basis. Zoë readily agreed. She needed a Bebe in her life right now. Zoë blamed herself for Therese's murder and couldn't get rid of the nightmares. Longer range, long after Zoë's nightmares stopped, Zoë would help

Bebe forget Dalton and deal with Jenny's murder.

Jonathan Winthrop called and I agreed to have lunch with him in Jasper, Winthrop's private dining room. On the way, I told Barry, his driver, I wanted to stop at the Apthorpe to see Amanda Diamond. Amanda and I hadn't spoken since Dee shot up Bebe's apartment, and I wanted Amanda to know I hoped she and I could remain friends.

The guard rang Amanda's apartment and told me to wait near the central gardens. I walked across to the bench where I'd sat two days ago, two days ago that seemed like two centuries ago. Amanda came out and walked toward me, hesitant to the point of reluctance, a questioning look on her face. The confident, flitting Amanda I'd met no longer seemed to exist. I extended my hand. She reached out, uncertain; her hand felt cold.

"I don't know—"

I cut her off. I didn't want an apology.

"I came to thank you for your help and for being a friend."

She seemed perplexed, though some of the tenseness in her face dissipated.

Amanda shook her head. "Still, I should have realized something was amiss when Dee called wanting to know if I'd meet with you. Dee and I hadn't spoken for years—we hadn't ever been that close—but with my divorce still fresh, human contact, no matter how distant, seemed a wonderful gift. I'm sorry."

"If anyone needs to apologize, it's Peter Zane. He's been a friend for years. He's the one who let me down, but in the end he also saved my life, so in time I'll likely forgive him."

"How is he? The paper said the bullet narrowly missed his heart."

"That's the dramatic version. I guess it makes better headlines than a shot in the shoulder. I plan to post his bail so he can start putting his life back together. Peter and jails aren't designed to go together."

"What do you think will happen to Dee?"

"I'm not sure. She's been charged with attempted murder. I don't know anything more."

"Hello Paige, Mrs. Diamond."

I spun around. David Amaroff walked up with Ed slobbering along behind on a retractable leash that seemed fifty feet long.

"I'm sorry about Mrs. Hunter." He said it more to Amanda than me, though I figured he meant it for both of us.

Amanda hugged him. Ed peed on the bench. David glanced at me, his cheeks flushed.

I embraced him and said, "We couldn't have done all this without your help, and Amanda and I are going to stay friends so I'll get to see you once in awhile."

His face brightened. So did Amanda's.

"I see you're back on the job with ugly Ed," I said.

He grinned. "Yeah, at least temporarily. Mr. Rockwell—you do know that's his real name—will be moving soon. He's off to a new assignment."

"So I've heard."

"I'm going to miss Ed," he said, and looked down at the bulging eyes of the panting, slobbering dog, whose stub of a tail started to wag so vigorously his entire rear end seemed about to launch.

"Me too," I said, and bent to rub the top of Ed's head. Ed deposited a glop of slobber on my pants and we all laughed. Then I embraced them both and ran to Jonathan's limo. I was due at Jasper, Winthrop twenty minutes ago.

Chapter 62

Pennington Jasper, George Kennedy, and Jonathan's father, joined us for lunch. Jonathan's outrageously casual new office attire of blue blazer and khaki slacks and open-necked shirt didn't help me feel any less under-dressed. Ed's slobber stain that ran from my knee to the lower part of my calf didn't help.

"You made quite a day of it yesterday," Pennington Jasper said. "I wish I could have been there in person to see it unfold."

An ancient black man, whom they addressed as Smeets, took our drink order. When he left, I asked Pennington Jasper if Dalton Croft had been on the boat.

"Sad business, that," Jonathan Senior said. "We've known him for a long time."

"We were trying to think if he'd given us any signs," George Kendall said, "but couldn't think of a single instance. He played everything like a pro."

"He is a pro," George Kendall said.

I shot him a questioning look.

"After law school, he spent four years with the CIA and trained as a Navy Seal. He opted out, like so many of us, lured by the big money earned by Wall Street lawyers."

Were they purposefully trying not to answer my question? At least when Xavier Lance had lied to me yesterday, he did it with three words.

"Was he on the boat?"

George Kendall said, "Xavier Lance's people described him as an expert at hiding in plain sight."

"Yes, but was he even on the boat?"

I glanced at Jonathan Junior who stood between his father and George Kennedy and wondered if he sensed my frustration.

George Kendall looked at Pennington Jasper as if

seeking permission to continue. Pennington Jasper nodded.

"They suspect he was," George Kendall continued. "There was a lot of scuba gear below, including underwater propulsion vehicles, and there was an escape chamber so he could have gone into the water without being seen."

"What about the canister? It was on the deck, not below. I handed it to the guy who held Jessie and he wasn't Dalton Croft."

"Time will be their enemy," Pennington Jasper said.

What did that mean? Did they get the canister or not?

Smeets returned with our drinks, and two ladies in starched black and white uniforms took our lunch orders.

"Cheers to you young lady for your bravery." Pennington Jasper raised his glass.

"Hear, hear," the others joined in.

Pennington Jasper took the seat at the head of the table and asked me to sit to his right. Jonathan sat on my right and Jonathan Senior and George Kendall sat across.

Once everyone had settled into their assigned places, I asked, "Did you say that the canister had been recovered?"

Pennington Jasper took his time taking a sip of his wine and replacing his goblet in exactly the same place it had been. Jonathan Senior, George Kennedy, and Jonathan Junior seemed inured to this slow motion deliberation.

"Alas that is the one failure of the exercise," Pennington Jasper finally said.

"So Praetorian won't be dismantled," I said. "Jenny's killers won't be brought to Justice. The people who tried to kill Abby, the people who murdered Therese and her mother won't be brought to justice; the people who kidnapped Jessie and were going to kill her won't be brought to justice."

"In time, Praetorian will, as you say, be dismantled. Meanwhile, thanks to you, we believe they will discontinue all their operations. You came closer to exposing its underbelly than anyone has in the thirty years of Praetorian's existence. Had we been able to switch canisters, Praetorian would have been totally disemboweled."

"You know why I wouldn't do that."

"Excuse me, Miss Harrington, I hadn't meant to suggest otherwise. The great success of the exercise is that you and you friend are safe. The rest is unimportant in that context, and I'm sorry if I conveyed that wrong impression."

No, you slippery old codger, what you meant to convey is that I should have given you the canister.

"We can take small comfort that the people you spoke of, with the exception of Miss Ross's killer, have been brought to justice."

"You mean they've been killed. They were the ones on the boat. Can I have their names?"

A man in a gray suit, who looked like one of the special agents at yesterdays meeting, tiptoed up to Mr. Jasper, whispered a few words, and then left.

Mr. Jasper pushed himself up. "You'll have to excuse us, Miss Harrington," he said, and nodded for Jonathan Senior and George Kennedy to accompany him. "We'll finish our discussions another time. Jonathan, please keep Miss Harrington company."

After they left, I asked Jonathan Junior if he knew what was going on. I also wanted to know if the gray suit had been at the meeting yesterday.

Jonathan didn't know what was going on, but did acknowledge that the gray suit was part of Pennington Jasper's private security force.

"The legal profession is getting more dangerous than it once was," I said.

"I detect a note of sarcasm, Miss Harrington, but as far back as I can remember, Mr. Jasper has had a security detail with him wherever he goes. Not seeing him with two or three security people would have raised more questions in my mind."

"But didn't you ever ask why? Weren't you the least bit curious?"

"Pennington Jasper is an eccentric. I've never been to his residence in Bronxville, but I'm told it has more security than the White House."

"I gather that level of eccentricity doesn't extend to your father and George Kennedy. At least I don't recall seeing fingerprint and eye scan entry devices when I visited your parents' apartment, though I wondered about the phalanx of young men and women with perfect bodies and short haircuts and grey suits hanging out in the lobby."

He chuckled, almost. "And probably a few not so noticeable—Abner Dodge doesn't travel without an entourage of armed escorts."

"Him I can understand. Mr. Jasper might be borderline paranoid."

He chuckled again, almost.

The door at the end of the dining room opened and Jonathan Senior came in. "There's something the two of you should see," he said. "We've got the TV on in the small conference room."

With that, he spun around and disappeared. Jonathan and I got up and followed. In the small conference room, Pennington Jasper sat in front of the TV, his hands folded on a cane I'd not seen him use before. George Kennedy stood to his right. Jonathan Senior moved to Jasper's left. Jonathan Junior and I came up and stood behind, all eyes locked on the screen.

Wolf Blitzer from CNN said, "To repeat this bombshell breaking news, two of New York City's most prominent lawyers have been found dead. Police divers pulled the bodies of Abner Dodge and Dalton Croft from the East River just within the last hour. Both had been shot execution style."

That's why Pennington Jasper, Jonathan Senior, and George Kendall had left. Who had called them? How did they know ahead of anyone else? Bebe! I had to get to her to make sure she knew and that she was OK with it. I pulled Jonathan aside and asked to use a telephone, and then his car and driver one last time.

ZOË AND AJIT were with Bebe when I arrived. I needn't have worried; since knowing of Dalton's involvement in Praetorian, she'd pretty much erased him from her memory banks. She acknowledged that she might have a few nightmares, but said they would have more to do with not killing Dalton in his sleep when she'd had so many opportunities.

She wasn't that shallow, that cold-hearted, but she constantly swirled in a level of society that feasted on the demented and lurid; her closest friends, the only people she really truly cared about, never pointed fingers at one another. In fact, I suspect her stature had raised a notch or two. For the next little while, she would be on everyone's coveted A-list.

Chapter 63

A few days later, Cameron Black was released from jail. I called Jonathan to see if he knew what was going to happen to Hebrides, now that it had lost Praetorian as its money source. Naturally, I also wanted to know what was going to happen to Cameron and Anne's marriage. Jonathan wanted to meet, and I agreed, so long as it wasn't at his office. I'd about had my fill of edifice JWK.

We ended up having lunch outside at Café Fiorella, the same place where Jonathan met with Tatiana Marchand and Cameron Black after Tatiana's and my hostile meeting. I'd not forgiven him for not telling me—this was my way of getting even.

As far as Hebrides and Praetorian were concerned, once the Department of Defense realized the nature of Jenny's brain child, it replaced Praetorian as the owner of Hebrides. The government was moving Jenny's lab and her engineering colleagues to a super secret military base, he thought in Nevada or Colorado.

"What about Jenny's and Anne's stock? Did the government take it also?"

"The government offered $200 million."

"How much did the august firm of Jasper Winthrop manage to get for them?"

"More, a lot more. I can't let you speculate on the amount, because I suspect it will appear in your article, and I don't want to be the unnamed source."

"I was going to say informed source."

"So, with her newfound financial independence, is Anne going to dump Cameron for her true love?"

He gave me an odd look.

"Don't tell me you haven't figured it out?"

"I don't have any idea."

"Anne and Tatiana."

His look said, 'Are you crazy?'

"It's true, believe me. Everyone thought you or Cameron had steered Jenny to Tatiana, when in fact it was Anne. Maybe not directly but she pulled all the strings."

"But in the end it was moot. Anne had no intention of stealing Jenny's share of Hebrides."

"Exactly!" I said. "Anne needed Hebrides to go public, so she could cash out and pursue a life of luxury without having to rely on Cameron's billions."

"And Tatiana made sure it was fair to both of them by talking at length to the underwriters. She's not a SEC lawyer, but her brother is a partner at one of the major firms, and I know she talked to him on several occasions."

"Jenny's problem was that she wouldn't sell her stock, and exercised her option to purchase Anne's stock. That gave her control, and she wouldn't agree to let Praetorian sell her invention to known enemies of the United States. That's what got her killed. Praetorian had already negotiated multi-billion dollar sales with foreign governments that wouldn't take kindly to being shafted."

"So Anne got a ton of money, though I suppose it isn't the same as Cameron's billions, or did he in fact lose his inheritance?"

"Oh gosh no, Cameron's billions are nicely intact, although I should point out that one billion is the same as the next."

"Is that billion singular or plural?"

"Did you say plural?"

I wrote several billions in my notes.

"Who gets Jenny's share?" I asked.

"Anne set up a number of education trusts for young women to attend MIT. She said that's what Jenny would have wanted."

I told him I wanted details to include in my story, and he gave me the name and number of the woman lawyer in charge of Jenny's estate. "Call me if she gives you a hard time," he added. "We had a conflict of interest since we handle Anne's affairs, and I steered the business to her."

"And Cameron gets out of jail only to return to an empty apartment."

He laughed. "It won't be empty for long. In fact, he wants your number."

"Whatever you do, please do not encourage him."

"Don't worry; I don't want the competition, although you might alert your friend Peter Zane. Cameron intends to ask him to make the introduction."

Why had I bothered hitting my savings to bail Peter out? Cameron Black could have simply tapped into his change purse.

Chapter 64

Three weeks later, Jonathon called to ask me to dinner before I embarked on my cross-country trip. Jonathan and I hadn't spoken for a couple of days and I hadn't brought him up to date on my change of plans.

"As it turns out," I said, "I'm not going to Calgary. Brad is going in my place. Abby needs more care than I could ever hope to give."

"Is she going to be OK?"

"She'll be fine, although Lisette, Brad's wife, who is a neurosurgeon, insisted she also go, so there really wasn't room for me."

"That doesn't rule out dinner."

I hated to let him down since he sounded so hopeful. "Jonathan, I'm really sorry, but I have a dinner engagement for this evening."

"Ajit?"

"I'd promised him a dinner at a restaurant of his choosing."

"Well, mark me down for tomorrow. Shall we say 8:00 p.m.?"

"That might be difficult. The restaurant he chose is in Virudhunagar, his hometown in southern India. We flew here yesterday."

I hung up to a wall of silence. Jonathan was angry, but he'd get over it.

A week later, Ajit and I returned to New York. My apartment in the Ansonia remained as it had when I left, a shambles. Ajit suggested I move in with him, but after giving the notion a brief moment of further thought, we both decided that idea spelled the end of a perfectly good relationship.

I took a room in The Beacon Hotel on 74th and Broadway, kitty corner from the Ansonia. In a week, a musician friend who owned an apartment in the Beacon said I could have a four month sublet while she went on tour in Europe. I'd start interviewing contractors in the morning. With any luck, maybe I'd get into my own place by Christmas.

I unpacked, had a shower, and went downstairs to the restaurant in the building. After dinner, since it was still early, I bought the latest *In Style* magazine and settled into a chair in the lobby. A moment later, the desk clerk walked across to where I sat.

"Miss Harrington, a gentleman dropped this off while you were having dinner."

He handed me a plain, letter-sized business envelope. Someone, at first glance I'd say a woman, had hand-written Paige Harrington across the front in green ink.

I set the magazine aside and ran my thumb under the flap. Inside was a single sheet of folded paper folded. I flipped it open, looked at the four printed words, and froze.

"Miss Harrington, are you OK?"

I couldn't believe what I'd just read. Or could I? Had a part of me known all along?

"Miss Harrington?"

I looked up. No, I'm not fine. I no longer own my life. Everywhere I go eyes will be watching and ears will be listening, deciding if I live or die.

"Yes, I'm fine. Did you happen to see who brought this?"

"An older man in a chauffeur's uniform. I remember his eyes; he had real cold eyes."

I looked at the paper again. Capital letters, printed: PENNINGTON JASPER IS PRAETORIAN.

My cellphone rang. I didn't recognize the number. I didn't have to. I knew who it was. I knew it had to do with the note in my hand. A shiver ran down my spine "Yes," I answered.

"Did you get my message?"

"Yes. I—"

Click.

I stared at the silenced phone. Yes, Mr. Rattner, I got your message.

THE END

McLeod divides his time between Western Canada,
where his two daughters and three granddaughters live,
and New York City's Upper West Side, where he and his
wife live with their two cats.

He has published two other novels, Death Spirits and
Barely Dead, which along with their reviews are currently available from on-line booksellers around the
world. Barely Dead is the first in his Paige Harrington
Mystery Series.

His blog features his short stories, some of which are
also in audio.

Web: http://wammac.web.aplus.net/